Jo Beverley

Lovers
AND
Ladies

THE FORTUNE HUNTER

AND

DEIRDRE AND DON JUAN

A SIGNET ECLIPSE BOOK

SIGNET ECLIPSE
Published by New American Library, a division of
Penguin Group (USA) Inc., 375 Hudson Street,
New York, New York 10014, USA
Penguin Group (Canada), 90 Eglinton Avenue East, Suite 700, Toronto,
Ontario M4P 2Y3, Canada (a division of Pearson Penguin Canada Inc.)
Penguin Books Ltd., 80 Strand, London WC2R 0RL, England
Penguin Ireland, 25 St. Stephen's Green, Dublin 2,
Ireland (a division of Penguin Books Ltd.)
Penguin Group (Australia), 250 Camberwell Road, Camberwell, Victoria 3124,
Australia (a division of Pearson Australia Group Pty. Ltd.)
Penguin Books India Pvt. Ltd., 11 Community Centre, Panchsheel Park,
New Delhi - 110 017, India
Penguin Group (NZ), 67 Apollo Drive, Rosedale, North Shore 0632,
New Zealand (a division of Pearson New Zealand Ltd.)
Penguin Books (South Africa) (Pty.) Ltd., 24 Sturdee Avenue,
Rosebank, Johannesburg 2196, South Africa

Penguin Books Ltd., Registered Offices:
80 Strand, London WC2R 0RL, England

Published by Signet Eclipse, an imprint of New American Library, a division of Penguin Group (USA) Inc.
The Fortune Hunter and *Deirdre and Don Juan* were previously published in separate Avon Books editions.

First Signet Eclipse Trade Paperback Printing, April 2008
10 9 8 7 6 5 4 3 2 1

The Fortune Hunter copyright © Jo Beverley, 1991
Deirdre and Don Juan copyright © Jo Beverley, 1993
All rights reserved

SIGNET ECLIPSE and logo are trademarks of Penguin Group (USA) Inc.

Set in New Baskerville
Designed by Ginger Legato

Printed in the United States of America

Dear Reader,

Welcome to *Lovers and Ladies,* which brings back into print two of my favorite novels, *The Fortune Hunter* and *Deirdre and Don Juan.*

Both are traditional Regencies that have long been out of print, and I know many of you are as glad to see them available again as I am. And for those of you to whom they are new, I hope you will enjoy discovering them!

I have always loved writing fiction set in the English Regency (which is the period from 1811 to 1820, when the Prince of Wales was regent for his father, the mad King George III). It's a short, complex, and rich period that's become familiar as the setting for Jane Austen's classic and wonderful romance novels.

The period has style in its long Georgian windows letting in light to shine on bright woodwork and the delicate furniture of Sheraton and Heppelwhite. We all know of the high-waisted

Empire dresses and the new, darker elegance of gentlemen's evening wear. Roads had improved, so people could travel the country and even visit the stately homes of the rich. Cities were increasingly lit by gas lighting.

However, the Regency could also be wild and wicked. In three of Jane Austen's Bennet sisters, we see the dimensions of their time: Jane Bennet is modest and well-behaved; Elizabeth Bennet is passionate and rebellious; and Lydia Bennet is wild and wicked.

My Regency fiction follows suit. Some novels are modest and discreet, some passionate and rebellious, and yes, some are wild and wicked. But as with the Bennet girls, there's always a happy ending.

The modest and discreet style of Regency romance is usually called the "traditional Regency." *The Fortune Hunter* and *Deirdre and Don Juan* are examples of this.

In a traditional romance, the stories stick closely to the social mores of the early nineteenth century. Certainly the aristocracy was wilder than the gentry, but even in the haut ton, there were rules, and consequences of breaking them, which make for interesting stories.

The Fortune Hunter and *Deirdre and Don Juan* have always been particular favorites of mine, because they explore the idea of beauty from opposite angles. In my books, extreme beauty is more likely to be a challenge than a gift, which is true to life, I believe.

In *The Fortune Hunter*, Amy de Lacy is a raving beauty, but all it brings her is the burden of being the one who has to try to snare a rich husband to support her brothers and sisters. In our times they could all have gone out and found jobs, but the options for Regency gentry were more limited; without money, their future is grim. In the end, of course, it's not beauty that matters.

In *Deirdre and Don Juan*, we have a young woman who lacks beauty. It was important to me that Deirdre not be an ugly duckling—a plain woman who would turn into a beauty with a minor makeover. Certainly her clothes are unfortunate, but she is what she is. When Everdon comes to value, desire, and love her, it is for Deirdre, the whole person, not for parts of her or despite her appearance.

And he fights to win her, as does Amy's Harry, passing a crucial test of love.

If you've enjoyed these stories, I have written many other romances set in the Regency period, some of these in the traditional style and others of the more dramatic type. The most recent is *Lady Beware*, which was published in June 2007. A new novel set a couple of generations earlier, *A Lady's Secret*, is on shelves now. You can find a complete list of my books, including free samples, at www.jobev.com.

You'll find lots of additional material there, including background details and pictures relevant to the novels. Come for a visit and enjoy. You can also sign up for my e-mail newsletter, which means you'll receive the latest news about my books and promotional activities. You can contact me at jo@jobev.com.

If you don't have access to a computer, you can write through my agent. Address a letter to me c/o The Rotrosen Agency, 318 East 51st Street, New York, NY 10022. I appreciate an SASE if you would like a reply.

A good book is such a treasure. May you have many in your life.

All best wishes,
Jo Beverley

THE FORTUNE HUNTER

1

I
T WAS A MERRY PARTY IN THE KITCHEN of Stonycourt in Lincolnshire, seat of the de Lacy family. For once a generous fire was roaring in the grate, a chicken had been sacrificed to make a feast, and the precious store of medicinal spirits had been raided to make a fiery punch. The four young de Lacys and their aunt sat around the scrubbed deal table toasting their good fortune and making grand plans for the use of their newfound wealth.

Stonycourt's two remaining servants—aged specimens—hunched on a high-backed settle close to the fire like two black crows, nursing mugs of hot punch but casting a jaundiced eye on the jubilation.

"A horse!" declared Sir Jasper de Lacy, youngest of the family and yet nominal head. "A hunter. A prime bit of blood and bone."

"New gowns," put in his twin sister, Jacinth, with a blissful smile. "Bang up to the mark and *not* homemade."

At sixteen, the twins were still very alike, for Jasper was of a slender build, fine boned for a boy, and Jacinth had insisted in following fashion by having her curly brown hair cropped short. She had declared that it was the only fashionable gesture that came free.

"A Season?" offered the eldest daughter, Beryl. She added, in the tone of one who speculates on fabulous wonders, "Almack's?"

Amy de Lacy, the middle daughter, smiled sadly. Beryl was one who dreamed of wonders, but always with a question mark after them. In truth, life had not served to raise Beryl's expectations. Though she had a sweet nature and a great many useful skills, no one could deny that she was plain— the sort of lumpy, sallow homeliness which could not be disguised by discreet paint or a stylish haircut.

As the daughter of Sir Digby de Lacy of Stonycourt and with a portion to match, Beryl could have expected to marry. That had all gone up in smoke two years ago when their father died and the tangle of bills and borrowings which had supported them in elegance had come crashing down.

Amy had suffered on her own behalf, for it was not at all pleasant to be poor, but she grieved more for Beryl, who was the kind of woman who should marry and have a home and children and now, doubtless, would not. Beryl was kind, skillful, and endlessly patient. She would make an excellent mother and she deserved a good, prosperous man to make her dreams come true.

"That's right," said the older lady seated at the head of the table, merrily tipsy beneath a tilted blue satin turban. "That's what's needed, Beryl pet. A Season. It'll be grand to be back in London, especially now peace is in the air. We'll soon have you married, then Amethyst, then Jacinth."

Amy winced. She had persuaded everyone else in the world to give up her ridiculous name in favor of Amy, but

Aunt Lizzie would not be moved. "My dear sister chose your name with loving care, Amethyst," she would protest, "and I will not betray her now she is in her grave." Put like that it made a simple change of name sound like a heinous sin.

But since Georgiana de Lacy had taken it into her head to call all her children after precious stones, why could Amy not have been Agate or Onyx? Or Sardonyx. Yes, she'd rather have liked being Sardonyx de Lacy.

But she would much rather have been called Jane.

She also wished Aunt Lizzie would not encourage the family tendency to flights of fancy. What else was to be expected, however? It seemed to be a trait which ran strong on both sides of the family tree.

After all, Amy's maternal grandparents—prosperous London wine merchants—had named their daughters Georgiana and Elizabeth after the famous Gunning sisters, clearly with social advancement in mind. In fact, they had achieved mild success. Lizzie had not married, but the beautiful Georgiana had married Sir Digby de Lacy of Stonycourt.

It was a shame, thought Amy, that this had so dizzied the Toombs family that they had sunk into penury trying to live up to their daughter's social heights. Some prosperous relatives would be very useful these days.

The trait of impracticality was strong on the paternal side, too. Amy's father had been a devout optimist and so delighted with his beautiful bride that he had been unable to deny her anything. He had extended his indulgence to each child without thought to his resources. They had been so happy, thought Amy wistfully, and the lovely house had frequently been full of guests and had rung with laughter.

She would give anything to have those days back.

"I don't think I would care for a Season really," Beryl demurred, coloring. "I'm a little old to be making my curtsy. . . ."

"Nonsense, pet," said Lizzie. "What do you say, Amethyst?"

Above all, Amy hated being faced with the choice of supporting these bubbles of fancy or exploding them. The truth was that Beryl was too old, and that, plain as she was, the chance of her making a match in London was slim indeed, but how could she say that? It wasn't as if Jasper's share in a winning lottery could support such an enterprise anyway, and she could still wring his neck for risking his hard-won book money on such an idiotic enterprise.

Everyone was waiting for her answer and so she said carefully, "I fear there simply isn't enough money. It's a drop in the ocean."

Dismay wiped away joy. Lizzie opened her mouth but it was Jacinth who got in first. "Amethyst de Lacy," she burst out, the use of the full name a protest in itself, "if you are going to be a wet blanket, I swear I will hate you forever!"

Amy pulled an apologetic face. "I'm sorry, Jassy, but we have to be sensible."

"*Why?*" demanded Jasper. "Look what sensible has achieved. We've been holed up here for two years like . . . like troglodytes, living from hand to mouth. No hunting. No dancing. No fun at all! It's only when I go and do something *unsensible* that we get anywhere!"

"Fine," snapped Amy. "And how are you going to build on this? Spend it all on *more* lottery tickets? Or perhaps you'd rather take it to the races?"

Jasper reddened. "I do seem to have a winning streak." At his sister's groan, he quickly added, "But there's no need for that. We have *five thousand pounds*!"

Jacinth cheered and offered another toast. Amy feared her little sister was on the go.

"Jasper," Amy said gently but firmly, "your masters say you

are very good with figures. How many hunters will the income from the money buy and keep? How many fine outfits? How many Seasons will it provide at the same time as it keeps up Stonycourt?"

"To hell with Stonycourt."

Aunt Lizzie gasped. "Jasper!"

"Sorry," he muttered. "But, Amy, the money will buy a lot."

"Not if you preserve the capital. If you can invest it to produce three hundred a year you will be doing well. That will provide a modicum of comfort but you should use some of it to pay down the encumbrances on the estate." Amy sought for a more cheerful aspect. "Of course, if you apply it all to the debt, then it will mean less time until it is cleared. Once we have paid all the debts, you can use the rents for income. We can slowly build."

"Slowly!" Jacinth burst out. "Slowly. That's what you always say. What about poor Beryl? She's twenty-three! She can't wait."

Beryl smiled sadly. "Don't you worry about me, Jassy. I know I'm not going to find a husband without a dowry, and this money can't provide one. Amy's right," she said with a sigh. "I'm afraid we're all going to be spinsters."

Jacinth looked aghast at this. She had obviously never previously applied the family's straitened circumstances to herself. "Not Amy," she declared spitefully. "She has only to stand on a corner of the highway to have men groveling at her feet!"

The moment the words were out she looked appalled, clapped a hand over her mouth, and then fled the table with a wail. Jasper scowled accusingly at Amy, then leapt up to go after his twin. Lizzie clucked and heaved herself up to follow.

Beryl placed a comforting hand over Amy's. "She didn't mean it."

Amy squeezed that hand but she said, "Yes, she did, and it's true. I wish to heaven I was plain as a barn door."

For Amy had the curse—as she saw it—of stunning beauty. Her hair was a glittering blond of such complexity of hue that the swains who regularly compared it to spun gold were not being as trite as it would appear. Her face was a charming heart shape; her nose straight but slightly upturned; her soft full lips were a perfect Cupid's bow, curved so that it was extremely difficult for her not to appear to be smiling. Her eyes were large and of a subtle dark blue lightened by flashes of lighter shades like a stream in the sun. Her skin, despite much time out of doors, was flawless.

Amy was just tall enough to be called elegant, and her form was sweetly rounded with a tendency to lushness in the upper part, which she particularly deplored.

Amy had never been at ease with her beauty, for it seemed to make people behave in very silly ways—men ogled and clustered, and women were frequently acidic—but she had borne it until the family's plunge into poverty. Then she had realized how it set her apart from her sisters, just as Jassy had said. Amy would always find a husband if she sought one, whereas Beryl—much more worthy of love—was unlikely to, and even Jassy, pretty as she was, might fail without a penny to her name.

So Amy had spent the last two years doing her best to obliterate her beauty. She had always had a taste for simple garments, and after her father's death she had stripped them of all trimmings and dyed the brighter ones into dull colors. Mourning had provided a good excuse, and those which had survived the black dye vat had been plunged into a brown one, with the explanation that it made them more suitable for work.

"But, Amy, dear," Beryl had said, "I cannot see why a brown dress is more practical than a pink one unless you mean that it will not look dirty when it is. I do not like that thought at all."

Amy had had no satisfactory response to that one.

She had used the same excuse, however—their new need to do the work once done by a dozen servants—to take to wearing her hair scraped back into a tight knot and covered by a cap. Beryl had found no logical argument against that, except that it was not very becoming.

Amy had hoped she was right, but neither clothes nor cap seemed to reduce Amy's quantity of admirers, and Amy wanted them reduced to zero, for she could not bear to marry while her sisters were left spinsters.

In desperation, she had made the experiment of having her hair cropped short like Jacinth's. That had been a disaster, and she was waiting impatiently for it to grow. For the moment there was no question of confining it at all. It rioted around her head like a cherub's curls, emphasizing not just her beauty but a childlike impression she abhorred.

"If you were as plain as a barn door," said Beryl with a teasing smile, "it would be even harder on us, dearest. I enjoy seeing your beauty."

Amy squeezed Beryl's hand again, touched by the sincere words. Beryl had no scrap of envy in her. "But perhaps I am too serious-minded," she said. "Since we never expected to have this money, it would do no harm to spend it on fripperies."

"It would do no good either," said Beryl, "except develop a taste for more. I'm sure you were right when you said it would be better to live very simply for a few years so that Stonycourt can be restored." She did not sound very sure.

"You are the oldest," said Amy. "If you think we should manage in a different way, please say so."

"Oh no," said Beryl honestly. "I have no notion at all. Left to myself, I suppose I would have carried on as Papa did, had it been possible to get credit. I am good at finding ways to manage on less, but I can't plan as you do, and figure out our finances, and how long it will take. . . . It would all be too depressing." She worried a groove in the table with her fingernail, then asked, "How long will it take, Amy?"

Amy had done her best to be vague on such matters, and in typical fashion, the family had not pressed her, but she would not shrink a straight question. "Four years," she said, "if we're very careful, and rents stay high, and there is no disaster such as the roof leaking. . . ." She stopped herself from listing all the unexpected expenses which could arise to throw her calculations into chaos. "In four years," she said cheerfully, "we should be almost free of debt, and Jasper's income will be adequate for Stonycourt to become a proper home again."

"That will be pleasant for Jasper," Beryl said, "but what of us?"

Amy felt as if a void had opened at her feet. In all her plans and calculations, she had never looked further than her cherished goal—to restore Stonycourt to the way it had been before their world fell apart. "We will live here," she said uncertainly. "There may even be a small amount for marriage portions."

But Beryl would be twenty-seven by then. Amy was suddenly aware that Jacinth was right. Beryl couldn't wait. "Perhaps we are holding too tight," she said. "We could reconsider selling some land and put the money aside for dowries. Uncle Clarence would approve that. He said as much."

Uncle Clarence was their guardian, though he lived in Cumberland and paid little heed to their affairs.

"Oh no," said Beryl firmly. "We agreed it would be disastrous to begin selling off the land. Four years is not so long." She sighed. "I do wish we could have some real tea, though." She went over to the stove and spooned dried chamomile into the pot.

Amy would have chopped her own heart and put it in the pot if there'd been any purpose to it. "A pound of tea would make a tiny dent in five thousand pounds, love," she said.

Beryl shook her head. "And gowns for Jassy, and a horse for Jasper. No, let's stick to our guns."

Jacinth came back, accompanied by Jasper and Lizzie. "Oh, Amy, I'm sorry," she said with a sniff. "That was a horridly catty thing to say."

Amy went over and hugged her. "Don't regard it, love. The only blessing of having this phiz is that *I* don't have to look at it all day. I'm sure it's very wearing. But you see, don't you, that we have to be careful for a little longer so Stonycourt can be Stonycourt again."

Jasper looked mutinous. "I don't think everyone's happiness should be sacrificed to a building."

"It's the home of the de Lacys, dear. We can't let it go, or fall down about our ears."

Beryl brought the teapot to the table. "Amy's right. But I think we should plan for what we are to do when everything is straight again. Jasper will want to marry, and his bride won't want a house full of spinsters."

Amy was touched by this sudden attack of practical thinking and disturbed yet again. Her faith in her own clearheadedness was being rapidly undermined. First she had assumed they would all be marriageable when their fortunes were stable again, then she had assumed they would all live on here happily as they had once done.

"I don't want to marry anyway," said Jasper nobly.

Beryl smiled gently. "Think of the succession, dear."

He went bright red. "Oh, true."

Jacinth looked resentfully at her twin. "But *I* want to marry. And what's to become of us if we don't? I won't become a governess or a companion. I won't."

Beryl poured her some tea and reverted to form. "You must look on the bright side, Jassy. It could all work out for the best. If you do have to seek employment, you and Amy are sure to attract the attention of the sons of the house and end up rich."

Amy shut her eyes. Such an adventure was one of her recurrent nightmares but the outcome would not be as benign as Beryl imagined. Since their poverty had become known Amy had received a number of sly propositions.

"I'm sure that would be very nice," said Aunt Lizzie doubtfully. Amy thought for a moment that her aunt was for once going to point out a folly, but she carried on. "I agree with Jacinth. Employment would not be at all pleasant and not at all necessary. A thousand pounds to each of us would be enough for us to live quietly in a cottage. Less if we all live together." There was a loud clearing of throats from the settle near the fire.

The two old servants, Mr. and Mrs. Pretty, had been butler and housekeeper at Stonycourt for thirty years, and when disaster struck they had been too old to seek employment elsewhere. When the other staff had been let go, they had stayed on, accepting room and board, waiting for the pension to which they felt they were entitled.

To which they were entitled, admitted Amy, even if Sir Digby had neglected such provisions. Lizzie Toombs looked sourly at the couple but said grudgingly, "And doubtless a thousand for the Prettys. The estate should be able to bear that, and if Jasper marries an heiress we'll all be well set."

"No, we won't!" cried Jacinth. "We'll be growing old in a cottage!" She looked around the table for reassurance. When it did not come, she burst into tears and fled again.

"What's the matter with her?" asked Jasper blankly. "If I did marry an heiress I'd see Jassy all right."

"I'm afraid that will be a while dear," said Amy. "I doubt you'll be able to marry a fortune for a good many years."

"Oh. Well then," he said carelessly, "I think *you* should. With your looks, you should be able to snaffle a duke as easy as falling off a chair."

There was silence. Then, "Of course," said Aunt Lizzie blithely. "What a clever young man you are, Jasper. We will use the money to take Amethyst to London. She'll be the toast of the town and marry a duke and we'll all be rich."

Amy felt as if she couldn't breathe. It must be the punch. "But what about Beryl?" she protested, the first defense she could think of. "The eldest should marry first."

Beryl laughed. "I couldn't catch a duke, dear. Nor would I want one. I will choose a husband with a small estate, a man who stays at home."

She was off in one of her dreams. As far as Beryl was concerned, "I will" was as good as done. Amy slapped her wits back into order. Was it possible? Marriage was a way out of poverty, after all, and she *would* do anything to make all right for her family.

"It would be madness to spend all the money," she said cautiously. "A thousand should be more than enough if we're careful. In fact," she added thoughtfully, "it may not be necessary to go to London at all. We live on the edge of the Shires, and it is still hunting season. There must be many wealthy gentlemen in this locality. As Jassy said," she added dryly, "I have only to be seen to slay."

"It would be much more fun to go to London," said Beryl simply.

Amy didn't have the heart to tell her it would be far too expensive for them all to go. Beryl's words merely stiffened her resolve to try other means. It would be perfectly horrid to be gadding about Town while Beryl and Jassy pined at home.

"If we are to do this," she said firmly, "we must remember that I will need to marry a very rich man, one willing to lay out a lot of money to bring the estate back into heart immediately and provide dowries for you and Jassy. I think on the whole I should look for an older man. A nabob, perhaps, or a wealthy cit."

"What!" declared Aunt Lizzie. "Marry beneath you when your mother struggled to raise herself up."

"We are not so high now, Aunt," Amy pointed out.

"You are a de Lacy of Stonycourt."

Amy shrugged. "Let us hope that makes me worth extra at market."

"But a gentleman who marries a golden dolly," said Beryl doubtfully, "raises her up to his status. A lady who marries a wealthy cit sinks down to his. I don't think you'd like that, Amy dear. You should marry the duke."

Amy shook her head. "If one offers," she said gently, "be sure I will consider him most seriously. But we must be practical. Money is our main object, accompanied by a generous disposition."

She summoned up a merry smile and raised her teacup. "To fortune hunting!"

Over the next days Amy marshaled her family like a general. Aunt Lizzie was set to writing to her acquaintance in London to discreetly inquire about rich tradesmen interested in marrying into the gentry. As Beryl had pointed out, such a marriage was not as popular as the linking of men of good birth with lower-bred fortunes, for it did not automatically raise a man up as it would a woman. But it did give useful connections, and the children could expect to step into the gentry if they'd a mind to, so it had some benefits to offer.

Jasper had returned to his school at Uppingham and was asking if there were any nabobs or such living in the nearby villages, here for the hunting. There was a degree of urgency to this. It was April and the hunting season was winding down as the crops began to grow. Soon all the wealthy Meltonians would be off to London.

Amy and her sisters took to paying especial attention to local gossip but were frustrated by the fact that all anyone wanted to talk about these days was Napoleon Bonaparte's abdication. This wonderful news would normally have delighted them, but Amy at least wished the dramatic events could have delayed for a little while so that people would still be interested in the minutiae of local life.

April progressed without anything being achieved. Aunt Lizzie received only gossipy replies from London full of plans for victory celebrations but lacking lists of wealthy bachelors.

Jasper wrote that he discovered there were a goodly number of avid hunters still in the area but the single men were all young bucks, and though well-breeched enough none were rich enough for their purposes.

Beryl and Jassy mulled over the local residents with care but could not keep it in their minds that a veritable Croesus was required, and his looks or age were of no account.

"There's that charming Mr. Bunting over at Nether Hendon," said Beryl one evening as they ate their mutton stew.

"He's tolerably handsome and I'm sure he has a sweet nature."

Amy forced a smile. "But if he has five thousand a year, I'd be surprised, Beryl."

"Five thousand a year is a comfortable income."

"But doesn't allow much for me to milk him of for Stonycourt," said Amy ruthlessly.

Beryl gaped. Aunt Lizzie frowned. "Amethyst, my dear, don't you think that was a little vulgar?"

Amy rested her head on one hand and gathered her patience. Then she looked up. "I'm sorry. It wasn't a proper thing to say. But there will be no point to this if I merely marry a man who will keep me in comfort. How could I live in comfort while my family suffers? So can we concentrate our efforts on finding another Golden Ball? Please?"

From the end of the table where they ate slightly apart from the family—by their own choice—Pretty cleared his throat.

"Yes, Pretty," Amy said.

"If I may be so bold, Miss Amethyst, I do know of a very rich man in this locality."

"Who?"

"There is a gentleman of the name of Staverley taken Prior's Grange in Upper Kennet. Talk down at the Jug and Whistle is that he is come from the West Indies very rich indeed and without wife or children that any knows of."

"Is he young?" asked Jassy excitedly.

"Is he handsome?" asked Beryl.

"Are we sure he's rich?" asked Amy.

"Anyone can be a trickster," said Pretty, "but it is the feeling of all that he's warm enough to toast with. Bringing in fine furniture, ordering all kinds of luxuries, hiring ample staff . . . and," he added with a slight sneer, which revealed long stained teeth, "paying on the knob for everything."

"There's no need for that, Pretty," said Amy sharply. "We pay on the knob, too, these days. No one will give us credit. How do I meet this man?"

"Amethyst!" cried Aunt Lizzie. "Do not be so precipitate. We must make the most careful inquiries."

Amy opened her mouth to refute this but then closed it. It was clear that if anything practical was to be achieved, she would be best advised to leave her family out of it. At least it seemed the Prettys could be relied on for help, even if it was only from self-interest. No bad thing, thought Amy. Self-interest could generally be relied on.

❧ 2 ❧

TWO DAYS LATER Amy was on the road to Upper Kennet, driving the family's only vehicle—a dogcart—pulled by Zephyr, their only horse. Perhaps Zephyr had once been an appropriate name for this broken-down animal, but no more. She had only been kept because there'd be little profit in selling her.

As the horse plodded along, Amy told herself not to be so ungrateful. They were fortunate to have a beast to pull the old cart when needed, and though Zephyr was old and slow she was steady and willing. *Clop, clop, clop* went the hooves along the road. Amy let the ribbons lie slack as she reviewed her plan, searching out flaws.

Investigation had failed to discover a reliable way of meeting Mr. Owen Staverley. According to Pretty he was past forty, of a stocky build and a taciturn manner. It was said he walked with a limp, but there was no report of other ill health. He occasionally went into Oakham or as far as Lincoln on business, but apart from that he stayed at home. Whatever had brought him to this locality, it wasn't the hunting, for he kept only a carriage pair and a quiet hack.

Having failed to discover a public place where she could "accidentally" encounter him, Amy had decided on a cruder but simpler course. She was going to have an accident outside his gates. To this end she had frayed Zephyr's reins close to the bit so that at a sharp tug they would break. The tack was in such a worn-out state that no one would ever suspect the damage to have been contrived. Of course, it would be clear to anyone with wits Zephyr needed no reins to control her, but Amy was willing to play the feebleminded wigeon if it suited her purpose. For once, her looks would be an advantage since they seemed to convince people she hadn't a wit in her head anyway.

She had told her family nothing of her plan in case they thought of some way to interfere. She was supposed to pick up some new laying hens from Crossroads Farm just beyond Upper Kennet. Five miles to get hens was not as outlandish as it appeared, for Mrs. Cranby had been the Stonycourt nursery nurse and could be depended on to give them good birds at a low price.

A sudden gust of wind swirled around and made Amy shiver. She looked up and found the sky was darkening. It had been a clear day when she set out, but it had taken two hours to get this far. Walking would have been faster, and if it was going to come on to rain she could perhaps have sought shelter at Prior's Grange without needing an accident of any sort. She told herself that a shower would make her piteous plight more touching, and a horse problem was more likely to engage the interest of the master of the house.

After all, it was not enough just to be given aid and shelter at the Grange; she needed to meet Mr. Staverley.

To avoid the possibility of being taken for a servant, Amy

had dressed as well as possible. Since it was her business to attract, she had borrowed a gown and bonnet from Beryl—without, unfortunately, being able to ask her sister's permission. The outfit was not in the latest style, but it had been made three years ago by the best dressmaker in Lincoln, and the quality showed still.

The cambric gown was in a clear shade of blue, worked with a white stripe design. It played up Amy's coloring well. The high-crown bonnet was lined with matching blue silk and trimmed with white roses and a plume. The plume kept tickling Amy's cheek and was the devil of a nuisance.

Amy blew the feathers out of her eyes and glanced at the sky again. Though a little rain would be useful to her plot, a downpour would be unpleasant and ruin all this borrowed finery. She reached behind to investigate the box under the backseat, looking for any kind of protection. She was rewarded by two musty old sacks and a moth-eaten rug. Not much, but they would afford some protection.

The sky was definitely darker and the wind was picking up. Amy shivered and pulled the rug around her shoulders for warmth. If she hadn't been trying to catch a rich husband she would have her warm red woolen cloak with her and be less likely to catch her death instead. She'd always known romance was a stupid business.

How far to go? Another mile or so.

She picked up the reins and clicked to Zephyr to go faster. The horse didn't alter her pace at all.

"Come on, Zephyr!" Amy cried impatiently. "You can't be any keener on a soaking than I am."

Clop, clop, clop. Zephyr only had one pace.

Amy let the reins go limp again and settled to watching the sky and calculating their progress. She could see the rise of Upper Kennet in the distance.

The wind grew stronger, whipping up twigs and last year's leaves, swirling dust into Amy's eyes. Perhaps some got into Zephyr's eyes, for she tossed her head a little and her steady pace faltered. Amy grabbed the reins but the horse immediately steadied to her usual pace.

Amy took off the bonnet before the plume broke and placed it in the box. It would have some protection there, and now she could pull the rug close about her head. She certainly was going to be a piteous sight when she reached her target.

Then there was a flash of lightning and a crack of thunder. Not overhead but not far away either. "Oh, heavens," muttered Amy, grabbing the reins. The one thing likely to stir Zephyr to excitement was lightning. The old mare was probably too tired to create a fuss, but Amy wished they were at Prior's Grange already. This was as much of a plight as she wished to be in.

She saw the rain coming. It swept over the fields toward her like a gray curtain, and when it hit it was sluicingly hard. Amy gasped and grabbed for the sacks to pull them on top of the rug over her head and shoulders. "Oh, poor Beryl's dress," she moaned.

Zephyr just dropped her head and plodded on.

There was a farmhouse of some sort on the right, with a light in a window. Amy thought of stopping to ask for shelter but she gathered up her courage. Just down this slight incline and up the next and she would be at the Grange. Now her situation was desperate enough to bring forward anyone's chivalrous instincts.

But the road had now become a stream. The wheels of the cart slipped one or twice, and Zephyr's pace faltered. A sign of uneasiness.

Suddenly a flash of lightning split the gray sky. It was

followed almost immediately by a deafening crack of thunder. Zephyr stopped dead, then began to toss her head and back them toward the ditch. Amy grabbed the reins. "Ho! Steady, girl! Steady."

The horse responded and plunged forward. This surprising surge of energy almost sent them into the opposite hedge. Amy hauled back on the reins.

The reins broke.

Amy let out a very unladylike curse. She leapt from the seat and sloshed her way to grab the horse's head.

Zephyr immediately quieted and stood inert, head hanging. The rain poured down, and Amy was literally soaked to the skin. Another flash of lightning. Another roll of thunder. Zephyr twitched, but Amy's soothing voice and a comforting hand on her nose were enough for the weary mare.

Amy wished she had someone to comfort her. The noise and power of the rain were numbing her. Or perhaps it was just the cold. It hadn't seemed a cold day for late April, but now that she was wet she was chilled through.

In a moment we can go on, Amy thought.

The rain was slackening a little—going from torrent to downpour. She gathered her resources. It couldn't be more than a quarter mile to Upper Kennet, sanctuary, and a fortune.

Then the thinning of the rain showed her the road ahead. Though the slope of the road was very gentle, it formed a little dip before curving up to Upper Kennet. That dip was now a pond with two small rivers pouring into it. Prior's Grange was on the next rise, but it might as well be in India for all her chance of getting herself and the cart there today.

Amy muttered a few more distinctly unladylike words.

She considered wading through herself and making her way up to the Grange, but apart from the fact that she couldn't abandon poor Zephyr here, her behavior would appear strange enough to raise embarrassing questions. She would have to seek shelter at the farmhouse, and there was the devil of a chance of finding a rich husband there.

Amy could have wept from disappointment, weariness, and cold. She was shivering as she pushed and cajoled Zephyr into turning. Her hands were numb, her half-boots were up to their tops in muddy water. She eventually got the job done and tugged the horse wearily back the way they had come. The slope had seemed nothing as they had come down it; now it was a mountainside.

Surely it was only a minute since she had passed that flickering light. Where was it? Visions of a warm kitchen, hot tea, and dry clothing were dancing in her head.

There. A light.

It was a small, square farmhouse with a barn to one side and another outbuilding to the other. Surprisingly there were two open gates, one at either side. Amy simply picked the nearest.

Sensing shelter, Zephyr's pace picked up a little. She gave no trouble as Amy led her into the barn.

When the rain stopped beating down on Amy's head it was a shocking relief. Amy leaned wearily against the horse's warm flank. She looked down. A dirty puddle was forming at her feet. Poor Beryl's dress.

She looked around. The storm had dimmed the day, but she could see this barn was rather ramshackle, probably unused. What sort of farm was this? She felt a trickle of unease at such evidence of neglect but stifled it. At least the barn was dry. The house would offer some kind of shelter.

Amy started to unharness the horse and rub her down, but her numb fingers were unable to perform the simple task. She blew on them, she tucked them into her relatively dry and warm armpits. It was no good, and her own shivering was getting worse by the minute. She could feel an impulse growing in her to burst into tears of misery. She had to get help.

She hated the thought of stepping out into the deluge, but across the muddy quagmire of a yard the warm golden light of a lamp glimmered in a window. She could see the shelves of a kitchen and could imagine the fire there, the warmth and aroma of the ovens. A haven.

Pointlessly, she dragged the soaked sacks further forward onto her face, then made a dash for it.

After three steps her feet went from under her. She slammed forward into the mud and slid for a yard or so. Stunned, she lay there winded. The mud was glutinously foul between her fingers. The rain beat down on her back. She could laugh or cry. She chose to laugh.

A fine beginning to her career as a fortune hunter. No one would want her at this moment.

It was tempting to just lie where she was, but Amy heaved herself up, her soaked muddy clothing like a millstone around her neck, and plodded carefully to the farmhouse door. It at least had a little porch covering it, and the rain stopped beating down on her head. She knocked. Nothing. She wiped her sodden hair back off her face with filthy fingers, picked up a stone, and beat on the door with that.

It swung open. Amy looked up to see a handsome, tawny-haired young man in shirtsleeves staring at her in astonishment.

Harry Crisp had been congratulating himself on staying indoors on such a day. His friends, Chart Ashby and Terance Cornwallis, had ridden out early to ride with the Belvoir, unwilling to miss a day's hunting this close to the end of the season no matter how unpromising the weather. Served them right. They'd be drowned rats by the time they found shelter.

He doubtless would have been with them, however, if he hadn't felt the need for a bit of time to think.

At Easter he'd taken his usual trip to Hey Park, his family home. Chart disliked his parents and went home as little as possible, but Harry was fond of his. They were a good sort. They gave him an adequate allowance, and despite the fact that he was an only child, they didn't fuss over him, or try to interfere with his fun. His father was deeply suspicious of London and clearly feared Harry would one day be ruined there, but even so he made no cavil at Harry's annual jaunts there with Chart. Yes, a very good sort.

Moreover, Lord Thoresby was still under sixty and Harry had reckoned, when he'd thought about the matter at all, that he had many years before he need think of settling down.

Now he knew that his father was not well.

Lord Thoresby's untypical petulance about it had been alarmingly convincing. "Load of nonsense," he'd grumbled. "Just because I've been dizzy now and then."

"Perhaps I should come and help you here, sir."

"Rubbish! And miss the last of the hunting? None of that. I have people here to do what's needed."

"There's only a week or two left," Harry said. "Hardly worth going back for." His father looked as well as normal but he couldn't persuade himself this was all a mare's nest.

"Won't hear of it," said his father firmly. "In fact," he added a great deal less firmly, "I . . . er . . . I was thinking it's about time you spent more time in London."

Harry stared at his father in astonishment. "I can't think why."

Lord Thoresby rambled on about gaining a bit of bronze, learning to know a flat from a sharp, and a great many other unconvincing reasons. Harry took the puzzle to his mother.

"Oh dear," said Lady Thoresby. She was a small, plump, pretty woman who had given her son his tawny curls and amiable temperament. "I hoped he wouldn't . . . You mustn't mind him, Harry dear. He's a little out of curl these days. Don't like to feel he can't do just as he wishes."

"But why would he want me to go to Town?" Harry demanded. "I could understand if he wanted me home, and I'm more than willing."

"Marriage," said his mother apologetically. She looked at her horrified son and chuckled. "It is a state slightly better than hell on earth, dear one, but there is no need to hurry."

"He wants me to—Almack's?" Harry queried blankly.

"No doubt you'll enjoy it when the time comes," she assured him. "After all, a handsome young man, the heir to an old title and a substantial fortune, will suffer few rebuffs. But as I said, there is no need as yet. And you may meet a bride elsewhere." Lady Thoresby looked up from her needlework. "I hope you know, Harry, that your father and I would accept any bride of your choice. There is no need to look for a fortune, or grand connections. Just find a warmhearted girl, dear. One who will make you happy."

Harry allowed his mother's comfortable tone to reassure him. Perhaps it was time for him to start thinking about settling down, but not for a year or two. He was only twenty-four, after all.

But then his father suffered another dizzy spell, almost falling down the stairs. The doctor examined his patient again and shook his head. "No way to say, Mr. Crisp. He must build up his strength and avoid overexertion and excitement. He could be with us for many, many years." Silently he conveyed the grim alternative.

Lord Thoresby would not hear of Harry staying and became agitated on the matter, repeating his opinion that Harry should go to London. Marriage and nurseries were not mentioned but were clearly fretting Lord Thoresby's mind. Harry had returned to Rutland to arrange for the moving of his hunters and tell Chart what was afoot. His friend would doubtless be horrified.

Loosely connected on the family tree, and almost exactly of an age, they'd been inseparable since their first days at Eton. Harry couldn't imagine going bride-hunting without Chart, but it was a devil of a lot to ask of even the closest friend.

And a wife was likely to interfere with his normal masculine pursuits to an inconvenient degree.

As he mulled over these depressing thoughts, he was occupying his hands with his hobby and trying to mend a small automaton. The lady with china head and limbs and a blue silk gown was supposed to dance to the music box inside. She should point a toe, turn, and move her head. All she could manage was a jerky twitch.

He was poking beneath her silk skirts, grinning at the thought that this was rather improper, when he heard a thumping on the door. Who on earth would be out in such weather?

As he opened the door, rain and wind swept in and he was confronted by a mud creature. Sodden sacks for a head. Mud for a gown. The sacks moved and he saw a pale face.

"Good Lord." He opened the door farther and gestured for her to enter.

The woman, or girl—it was hard to say—staggered in, and he could shut out the noise and the cold, wet air. He looked blankly at his visitor and took in the growing pool of mud under her feet. Firkin, Corny's manservant, would have pungent words to say.

Consigning Firkin's future words to the devil, he said, "You must come into the kitchen." He directed the creature along the passage and into the warm room. Her shoes made slurping sounds as she plodded along.

Once in the room he looked at the trail behind her and said, "Er . . . perhaps you could shed some of your covering here."

Amy was coming back to some kind of sanity. She was still shivering cold and wetter than she'd been since she fell in the horse trough, but there was warmth about, and no wind, and no rain. "Who are you?" she asked the young man. He was clearly no farmer.

He gave her a small, elegant bow. "Harry Crisp, at your service, ma'am. You really should get out of those clothes. I'll find some towels and a blanket."

He turned away, and Amy said quickly, "You can't be alone here!"

"Can't I?" he asked with a raised brow. "Oh dear."

Amy didn't know what to do. "I can't possibly stay here alone with you," she said.

It occurred to Harry for the first time that this soggy mess spoke in the manner of a gentlewoman, and clearly a young-ish one. It was a delicate situation. "Awkward, I grant you," he said. "But what else are you going to do?"

"I suppose," said Amy faintly, "I'd better go back to the barn and my horse." Her teeth started to chatter. Her nose was running. She sniffed.

"What good would that do?" he asked. "No one would know whether you'd been inside or out so why not stay in where it's warm and dry? You have a horse? Is it cared for?"

"N-no!" Amy wailed. "My hands were t-t-too c-cold!"

Harry had a strong urge to gather this waif in for a consoling hug, but apart from the mud, she'd doubtless set up a shriek of rape. "Don't worry about a thing," he said reassuringly. "Just wait a minute."

He ran up the narrow wooden stairs to the bedrooms and collected a stack of towels and a spare blanket. He didn't know whether the girl would have the wit to use them, but he'd do his best to see she didn't catch her death.

Back in the kitchen, she was standing as he had left her. He had the strange image of the mud drying and leaving her a grotesque brown statue in the kitchen of Coppice Farm. "Here, ma'am," he said as he placed the pile on the table. "Make yourself as comfortable as you can, please. I'll go tend to your horse."

She didn't move. Harry shrugged. He didn't think he should strip her by force, though it might come to that if she was still fixed there when he returned.

He went into the passage, pulled on the heavy oilskin cape which hung there, and plunged out into the downpour.

Amy heard his footsteps and the slap of the door as it closed behind him. She just stood there. To move seemed altogether too much trouble and she wasn't at all sure what was the right thing to do. But then something told her it was very bad to be standing here getting colder and colder with her teeth chattering. She moved toward the stove, which had a fire in the center. Her shoes went *squelch, squelch*. She looked behind at the muddy trail she was leaving and bit her lip.

She shed the sacks and rug, dropping them in a tidy pile in the corner. She stepped out of her shoes and abandoned them, too. She grabbed a towel and rubbed her face and hair, feeling the circulation coming back to her skin. But the rest of her was still so chilled.

As he had said, she needed to get out of all these sodden clothes. She couldn't! Then she sternly reminded herself that she was dedicated to pure reason. It made no sense to preserve her modesty at the cost of her life. But she had better do it quickly before her host returned.

She struggled her way out of her gown. She couldn't manage the lowest button with cold fingers, and so in the end she tore it free. The poor gown was done with anyway. That only left her shift and cotton stockings. The stockings were quickly done with and she rubbed her damp legs vigorously with the towel, gasping with pain and relief as the circulation began again.

She saw the way her wet shift clung to her legs and giggled. Some dashing women were said to damp their skirts. She'd certainly gone to extremes in that regard. That reminded her that a young man was going to return at any moment and she was standing here as good as naked.

With a little cry she wrapped the blanket around her but it had scarcely touched her when she realized that it would only get wet from her wet shift. It might be her last bastion of modesty, but it would have to go.

She tore it off and frantically wrapped herself tentlike in the blanket. But that would never do. Her arms were imprisoned inside and if she moved, the whole thing gaped down the front. Ears straining for sound of her host's return, Amy wound the blanket around her body beneath her arms and tucked the end in securely. It was, she told herself, as decent as any gown except for her bare shoulders. She took up two of the small towels and tucked them down the back of her "gown," then crossed them over at the front and tucked the ends in under her arms like a fichu.

There was a small mirror on one wall and Amy peered into it. Her outfit actually looked very respectable. It wasn't of course, but it was the best she could do, and if her host was a villain it surely didn't matter what she was wearing.

She was still a mess. Though her hair was merely wet, her face was streaked with mud. She tried the pump at the sink and found it worked. She scrubbed at her face until it was clean.

Then she allowed herself to go over to the stove.

The warmth washed over her, making her feel dizzy. There were two chairs there and Amy sank into one. She rested her feet on a convenient footstool close to the stove and held out her hands to the warmth, shuddering with the relief.

Hell might be pictured as flames, she thought, but this was surely heaven. She took a towel and rubbed at her hair, then tilted her head toward the heat. For once the crop was useful; it should dry in no time. As she ran her hands through it to speed the process, she looked around thoughtfully.

It was a very plain kitchen. There was the stone sink with the pump and a bucket underneath to catch the drainings. In the center of the room was a deal table and four chairs. To her right were the cupboards she had seen through the window, their contents hidden behind closed doors. Against the far wall stood a dresser with some pottery plates and cups upon it and three silver tankards. They struck her as strange in such a simple household.

But then her host did not belong in this place either.

It was not these things which struck her most, however, though she could not quite decide what did.

After a moment she realized. There was no aroma. She'd never before been in a kitchen without the smell of food.

There was nothing cooking on the stove and, she would guess, hadn't been all day. There were no herbs hanging from the beams, no strings of onions and garlic.

The only sign of food at all was a loaf of bread on the table, along with a crock of butter and some cheese. Was that all her host ate? Perhaps he, too, was a victim of sudden poverty.

Amy became aware of hunger. She longed for some bread and cheese and a cup of hot tea.

There was a blackened kettle keeping warm to one side of the hob, but Amy had no way of knowing where the tea-making things were, if indeed the house could afford such a luxury. Besides, it would be overbold to make so free with someone else's kitchen.

Amy wished her host would return quickly, but then she recalled her state of dress. She might be fully covered but she felt half naked. Moreover, she realized, all her clothes were in that muddy pile in the corner. She no longer had any real clothes fit to wear.

She heard the back door slam and booted footsteps in the passageway.

❧ 3 ❧

H ARRY SHOOK OFF THE CAPE and hung it up, grimacing at the muddy trail into the kitchen. Was it better to clean muddy floors when wet, or was one supposed to leave them to dry like clothes? He hoped the latter. Firkin had been given the day off, and with this weather he'd likely not bother to come back before tomorrow.

Harry sat on the bench and used the bootjack to pull off his wet boots, then put on his slippers.

He wondered who his unexpected guest was. She'd spoken like a lady but that worn-out old cart and the worn-out old horse in the shafts argued at the best genteel poverty.

He supposed she was a penny-pinched spinster of uncertain years and was now in a state of the vapors about being alone with a daring rogue. Well, he'd be charming to her and soon reassure her. He had a gift for charming females of all ages.

Reassuring smile in place, he walked into the kitchen.

And stopped dead.

Sitting beside the practical, mundane stove was an angel in a blanket, looking up at him with huge blue eyes.

Suddenly it registered. Frightened eyes.

Instinct took over. With scarce a moment's hesitation he said cheerfully, "Your nag's taken care of. I moved her into the stables, rubbed her down, and gave her a feed." He swung the kettle over the heat. "I'm sure you can use a cup of tea. I'm afraid I've not much food. Just bread and cheese and a Melton pie." He braced himself and looked at her. Still an angel, but a lot less frightened.

He risked a smile. "Would you like some?"

She smiled back. He could feel his heart begin to pound. He'd seen a lot of lovely women, but he'd never seen one as beautiful as this. Vague notions of fairies and bewitchment began to dance in his head, but he dismissed them. She was all too obviously flesh and blood, and here he was in a situation where it would be positively caddish to show how he felt.

It was an effort to keep the calm smile in place but he made it.

"I would like a piece of pie," she said softly. Her voice was as well bred as he'd thought and very musical.

He went and cut a slice of the pie. "Do you want to eat it there?" he asked.

The angel stood warily, holding on to the blanket. Harry watched, fascinated, unable to suppress the wicked hope that it might come loose and fall. But it stayed secure. With the cream wool down to the floor and the white towels over her shoulders the young woman looked like an Egyptian goddess except that Egyptian goddesses did not have clear blue eyes and an aureole of spun-gold curls.

She sat at the table and started in on the pork pie, her hunger confirming the fact that she was blessedly human. Harry made the tea, using the time to strengthen his self-control. When he was sure he could treat the vision like his aunt Betty, he carried the pot to the table, along with two cups, a pitcher of milk, and the sugar bowl, then sat opposite. If all he could permit himself was a feast for the eyes, then at least he'd make the most of it.

"I must apologize for the state of the hospitality," he said lightly. "We only have one servant here and he's gone off to visit his sister. He was supposed to be back tonight, but with the weather he won't bother."

"We?" she asked, startled.

"It's all right," he reassured her. "They won't be back either. They'll have racked up somewhere." He saw her relax and was pleased at how she trusted him. He just hoped he could prove worthy of that trust. "Coppice Farm belongs to my friend, Terance Cornwallis," he explained as she ate. "I'm staying here for the season with another friend, Chart Ashby."

"Meltonians," she said with a trace of anxiety.

Harry could understand that. The avid hunters were little enough trouble when the scent was up and the hounds running, but if weather canceled the hunts, boredom often led to mischief.

"Not really," he said. "Meltonians are the great guns, the top of the trees. We've a way to go yet." Now that it had brewed, he poured tea into their cups. "I would like it if you would give me your name."

She was startled, which certainly did nothing to mute the effect of her eyes. She had clearly not thought that he did not know her. "Amy de Lacy," she said readily. "Of Stonycourt."

His first impression had been correct. She was a lady. A wild thought began to take possession of his mind. If he had to marry, why not marry an exquisite creature like this? Then he'd be entitled to look at her as much as he pleased and discover if the form beneath the blanket was as promising as it appeared.

He took a breath and stopped his imaginings before they appeared on his face. "I'm afraid I don't know the area very well," he said. "Is Stonycourt near here?"

She sipped from her cup of tea and gave what seemed to be an excessive sigh of pleasure. "About five miles away, over the Lincolnshire border."

"You're a long way from home."

Surprisingly, she colored. That did nothing for his control either. She looked like a naughty, tempting cherub. "I . . . I was supposed to be picking up some layers. We didn't expect such weather."

"No one did, or I doubt even my hunting-mad friends would have gone out."

She tilted her head to one side, and there was a glint of teasing humor in her eyes as she said, "And are you not hunting mad?"

He laughed. "Caught, by Gad! Don't tell anyone."

"Certainly it's a heresy among men," she agreed.

"It's not that I don't like the sport," he assured her. "It's just that I'm not *mad* for it. There's nothing like a fine run on a clear crisp day, but to be slogging along on a soggy one is something I can do without."

Amy was feeling most peculiar. It was not just the rain and the cold followed by dry and warmth; it wasn't even the fact she was sitting here most unconventionally dressed, alone with a gentleman; it was the way he was behaving.

It wasn't that he was unaware of her looks—she'd seen a betraying flicker or two of astonishment. That didn't bother her, for without vanity her mirror told her every day that a person would have to be blind to not notice her beauty. But there was no heat in his eyes that made her want to hide, nor adoration to make her squirm. And he'd not said one word that could be construed as flirtatious.

It was like talking to Jasper.

It was wonderful.

She dared to tease again. "Did you read the comment of William Shenstone that the world may be divided into people that read, people that write, people that think, and fox hunters?"

He grinned. "He'd be strung up for that, these days." He reached for the teapot and refilled their cups.

He was a handsome man, Amy thought, and handsomer when he laughed. She wasn't used to looking at men—she was more accustomed to avoiding them—but now she cautiously indulged a desire to study him.

He had light brown curly hair, hazel eyes, and a clean-cut face, but that wasn't the measure of his handsomeness. It was more the play of expressions on his face, particularly the teasing twinkle that could brighten his eyes and the way those eyes crinkled when he smiled. He was a man who was not afraid to smile.

She finished the last of her pie and tea and refused his offer of more. "When do you think I will be able to leave?" she asked.

"There's no way of telling," he said. "It's still throwing it down, and the roads will be in a terrible state even when it stops. I honestly don't think your horse would make it five yards in this, never mind five miles. I'll lend you one of ours if you want but we've only regular saddles. I'd come with you, of course, but it would still be a devil of a ride. Will your family be very worried?"

"I suppose they will," said Amy, "but it would be madness to go out just yet." She looked up anxiously. "But all the same, I can't spend the night here."

He smiled, and that warm smile allayed her anxiety like a potion. "For all that it's so dark out, Miss de Lacy, that's just the storm. It's not quite three yet. There's plenty of time. If the worse comes to the worst, we'll walk over the hill to Ashridge Farm. The Coneybears will make you welcome, and your reputation will be safe there."

Amy frowned thoughtfully. "This obsession with nighttime isn't very rational, is it? After all, there's nothing to stop us—" She caught her breath and stared at him. This wasn't Jasper.

"Not very rational, no," he said calmly, though she could see the twinkle in his eyes. "But as that's the way the world sees it, that's all we need to deal with."

"That's not quite the way the world sees it," she pointed out firmly. "There could be trouble just about me being here, especially dressed like this."

"But you look charming. You could set a new fashion."

Harry almost added that a beauty such as she could wear sackcloth and set a fashion but realized in time it would be a mistake. It really was incredibly difficult to treat this woman as if she were a sister. He didn't even have any sisters.

He pulled up a mental image of Chart's boisterous sister, Clytemnestra, and tried to think how he handled her. Just as if she were a boy. He realized his companion was speaking.

"It would have the advantage of economy," she agreed dryly. Then she frowned. "I have also to be concerned, however, about what I am to wear when I leave."

Harry was startled. He looked at the muddy pile which was her clothing. "And the only spare clothes in this house," he said, "are men's."

"That would stir up the dust," she said. She was trying for a blasé tone but her anxiety showed through. "If I return home in any change of clothing, questions are sure to be asked. I do not wish to cause you any embarrassment."

Harry was considering that this might be the time to propose to her and soothe her fears, but his instinct told him it would not be a good idea.

She rose and went to inspect the muddy pile. "I think I'd better try to wash the dress."

"I can't imagine it will do any good."

She looked a reproach for such negative thinking. "What other choice do I have?"

Skeptically, Harry pulled out a tin tub and put it on the table. "I think this is what Firkin does the wash in if he does, but we have a woman in once a week for such things. What else do you need?"

"Water," Amy said. "Hot would be best, but I think we must make do with cold. There's no time to heat any if this is to be washed and dried. I need soap. I don't suppose you have any borax?"

"Not as far as I know." Harry passed over the bar of soap, then applied the pump and filled a bucket with water. As he poured it in the tub, Amy was paring fine strips off the soap into a dish full of the last hot water from the kettle.

Two buckets of water half filled the tub, and Amy poured in the liquid soap. Then she picked up the muddy lump which had been Beryl's blue stripe cambric and carried it at arm's length to the tub. Being careful not to splash herself, Amy sloshed the dress around and the water grew very muddy, very quickly.

"Good Lord," said Harry. "It's blue."

"Was," Amy said sadly. "It was my sister's favorite dress."

Harry was about to ask why she had been wearing it, especially on a mundane trip to pick up hens, but held his tongue. His original assumption of poverty was doubtless correct, and there could be all sorts of embarrassing reasons for the act.

He watched as she picked up the dress and banged it

down, working out the dirt as best as she could. There was something strangely erotic about this delicate-looking beauty up to her elbows in suds. Perhaps it was seeing the silky roundness of her arms proving to be so capable.

She stood up with a sigh. "I think we'd better try fresh water."

Harry obediently tipped out the dirty water and filled the tub again. He'd never even considered the matter of laundry before, and here he was taking an active part. It was obvious that Amy de Lacy was familiar with the process. More evidence of abject poverty.

He imagined this poor family come down in the world and living in a cottage with only one good dress between them. It doubtless explained Miss de Lacy's self-possession while dressed so strangely. Perhaps, he thought—allowing his imagination full rein—they all wore blankets at home while waiting for their turn with the dress.

She was going to be overwhelmed when he asked her to marry him. He would provide all the comforts of life for her destitute family, and she would fall deeply in love with him.

"Do you have just the one sister?" he asked as she worried over the dress with the bar of soap, trying to get out some of the dirt around the hem.

"No, two," she answered readily. "Beryl's my older sister and Jacinth's my younger."

"Do you have any brothers?"

"Just one. Jasper."

He made the connection. "Beryl, Jasper, Jacinth, all living at Stonycourt. Your parents must have been of a humorous disposition."

She looked up with a rueful smile. "Whimsical, at least."

"They should have called you Sapphire." It was out before he could stop it.

She looked slightly disappointed in him but merely said, "Or Aquamarine."

"How did you escape with Amy?"

"Simple good fortune," she said, once more bent to her work.

In the end she had to accept that she'd done all she could. The gown was now blue and the stripes could be seen, but there were heavy dirt stains fixed in the material, particularly around the hem. Amy hauled the garment out of the water and wrung it out as best she could, which wasn't very well. "I don't suppose you have a mangle," she said.

"I'm afraid not."

She looked around thoughtfully. "Do you mind the floor getting wetter?"

Harry looked down at the stone flags, which were awash with muddy water. "All the better to wash it with, I'd suppose."

She passed him the bodice of the dress and took the hem end herself. "Twist."

"Twist?"

He saw what she was doing and began to turn the cloth in the opposite direction, keeping it taut all the while. Water began to pour out.

"This can't be doing the garment much good," he pointed out.

"This garment is past its last prayers," said Amy, twisting harder.

"Perhaps I should buy you a new one," he said.

"Why?" she asked with a blankly mystified look. "This is none of your doing."

Harry accepted it. He could hardly explain that he didn't want his future wife in rags, but he began to plan a wardrobe for her. He had never been much interested in women's clothes, but now he imagined Amy in cerulean blue silk with silver net; in dusky pink muslin trimmed with blond; in pristine white with roses in her hair.

He realized the work was getting harder as the dress became tight and began to twist on itself. Amy continued to turn her end, grimacing with the effort, determined to squeeze every last drop she could.

The dress coiled into a tighter and tighter bundle, and Harry and Amy were drawn closer and closer together. When Amy gave the final, grunting twist and said, "There!" she looked up and found herself inches from him.

Her mouth went dry and her head felt light. It was all that effort. She saw the fine chiseled shape of the end of his nose and thought it very pleasing indeed. She raised her eyes, and there was a warmth in his which shivered through her in the strangest way.

They were just standing there. She pulled the dress from his hold and hurried over to hang it in front of the stove, being careful that it couldn't catch fire.

That would be typical of today, she decided, that her clothes and her very shelter burn down around her ears.

As she stretched the cloth to try to lessen the creases she wondered what had made her feel so funny. It was this situation. In this predicament it was hardly surprising that she felt peculiar. For the first time in her life she would quite like to have a case of the vapors if she had any idea how to do it. She could at least appreciate the appeal. Just to let go, give up, and let someone else take care of everything.

Let him take care of everything?

She checked that her drapery was all securely in place and turned. He was looking out the window. He glanced at her. "Still very heavy," he said easily. "I think it will be at least an hour before it stops."

So he hadn't felt anything strange. That made her lapse

even worse. Here was the one man she had met who treated her as a normal person and she was turning silly.

He was saying something else. "But you'll need that long for your dress to even begin to dry. You know," he said as he left the window, "I don't feel it's at all wise for you to try to travel five miles in damp clothes on a chilly day."

"What else do you suggest?" Amy heard the edge of sarcasm in her voice and regretted it. She *was* dreading the trip home.

"You could go to Ashridge Farm, and I could ride over and reassure your family. Do you have parents still alive, by the way?" The question seemed to have importance for him.

"No, my father died two years ago, my mother six."

"I'm sorry. Who is your guardian, then?"

"My uncle, but he doesn't live with us. We have an aunt to lend us respectability." She couldn't understand why he seemed to find this displeasing, too. He must be a very high stickler. What would he think to find out that the de Lacys lived almost entirely in the kitchen—certainly in the winter months—and did almost everything for themselves because they felt guilty at asking anything of their two elderly and unpaid retainers?

"About Ashridge Farm," he prompted her.

Amy gathered her wits. "I suppose it is my only option," she admitted. "If you don't mind riding over to Stonycourt."

"I will be delighted," he said with a little bow.

He seemed to have turned rather serious. Amy felt uncomfortable with the lull in conversation and so she walked over to the table, hitching up her blanket so it didn't trail on the muddy floor. She studied the doll there. "It's an automaton!" she declared in delight.

He came to join her. "A broken one."

Amy sat down and touched the silk skirt with a gentle

finger. "She's lovely. I had a doll once very like her. French, I think."

"Yes, but the mechanism is German. I'm mending her."

"Why?"

He looked up a little coolly. "Because otherwise she'd go on the rubbish dump."

Amy realized her question had seemed unfeeling and flushed. "I meant, why you?"

He sat down in front of the doll. "It's a hobby. I like to fix things, and these are often so beautiful it seems very worth the trouble. My mother finds them for me."

"You haven't told me anything of your family," she said. It was only a second later she knew that the curiosity she felt about this man was unwise.

"I'm an only child," he answered readily. "My mother and father are still living. Down in Hampshire."

"You're a gentleman," Amy said and tried to revive her teasing note. "You spend winter hunting, spring dancing and gambling."

"I don't gamble," he said with a lazy smile. "And I spend the summer sailing."

Amy's heart gave a little lurch. "Oh, I envy you!" Then she wished it unsaid. It was not wise to show one wanted things.

"You like to sail?" he asked. "Strange for a person living in the middle of the country."

"My father took us once with a friend," she said primly. "It was very pleasant." It was one of the best times of her life, but she didn't want him to know that.

He looked at her quizzically but then moved the automaton a little. "When I was interrupted," he said with a smile, "I was trying to see the state of the spring at the top of this lady's leg. I'll feel better about such a delicate operation now she has a chaperon."

Amy grinned at the thought. "Does my charge have a name?"

"Not as far as I know. Why don't you christen her?"

"Jane," Amy promptly said.

He looked at the elegant lady with the silk clothes and the high-powered hairstyle. "She doesn't look like a Jane to me, but if you wish." He began to inch his fingers up the doll's leg.

Amy giggled and felt herself color. "As Jane's chaperon, I don't think I should allow you to do that, sir."

"Think of me as her doctor," he said, and something in the way he said it set Amy's heart speeding. She was determined not to embarrass herself by showing it.

When he lifted the skirts to reveal layers of silk and lace petticoats, she protested again. "Really, sir! Can you not, as some doctors are supposed to do, examine by feeling alone?"

His eyes twinkled. "I'm afraid not." There was more to the words and the smile. Or Amy felt there was more. As his sensitive, long-fingered hands moved Jane's pale, porcelain leg Amy felt her face heat. She imagined his hands on her own leg.

He lifted that leg and stretched it.

Amy leapt to her feet.

He looked up and there was a flicker of humor in his eyes. "Is something the matter?"

"The dress," Amy gasped. "I must turn the dress!" She fled over to the hearth.

Parts of the gown were dry, but other parts were very damp. Amy rearranged the gown so that the thicker parts of the bodice and sleeves would be close to the heat, wishing she was near something cold, not hot, so she would have a chance to cool her burning face.

She couldn't think what had come over her. She had never had such thoughts before in her life. And with poor Mr. Crisp. The one man who had not ogled her, or protested his devotion, or done anything at all to embarrass her. And here she was having lewd thoughts about him.

When she'd finished with the dress, she sat in the chair by the fire but still watched him from half a room away.

He looked over. "Are you cold? There are more blankets."

"N-no." Amy swallowed. "I'd better keep an eye on the dress. It might scorch. I can preserve poor Jane's virtue from here."

He accepted it and they sat in silence as he worked, only the crackling of coal and the ticking of the kitchen clock to disturb the peace. His fingers were constantly entangled in the silk and lace of Jane's petticoats, and Amy's thoughts were extraordinary.

Then Amy realized the rain had stopped, and a glance at the window confirmed this. There was even a lightening as the clouds lifted, but the natural darkness of evening was gathering.

She glanced at the clock. "It's five o'clock," she said. "I should go."

He looked up from his work. "So it is. We'll go in a minute, but I think I've fixed part of Lady Jane. It was just a loose connection. Come and look."

As if pulled by strings, Amy moved back to the table. He gave the key a few turns. A sweet, tinkling minuet started and the lady turned slightly. Her leg began to rise in an elegant and amazingly realistic manner.

There was a *ping*, and it collapsed limp again as the music slowed and stopped.

He laughed. "A long way to go yet, I'm afraid."

Amy touched the silk skirt. "She will be lovely when she works, though."

"Yes."

She looked up and their eyes met. Amy knew there was something she wanted to say, but didn't know what it was.

His smile was rueful as he stood up. "You're right. It's time to go. I think it might be best if we don't tell the Coneybears you have been here at all. We can say you sheltered in the barn and only asked my help when the rain stopped."

"That sounds nonsensical to me," protested Amy.

His warm hazel eyes twinkled. "And you do not like to be thought foolish. Do you always do the sensible thing, Amy de Lacy?"

"I try," retorted Amy, for some reason feeling defensive. "You probably don't think that very womanly."

"Don't I?"

He was laughing at her. She quickly turned away. "I don't suppose so," she said. "You would doubtless approve of me far more if I had fainted out in the road and were sinking into the grave from inflammation of the lungs!"

"Now that makes *me* sound remarkably foolish."

He had come up behind her, and she could sense the warmth of his presence there. His hands settled over her towel-covered shoulders and turned her around.

Amy felt breathlessly dizzy as she looked up, and completely adrift. What was she doing? What was she supposed to be doing? What did she want to be doing?

He lowered his lips and touched them to hers. It was the lightest touch, velvet soft and warm. It was lovely.

Amy jerked her lips away but his hands prevented further escape.

"I'm sorry," he said gently. "I shouldn't have done that." He did not sound repentant.

"No, no," she stammered. Then, "Yes. I mean you shouldn't have. We shouldn't have. . . ." His hands were still on her shoulders, a firm warm pressure that seemed to be seeping down into her as the damp chill had done so many hours ago.

"Perhaps not," he said, and his thumbs made little circles against her collarbone. "But it was not so terrible a sin." His right hand moved like a warm breeze across her shoulder to her bare neck. She gasped as she felt the soft brush of his fingers against her skin. She knew from his expression that he was thinking of more sinful things, and here she was, doing nothing to stop him.

He caught his breath and moved a yard or two away. "I do beg your pardon," he said. He looked around, as if at a loss, and his eyes fastened on her gown. "Perhaps your dress is dry."

Amy forced her limbs into movement and went to the dress. It was dry in parts but not in others but she had no intention of lingering here a moment longer. She knew what was happening here and it mustn't. It had only been a couple of hours. It was not too late. "It's dry enough," she said. "My family will be concerned. We must go to the farm quickly so that you can take a message to Stonycourt."

"Of course," he said, as if nothing significant had happened. But the power of the look in his eyes contradicted his tone and sent a shudder through her. "I'll just go upstairs and dress more warmly. You can put on your dress."

When he'd gone, the madness faded a little. Amy looked at her clothing in despair. For a supposedly sensible couple they'd not done very well. They'd done nothing about her shift, stockings, and shoes. What had they been thinking of?

❧ 4 ❧

AMY SPENT A FEW MOMENTS trying to gather the forti-
tude to put on her sodden, dirty shift but could not do
it. Anyway, it was clearly nonsensical, and now above all times
was the time to be sensible.

With a shudder she wriggled into the wet stockings. She
could disguise the lack of a shift but she could hardly go
barefoot and if she was to put on the soaking shoes she
might as well bear the stockings. Then she put on the dress.
At least it was warmly damp, not clammy.

When she came to fasten it she remembered the bottom
button. Well, there was nothing to be done about it.

He cleared his throat outside the door. "Is it all right for
me to come in, Miss de Lacy?"

"Yes," she said.

He frowned when he saw her. "The sooner we get you to
Ashridge and into dry clothes again, the better. Take the
blanket to wrap around yourself."

Amy picked it up but said, "There is a button missing at the back of my gown. Do you have a pin to fasten it with?"

He came to look. It only then occurred to Amy that without her shift he would be looking at her bare back where the dress gaped. She didn't know why that seemed so dangerous, but it did.

"It doesn't matter," she said quickly.

"Hold on," he said, hands on her shoulders again, but impersonally. "I can fix it with my cravat pin."

Amy pulled herself out of his hold. "Don't be silly! That *would* set the cat among the pigeons."

He grinned. "I suppose it would. Never mind. It's only a small gap and it will be covered by the blanket. All set?"

As they walked down the passage toward the door, he said, "Look, there's an old pair of pattens here, belonged to Corny's aunt. Do you want to borrow them?"

"I think my shoes are past protection, but the pattens may keep me out of the mud." She tied them on and found the fit tolerable. The iron rings raised her a good three inches so that her eyes rose from his chin to his nose. She wasn't sure why this seemed significant.

She turned and *clink, clink, clink*ed her way to the door.

"I don't know why you women insist on wearing those things," he said. "A pair of boots would be better."

Amy turned. "And needing a jack to get in and out of. Not very practical for a farm woman who's in and out all the time."

"And who has to clean the floors," he acknowledged. "I see what you mean."

He opened the door and they went out. The air was heavy with moisture and chill, too, but the wind had died down. Within her blanket, Amy was not too cold, though she knew her legs and feet would soon be frigid.

She was more concerned, however, with pondering this

man's reaction to her contradiction. Experience had taught her that men did not like being told they'd said something silly, but she always forgot and told them anyway. This Mr. Crisp hadn't seemed to mind at all.

They crossed the muddy, bepuddled yard to a stile. Amy had to take his hand as she climbed over it, and the touch reminded her of that kiss. She looked at him, met his eyes, and looked away. This would not do at all.

They followed a footpath across a field of sheep and lambs, and Amy was glad of the pattens, which kept her feet above the soggy ground. The sheep watched the humans as they passed; the lambs gamboled forward and back, daring each other toward danger.

"Lambs are endearing, aren't they?" he said.

Amy thought so, too, but wanted no part of sweet sentiment today. "It's a shame they'll soon look as stupid as their mothers," she said flatly, "or end up as roast or stew."

He looked at her sharply. She met his eyes and saw his shock. That should nip any romantic nonsense in the bud.

But she was aware of a leaning toward sentiment herself, a desire to delight in lambs and courting birds, spring flowers and pretty ballads. She stamped on it firmly. She had to be ruthlessly practical.

It all came of having such an impractical family. How could she give in to nonsense when she had a brother who spent his book money on lottery tickets, sisters who believed that wishes would come true, and a father who had given no thought to the future.

Sir Digby had not been a desperate, haggard debtor; he'd been as happy as a bee in honey as long as he could somehow continue to provide fine wines, rich food, silk dresses, and prime horses for his family.

Amy couldn't understand such a mentality at all.

"Don't look so worried," her companion said. "It'll take me no time at all to ride over to your place and reassure your family."

She realized they must have been walking for some time. They were coming to the end of the sheep pasture; Coppice Farm was behind some trees, and another, more prosperous farm was ahead at the top of the rise. Presumably Ashridge.

"I'm sorry. I was woolgathering."

He smiled. "Very appropriate among a field of sheep, and these seem to have a fine thick fleece."

They came to a gate. As he opened it he picked a long tuft of wool from the hedge. After they were through and the gate was securely shut, he gave it to her with a smile. "A fleece for your thoughts?"

She took it and rubbed it between her fingers, feeling the grease in it. "Just family troubles, Mr. Crisp." She determined to make sure he had no illusions. "You'll doubtless have realized we don't have much money."

"I don't think any the less of you for it."

"So I should think," Amy retorted. "Money isn't the sole determinator of quality, Mr. Crisp."

He raised his brows. "Has anyone ever told you you've got a damned sharp edge to your tongue, Miss de Lacy?"

He was daring to criticize her. "Yes," she said. "Doubtless the same people who tell you you've got an uncouth edge to yours."

"Uncouth!" He caught his breath and his temper. "All I meant, Miss de Lacy, was that I don't look down on you or your family for being poor, as I'm sure other people do, it being the way of the world. Is that deserving of rebuke?"

"I—" Amy caught herself, too. What was going on? She was normally the most moderate of people. "I am sorry," she said sincerely. "And after you've been so kind. I'm just not myself, Mr. Crisp, and you're right, there are family problems, but not ones I can discuss with a stranger. Please excuse my outburst."

They had come to a stop during their spat, and now he touched her elbow to urge her on toward the gate which led into the yard of Ashridge Farm. "You are excused. This must have been an ordeal." He stopped by the gate and smiled at her in a way that reminded her of that strange time in the warm kitchen. "I don't suppose you could bring yourself to call me Harry, by way of reparation."

Amy felt a pang of alarm. "Of course not," she said, rather more sharply than she had intended.

"No, of course not," he repeated without offense as he ushered her through the gate. "But despite our brief acquaintance I feel very at ease with you, almost like a brother. I have no sisters, though, so I don't know how a brother really feels."

Relieved at his light tone, Amy grinned at him. "Blue-deviled, I think. Jasper seems to think his sisters are his cross to bear."

He smiled. "My friend Chart appears to feel the same way, but protective, too. Toward his younger one at least."

"Poor Jasper has only older sisters. Even his twin came into the world ahead of him."

They crossed another muddy yard, and the farmhouse door opened before they got there. In it stood a pretty, brown-haired, brown-eyed girl in cap and apron. "Good day to you, Mr. Crisp."

"Good day, Meg. This lady got caught in the rain near our place. I was hoping your mother would give her shelter for the night. Then I can ride over and tell her family she's safe."

The girl was already standing back and urging them in.

In moments, Amy was in a proper kitchen. Pots were

bubbling on the hob, filling the place with warm, aromatic steam. Five loaves sat cooling, adding their own perfume. A big pie sat on a table already laid for dinner.

Mrs. Coneybear came forward. "Oh, the poor young lady! Come stir the gravy, Meg, while I see to things. Why," the gaunt woman said as she came toward them, "it's Miss de Lacy, isn't it?"

"Miss Amy de Lacy," Amy said. "I'm surprised to be recognized so far from home."

The woman chuckled. "Once seen, never forgotten, dear. Saw you at Stamford market last year. Are you wet? Oh dear, you are. You'll catch your death. Now, Mr. Crisp, if you're to ride over to Stonycourt, you'd best be on your way. Night's coming."

And so Amy found her good samaritan gone without a special farewell, but she scarce had time to consider if this was a good thing or not as she was sent off with a talkative Meg to find dry clothes.

"Put us all in a tizzy, I'll tell you, having three fine young gentlemen a-come and live next door. Very nice, they be, when all's said and done. They come over now and then to get milk and eggs and such, seeing as they mostly have just the one servant."

She opened a wardrobe within which the clothes hung on hooks and pulled out a green print gown. "Here, try this, miss. It'll doubtless be a mite tight around the top, but it's this or nothing, for Ma's flat as a board, despite having bore five kiddies."

She cheerfully helped Amy out of her gown and didn't say anything about the lack of a shift but produced one of her own. Amy wondered what she was thinking, and could feel her face heat up. She wanted to protest her innocence but knew that would be the worst thing to do.

"Yes," Meg went on, "Ma said it was as well I was already smitten with Martin Howgarth before those three turned up, or I might have gone and done something silly."

Was that a sly dig?

"Course, that Mr. Ashby's the handsomest. But he's got a bit too much of an air to him for my taste. Grandson of a duke, he is, so they say. And Mr. Cornwallis, he's a lovely man, but ever so shy. He stays here most of the year, so we see a lot of him. Ma has him over for dinner every now and then. She seems to think he'll starve to death, though you only have to look at him to see that t'ain't likely to be his problem."

Amy was in the dress and Meg was forcing the buttons together. "I'm not sure it will fit," Amy protested.

"Course, it will," Meg said cheerfully, and gave another tug, which rendered Amy nearly as flat as Mrs. Coneybear. "Which do you think's the most handsome?" Meg asked.

Amy found once the buttons were fastened, it was not too uncomfortable. In a small mirror, she could see the effect was rather like a Tudor stomacher. Her bosom was flattened out. She was thinking of adopting the style when she remembered she was supposed to be flaunting her assets, not concealing them.

"Well?" Meg prompted.

Amy remembered the question. "I . . . er . . . only saw Mr. Crisp. I'm not sure any other gentlemen were at home."

"Out hunting," said Meg, with a nod of her head as she gathered up the dress and stockings. "Mad for it, they be. I'll put these in to soak, will I?"

"Do you think it will do any good?" Amy asked.

"Can't hurt," said Meg, heading for the door. "Come you down. The men'll be in for dinner in a moment. I think Mr. Crisp is nicest. And he's good enough looking when he smiles. He's got a lovely smile."

"Yes," said Amy wistfully. "I suppose they're all very rich," she said, not really believing it.

"They're not short a groat," said Meg with a flashing grin over her shoulder. "Mr. Ashby paid a hundred guineas for a horse a few weeks back. A hundred guineas! Da couldn't get over it. But I don't reckon they're rich by your standards. Mr. Crisp and Mr. Ashby are oldest sons, though, so they'll come into a fair bit one day I suppose."

Not soon enough to be any use to me, thought Amy.

Meg dumped the dress and stockings in a tub and disappeared. In a few moments she was back with a large bucket of hot water. She pumped in some cold, then added hot, then threw in some softened soap and some liquids.

"What are they?" Amy asked.

"Turpentine and hartshorn. Works a treat on stuff like this."

Full of energy, Meg grasped a dolly-stick and started to pummel the garments with it. Amy felt exhausted just watching her.

"They'll never be the same, but they might be wearable," Meg said cheerfully. She considered Amy as she worked. "You're a grand looker, miss. Mr. Crisp was giving you the eye." She gave a cheeky wink. "You interested in him?"

"No," said Amy quickly.

Meg accepted it. "I suppose most men make a sheep's eye at you," she said without a trace of envy. "He's going to be a lord, though, one day. You could do worse."

"He is?" He'd avoided giving her that information. Amy wondered why.

Meg nodded. "Can't remember lord of what. There!" She hauled out the dolly and hung it on the wall. "We'll just let them soak." There was a shout from the kitchen. "Come on,

Ma'll need my help, and you look as if you could do with some food."

Amy trailed slowly after. She realized her day's misadventures had exhausted her, but she wondered if she had ever had the bursting vitality of Meg Coneybear. Perhaps it was as well fate had destined her to be ornamental rather than useful.

She shook off that depressing thought and told herself it was simple lack of food that made her so mawkish.

If that was the problem, she had come to the right place to solve it. Even in their prosperous days, the de Lacys had not eaten with the gusto of the Coneybears. She could quite see that the thought of the young men living on bread and cheese would wound Mrs. Coneybear to the heart.

Ten people sat to the table, including Amy. There were Mr. and Mrs. Coneybear, Meg, three robust sons, two working men, and a healthy young giant who turned out to be Martin Howgarth, Meg's intended. Amy understood why Meg had not had her head turned by the young gentlemen at Coppice Farm, for Martin was handsome enough and plainly adored the girl.

His warm attention to his bride-to-be had a strange effect on Amy. She wished she was loved like that. She wished she had some chance of being loved like that. A mercenary marriage seemed unlikely to produce that kind of devotion.

The huge pie was steak and kidney, and it was served with masses of potatoes, turnips, and greens and great slabs of bread and butter. It was followed by a choice of damson pie or bilberry, both with custard. The men consumed vast quantities, washing it down with home-brewed ale. When they'd finished, they sat nibbling at cheese, just to keep starvation at bay.

Amy had seen all the men's eyes widen at first looking at

her, but they'd been too concerned with the food to make anything of it. Now, however, as Meg and her mother cleared the table and the pipes came out, Amy saw a selection of looks directed at her. Mostly they were just frankly admiring, though Amy feared the youngest Coneybear son had a touch of idolatry in his eyes. And one of the farm workers had a lustful gleam in his eye.

She decided it was time to disappear. She rose to her feet. "Thank you for the meal, Mrs. Coneybear. It was delicious. I'm afraid, after my adventure, I feel very tired. Could you show me where I could sleep?"

The lustful man sniggered, but a stern look from Mrs. Coneybear shut him up.

"Course, dear," the woman said. "You can sleep with Meg. Just you go up. Meg'll come up in a minute with a hot brick."

"Oh, that's not necessary."

"We don't want you taking pneumonia, Miss de Lacy. You do as I tell you. You'll feel more the thing in the morning."

Amy was no sooner in the bedroom than Meg scampered in after her, pulled out a flannelette nightgown, and gave it her. Then she was gone.

Amy changed and slipped into the bed, which was not very cold. Within minutes Meg was back with the brick wrapped in layers of flannel. She pushed it in by Amy's feet. "One thing," she said cheerfully, "you'll have the bed right cozy for me by the time I come up."

At the door she turned. "What d'you think of him, then?"

For a second, Amy assumed she meant Harry Crisp, but then she realized her mistake. "Mr. Howgarth seems a pleasant man, and very handsome."

Meg's face lit up in a starry smile. "Isn't he? We're to be married come June. I can hardly wait."

Her meaning was earthy and direct and wholesome.

After she'd gone, Amy lay thinking of that amiable giant: of his warm lazy smile following his darling as she bustled about the room, of his solidly muscled forearms and his hairy chest showing at the vee of his open shirt.

The thoughts slid over, somehow, to Harry Crisp. She had seen no part of his body except his hands and face. Would she see him again? Or would she be returned home by the Coneybears?

She shouldn't see him again. She was a fortune hunter, and he didn't have the kind of fortune she required. And he seemed able to stir in her wanton thoughts the like of which she had never experienced before; thoughts which made her want to consign Owen Staverley and all other wealthy bachelors to the devil.

She wiped away a slow trickle of tears. They were just tiredness. That was all they were. Amy fell asleep before Meg joined her and woke after the girl had gone. That was hardly surprising, for she could tell by the sun that it must be the middle of the morning. Feeling like a slugabed, she leapt out of bed and washed her face and hands in the water provided. She felt a great deal more like herself and able to face anything.

She remembered her weak, sentimental feelings of the night before and laughed, dismissing them as the product of an overly tired mind.

To her amazement, Beryl's dress was laid on a chair, faded but with nearly all the stains removed, and pressed almost to elegance. Her poor mistreated stockings were snowy white and, she saw when she picked them up, neatly darned in two places where there had been no darn before.

She detected Meg's indefatigable work and sighed. She felt such a useless, ornamental creature next to the robust girl. It was both reassuring and disconcerting to remember that Martin Howgarth had not given the beautiful Amy de Lacy a moment's more attention than he'd had to, but had cared only for his bride-to-be. Clearly a man who knew a treasure when he found one.

Had they walked out together last night, Meg and Martin, holding hands in the moonlight, talking of plans for their home and their family? Perhaps stopping for a kiss.

Amy walked down the stairs to the busy kitchen. She could hear Meg and her mother chattering away accompanied by the clatter of constant work. The chatter was mostly Meg's. Amy smiled, realizing that even after such a brief acquaintance, she would miss the girl.

She walked into the kitchen and stopped dead. Three young men were tucking into huge plates of sausage, eggs, and fried bread.

The one facing her, a rotund young man with gingerish hair, froze, a forkful of food midway to his mouth.

Alerted, the other two swiveled.

Harry Crisp rose to his feet, his charming smile lighting his face. "Miss de Lacy. You are looking a great deal better."

Amy gave him her hand and a smile and turned to his companion. The second man grinned at her appreciatively as he slowly rose to his feet. He was as tall and broad as Harry Crisp, but dark haired and gray eyed. He was an altogether handsomer and bolder specimen. His fine eyes gleamed with appreciation, yet Amy could not take offense. It was the unabashed acknowledgment of one fine bird for another.

Harry followed her eyes. "Allow me to present my friends, Miss de Lacy. Chart Ashby and Terance Cornwallis."

By this time the rotund one had come to his senses. He dropped his fork and got to his feet to stammer an incoherent greeting.

Chart Ashby took her hand and kissed it with lingering

expertise. Amy just gave him a humorous look; she knew the type. It was Harry Crisp who took offense, drew her away, and guided her to a seat at the table. The gentlemen all sat down. Meg bustled over with a plate full of food and a mug of tea, which she placed before Amy with a cheerful smile.

Amy wondered how she could eat a fraction of it, but clearly the men would not feel happy about eating until she was, so she started.

When she'd swallowed the first mouthful she turned to Harry Crisp. "Were my family worried?"

He frowned slightly. "Not really. I suppose they know you're a sensible person who would seek shelter." He looked up at her gave a slight wink, which reminded her that they shared secrets.

Amy colored and broke eye contact. This caused her gaze to fall on the handsome Mr. Ashby, who was looking intrigued. She felt her face heat even more. He had the look of a man who noticed things and would not be above making mischief if it suited him.

"They certainly know I'm sensible," she said firmly and cut another piece of sausage. "I'm famous for it. I hope they made you welcome." She considered the delicious sausage and remembered that yesterday's dinner was to have been potato pie. Looking down at the feast on her plate, she wondered what he'd made of it.

"I came straight back," he said, "in case you needed reassurance. But you were already in bed. Mrs. Coneybear gave me some leftovers."

"Mrs. Coneybear's leftovers would delight the Regent himself," said Chart Ashby, directing a brilliant smile at the farmer's wife.

There was a touch of red in the woman's cheeks as she grinned. "Go on with you, Mr. Ashby."

He turned the same smile on Amy. "Fortunate for us you were so far from home, Miss de Lacy."

Amy stiffened. She found his manner altogether too warm. "What do you mean by that, sir?"

His smile broadened. "Why, only that you have given us an excuse to come begging at Mrs. Coneybear's table."

Amy felt tricked into the wrong. Thank heavens this man had not been alone at Coppice Farm yesterday. Heaven knows what would have become of her. She saw a look flash between Harry Crisp and his friend, and with a smile Mr. Ashby returned his attention to his food.

Harry said, "I believe your aunt was concerned. It appears you hadn't made it clear where you were going. But your sister was sure you would be safe, but for some reason she seemed to think you would be at Prior's Grange at Upper Kennet."

Amy could feel guilt rise in her cheeks. "I wonder why," she said lightly, then lied shamelessly. "I'm afraid Beryl thinks she has powers of precognition. She likes to guess things, but she's rarely correct."

Chart Ashby laid down his knife and fork. "If she guessed Upper Kennet with nothing to go on she got remarkably close. Perhaps you should charge for her services."

"A miss is as good as a mile, as they say," Amy retorted and addressed herself to Harry. "I must thank you again for riding over, sir. And now, will Zephyr be fit for the return journey?"

All three young men appeared to have a choking fit at the name. Amy struggled but then she burst out laughing. "It is ridiculous," she admitted as she wiped away tears. "But she was probably young and speedy once."

"Not with those hocks," said Mr. Cornwallis seriously.

Amy looked at him. "Oh dear, and I'd always consoled myself with the thought of her flighty youth."

Mr. Cornwallis colored and stuffed more fried bread in his mouth.

"Whatever her past," said Harry, "she appears as able as she was yesterday, and I've mended the ribbons. I think you can make it home, but of course we'll escort you to make sure."

"Oh, that's not at all necessary," Amy said. She needed to put the full five miles between herself and Harry Crisp as soon as possible.

"It assuredly is," he said. "Besides, Corny's fellow, Firkin, did try to get back yesterday and slipped and twisted his leg. He's laid up at his sister's for the next few weeks. We thought we'd ride over to a friend of ours after seeing you safe, see if he can put us up for a day or two while we find a replacement." He winked up at Mrs. Coneybear. "We did ask if we could hire Meg, but her mother won't have it."

Mrs. Coneybear gave a wry smile. "Quite apart from the fact that I need her here, Mr. Crisp, as they say around here, 'tis a foolish shepherd what puts sheep in with wolves."

Meg giggled and flashed a look at Chart Ashby. He made a gesture of mock alarm. "Don't flirt with me, girl. Martin'll tear my arms off!"

"That he will," Meg said saucily and went off on an errand with a laugh and a swing of her hips.

Her mother sighed. "I'll be glad to see that one safely wed. So you'll be away a few days, sirs. I'm sorry to hear about Josh Firkin, but I'm sure I can find you someone if you want me to look."

As they discussed this, Amy messed aimlessly with the remains of the food on her plate, until she realized what she was doing and stopped it. Why did she envy Meg so?

Because Meg was so sure of her place in her family's affections, and in those of her husband-to-be. And doubtless in the Howgarth family, wherever they were.

These days Amy's family seemed to see her only as a task-master and a wet blanket, and Jassy, at least, envied her beauty. The future offered little chance of improvement. Either she must continue to bully her family into economy or sell herself to the highest bidder. She could hardly expect a man who bought beauty to have the kind of wholesome warmth Martin showed for Meg. And if she married an older man for his money, his family would surely all hate her.

A hand covered hers. She looked up. It was Harry Crisp. They were alone. She could hear Mrs. Coneybear talking to the other men outside.

"What is it?" he asked seriously. "Do you not feel well?"

Amy pulled her hand away. "I feel perfectly well. Are we ready to go?"

She would have left the kitchen, but he detained her with a gentle hand on her arm. "You are unhappy, Miss de Lacy. I wish you would tell me why. Is it your family?"

Amy had the strangest urge to lean against his broad chest and have all her problems soothed away.

He spoke again. "I couldn't help but think your family were not as concerned as I would expect, Miss de Lacy."

"Don't criticize them," she said sharply, stepping away. "It is as you said. They knew I could take care of myself."

He stiffened and removed his hand. "I'm sure you can, too," he said coolly, "but I would still be concerned if you were out in a storm."

Despite the coolness, there was a message in his eyes which a part of Amy hungered to read but another part knew would be disastrous. "You have been very kind, sir," she said flatly, "but my safety, and my high or low spirits, are none of your concern."

With that she finally made her escape.

❧ 5 ❧

TRUE TO THEIR WORD, the three young men escorted her home, but Zephyr's ambling pace was too much for their patience, and they took turns at racing off across nearby fields and setting their mounts at a variety of obstacles, often at hair-raising speed.

Amy couldn't help thrilling at their magnificent horsemanship, even as she told herself they were reckless fools and that Mr. Owen Staverley would prove to be a quiet, restful companion in life.

Harry Crisp chose to escape rather less often than the others, and showed less impatience with ambling alongside the cart chatting to Amy.

"You're going to have to retire poor Zephyr soon," he said at one point.

"I know," said Amy with a sigh. "But that will leave us entirely without transportation." She was perfectly happy to hammer home their destitution in order to squelch any inconvenient tendencies on his part.

"You could replace her for a few guineas," he pointed out. "Surely that would be a good investment."

"A few guineas may seem nothing to you, sir, but we simply do not have it to spare."

She saw him raise his brows skeptically, but he did not persist. "Then I suppose you will have to depend on neighbors for assistance. When you need to go into Stamford or such like."

"I am sure they will be pleased to help if it should become necessary," Amy said, hearing the chill in her voice. It was perhaps ungracious, but she felt as if she were being interrogated. The fact was that their friends and neighbors had been very kind, but the de Lacys had refused most offers of help. They could not be forever accepting hospitality they could not return.

"Miss de Lacy," he said with a frown, though not unkindly. "I fear you are ill advised. It can happen to anyone, to fall on hard times, and I am sure your friends and neighbors would take pleasure in helping you until your family has restored itself."

She looked up at him in irritation. "You make it sound," she sharply, "like a frosted plant which will grow lush with time and sunshine, sir. In fact, the family is a group of people who are teetering on a razor's edge between destitution and a chance of a prosperous future. Only hard work and constant vigilance will prevent disaster."

"I think you worry too much," he said blandly, making her want to hit him. "But if so, all the more reason to let your friends and neighbors help you."

"Your mount is looking restive, Mr. Crisp," she said pointedly. "Would he not enjoy a gallop?"

He looked thoughtfully at her, not obviously dismayed by the dismissal. "It does all creatures good to run free," he said and turned the big bay toward the fields. He entered decorously enough through a gate but then set an alarming pace toward a fence and flew over it, then headed for the next.

In this low-rising countryside, it was easy to watch his progress over hedge and fence and gate. He was a fine rider—courageous but also considerate of his horse.

Amy sighed, wishing she were riding with him. If she still had Cloud, her favorite mount, she could offer a fair challenge. She had usually held her own against Jasper, and the four years' difference in age surely didn't matter in such things, as his best horse, Caligula, had been a hand taller than Cloud.

They seemed so long ago, those carefree times. Riding parties, dancing, picnics. The hunt had met at Stonycourt once a season, the mounted host taking a stirrup cup before setting off. The de Lacy men had always been among the best mounted.

They could regain it all, she told herself firmly, with prudence and management. The hunt would meet again at Stonycourt, with Jasper as the host. There would be dowries and a Season for Jassy, at least. All it needed was management and a rich marriage.

Harry Crisp headed back, flat out, aiming to leap the high bushy hedge onto the road behind her. She gasped and twisted to watch.

The bay gathered and soared over the brush without fault. But a plover was flushed and flapped up noisily from beneath the horse. The horse landed awkwardly, almost going down. Heart in mouth, Amy saw the skill and strength used to hold him and right him.

Harry leapt off and went to the jibbing, trembling horse's head to quiet him.

Amy pulled up Zephyr and ran over. "Is he all right?" The damned man could kill himself with that sort of insanity!

"Yes. Just bothered a bit. There, boy," he said, rubbing the bay's nose. "It's my fault, not yours." He looked ruefully at Amy. "I should know to be cautious with that kind of thick hedge."

She nodded sternly. "Yes, you should. I don't know what you were about."

He smiled lazily. "I was trying to impress you, of course."

Amy stared helplessly at him, then, face rosy, she hurried back to the dogcart. The way her heart had leapt at his words was positively terrifying.

For the remainder of the journey, Harry Crisp rode decorously alongside the cart but in silence. Amy was aware of him, however, all the time, whereas Chart Ashby and Terance Cornwallis could have ridden off the edge of the world without her being any the wiser.

When they turned in the gates of Stonycourt, all three men settled to riding nearby, looking at and admiring the rolling meadows and occasional stands of trees. There had been a great many more trees once, but they had been felled, some by her father to provide money for extravagances but most since his death to feed the gaping maw of their debts. They would all have gone except that Jasper had put his foot down and declared he refused to have his land completely deforested.

Nothing Amy had said had moved him.

Now Amy admitted Jasper might have had a point. To a person who had never seen it in better days, Stonycourt Park looked well enough today.

"I am perfectly safe now, gentlemen," she said as the house came in sight. "I thank you for your escort."

"Not at all," said Chart Ashby. "Take you to your door, Miss de Lacy. This is a very pleasant property."

In the spring sun the house and grounds did look almost as they had. It brought tears pricking at Amy's eyes but it was also undoing all her good work in deterring Harry Crisp.

"Burdened with debts," said Amy bluntly.

"But full of potential," said Chart, looking around with a shrewd eye. "Fine land."

Amy cast a quick glance at Harry Crisp to see if he was as impressed as his friend. His face was unreadable. "All leased," she countered, "and the income being used to pay interest and reduce debt."

"What? All of it?" asked Chart, startled.

"Yes," replied Amy firmly.

Amy loved Stonycourt, but at this moment she could have wished it a moldering ruin. Instead it rested in placid beauty in its landscape, as handsome as ever. It was a substantial, plain three-story stone building with a two-story wing at each side. There was no ornament to it at all—not even a portico over the door. It owed its beauty to perfect proportions and simplicity. It would take a long time for poverty to take those away, and the fact that there now were sheep grazing right up to the drawing-room windows meant that they had a well-groomed sward in all directions.

"Why?"

Startled out of her thoughts, Amy realized it was Harry Crisp who had spoken. "Why what?" she asked.

"Why does all the income go to service the debt?"

"Is that any of your business, sir?"

He raised a brow. "I suppose not, but you seem determined to air your family's woes, and I am curious."

Amy could feel her cheeks heat. "It was not my intention to burden you with my family problems. I merely find it detestable to be pretending to be something other than the truth. As for our financial arrangements we do not starve and my brother attends school, but we prefer to live simply for a few years to set the estate on a sound footing once more."

"Very frugal," he said without obvious approval, "but I think the estate could bear the burden of a few indulgences. Another nag, for example. I'll act as your agent to buy one if you want." When she did not immediately agree, he said with an edge, "I engage to pay less than the cost of that dress you ruined yesterday."

Amy could think of nothing to say. He thought her the sort of featherheaded fool who would fret about a guinea or two while carelessly ruining a valuable garment, and there was no explanation she could make. She was relieved that they had arrived at the house at last.

Beryl appeared, flushed with excitement, trailed by the ever-watchful Prettys. Amy made the introductions but managed to forestall Beryl's attempts to invite them in.

Then Aunt Lizzie appeared to support Beryl, but Amy grimly prevailed and soon the men were mounted again.

But then Chart Ashby said, "Hume House is only a couple of miles cross-country from here, Miss de Lacy. Can I hope we'll be welcome if we call to see how you are?"

What could she possibly say but yes?

"Three handsome heroes!" declared Beryl ecstatically as soon as the door was closed. "Amy, dearest, you've outdone yourself. One for each of us!"

"But why you didn't want to invite them in, Amethyst," said Aunt Lizzie, "I cannot imagine. Very rag-mannered."

"What on earth could we have offered them?" Amy demanded. "I doubt they have a taste for chamomile tea."

"I doubt I have either," sniffed Lizzie. "I don't know why you won't let us buy just a little bohea to add to it. Anyway, I do believe there is a quarter bottle of brandy left. That would be more to their taste."

"After our grand lottery party," said Amy, "that is all we have. We had better preserve it carefully, not waste it."

"It wouldn't be wasted," Lizzie pointed out. "It would be more in the way of an investment. You have to make men comfortable if you wish to attract their interest, Amethyst."

"I have no desire to attract their interest," said Amy firmly.

Beryl laughed her disbelief. "But they are handsome and charming and all you could desire!"

Amy said, "Except rich."

This was drowned by Aunt Lizzie's, "Shame about London, though. They say Tsar Alexander's going to be visiting in June."

Amy could feel a familiar exasperation creeping up her neck to form a headache.

Pretty, who was hovering—in case there was something to be learned rather than making himself useful—muttered, "I thought you was off after that Staverley gent, Miss Amy."

"So I was, Pretty," said Amy crisply. "For heaven's sake, Beryl, those poor young men just assisted me. Are you going to shackle them for it?" When she saw the hurt disappointment on her sister's face she was immediately contrite. "I'm sorry, love. Indeed, Mr. Ashby did say he might ride over to call. Perhaps you can engage his interest."

Beryl brightened a little. "Is he the dark one? Oh no. I'm sure he's too much of a high-flier for me. What about the portly one with the friendly smile?"

Amy was going to protest her sister's self-denigration, but had to acknowledge that it was true. It was impossible to imagine the arrogant, though charming, Chart Ashby and her plain, sweet-natured sister having anything in common.

"Mr. Cornwallis," she supplied. "He's very shy, so I haven't shared more than a couple of words with him, but he does seem very pleasant." There was no harm in encouraging Beryl's dreams a little, and heaven knows, if she could find herself a husband, that would be one less person depending on Amy for survival.

Beryl linked her arm happily with Amy's and led her toward the kitchen. "So that leaves the two dashing ones for you and Jassy."

"Jassy's far too young!" Amy protested. "Where is she anyway?"

"She's walked over to the Burford's to visit Amabelle. Tell me all your adventures."

Amy wasn't up to objecting to Jassy's outing, though she would return discontented and with a charity package from Amabelle Burford's mama. She decided to give Beryl and Aunt Lizzie the official version of her adventure and mention nothing of the hours spent in a blanket in Harry Crisp's kitchen.

Aunt Lizzie frowned as she made the herb tea, both at the concoction and the story. "Why did you linger in the barn in your wet clothes, you silly girl? You could have caught your death!"

"But I would have had to cross the yard to get to the house, and it was raining so hard," Amy pointed out. "And it was a good thing I stayed where I was, for Mr. Crisp was all alone in the house. That would never have done."

Aunt Lizzie got a calculating look in her eyes. "Seems to me it would have done very well indeed, dear. He'd have been smitten . . . likely have become a bit carried away . . . honorable thing and all that."

Amy felt sick at the thought and took a deep breath to stop herself saying something unforgivable. "That would have been disastrous, Aunt," she pointed out. "He's not rich enough."

Lizzie splashed boiling water on the leaves. "Ugh. I don't care what you say, this might be good medicine but it isn't *tea*. You can carry this fortune-hunting thing too far, Amethyst," she said. "A bird in the hand, and all that. He's doubtless warm enough to keep you in comfort and to help your sisters along a bit. Don't be greedy."

Amy sat down at the table, feeling as if she'd stepped back into a quagmire after a few brief hours of relief. "Even if that were so," she said, "how could we all marry and go away, leaving Jasper here at a Stonycourt crippled with debts? And the Prettys must have their pension," she continued, "and you, Aunt, should have enough to live in comfort in London near your friends."

"That would be nice," admitted Lizzie. "You're a kind, thoughtful girl really, Amethyst." She brought over the tea, and the other women sat down at the table. "Are you sure they're not rich?" she asked.

Amy realized she didn't know for sure, but she wanted to squelch these notions. "Not particularly," she answered firmly. "They all will have to wait years before they are in control of their fortunes. They aren't in a position to pour money into the estate or provide dowries."

"You mustn't worry about us, dearest," said Beryl. "Truly, I am quite resigned to being a maiden aunt. I will dote on your children. I will look after Jasper until he finds a bride and then go where I can be most useful."

She was being completely honest, thought Amy, which made it even worse. Beryl the dreamer had bravely scaled her dream down to fit her circumstances. Amy was determined she should have more. "Beryl, that is all nonsense," she said briskly. "I have no particular interest in any of my rescuers, or they in me. In fact, in Mr. Crisp's case, it was refreshing to encounter one male who did not lose his wits over me. That dratted storm ruined my plan to meet Mr. Staverley, but I will think of another." She looked ruefully at the dress. "I am sorry about this, Beryl."

Beryl drained her cup and got to her feet. "All in a good cause," she said. "It's time you stopped wearing your usual dismal clothes anyway. Let's have it off you and see what can be done. It has at least held its shape."

Amy followed her sister upstairs. "I'm afraid it's beyond repair, dear."

Beryl looked at the dress again. "We'll see. I think I'll dye it a darker shade and put a flounce around the hem to hide the stains. You'll be surprised."

In her room Amy stripped off the hard-used garment and passed it over. She wouldn't be surprised if Beryl managed to revive it. She was very good at that sort of thing. She saw Beryl looking at her shift in surprise. "That isn't yours."

"No," said Amy praying that she wouldn't blush. "It belongs to the daughter of the farm where I stayed the night. Mine was completely ruined."

"I don't see how it could be more ruined than the dress," Beryl said with mild disapproval. "I'm sure I could have mended it. Really, Amy," she said as she left, "sometimes you just aren't very practical."

Amy collapsed on the bed in giggles.

Eventually she sobered. She'd left her shift in Harry Crisp's house, and it was monogrammed. Beryl insisted on embroidering their initials on all their personal garments. What would happen if it were found?

Piers Verderan, Lord Templemore, was in the stables of Hume House when Harry, Chart, and Corny rode in. He was studying the gait of a fine gray Thoroughbred which was being led around by a groom. Verderan, as he still preferred to be called, was a handsome, elegant man with crisp, dark curls, which gave him a distinctly devilish look and contributed to his nickname of the Dark Angel.

He looked at the trio with a sigh, but there was a smile in his deep blue eyes. "Can't be the faulty roof this time," he said.

"Faulty servant," said Chart blithely as he swung off his horse. "Broken leg. If it ain't convenient, Ver, it don't matter. Melton will be pretty empty this time of year."

Verderan smiled, an open smile which would have startled his acquaintance a year ago. "But life's been so dull these last weeks," he said. "Renfrew was our sole hope of enlivenment, but he's buried in his plans for this place. Once we remove, he's to take it all in hand." He turned to the groom holding the gray. "He looks fit, Pritchett. Put him in the paddock."

Another groom came forward to take the guests' mounts, and the gentlemen moved toward the ramshackle old house.

"Good God, Ver," said Harry, "Renfrew'll do the whole place in shades of yellow!" Kevin Renfrew was known for always wearing yellow. He said it brought sunshine into even the dullest day. Verderan's wife, Emily, had christened him the Daffodil Dandy.

"More than likely," said Verderan urbanely. "It should brighten this part of Leicestershire considerably."

They entered the house through a side door into a moldering estate room and passed into the dingy hall. There they encountered Emily Templemore.

Her ready smile was wide and warm. "Oh good," she said. "Guests."

She came to stand by her husband, and he wrapped an

arm around her waist. "Just what we need, yes?" he said. He looked down at her and his friendly smile became something much deeper, which she echoed. "We're four months married and life's becoming tedious. We've only Randal, Sophie, and Renfrew here to amuse us in the evenings." Verderan looked up at the three. "I do hope you have some enlivening activity to share with us."

"Randal's back?" said Harry. "Good."

"We might," said Chart, with a sliding, puckish look at Harry. "Know anything of the de Lacys of Stonycourt?"

Later that night, as they prepared for bed, Harry said to Chart, "I'll thank you to keep your fingers out of my business!"

"So it is your business, is it?" queried Chart. He looked at his clothes. "I don't know why I gave Quincy the month off. My wardrobe is degenerating into rags."

"Pick 'em up," said Harry unsympathetically as he folded his own clothes. "You're not as useless as you make out."

With a smile, Chart obeyed. Hume House was not large, and some rooms were so neglected as to be undesirable, and so Corny was sharing with Kevin Renfrew while Harry and Chart shared this chamber.

As Chart folded his clothes he produced, as if by magic, a soiled rag. "Now, what is this?" he asked of no one in particular. He unfurled it, and it was clearly a lady's shift. He waved it in the manner of a matador with a cape.

Harry made a grab for it. Chart dodged. They tumbled to the floor and soon it was a full-fledged wrestling match.

In the end they cried quits and lay back in exhausted satisfaction. Harry looked for the source of contention and found it torn in two. It seemed a shame.

Chart sat up, arms around knees. "Care to tell me?"

Harry balled the rag up. "It's not what you think."

"What do I think?"

"That Miss de Lacy and I had a pleasant romp while the storm raged."

"I don't think that."

Harry looked at him. "You don't?"

"She didn't have the look of a well-pleasured lady, and you didn't look as bedazzled as I'd expect in such a case. But if you try to tell me that tale again of her skulking out in the barn until the rain stopped, I'll call you a liar."

Harry tossed the ball of cloth into a corner. "She came in for help. She was like a drowned rat and covered head to toe in mud. We had to get her out of those wet clothes."

"Oh-ho!" Chart chortled.

Harry waved a warning fist in his face. "*She* got herself out of her wet clothes while I saw to that sorry excuse for a horse." He rose and went to put more coal on the fire. "When I came back she was wrapped in a blanket and a couple of towels." He turned to look at his friend. "Have you ever seen such a beauty?"

"No," said Chart simply.

Harry frowned. "Do you feel at all interested in wooing her?"

Chart got to his feet in amazement. "*Wooing her?* God, no. I could sit and look at her now and then, as I'd look at a piece of sculpture." He studied his friend in concern. "Not thinking of doing something stupid, are you?"

The moment had come.

Harry had found an opportunity to speak to his cousin Randal and had his feelings confirmed. It was more likely that his parents were downplaying the seriousness of the situation than exaggerating it, and in that case it would undoubtedly be best for him to put their minds at rest by marrying and setting up his nursery.

After meeting Amy de Lacy and spending an evening with Randal and his wife, Sophie, and Verderan and Emily, the notion was no longer so intolerable.

The Ashbys and the Templemores were loving couples in very different ways. Randal and Sophie had married in August but it hadn't, as some had hoped, sobered them. They still treated life as a delightful game, but it was now a game they played as a team.

Verderan and Emily had married just before Christmas and disappeared for a long honeymoon. They had only been back a month and Harry had seen little of them in that time. He was amazed at the change in Piers Verderan. No, not really a change, merely a heightening of his virtues and a marked diminution of his vices. His tongue was noticeably less sharp and his notorious temper seemed nonexistent.

Emily Templemore was not a Sophie. She was eight years older and of a much quieter disposition. She and Verderan loved in a quieter, more subtle way, and yet their love was as clear in the air as the perfume of roses.

Harry remembered Emily Grantwich in the days before she and Verderan had sorted out their affairs. She'd been weighed down by concerns, mostly to do with family. It seemed to him Amy de Lacy was similarly burdened. Was it possible he could bring a glow to Amy's eyes like the glow in Emily's?

Chart was looking at him with horror.

"My father's ill," Harry said. "He wants me to go to London and find a bride."

"Lord," said Chart, looking for all the world as if he'd just been told his friend had a fatal disease.

"It's not that bad," said Harry with a wry smile. "Look at Randal and Ver."

"They're six years older," Chart pointed out. "I've no mind to be tied down just yet."

"You don't have to. You've got a healthy father and a younger brother. And you don't have a title to carry on."

"Much to my father's disgust," said Chart. "So you're really going to do it? Almack's, the lot?"

Harry grinned. "Perhaps not." At Chart's look he said, "Amy de Lacy."

Chart frowned. "Are you sure that's wise? After all, what do you know of her other than that she's a raving beauty?"

Harry walked over and got into bed. "We did talk," he pointed out.

Chart extinguished the candles and joined him. "And?"

"She's easy to talk to. She has a sense of humor. She's very sensible. After all, Chart, most girls would have thrown fits to be in such a state, and would probably have rather frozen to death than done the sensible thing and take off their clothes."

Chart was lying back with his hands behind his head. He chuckled. "True enough. Remarkable just how reluctant most females are to strip down, no matter how sensible it might be." He sobered. "Don't bite my head off, old man, but are you sure she didn't hope for something more than talk?"

Harry leaned up on one elbow. "I'm sure. She was in a fine state of nerves."

"Quite reasonably if she'd set out to seduce you. I will credit her with being a virgin. Emily said her family's all rolled up. It wouldn't be surprising if a beauty like that decided to catch herself a good husband by unconventional means." He looked at his friend. "Going five miles for some broody hens sounds a bit rum to me."

Harry leaned back. He didn't like Chart's words, but he had to admit there was some sense to them. "She could hardly have planned the storm. No one expected it."

"True, but she could have planned a broken rein. Look at

it logically. She sets out to go five miles for something she could have got closer to home. She'd dressed in a smart gown when they're apparently impoverished. Did you notice that Emily said the beautiful Miss de Lacy is in the habit of wearing extremely dull, unornamented garments?"

"I noticed," said Harry.

"There was a bonnet in the box," Chart added, rather apologetically.

"What?"

"In the box of the dogcart. There was a very smart bonnet—blue silk lining, striped ribbons, the lot. I'll go odds she would have looked very fetching in it."

Harry sighed. The fire crackled. Far off in the hall, the old clock wheezed its way through the twelve strokes of midnight. "It doesn't matter," said Harry at last. "I don't blame her for trying to catch the interest of an eligible *parti*. After all, life must be miserable if they're as poor as it would appear, especially with some idiot insisting they live like the workhouse poor until they're out of debt. Doubtless that fusby-faced sister."

Chart shrugged. "As you will. Just as long as you're forewarned. Beauty's a damned dangerous thing, and once you swallow the bait you'll have the whole family on your hands." He rolled over and settled himself for sleep. "One good thing. If you can fix it all with Miss de Lacy, you won't have to do the Season. I'd probably think friendship required me to tag along and guard you from your better nature."

6

THE NEXT DAY, Chart and Harry announced their intention of riding over to Stonycourt to inquire after Miss de Lacy's welfare. Corny declined to accompany them, saying he had become quite interested in Kevin Renfrew's plans for Hume House. It was more a case, they knew, of him not being one for the ladies. Emily gave them a basket of food to take over with her compliments, instructing them to be sure to give it tactfully.

Later, as they trotted down the drive to Stonycourt, Harry said, "This is a fine property. Surprised someone could run himself into the ground with this."

"Mortgages," suggested Chart. "Gambling more than likely. Things like that," he pointed out, "run in families."

Harry gave him a disgusted look and speeded up, eager to see Amy de Lacy again. Would she be the warm, unconventional delight of the kitchen, or the cool young lady who had fobbed them off so efficiently yesterday?

And why, he wondered, had she turned frosty? It could

have been a delayed attack of missishness, but he did not judge that to be in character. Perhaps it was maidenly shyness in the face of her own warm feelings.

Chart's voice broke into his reverie. "I'd ask why you had a besotted grin on your face if I felt I really wanted to know."

Harry just grinned at him. After all, duty and inclination were coming together in a most satisfactory way, and he felt sorry for Chart, who clearly had no notion of the delights of falling comfortably in love.

They dismounted in front of the house, and when no groom appeared, tethered their horses. Harry went up the three shallow steps and rapped the knocker. Nothing happened. He rapped again.

He had his hand up to try a third time when the door swung open and Amy de Lacy stared at him, rendering him speechless.

He'd forgotten just how beautiful she was.

She was wearing a plain gown the color of weak, milky tea, largely covered by a black apron. There was a smudge of dirt across her cheek, and her gilded curls were an untamed riot with a cobweb draped across one side.

She was exquisite.

"Oh," she said. A hand fluttered to her hair and was restrained.

Harry gathered his wits and bowed. "Good morning, Miss de Lacy. Mr. Ashby and I came to see if you had recovered from your ordeal." He was aware of Chart beside him, tipping his hat.

She just stared at them with those mesmerizing blue eyes, and Harry felt like bursting into a chorus of Tom Moore's latest ditty. "The light that lies in women's eyes/Has been my heart's undoing."

"Why, it's Mr. Crisp and Mr. Ashby." The welcome came

not from Amy de Lacy but from her plain sister. "How lovely of you to call. Do please come in."

Harry bludgeoned his wits into order, tore his eyes away from his beloved, and managed to greet Miss de Lacy civilly.

Amy allowed Beryl to take over, though she knew she should forbid them to enter the house. But how?

She'd been frozen, panicked by the flash of searing excitement which had jumped through her at the sight of him. She'd wanted to slam the door in his face and yet had known that was impossible. Now she wanted to run and hide in her room until he left.

"We are rather busy," she said.

A beaming Beryl was already shepherding them into the little-used and chilly drawing room. "You will stay for tea, won't you, Mr. Crisp, Mr. Ashby?"

"We'd be delighted," said Chart Ashby with a quizzical look at Amy. "Perhaps we can make a contribution." He proffered the basket. "Lady Templemore, our hostess, insisted in sending an invalid basket. I can see Miss de Lacy is recovered, but can I hope you will make use of it anyway? Lady Templemore will be hurt otherwise."

"Oh, how kind," said Beryl. She glanced at Amy for guidance, but Amy was too swamped by personal problems to worry about unwelcome charity. Beryl reached for the basket with enthusiasm.

Chart Ashby held on to it. "It is a trifle heavy," he said. "Perhaps I should carry it for you." He cast a meaningful glance at Harry and Amy.

"Oh yes!" declared Beryl, who'd just helped Amy move wardrobes as they did the spring-cleaning. "That would be so kind." She quickly led the way to the kitchens.

Amy looked around and realized she was alone with Harry Crisp. "Oh dear."

"My dear Miss de Lacy," Harry said with a teasing smile, "you are surely not nervous to be alone with me. We've weathered worse than this after all, and the door is safely open."

Amy could feel her cheeks heat. She found herself fiddling with her apron and stopped. "Yes," she said. "I mean we have, and I'm not . . ." This would never do. She wished he weren't here. She wished the room weren't so shabby. She wished she were still the wealthy Amy de Lacy, dressed in modish style and receiving a handsome gentleman without thought of her duty to marry riches.

She realized she was still in her work apron and pulled it off. Then, unsure what to do with it, she tucked it under a cushion. "It is a lovely day, isn't it? I do hope you had a pleasant ride."

He was looking at her with warm amusement and considerable tenderness. It was as if they were back at Coppice Farm. Her anxiety melted away and she laughed. "That was ridiculous, wasn't it? I don't know why I should be ashamed to be seen in an apron when the whole world knows we have to do for ourselves. Won't you be seated, Mr. Crisp."

She took a straight-back chair and he took another close beside it.

"We are all driven by convention," Harry said. "I don't think the worse of you for having to do menial work. But I think it a shame."

Amy smiled ruefully and looked down at her hands—not ruined yet, but rougher than they used to be. "So do I, but then I think that there's no reason I should be exempt. Why should one woman heave furniture and another idle her days away?"

"Is that what you've been doing?" he asked, startled. He picked up her right hand and studied it with a frown, tracing a line of dirt with one finger.

Amy tried to pull away. "I must go and wash."

He held on. "That doesn't matter. But you do have servants," he said. "I surely saw one yesterday."

He continued to hold her hand, and the warmth of his skin against hers was . . . distracting. "Pretty and Mrs. Pretty," she said unsteadily. "But they are more pensioners than servants. They have worked at Stonycourt all their lives and deserve a pension." His thumb was rubbing against her skin. "There's . . . there's no money to pay for it. So they live on here. It's that or the . . . the workhouse. Please let me go!"

"Why?" he asked.

Amy could have cited propriety but instead she said weakly, "My hands are so dirty."

"I don't mind," he said and raised her hand for a kiss. Then he released it.

She was a regular Cinderella, Harry thought, having to struggle not to show his anger at her lazy servants and her ugly sister. More than ever he wanted to sweep her into his arms, kiss her, and carry her off to Hey Park, where she could idle her days away in peace.

She leapt to her feet and moved away from him. How shy she was. "Jasper and Jassy help," she carried on. "But Jasper is at school most of the time—he boards at Uppingham—and Jassy has her lessons, too. Aunt Lizzie does a great deal of the cooking, but she's too old to do heavy work."

"You're too delicate to do heavy work," Harry said firmly.

She turned to him in surprise. "I'm not the slightest bit delicate," she said. "You mustn't be deceived by my appearance." She walked over and picked up a sturdy chair, raising it above her head. By the time he was on his feet to assist her, she had already set it down again. "See?"

"So you're a female Atlas," he snapped, filled again with a

burning desire to claim her and put an end to such foolishness. "That doesn't mean you should be doing such things."

"Rooms need to be cleaned," she pointed out, "and that means furniture must be moved. So, we move it."

"This is all nonsense," he said. "You may be in straitened circumstances, Miss de Lacy, but this degree of hardship cannot be necessary. You are being shamefully ill used."

"By whom?" she asked, appearing to be genuinely at loss. She was such an innocent darling.

He hesitated to name her hard-hearted family since she seemed devoted to them, but he had noticed that the sister had been wearing quite a tolerable green spring muslin while Amy was in little more than a rag.

He was saved when Beryl bustled into the room, followed by Chart Ashby bearing the tray, and an older lady carrying a plate of cakes. A cruel aunt instead of a stepmother.

"Tea!" the older woman declared with a degree of emphasis which seemed uncalled for.

They all sat as tea and cake were dispensed. Harry noticed that both the sister and the aunt raised their cups to their lips as if the china contained a sacred beverage. After the first taste they sighed softly in unison. He glanced at Amy, but she held her cup and saucer forgotten in her hands.

"Do you not care for tea, Miss Amy?" he asked.

She started and looked down. "Oh, yes." She sipped and then smiled. "It is good, isn't it?"

It occurred to him at last they perhaps were not able to afford tea. True, it was expensive, particularly since the war, and was always kept in a locked caddy, but he'd never known anyone before who could not afford it. Even the tenants at Hey Park would have an ounce or two in a tin for the occasional cup.

A proposal hovered on his lips. He could put an end to

this here and now—provide tea, wine, and good food; dress Amy as befitted her station; and hire servants so she ceased such foolish, dangerous activities. But she deserved better than such a hurly-burly offer.

He realized Chart was adroitly holding up their end of the conversation and began to take part himself. The sister and aunt were less honest than Amy and attempted to keep up appearances, but he still gathered a bleak picture of their situation. He couldn't help but wonder if they would be better advised to sell up and live in modest comfort, but it would be time to look into such things when he was part of the family. They were obviously in need of proper advice. The new baronet was a mere schoolboy, and the trustee lived in Cumberland and paid little attention to their affairs. Harry gathered he was a poet of sorts.

He'd bring in his father's man-of-business and the Hey Park steward to assess the situation and decide what should be done for the best.

Amy relished her tea, even though she knew this whole event was a disaster. It was as Beryl had said; it would be so much harder to go back to herbs after savoring bohea. Moreover, Beryl and Aunt Lizzie were enjoying this little party so much that they would stretch it out as long as possible, when Amy knew she needed to have Harry Crisp leave.

She just couldn't seem to stay sensible, especially when he touched her.

She recognized the warning signs. Yesterday he may have treated her as a brother—for most of the time, anyway—but today he had a different look in his eye. If she wasn't very careful he would propose to her, and she didn't want to have to hurt him by a refusal. To worry her more, there was always the danger that she wouldn't manage to refuse him at all.

If he were to touch her, perhaps kiss her . . .

"Amy!"

Amy looked up suddenly and would have spilled the tea if there had been any left in the cup.

"What were you about?" Beryl asked. "It looked as if you were trying to read your future in the leaves."

They had played that game in the good old days. She grinned and peered into the cup. "Let's see. Goodness, I have a very twisty road here. Life is going to be complicated in the future, I fear. But I have a tree. That," she said with a flashing look at Harry, "means sturdy good health."

He leaned over to look. "How can you see a tree in all that? It's just a splattering of tea leaves."

"Oh ye of little faith. *I* can see a tree. And a road."

"And what of marriage?" he asked lightly. "Is that not what all young ladies seek in the leaves?"

Amy realized she had allowed herself to slide into warmth again and drew back, but he had his hand on her cup and she could not retreat far without a struggle. "A ring signifies marriage," she said.

He looked and then smiled at her. "I see a very clear ring."

"Oh, Amy," declared Beryl. "How lovely!"

"It is marred by a cross," countered Amy.

Beryl's face fell. "Oh dear."

Harry shared an indulgent glance with Chart Ashby. "And what does that mean?"

"It means," said Beryl seriously, "that Amy will experience many difficulties before she marries and is in danger of failing to find true love there."

Harry glanced into the cup again and then surrendered it to Amy. "I hope I do not offend, ladies, but I don't think that is a good prediction of Miss Amy's future at all." It was time for them to take their leave, and with some reluctance he led the way.

As they rode off he turned to Chart. "Well?"

Chart shrugged. "I don't know. She seems charming enough. I suppose you could do worse. I suspect she'll want you to lay out a lot of blunt on the place."

"My father won't mind helping them out, providing some comforts. As to the estate, we'll have to see if there's anything to save. They seem to be in desperate straits."

They discussed estate management on the way back in a competent manner which would have surprised and delighted their parents.

Back at Hume House, Harry announced his intention of asking Amy de Lacy to marry him as soon as it seemed appropriate, and was pleased to find that no one had any objection to raise.

Amy tried to put Harry Crisp out of her mind, which wasn't easy when Beryl and Lizzie dwelt on the visit all the time. Jassy, returning from yet another visit to Amabelle's, was put out to find she had missed the beaux, and so she stayed at home the next day.

"They won't call again," said Amy.

"Who?" asked Jassy innocently.

"The king and queen," Amy retorted. "But if you think we might have visitors, make yourself useful and dust the drawing room."

Aunt Lizzie, she noticed, was polishing the tiles in the front hall, and Beryl had gone out to look for flowers—both in their best gowns. Amy shook her head and went off in her workaday brown bombazine to take the kitchen scraps to the pig.

This was her latest project. After all, most of the tenants had a pig. Augustus would survive almost entirely on scraps and then, come winter, provide bacon, ham, and sausage.

As she tipped out the bucket for the eager fellow with his

comical flapping ears, Amy wished Jassy hadn't christened him. She scratched him behind one ear as he snuffled around for the choice bits. "How are you, then, Augustus?" she asked. "That's right. Eat up. I don't suppose it will help when the time comes, but I'll make sure you're as happy as possible until then."

Augustus looked up and gave a strange little snort of disbelief. "Oh dear," said Amy.

"Do you always talk to the livestock?"

She whirled around to find herself face-to-face with Harry Crisp. "What on earth are you doing, creeping up on me like that!"

He looked down at his top boots. "I don't think it's possible to creep in boots on a gravel path, Miss de Lacy. I think it was more a case of you being enthralled by your companion."

"Nonsense," said Amy, face flaming. "I was merely feeding him. Fattening him up. They . . . er . . . feed better when talked to."

Harry looked over the sty wall. "He seems to be eating well still."

"Because of the sound of human voices," said Amy triumphantly.

Harry leaned against the wall and grinned at her. "Then I suppose it is our duty to stay here and talk."

Amy picked up the bucket. "I have work to do."

He took the bucket from her and held her hand. "The lowest laborer is entitled to a rest." He looked over the sty wall again. "I see you were correct. The poor pig has stopped eating. We must talk more."

Amy looked down and saw he was telling the truth. Augustus was not rooting in the trough but looking up longingly. She knew it was not foolishness, but his expectation of the treat she always brought in her pocket and gave before she left—an apple, a carrot, sometimes a piece of leftover pie or stale cake. Today, because of Lady Templemore's bounty, she'd stolen a buttered scone for him.

"I was fooling," she said. "I could recite *The Corsair* and make no difference to his eating."

Augustus rested his snout against the top of the wall and squealed demandingly.

"He protests that. *Can* you recite the *The Corsair*?"

"Of course not. I doubt even Lord Byron can."

"Perhaps you should just relate the story of your life," he suggested with a smile. "For the pig's sake, of course."

Amy gave him a disgusted look. "Augustus couldn't care a fig for my history." She pulled out the scone. "This is what he wants." She tossed it into the sty. The pig gave a snort that said, About time, too, gulped it down, and went back to eating.

"You see," said Amy. "Just like all males. Cupboard love." She walked briskly back toward the house and he kept pace with her, the bucket clattering against his leg.

"Do you really have such a low opinion of men?" he asked.

Amy regretted her tartness. She slowed her pace and said, "I'll have to hope it's not true. My cupboard, after all, is bare."

He put down the bucket and stopped her with a hand on her arm. "Hardly that, Miss de Lacy. There are other riches than money."

Oh dear. I've forgotten to be careful and we're in trouble again. "If you mean my beauty," she said prosaically, "I have no desire to be married for looks. What would become of me in a few years when they fade?" *And yet that is what I plan to do.*

She pulled against his hand, but he merely brought his other hand to her other arm to hold her more firmly. "I shan't let you run away just yet. You know you have nothing to fear from me."

Oh no, I don't.

"I don't deny that you have beauty, Miss de Lacy, but you also have courage, honesty, and a warm heart. It extends," he said with a smile, "even to the porker. May I hope it extends to me?"

Amy could feel panic growing in her. It would be so easy, so wonderful, to say yes. He would make her happy. He would give Beryl and Jassy and even Lizzie a comfortable home, perhaps even give her sisters a small dowry each. He would help Jasper, and after all, it would not be so terrible to lose some land, and some of the silver and pictures. . . .

"Miss de Lacy?" he prompted. "Amy?"

But it would be utter selfishness. She would be the only one to benefit when she could provide everything that was required. "I am grateful to you, of course," she said woodenly.

"You know that isn't what I mean," he said gently. "Amy, will you marry me?"

Amy stopped breathing. She knew that because she noticed when she needed breath to say, "No."

Color touched his cheeks. "A bit abrupt," he remarked. "Could you give me a reason? I'm healthy, wealthy, and willing. Where lies my shortcoming?"

Amy swallowed and took refuge in the banal. "We hardly know each other, sir."

Foolishness was always unwise. "I feel I know you better than any number of young women I've danced with, and walked with, and been acquainted with for years."

"I don't know you at all," Amy persisted.

"Don't you?" he queried. "Well then, have I your permission to visit you, so that you may get to know me better?"

She was hurting him. She hated this. But it was unfair of him to badger her so. "I don't think so."

"Miss de Lacy," he said with a touch of impatience, "if you have taken me in dislike, or if you are already pledged to another, I wish you would tell me directly. Otherwise, these dillydallyings of yours are very strange."

At this reproof, Amy applied all her strength, and she wrenched herself out of his hands. "Strange?" she echoed. "I always thought a man was supposed to take no for an answer, sir. Instead, you're hounding me to death. Two days ago we were total strangers." She raked her hands distractedly through her hair. "Why on earth *would* I want to marry you?"

"Because I can rescue you from poverty, if nothing else," he said, looking every bit as distraught as she. "You may not be ready to agree to marry me now, Miss de Lacy, but you have no reason to dismiss me out of hand, unless your beauty has so gone to your head that you are holding out for a better catch. I think I am entitled to a logical reason for your refusal to even consider my suit."

Amy welcomed the rare surge of temper, for it swamped the pain. She hissed in a breath through her teeth. "Very well, sir," she snapped. "If you want logic, you may have it!" She looked him straight in the eye. "I *am* holding out for a better catch. I plan to marry a fortune, and you are nowhere near rich enough." She laughed at the shock on his face. "I could be wrong, of course, our acquaintance being so slight as to be nonexistent. If you are a regular Croesus, pray tell me now and I'll say yes, and thank you, sir, and be as grovelingly grateful as you clearly expect me to be."

"I do not—"

She interrupted him. "But you're not a Croesus, are you? And so you're no use to me, Mr. Crisp, for all that you're a handsome, pleasant young man. I intend to marry only an immensely rich man."

He turned white. "You bitch."

At the end of her tether, Amy hit him, knocking his head sideways with the force of it. The sound cracked, and in seconds the scarlet mark was on his face like a red flag. Manual labor developed the muscles remarkably.

"Amethyst!" gasped Aunt Lizzie.

Amy turned, horrified, to see Aunt Lizzie, Beryl, Jassy, and Chart Ashby gaping at her. She wished the earth would swallow her. How had she ever become so lost to proper behavior? She turned, seeking adequate apologetic words.

Harry laughed in her face. "I should have known," he said. "Even your name is false. You're not an Amy, you're an Amethyst—beautiful, cold, hard. And for sale to the highest bidder."

Amy forgot apologies. "Leave!" she commanded and pointed dramatically toward the distant gates. "And you will never be welcome here again."

Harry looked her over. "There is certainly nothing here to tempt me." He bowed curtly to the other ladies and stalked off.

Everyone simply stood frozen.

After a moment Chart Ashby made an elegant bow. "Apologies, ladies. 'Fraid we'll have to miss our dish of tea."

No one said a word as he followed his friend, but then Aunt Lizzie said, "Amethyst . . ."

Amy burst into tears and fled to her room.

When Chart arrived at the drive where they had left their horses, Harry was already at the end of the drive, heading away from Stonycourt at a gallop. Chart made no hurry about following. A long, blistering, lonely ride was probably what his friend needed right now.

❧ 7 ❧

CHART SAW NO SIGN OF HARRY during the leisurely canter
back to Hume House. That didn't surprise him. If he'd
been assaulted by his beloved, he'd doubtless disappear to
lick his wounds.

Chart was mildly puzzled over the behavior of the beautiful Amethyst. Harry Crisp would be quite a catch for her, so
why the furor? He couldn't imagine that Harry had done or
said anything to truly warrant such outrage. That wasn't in
Harry's style. Too sweet-natured for his own good, was Harry,
and especially gentle with ladies of all degrees.

When he strolled into Hume House he expected inquiries as to Harry's whereabouts. Instead he was greeted with,
"What's got into Harry?"

They were all in what passed for a drawing room—
Verderan, Emily, Randal, Sophie, Corny, and Renfrew. It was
Randal who had spoken. He was a spectacularly handsome
man with golden curls and bright blue eyes made for teasing.

In their school days he'd been the Bright Angel to Verderan's Dark, but he had left the nickname behind.

"Why d'you ask?" Chart replied.

"Because he stormed in here like a Fury," Randal said, "grabbed a decanter of brandy, and headed for your room. There was a crash a while back but it didn't sound fatal."

"Lord," said Chart, rather awed. He tried to remember the last time Harry had lost his temper. He didn't think Harry ever had.

"He can wreck the place if he wants," said Verderan. "I'm sure there's nothing of value. But we'd rather not have a corpse in the house."

"What happened?" asked Randal seriously.

"I'm not sure," said Chart. "We rode over, and when we spotted the beautiful Amy in the kitchen garden Harry went over to do a spot of wooing while I went up to the house. The other ladies fussed and prepared tea, but when Harry and his beloved didn't come in we all went to find them. We came upon them on the path in a grand heat. He called her a bitch. She hit him and ordered him off the estate. He seemed to be in a taking because her name's Amethyst. I don't know why."

"Amethyst," said Emily. "I only ever heard her called Amy, but it makes sense. They're all named for stones."

"'Beautiful, cold, hard, and for sale to the highest bidder,'" said Chart. "That's a quotation."

"Harry?" queried Randal in amazement.

"Harry."

Everyone in the room took time to ponder this. They all knew Harry Crisp to be an equable young man with beautiful manners.

Kevin Renfrew said, "There speaks a man in love." He appeared completely serious and everyone took it that way. Renfrew had a gift of seeing the best and the truth in everyone.

"In that case," said Verderan dryly, "I think we should give him a few pointers on a more subtle wooing technique."

"Ha!" scoffed Emily. "Who's claiming to be an expert? As I understand it, Sophie had to woo Randal, and you just teased me to death."

"At least you never hit me," he responded with a smile.

"I tried at least once. You were just too quick for me."

"Then perhaps we should teach Harry that, too." He kissed her hand and sobered. "I think someone should go up and make sure he isn't putting a pistol to his head. Volunteers?"

"He wouldn't," protested Chart. "Over a woman?"

Randal got to his feet. "You obviously lack all sympathy with pangs of the heart. And it should be kept in the family. I'll go."

Randal knocked on the door. When there was no answer, he opened it and walked in. Harry was sitting by the window, staring out. The crash had obviously been the decanter, which lay shattered in a corner. From the size of the puddle and the strength of the fumes, very little if any had been drunk.

"You prefer to inhale your solace, do you?" said Randal.

Harry didn't turn. "It's all right. I'm neither going to drink myself to death nor shoot myself. Not over a heartless, deceiving bitch."

Randal closed the door. "I'm more concerned that you might walk out and offer for the first woman you see, just to prove how little this one means to you."

Harry did turn at that, sharply. "She means nothing. We only met two days ago."

Randal went to lounge in a chair. "There seems a remarkable amount of heat for such a brief acquaintance. As a senior member of the family, I have to ask. Did you dishonor her?"

"No," said Harry sharply, color returning to his cheeks.

"But today you asked her to marry you."

"Yes."

"And she said no."

"Yes."

Randal steepled his fingers and considered his cousin. "How did such a simple discussion come to blows?"

Harry got to his feet. "That's none of your damn business. There's no cause for concern. I'm not a danger to myself or anyone else. I will doubtless never set eyes on the alluring Amethyst again, for which I am immensely grateful." He flung open the window. "Best get rid of these fumes before night, or we'll go to bed sober and rise drunk."

Randal shrugged and got to his feet. "What are your plans, then?"

"Hunting's just about over," Harry said. "I suppose I'll visit my parents, then settle myself in Town. Run my eye over the latest crop of fillies," he said callously, "and pick the one that takes my fancy most. Might as well go for a handsome portion while I'm at it, I suppose. Any younger children will thank me." He looked at Randal with a slight, humorless smile. "That's how it's done, ain't it?"

"Oh, surely," said Randal dryly. "And be sure to check the soundness of her teeth and the width of her hips." He went to the door. "Are you leaving tomorrow, then?"

"Why not?"

"Why not indeed." With that Randal left and went thoughtfully downstairs. There he related most of the conversation to the others.

Chart groaned. "That means I'll have to do all that social nonsense, too."

"Excellent idea," said Randal. "He needs a close eye kept

on him. In fact," he said with a smile at his wife, "I think the Season calls us too."

"Oh good," said Sophie with a brilliant smile. "I'll be able to show off my prize."

"My thought entirely," said Randal and wound one of her auburn curls around his finger.

Verderan said, "Tempting though it is, I think we will give this circus a miss." He took Emily's hand and kissed it. "I have yet to show Emily my principal estate and we intend to live quietly for a while. It is near London, however, on the river near Putney. You will be welcome if you decide you need some country air." He smiled around. "If you wonder why we are settled on bucolic idleness, it is because by next year, there will be three Verderans in the family."

The meeting turned to celebratory drinks.

Chart found the claret soothing, and he began to take a brighter view of the future. He'd always had a bad feeling about Amy de Lacy, and Harry was well rid of her. When he bethought himself that the final defeat of Napoleon Bonaparte was likely to turn the Season of 1814 into a gala affair, Chart was actually beginning to look forward to the adventure. Until Randal took him apart.

"Chart, since you're likely to be the man on the spot, keep a close eye on him."

"He won't do anything silly," said Chart. "He's seen that woman for what she is."

"Perhaps. There may, however, be a natural tendency to offer for the first tolerable woman he sets eyes on. Not a good idea."

"No?"

"No."

"And I'm supposed to stop him?"

"I'm sure you're up to the task."

On the whole, Chart thought, the next few months were going to be hell.

If Amy had known of these sentiments, she would have echoed them.

Her family were horrified with her. Not only had she been intolerably vulgar, she also had summarily disposed of two handsome, comfortably circumstanced young bachelors.

"And after all, dear Amethyst," said Aunt Lizzie at the end of one of her daily laments, "even in the tediously mercenary standards you seem to have espoused, you might have thought that a bird in the hand is worth two in the bush and kept him dangling. Then, if it turned out that you did not want him, Beryl and Jassy would have had a chance."

The Prettys were the only ones who seemed to approve. "You can do better than a stripling like that, Miss Amy," mumbled Mrs. Pretty around a mouthful of loose teeth. "You go after that Mr. Staverley again. He's a warm man and no mistake, and in control of his own."

Amy, desperate to prove to her family that she could rescue something from the debacle, set out to do just this. She pondered a number of fanciful plans, but the fact was that she couldn't take to haunting a spot five miles away from Stonycourt without causing talk.

The first trip to get the layers had in fact been plausible, and Amy repeated it two days after her disgrace. She lacked the nerve to stage some kind of accident as she passed the gates of Prior's Grange on the way to Hetty Cranby's. She told herself she would think of a good excuse on the way back. Perhaps she could fray the reins again.

But Hetty Cranby made it clear the whole area knew of her misadventure—the edited version, at least—courtesy of the

Coneybears. Another identical accident so close by would be bound to set people thinking. Any accident at all would be suspicious. Amy drove back past the solid, prosperous, newly painted gates of the Grange and gave a wistful sigh.

She had to pass Coppice Farm both coming and going, but she encouraged herself with the knowledge that the inhabitants were far away. As she passed it on the return journey, however, she remembered that she had left her ruined shift there. It was presumably just lying in the kitchen, since the three young men no longer had a servant and were hardly likely to tidy the place themselves.

She pulled Zephyr up. What she ought to do was go in and retrieve it before someone else came across it. With her story buzzing around the area, and *A de L* embroidered upon it, someone would be sure to put two and two together.

It was the last thing she wanted to do, but she pulled into the yard. She sat there, listening, wondering what she would do if, by some terrible mischance, Harry Crisp came out to see who the visitor was. The local grapevine had been definite that all three young men had left the area the day after that horrible meeting, but the grapevine could be wrong.

She found she was actually shivering with nerves.

The place was clearly deserted, however. It was silent, and there was no smoke rising from the chimney.

Amy climbed down and went to knock timidly at the door. Then she knocked more firmly. When there was no answer, she lifted the latch and went in.

The building had the dead feel of a house left empty for some time and it was as she had thought—little attempt had been made to clean up. The trail of mud down the passageway and into the kitchen was still there like a ghostly memory of her adventure. There was the tub in which she'd washed the dress. There was the dried mark of the muddy puddle they'd made when wringing it.

Realizing she was just standing here, where she would hate to be discovered, Amy hurried to the hearth where she had dropped the garment. There was no sign of it. She checked all around the room but it simply was not there. Growing frantic, she searched the scullery and the yard outside the scullery door, in case it had been thrown away.

It was nowhere to be found.

Amy took a deep, steadying breath. Could she hope that he'd burned it?

Why would he do that?

She checked the cold ashes in the grate but they could tell her nothing. She hunted through the room again, hopelessly but driven.

What if he'd taken it?

What could he do with it?

She'd heard tales of young rascals laying bets on a lady's dishonor and producing an intimate garment as proof. Despite the warm sunshine, she shivered and hugged herself. Surely Harry Crisp wouldn't do such a thing.

From their first meeting, she would never have thought so, but now . . . she'd hurt and offended him. She shuddered when she remembered the way he'd said, "You bitch." How those warm brown eyes had turned hard and cold. She'd never imagined a man saying such a terrible thing to her, but he was right. She was the lowest of the low, a fortune hunter.

She looked at the plain, bare table and saw an oily stain where the automaton had stood.

Lady Jane was gone, of course. Amy remembered his long, sensitive fingers trying to mend the doll. Remembered the way he had made her feel as he ran his hands up the doll's fragile leg. How he had made her feel when he had touched her skin.

That man would never unjustly ruin a lady any more than he would smash that delicate toy. But the man she had made with her cruel words might.

With a last, sad look around at the dismal remnants of the magical afternoon, Amy left Coppice Farm.

It was Pretty who dug up the information which enabled Amy to make her next foray after Staverley.

He came sidling up one day as Amy was scrubbing the family wash in the huge tub. "Don't do that, don't," he said. "Ruin your hands, that will."

"Volunteering?" asked Amy wearily. Her patience with everyone was wearing thin.

"Rheumatics," he said by the way of excuse. "Got some news of that Staverley gent."

Amy looked up and brushed her hair back from her brow with a wet hand. At this moment, she felt too weary to become excited about her prey but she said, "What?"

"Grounds of Prior's Grange have some sort of old stone building. Everyone thought it was a croft or such like. Yon Mr. Staverley's taken it into his head it's part of the old monastery. He's setting to have it cleaned up so as to have his own real Gothic ruin. Very excited about it, he be. Probably like to share his interest."

Amy looked at the old man thoughtfully, then nodded. She left the clothes to soak and went in search of Beryl.

"We have developed a passionate interest in the Gothic," Amy told her.

"We have?" Beryl was engaged in making new slippers for Jassy.

"Yes, and you are going to write to Mr. Owen Staverley and ask his permission to visit the ruin on his estate and sketch it. We still have some sketching pads, do we not?"

"Yes, but . . ."

"And I will come with you."

Beryl put aside her work. "I don't know, Amy . . ."

"Come on, Beryl. You used to love sketching romantic ruins!"

Beryl smiled. "Well actually, I *would* like to see it, and before Mr. Staverley 'improves' it. He'll probably put a tower on it, or the like."

"Doubtless. It's as well you do have a genuine interest in such things. You'll have to prime me with clever questions and be prepared to interrupt if I run out of things to say. But after all," she said grimly, "I will only have to smile and look beautiful, won't I?"

She returned to the washing. Beryl considered her thoughtfully, slippers forgotten in her hands.

Thus it was that one morning in May, Amy and Beryl drove past Coppice Farm on their way to the Grange. Amy was intensely grateful that Beryl didn't realize the significance of the place.

Beryl had written a note and Mr. Staverley had responded quite warmly, encouraging them to visit and promising to show them the building himself. Amy wished she felt more uplifted now the moment was at hand, but at least she would be grateful to have it all done with.

Beryl was dressed in a very pleasing cream muslin, which looked as fine as could be because it was far too impractical to have been worn for housework. Amy had insisted on wearing the refurbished blue. If any mischance occurred, she didn't want to ruin another of Beryl's small stock of pretty gowns. In fact the blue cambric had turned out remarkably well dyed a deeper shade and with a striped flounce to hide the stains around the hem.

It was unfortunate that it held indelible memories.

On consideration, Amy had decided that she had overdone things last time, and so both she and Beryl wore their warm, red, hooded cloaks, universal everyday wear of ladies in the country. The cloaks lessened any impression that they might be dressed for effect.

When Zephyr plodded through the handsome gates and up the well-groomed drive to Prior's Grange, Beryl looked around at the smooth meadows and well-tended flowerbeds and said, "Oh, how pretty it is."

"Yes," said Amy sourly, for she was keyed up with nerves. "But that was never the Prior's Grange."

Beryl looked ahead at the house and chuckled. "Assuredly not." It was a slightly shrunken Palladian mansion, all white stone and pillars. "There was a monastery here, though, Amy, so presumably there was a grange. And as Mr. Staverley has just bought the place, he cannot be held responsible for the misnomer."

"He bought it," said Amy as they pulled up.

Beryl looked at her in concern. "If you have taken the place in dislike, you will not want to live here, love."

Amy forced a smile and laughed. "I haven't taken it in dislike. It is actually a pleasing house, with a slightly strange name. I promise, if this gentleman offers his hand and his heart, I won't hit him for his impudence."

Beryl looked worried, but Amy stalked up to the door and applied the gleaming knocker. This brought a footman, and Mr. Staverley hot on his heels.

He was not a prepossessing man. He was rather short in stature, but with a heavy chest and a head a little too large. His hair was a thinning brown, muted by gray, and his eyes were a very ordinary blue. His skin was darkly sallow, doubtless due to his years in a hot climate.

"You must be the Misses de Lacy," he said abruptly, not looking too pleased at the discovery.

As Beryl confirmed this and made a few conversational comments, Amy decided this plan wouldn't work either. Owen Staverley wasn't interested in them. He'd hand them over to a servant and that would be the end of it.

She couldn't be altogether sorry. She didn't want to marry this monkey of a man, but she remembered her task and steeled herself to do her best. When Beryl introduced her, she fixed on her face what she hoped was a demure smile and watched for any warmth or admiration in his eye.

He looked at her fixedly, blinked, then turned away without reaction or comment. "Come along, ladies. Let me show you the building in question. As you have an interest in these things, I'll welcome your opinion."

Amy sighed. So much for her reputation as a slayer of men. Even as a fortune hunter she was a sorry specimen.

Two hours later Amy was counting over all the useful things she could have done with this afternoon. She could have weeded the vegetable garden, mucked out Zephyr, washed some windows, taken down the winter curtains to put up the summer ones, patched her gray merino.

Heavens, she could have curled up by a window in the sun and read a book—a rare luxury these days.

Instead, she wandered around on Mr. Staverley's left as he conversed at length with Beryl on his right about monastic architecture. True, she had been given the opportunity to sketch the small stone hut, which was the center of interest, but though she was tolerably skilled at art she could make nothing inspiring of it. If it was a monastery chapel, she'd eat the drawing pad, board and all.

It was Beryl who somewhat hesitantly expressed these doubts, causing their surly host to frown even more.

"But I do think it may be an acolyte's cell, Mr. Staverley," Beryl quickly added. "That would be much more interesting, and could mean the building is older than you think. I am no authority, but it may even date as far back as the twelfth century."

"Twelfth century, eh?" he barked, and marched about a bit. "Hmm. Come back and drink some tea, ladies. We must discuss this further!"

Must we? thought Amy as she collected her materials and followed the other two. Her laggardly progress was not noticed.

Yet another man not obviously smitten by her charms. That made Martin Howgarth, Terance Cornwalis, Chart Ashby, and Mr. Staverley. And whatever he might once have thought, Harry Crisp surely wanted nothing to do with her anymore. Now that she needed her allure it seemed to have evaporated. Had it gone, or was it perhaps something that shone the brightest when she was trying to conceal it?

She had to consider this seriously, for since Mr. Staverley was not going to oblige her with an offer, it would have to be London. The shocking expense involved meant that she *must* succeed. Should she dress with puritan simplicity and maintain a sober countenance, or should she deck herself out in fashion and simper?

"Amy, dear, is something the matter?"

Amy realized she had actually stopped still to ponder this, and her sister and Mr. Staverley were ahead on the path, waiting for her.

She hurried after them. "No, nothing at all," she said gaily. Feeling she had to offer some explanation she added,

"I was just taken by the beauty of a birdsong and had to stop and listen."

Mr. Staverley gave a kind of snort and hurried them on to the house like a bad-tempered sheepdog.

Once there he arranged for the housekeeper to take them to a room where they could wash their hands before tea.

"Well, Amy?" asked Beryl excitedly as soon as they were alone.

"Well what?" Amy replied shortly. "The man clearly is not interested."

"Oh, I'm sure he looked at you particularly a number of times!"

"Truly?" Amy couldn't be sure whether this was Beryl's wishful thinking or not.

"Truly." Beryl checked her hair in the glass. "You didn't seem to want to join in the discussion of the building, so it was doubtless difficult for him to express his interest. It will go better during tea, you'll see." She looked around the room. "Pretty was quite correct. Everything is of the best and in very good taste."

Except the owner, thought Amy, but she accompanied her sister back to the salon determined to do her duty if the opportunity should arise.

"Ah," said Mr. Staverley, in his abrupt way. "Tea in here as you see. You'll pour, Miss de Lacy."

Beryl looked as if she would defer to Amy but went to sit before the tray and dispense. Amy looked at the table laden with sandwiches and cakes and felt her spirits lift. At least something good would come out of this. She wondered if there was any possibility of smuggling some of the delicious fruitcake home for the others.

Beryl suddenly spoke in a loud voice. "My sister was remarking how handsome this house is, Mr. Staverley."

Amy remembered her duty. "Indeed yes, Mr. Staverley. An excellent property."

"Place was a mess when I bought it. Sold for debts. World's full of fools. Didn't even know that building was anything but a croft."

Within moments the conversation was firmly back on medieval architecture. Beryl flashed Amy an imperative glance, but Amy could think of nothing sensible to say. She failed to see how her talking like a fool would advance her cause. She devoted herself instead to looking interested and beautiful while she planned a slightly different arrangement of the kitchen garden, which might prove economical of time.

As soon as they were on their way home, she said, "That's that, then. It has to be London."

"He may just be shy, dearest," said Beryl.

"Shy!" scoffed Amy. "He doesn't know the meaning of the word. He's a bad-tempered, selfish man and I'm glad he isn't interested."

"Oh dear. I can't help but feel you are being harsh. I found him most intelligent and considerate. But if you have taken him in dislike, dearest, you assuredly must not consider marrying him for a moment."

"I could marry him for a moment," retorted Amy. "It's the 'till death do us part' bit that's daunting."

Hearing her own words, she burst out laughing and Beryl joined in. But it wasn't funny, Amy thought. Who was she going to have to tie herself to for the rest of her life?

A picture invaded of a tawny-haired young man with a fine strong body, and a mouth made for smiling. Romantical nonsense, she told herself firmly.

By then they were passing Coppice Farm. Amy turned her head away. Romantical nonsense was amazingly potent in its power to make fools of the wise.

8

THREE WEEKS LATER, Amy stood in the lush drawing room of 12 New Street, Chelsea, with very cold feet despite it being a warm day in May. She was fully embarked on fortune hunting, and she *had* to succeed. It was all so horribly expensive.

Even though she, Beryl, and Jassy had worked together on her fine new wardrobe, some items had had to be purchased, and the cost of material alone had amounted to a frightening sum. The coach fare for her and Aunt Lizzie, along with the charges for food and lodging along the way, had been another burden.

There would be more expenses in the future, for though their hostess—Lizzie's cousin, Nell Claybury—appeared delighted to have them visit for as long as they pleased, there would be tickets, vouchers, and vails.

"Come sit down, Miss de Lacy, please," said Mrs. Claybury cheerfully. "I know after traveling for days you feel you never want to sit again, but truly you will feel better for a cup of tea." The plump lady patted the seat beside her and Amy went to take it.

Aunt Lizzie's cousin Nell was a still-pretty woman in her fifties, and if Amy suspected her chestnut curls owed something to artifice, she had to admit that it was well enough done so that one could not be entirely sure. The lady also appeared to have an amiable temperament and a genuinely kind disposition. More than these, however, it was the shrewd common sense she detected in Nell Claybury that attracted Amy.

"You are a treat for the eyes, Miss de Lacy," the woman said frankly and turned to Aunt Lizzie. "I can quite see why you wanted to bring her to Town, Lizzie. She'll make a fine match, no doubt of it." She glanced at Amy. Heaven knows what she saw there. Amy thought that her expression must have hinted at her fears, for Mrs. Claybury quickly went on, "But no need to talk of such things just yet. So tired as you both must be. After tea you must go to your rooms and have a nice lie down. We'll have a quiet dinner, just the three us, and then you can have an early night. Tomorrow I'll show you some of the sights. You'll like that, my dear," she said kindly to Amy, as if Amy were a child. "We'll go to the Queen's Palace. You may catch sight of the queen, or one of the princesses."

Amy sipped the excellent tea and let the chatter wash over her as Nell told of her life alone here since her husband died some two years since. Her two sons, both occupied in the family ship chandlery, chose to keep their own establishments, and so this fine house, built ten years ago, was left just to her. Her two daughters were married and living away from London.

"So you can see how pleased I am to have company, and an excuse to gad about!"

Amy smiled. The pleasure was clearly genuine, and it lightened her burdens to think that this kind lady was going to benefit from the enterprise. All that remained was to be sure that Aunt Lizzie was correct in saying that Nell Claybury moved in the highest circles of the city. The house and its location were very promising.

New Street had been as recently built as its name suggested, and if one were set down here by magic, it would be hard to tell one was not in Mayfair; there was even a square, Hans Place, very close by. Instead of the most fashionable part of Town, however, this was an area of rich merchants. Many of the surrounding streets were of simpler houses, doubtless inhabited by the ambitious clerks who worked in the city.

Next day Amy thoroughly enjoyed the carriage tour of London, as if she truly were a child being given a treat, and she stored up all the details so that she could write of them to the family back home. And soon, if she was successful, her family would be here to delight in the sights themselves.

The sun was shining, and the city appeared at its best despite the noise and dirt. Trees were in bright leaf in the parks and squares, and flowers made brave splashes of color.

Everyone, even those in rags, seemed cheerful now that the Corsican Monster was safely tucked away on the island of Elba, and Bourbon cockades and fleurs-de-lis had sprouted with the spring flowers. In various places preparations were already under way for the grand victory celebrations which would mark the visit of the tsar of Russia and the king of Prussia.

The Claybury coachman took them past a host of fine buildings, new and old. The Houses of Parliament, the Royal Exchange, and Westminster Hall had graced London for centuries; Somerset House, the Royal Circus, and the Lord Mayor's House were new additions. Mrs. Claybury promised

Amy visits to many of these places in the weeks to come. Almack's Assembly Rooms were pointed out, and the homes of some of the famous—Holland House, Carlton House, and Devonshire House.

Amy thanked her warmly, for she could see the lady took genuine pleasure in pleasing others, but she couldn't help a pang of dismay. Here she was gawking like a yokel at places to which she was entitled entry by birth.

Had she come to London as Amy de Lacy of Stonycourt, the daughter of a rich baronet, rather than the poor guest of a merchant's widow, she might well have attended a ball at Holland House, and received vouchers for Almack's. It was more than likely that she would have attended an event at Carlton House.

But she firmly put such unworthy repinings behind her. She had set her course and would hold to it. Her family depended on her.

That very evening she was given the opportunity to begin. Their hostess had an invitation to an evening of cards and music to which she had been urged to bring her guests.

"Clara Trueblood always does things very well," said Mrs. Claybury. "There'll be plenty of younger people for Amy, and," she added meaningfully, "some older, warmer ones, too."

Amy had insisted that their hostess know of her plans, but this plain speaking made her color.

"Don't you be missish, dear," said Nell comfortably. "Most young ladies are out to make a good marriage, and with your looks you'll have no trouble at all. There's a lot to be said for knowing what you plan to make when you start to bake. Not but what," she added thoughtfully, "you might do better to introduce yourself to some of your highborn connections and move in better circles. Looks like yours come once in a decade, dear."

Amy had regained her composure. "It would not serve, ma'am. It would be much more expensive to cut a dash in Mayfair. Even the rent of a house is beyond us. Besides that, many of the ton are land rich but not overendowed with cash to put into Stonycourt."

"You had best make sure any gentleman who courts you is willing to lay out his blunt, dear, or you could get a sad surprise, be he ever so rich."

"Oh, I know that," said Amy. "I intend to be completely honest about it when the time comes."

Nell nodded, but she still looked dubious. "Even if you are seeking a wealthy city man, it would do no harm for you to attend a few fashionable affairs. In fact, it would doubtless raise your value considerably."

Amy experienced a stab of alarm. Cutting a dash among the ton was no part of her plans. "I do hope not, ma'am, for I have no intention of moving in those circles. I doubt if I could anyway. Our connections are limited. My father had only one sister and she lives in Cumberland. I have cousins but I don't know if they are in Town. There are doubtless friends, both from school and from home, but not close enough for us to expect them to sponsor me." She smiled at Mrs. Claybury, for she had developed a genuine fondness for the lady. "Not everyone is as generous as you, ma'am."

The woman colored with pleasure. "Oh poo. I simply hate being here all on my own. The next few months are going to be the most delightful I've had in years. The whole of London will be in festival for the victories, and I will enjoy it a great deal more in young company. Besides," she added naughtily, "I can't wait to see all the gentlemen of my acquaintance make perfect nodcocks of themselves over you."

Amy joined her new friend in laughter and felt a good deal better about everything.

• • •

The Claybury party arrived at the Truebloods' rout fashionably late, and to Amy's eyes it appeared grand enough to be a ton affair. The hosts had hired rooms at the Swan, and by the time Amy and her party arrived, those rooms were pleasantly full of a hearty throng. The gentlemen were all fine; the ladies smart. There was no shortage of beautiful garments and costly jewels.

Tables were set up in one room and were being well used by card players. Amy was pleased to see, however, that there was none of the tense atmosphere she would expect from high gaming, and the coins in use were mainly pennies, thruppences, and sixpences. It didn't appear anyone was likely to lose their all here.

Another room was arranged for rest and conversation and included lavish amounts of food and drink. A great many of the older people were settled there.

A third room was a ballroom, where a trio worked away in one corner, playing cheerful country dances. Despite her determination not to take pleasure in this mission, Amy's toe began to tap. It had been so long since she had attended a dance. She waited for some gentleman to ask her to dance and did not have to wait long.

Heads had turned as they passed through the rooms. People had stared. Amy had always attracted attention, even in the dull clothes she had chosen in the past. Dressed as she was now in a pale pink silk gown with bodice of deep pink satin trimmed with beads, she knew she was unignorable. Especially, she admitted ruefully, as the bodice was fashionably low. It had been Beryl who had insisted on that, and Amy rather wished she hadn't given in. She felt horribly exposed.

But that, or her other endowments, attracted the young

men like a blossom attracts bees. They gathered, they hovered. Amy wondered which would prove boldest.

It was a bright-eyed and dashing young man called Charles Nolan. He had fashionable windswept dark hair and too many showy fobs.

"He who hesitates is lost," he quoted cheerfully as he led her into the set.

Amy smiled at him. "Are you usually so quick to act, sir?"

"Of course. I find it serves me well. I am fast making my fortune by means of seeing opportunities and taking them."

He clearly intended this to be a point in his favor, but Amy immediately crossed him off her list of possibilities. Up-and-coming hopefuls were of no use to her. She had never expected to find her fortune attached to a young man anyway.

Mr. Nolan was succeeded by Mr. Hayport; Mr. Hayport by Mr. Jackson. She was careful to appear amiably featherheaded, for she had settled on that role. Her appearance seemed to lead people to leap to that conclusion anyway, and so she would allow it, as gentlemen appeared to be much happier without a challenge to their own intellects.

None of her partners were eligible but Amy enjoyed herself tremendously. Then her conscience began to prick.

This would not do at all. She would never meet the older, richer men while prancing on the dance floor. When the next partner presented, she pleaded exhaustion and asked him to take her to the refreshment room.

He collected wine for them and sat beside her. This gentleman was Peter Cranfield. He was a little older than her previous partners and of a more serious disposition. He did not seem at all put out to be spending his time with her in conversation rather than dancing.

He tactfully made it clear that he came of a very wealthy family, but he also told Amy that he was one of three sons who would inherit the business and their father was still hale and hearty. Amy felt rather sorry for him, for he clearly thought himself a very fine fellow. She hoped this prime article wouldn't precipitately propose.

Amy missed a great deal of Mr. Cranfield's subtle self-advertisement in a fruitless review of a certain disastrous encounter. Even though the result could never have been different, she had wished and wished again that her last moments with Harry Crisp had not been so horrible.

"Well, Peter, you have carried off the prize. I admire such enterprise."

Amy looked up quickly to see an older man by their table. He was a trim man with silver hair, fine bones, and heavy-lidded gray eyes.

Mr. Cranfield rose, rather reluctantly. "Thank you, Uncle. Miss de Lacy, may I make known to you my uncle, Sir Cedric Forbes?" Amy acknowledged the introduction. "And this, Uncle, is Miss Amy de Lacy of Lincolnshire. She is a guest of Mrs. Claybury."

Sir Cedric sat at the table. Despite his age—for he must have been in his fifties—he was still a handsome man and had an air of intelligence and authority.

He immediately took over the steering of the conversation. Not a mention of money now, but talk of the Frost Fair in February and the great snows which had followed; anticipation of the coming festivities and the political implications of peace. Amy enjoyed it tremendously, then began to fear she was appearing too intelligent.

"La," she said, with a flutter of her fan, "I cannot wait to see the tsar, Sir Cedric. He is said to be remarkably handsome."

Sir Cedric appeared amused but he also showed admiration. Amy's heart began to beat faster. Was this the one?

He was surely in control of his own fortune, but how great was it? There was nothing to tell from his appearance, which was elegant but unostentatious.

If he did prove suitable, she would be Lady Forbes, which would soothe her family.

"Handsome men are not that rare a sight, Miss de Lacy," he said in response to her inanity. "You will doubtless see many during your weeks in Town."

"Oh, I do hope so," fluttered Amy, feeling a perfect fool.

Sir Cedric turned to his nephew. "I am sure you have a partner awaiting you, Peter. I will take care of Miss de Lacy until she feels ready to dance again."

Mr. Cranfield took a disgruntled leave and Sir Cedric turned back to Amy. "Some more wine, Miss de Lacy?"

"That would be delightful, Sir Cedric."

As soon as it was provided, he considered her with appreciation and a glint of something which could be friendly, teasing, or flirtatious. "Do you concern yourself only with looks then, young lady?"

Trapped in her act of silliness, Amy almost blurted out that she also concerned herself about money. What would this man want to hear? At his age he doubtless took life very seriously. "Indeed no, Sir Cedric," she said, muting the simper a shade or two. "I do delight in a man of character and intelligence and I love to hear an erudite discussion."

"How unfortunate then," he said with a twinkle, "that the debating society at the Athenian Lyceum has ceased to meet. But we now have the Surrey Institution, where excellent lectures are given on a great many interesting subjects. If you would like, Miss de Lacy, I would be delighted to escort you and your aunt there one day soon. I know that Mrs. Claybury has little interest in such events."

Amy wasn't sure she did either but she expressed enthusiasm for the plan. He then discussed a bewildering range of intellectual diversions available in the capital until another young hopeful came to beg a dance.

Amy longed to be back on the floor but did not want to offend her potential Croesus.

"Please, Miss de Lacy," he said, "if you are rested, go and prance with this young fellow. I rarely dance anymore but I would not deny you the pleasure. I will make all the arrangements with your aunt for our visit to the Surrey Institution."

As she left the refreshment room, Amy felt as if she had acquired a tutor rather than a suitor, but having made such hopeful progress she abandoned herself to the joys of the dance until the early hours of the morning.

The three ladies were tired but content on the way home.

Aunt Lizzie had spent most of her time in the card room playing whist, a pleasure denied her since Sir Digby's death, since only Beryl and Amy could play a decent game, and Amy found little pleasure in it. Together with the enjoyment, she had the satisfaction of ending the evening six shillings the richer.

Nell Claybury had enjoyed her wide circle of friends. "And I declare," she said, "you danced every dance, Amy. You were a grand success. I expect my knocker to be constantly on the go now that you have been seen."

Though she knew it was true, Amy demurred. "Many of the callers will be for you, Mrs. Claybury. Whenever I looked around you were on the floor, too."

"I confess, I do love to dance," said Nell with a twinkle, "and there are usually some gentlemen gallant enough to take pity on an old lady."

Amy grinned at her. In her youthful pale green silk, Nell looked a good deal less than fifty. "I swear," Amy said, "I don't know how I am to catch a rich husband with you as competition."

"Flummery. And I doubt I have the mind to marry again. Did you meet anyone who interests you, dear?"

Amy was hesitant to put her hopes into words, but she needed to know the extent of Sir Cedric's wealth and so she named him.

"My dear!" declared Nell. "He is a regular Midas. Or is that who I mean? Forbes Bank, you know."

Amy didn't, but a bank sounded just what she needed.

"Of course he is rather old," said Nell, "but still very handsome and so charming. He and my husband were good friends, but I haven't seen much of him these past few years."

"Is he a knight or a baronet?" asked Aunt Lizzie.

"Just a knight. For services to the realm," Nell said, then winked. "Something to do with Prinny's debts."

Aunt Lizzie wrinkled her nose but said, "Still, it will not be intolerable to have you Lady Forbes, Amethyst. It will sound quite well at home. He spoke to me about an entertainment he plans. He did seem to be a man of sense and elegance. No doubt he will do."

"Let us not go too fast," protested Amy. "His interest may be no more than avuncular."

Nell Claybury chuckled. "I doubt any man's interest in you is merely avuncular, Miss de Lacy. I declare the temperature in those rooms rose five degrees as you passed. You must live an interesting life."

Looking out the carriage window at the dark streets, Amy made no reply. She did not find her life interesting. Now that the excitement of the evening was behind her, and a victim was singled out, she realized her life was intolerably bleak.

● ● ●

"Wednesday night is Almack's night," Chart chortled as he entered the handsome rooms he and Harry had taken in Chapel Street. With a man and wife to take care of domestic matters and Quincy and Gerrard to turn the young men out smart, they were very comfortable indeed. Or would be, he reflected, if Harry were his normal, lighthearted self.

Certainly Harry was acting the part tolerably well. He laughed at jokes and even told one now and then. He took interest in games of chance, pugilistic exploits, and salacious gossip. But there was a bitter edge to him that Chart had never seen before, and he was drinking too much.

Damn Amethyst de Lacy.

"Oh God," groaned Harry from where he sat slumped in a chair, cradling a glass of claret. "There'll be more than enough Wednesdays in the Season. I can't face it tonight."

"There are not that many Wednesdays in a Season," countered Chart firmly, "and when I talked my mother into getting us vouchers, I promised we'd be there tonight in case Clyta needs a partner."

Harry sighed and pushed up out of his chair. "Oh well, if it's for the lovely Clytemnestra."

"And for you," said Chart. "The sooner you settle on a bride the better."

"I've been doing the pretty at receptions and soirées for weeks, haven't I? Nothing but frightened sparrows and brazen hussies."

Chart restrained the urge to plant him a facer and knock some sense into him. "And which of those is my sister?"

Harry smiled, and looked for a moment like his old self. "Either a frightened hussy or a brazen sparrow. Has she decided quite what style she wants to develop?"

"No," said Chart with a sigh. "She's bold one moment and stammers the next. I hold it's the mixed influence of my eldest sister, Cassandra, who has herself wrapped up so tight I'm surprised she can walk, and a lingering adoration of my scandalous sister, Chloe. At least with you there and Randal—for he's promised to attend—she won't be a wallflower."

"She won't anyway," said Harry. "She's a handsome specimen. Tell you what, Chart. Why don't I offer for Clyta? Solve all our problems."

"Over my dead body." Chart was as startled by his own words as Harry was.

The two friends looked at each other.

"May I ask why?" Harry asked coolly.

"Gads, I'm sorry," Chart said. "I didn't mean it like that. If you develop a fondness for her, nothing would please me more. But," he added firmly, "I don't want Clyta in a marriage of convenience. I'm sure they turn out damned inconvenient in the end."

❧ 9 ❧

HARRY DANCED WITH CLYTEMNESTRA ASHBY TWICE and tried to induce by force a feeling of connubial warmth. It would be wonderfully convenient, but it didn't work.

She was a shapely young woman of average height and was blessed by a mass of dark curls, very fine blue eyes, and an excellent figure that could almost be called lush. She had looked womanly since she was fourteen, and now, with a coating of bronze, she could pass for a matron, which, in Harry's opinion was unfortunate. Inside this glittering shell she was clearly still the young, rather gauche girl he had so often encountered at Chart's home.

Her behavior, as predicted, wavered between over-fulfilling the promise of her appearance or lapsing into a hot-cheeked awkwardness more suited to a school-room. Harry could understand Chart's protective concern. It would be easy for a man to get the wrong idea about Clytemnestra Ashby.

Harry felt the same concern, but it was all brotherly. He could not imagine taking Clyta to wife.

As he held hands with her and danced down the line, he remembered how hard it had been to pretend to merely brotherly fondness with Amy de Lacy, the excitement he had felt at merely being in the same room as her. Would he ever feel that way about anyone else? Then he cursed himself for this weakness.

"What?" asked Clyta, missing a step. Her eyes were wide with alarm. "Did I do something wrong?"

He'd sworn aloud. "No, of course not," Harry said with a reassuring smile. "I . . . er . . . I just remembered something I've forgotten to do."

She looked at him dubiously as they settled to their places at the end of the line.

"Truly," he said across the gap.

She was reassured and smiled as they stepped together and joined hands. It turned into something twistedly seductive. "Not very flattering," drawled Clyta with a sultry look worthy of the demimonde. "Your thoughts should all be of me, sir."

Harry suppressed a groan. "Do stop that, Clyta. Just be yourself."

She flushed again. "But I am." They danced around each other. As they separated, she added anxiously, "I think."

Harry gave thanks he didn't have to steer Clyta through her first Season.

Other than Chart's sister, Harry followed his usual policy and worked his way methodically through the most eligible young women. He was determined to meet as many as possible so as to give himself the greatest chance of encountering a tolerable one. Amy de Lacy couldn't be the only charmer capable of stirring his blood. He had no fixed criteria and tried whatever presented—pretty or plain, witty or shy, tall or short. But he tried the rich ones first. Might as well marry a fortune as not.

There was not a one he felt any desire to share his life with. When he danced with the pretty Miss Frogmorton, who was quite an heiress to boot, he found himself wondering what this pattern card of perfection would do if caught in a deluge. It was impossible to imagine.

And why the hell was Amy de Lacy fixed in his mind like a family ghost?

It was all so depressing that when Randal's wife boldly asked him for a dance, he agreed.

"Are you so short of partners, Sophie?" he asked.

"Not at all," she replied. "I merely thought you deserved one dance of pleasure."

"And what is that supposed to mean?" he demanded.

She gave him a saucy look. "You know perfectly well. If you want my advice—and you don't, of course—you'll stop looking so hard."

"If I just ignore the problem, my future bride will appear one day like a genie from a bottle?"

Sophie laughed. "What a lovely thought!"

He couldn't help but laugh with her. It *was* a great relief to be with someone simply for the pleasure of it. "For some reason I doubt that a bride from a bottle would be suited to life at Hey Park."

This time he could dance without ulterior motives, and by the time the set was over he was feeling relaxed and more like himself than he had in weeks. As they strolled over to join Randal, Sophie asked, "What of Amy de Lacy? Do you still think of her?"

It was like a dash of icy water. "No," Harry said sharply. "Why would I?"

"Merely to rejoice in such a lucky escape," said Sophie lightly. "After all, I doubt there's a lady in this room who would reject your suit, never mind slap you for it."

Harry handed her over to her husband and stalked off without a word.

Randal looked down at his wife and raised a brow. "Distinctly frosty," he said. "Why do I have the feeling you've been meddling again, minx?"

She dimpled. "Because you know me so well? Harry's never going make a good choice of bride until he clears. Amy de Lacy from his head."

"And you intend to help him with his spring-cleaning? Sophie, from whence do you get this lamentable tendency to interfere?"

"I don't know," she said unrepentantly. "But I'm very good at it. Did I or did I not bring about the happy union of Ver and Emily?"

"I think they would have managed well enough on their own."

"Ha! There speaks the man who would have let me marry Trenholme out of a misguided sense of nobility."

He laughed. "Perhaps. I would probably have snatched you away at the altar like Lochinvar."

"Would you?" asked Sophie, much taken. "Then I wish I had accepted him."

He shook his head. "You're incorrigible. But at least in this case there's little mischief you can do, with Harry here and Amy de Lacy in Lincolnshire."

"No?" queried Sophie sweetly. "But this very morning I received a letter from Emily. They are on their way to Hampshire, but apparently as they left, gossip said that the beautiful Miss de Lacy has come to London for the Season. We could meet her anywhere." With a naughty grin at her alarmed husband, she swept off on the arm of another partner.

● ● ●

Amy and Aunt Lizzie were escorted by Sir Cedric to the lecture at the Surrey Institution. It proved to be on the plants of the Amazon. It was stupefyingly boring but afterward Amy eagerly accepted an invitation to attend another one the next week on the principles of steam locomotion. Sir Cedric was clearly interested in her, and he was exactly what she had come to London to find. She was not surprised, however, when Aunt Lizzie declined the treat, saying Amy hardly needed a chaperon to such an event.

Her aunt was pleased enough in the meantime to accompany Amy and her admirer to the Royal Academy, and to the British Museum to see the Egyptian antiquities. In her visions of a London Season, Amy had never imagined it to be quite so *educational*.

Each evening, however, there was a soirée, a rout, or an assembly to attend and ample opportunity to dance. Amy received three proposals in the first week, but, though at least one was unexceptionable, none of the gentlemen was rich enough for her purpose. At least, she thought wryly, she had learned to be a little more gracious in her refusals.

All her hopes lay with Sir Cedric.

Their second trip to the Surrey Institution was the first time they had been out alone, and Amy was excited and yet nervous. If Sir Cedric suddenly became loverlike, what should she do?

"And are you enjoying your time in London, Miss de Lacy?"

"Very much, Sir Cedric. Everyone is most kind."

"I must confess that I am a little surprised that you are not moving in the higher reaches of society to which you are entitled."

Amy flicked a glance at him. Was he suspicious? She made a decision. "We can't afford it," she said bluntly.

He nodded slightly as if she had confirmed something he already knew. "But you would have no objection to attending fashionable events?"

"No," she said. "I have no family or close friends to sponsor me, however."

"If you accompany me, you would need no sponsor." He smiled at her unguarded look of amazement. "The barriers of Society are flexible, Miss de Lacy, particularly before the pressure of wealth. I receive a great many invitations and attend what functions please me. I would like to see you shine in your appropriate setting."

"I do not consider myself above my present company, sir."

"And I admire you for it. But you are above it, Miss de Lacy. You could have all London at your feet."

Amy was torn between a natural desire to enjoy the social pleasures she had been raised to expect, and a feeling that it would be most unwise. "Why do you wish to do this for me?" she asked.

He smiled slightly, almost ruefully. "I think it important, that is all. I have already received an invitation to Carlton House, to the fête for the victorious allies in July. If you are still in Town at the time I would like you to accompany me. And your aunt, of course."

Amy felt a tremor of nervous anticipation. This must presage an offer, and yet that question mark—"if you are still in Town"—made it uncertain. Did he need encouragement?

He did not seem to be at all unsure of himself as he continued, "And the Russian Embassy is to hold a reception in two weeks. Will you accompany me to it, Miss de Lacy? The haute ton will be there in force, and you did say you wished to see the tsar."

It was no part of Amy's plan to mix with the fashionable

elite, but she suppressed her qualms. "I would be pleased to attend," she said firmly.

This second lecture proved to be a little more interesting than the first, as there were a number of models which hissed and turned under the influence of steam. The lecturer was concerned with the use of steam in industry and transportation. He claimed steam could one day replace horses, but Amy found it difficult to imagine a teakettle trundling up the North Road.

The steam made her think of kitchens, though. How useful it would be if steam could turn a spit, or power a dollystick to pummel a load of washing. She remembered Meg Coneybear and her energy, and the amount of work she would have on her hands all her life.

Harry Crisp would be interested in things like this, she thought, remembering the automaton. She wondered if he ever designed machines.

The lecturer was detailing some physical principle, which Amy found boring. She took to studying the assortment of people packing the lecture hall.

She and Sir Cedric were sitting at the front of the first gallery. Below them, on the floor of the hall were nine rows of banked seats, giving everyone an excellent view of the stage. Her eyes wandered the audience, which included all types of people, from the ton to threadbare students, scribbling notes.

It was because she had been thinking about Harry Crisp that one man looked like him.

Very like him.

The same crisp, tawny curls. Straight, broad shoulders . . .

A tingling chill passed through her. It couldn't be. It had to be her imagination. The gentleman was in the third row in the hall. She could really only see the back of his head and one ear.

But it was Harry Crisp. She knew it, and felt this urgent desire to leap to her feet and flee.

It was impossible, seated as they were in the middle of a row. Anyway, nothing would serve better to draw attention to her, especially as the lecturer had paused to set up his next demonstration. People were conversing with their neighbors and glancing around. Amy wished she could slide down and hide.

Harry turned to speak to a pretty young lady by his side, smiling at her words. Amy felt her teeth clench together at the sight.

Sir Cedric asked how she was enjoying the lecture. Amy turned to him with a brilliant smile and assured him she was fascinated. Harry Crisp was nothing to her, nothing.

But as the lecture resumed, her eyes were drawn back to him and his party. The young woman leaned to her other side to make a quiet comment to a handsome blond man. Perhaps he was her partner, not Harry. On Harry's other side was a gray-haired man. Amy ignored the speaker and studied the trio for any further sign of their alignment.

Did people really feel eyes upon them? The blond man turned. His eyes locked with Amy's and he stared at her. He was truly the most handsome man she had ever seen and she found she could not look away. Amy feared she was going mad. Then his lips curved in a thoughtful, intrigued smile before he turned away.

Short of breath, Amy concentrated her gaze on the stage and planned how she could get herself and Sir Cedric out of the building ahead of the crowd.

They were seated not very far from the stairs, but Sir Cedric had, on the last visit, showed a habit of waiting for the crush to abate before leaving. That would be disastrous, for she would be fixed here like an object on display as the people filing out of the lower hall passed within feet of her. Instead they must be first out.

As soon as the lecture was over, she put her hand to her head. "Oh, Sir Cedric. I feel faint. Please, let us leave quickly!"

He was all concern. "My dear Miss de Lacy. You should have spoken before. It will be far better now to wait a few minutes rather than leave in this crush." He used his program to fan her vigorously.

The moment had been lost and the stairs were already filling. She could see Harry Crisp and his friends already on their feet. They would turn at any moment. The blond man did turn his head slightly and raised his brows to see her sitting there.

She leapt to her feet. "I will feel better if I am moving," she declared. "Please let us go."

"Very well," said a worried Sir Cedric. "Come along." He put his hand on her elbow and steered her toward the stairs. Once there, however, the pressure of his hand turned her down them, not up.

"What are you doing?" Amy cried.

"You are not well, Miss de Lacy. There is an exit behind the stage. I am sure we will be able to use it."

Amy pulled out of his grasp. "I am already much recovered," she insisted and turned to join the line leaving the hall.

But the damage had been done. Harry Crisp had seen her. He went pale and almost looked as if he would speak, though there would be no point at such a distance unless he were to bellow. Then he turned his attention back to his companions.

It was not a cut. At such a distance there was no question of such a thing. But it felt like one to Amy. It felt like a sword in the heart. Seeing him again, she realized her feelings went far deeper than she had ever thought possible after such brief acquaintance.

If only, if only, her father had not been so foolishly improvident, how happy she could have been.

In the carriage, Randal opened the subject with ruthless good humor. "That, I suppose, was Amethyst de Lacy."

Harry was staring out of the window. His head jerked around. "Why do you suppose such a thing?"

"I was told she was a diamond of the first water, and they don't come any more beautiful than that. Or at least, she's the only raving beauty I can imagine staring at you in such a way."

"Staring?"

"Assuredly."

"Damn impudence!" snapped Harry, then colored. "Sorry, Sophie."

"Not at all," she said amiably. "Was I the only one attending to the lecture?"

"I was attending," said Harry, and proved it by grimly discussing steam engines all the way to Mayfair.

When Randal dropped him off in Chapel Street, however, Harry asked as if impelled, "Who was that old man she was with? A relative, I suppose."

"Quite possibly," said Randal. "I think it was Sir Cedric Forbes, the banker." His mouth turned up in a wicked smile. "Doubtless a very high bidder."

Harry slammed the door of the coach.

As the coach rolled off, Sophie said, "Was that not a little unkind?"

"'Tis cruel to be kind," Randal mused, absentmindedly

drawing his wife into his arms. "I think your instinct is once more correct. It is time to meddle."

"But if she was with a rich, old banker she really is a fortune hunter. Harry is well rid of her."

"But does he know that? And she may have declared herself a fortune hunter, but the girl I saw back there was looking at Harry as if he were a lost treasure." He looked down at Sophie and smiled. "As if he were something very precious which she could not have. I know that feeling."

Sophie colored. "You only ever had to ask."

"It didn't seem that way at the time."

"You think this, too, may be a misunderstanding?"

"I don't know, but like all happily married people, I want to propel my friends into the same state. I do not see either Harry or the exquisite Miss de Lacy heading that way, and I think it behooves us to try to steer them aright."

Chart was summoned to Upper Brook Street. To Randal and Sophie's surprise he brought his sister Clyta with him.

"She has an important contribution to make," he announced.

Clyta looked flustered but said, "Amy de Lacy was a school friend. She was always kind to me. I'd like to help her if I can."

"Well," said Randal, "we're not at all sure the objects of our concern will appreciate our meddling, but you could certainly play a strong part in our plans."

"What are our plans?" asked Chart.

It was Sophie who outlined them. "Amy de Lacy and Harry only really met a few times. There was the storm, the tea party, and a few moments in the garden." She wrinkled her brow. "It almost defies belief that they could have got in such a muddle over tea."

"Really?" queried Randal with a heavy-lidded smile. "I remember a tea party at Maria Harroving's and some cakes . . ."

"Yes, well," said Sophie, turning rosy. "But that was hardly the first time we'd met."

"Nor was tea the first time Harry met his fatal charmer."

"No, that was the storm," said Chart, "and we don't know what happened there."

"What we do know," said Sophie, taking control again, "is that neither of them was unaffected. Two meetings later he asked her to marry him and she hit him. Neither action indicates indifference. Clyta, does it surprise you to hear that Amy hit him?"

"Yes," said Clyta, eyes very wide. "Amy is gentle and sweet. She doesn't give in to unkind impulses."

Sophie nodded and continued. "Harry acts like a scalded cat if ever the woman's name is mentioned, and if Randal is correct, she was looking at Harry with her heart in her eyes." She frowned at her husband. "It doesn't make sense when she rejected him."

"And dash it all," said Chart, "they only met three times, and two of them were so brief as to be of no account!"

"So who believes in love at first sight?" mused Randal. "The point is, be it love or infatuation, it is a case of absence making the heart grow fonder. We must bring them together so they can either work out their differences or work out their obsession. Moving as they do in different circles, this will not be easy."

Sophie said, "A little investigation has revealed that she is staying with a Mrs. Claybury in Chelsea. A ship chandler's widow. A wealthy lady but not one who moves among the ton. That doesn't make sense either," she said with a sigh. "This is all a conundrum. I can't wait until it is solved." She looked, bright eyed, at her husband. "Shall we invade the cits, Randal, Harry in tow?"

"I fear he'd have to be in chains," Randal replied.

Clyta spoke up. "Why don't I simply invite her to my ball next week? I'm sure she'd like to come."

Everyone smiled. "Perfect, and perfectly simple," said Randal. "Congratulations, Clyta. But deliver the invitation in person, cousin. She may take a little persuading now she knows Harry is in Town."

When Clytemnestra Ashby called, Amy began to feel she was assaulted on all sides.

After the encounter, if such it could be called, with Harry Crisp at the Surrey Institution she had revoked her acceptance of Sir Cedric's invitations to the Russian Embassy and to Carlton House. She could not, would not, move in circles where she might encounter Harry Crisp face-to-face.

Sir Cedric, however, was proving to be unfortunately persistent and had recruited Aunt Lizzie and Nell Claybury to his side. Amy had no idea what he thought to gain from it, for Aunt Lizzie clearly supported Amy's move into higher circles in the hope that she would find a better match.

"I have always said it," Lizzie declared as they retrimmed Amy's pink dress with blond lace. "You have only to be seen."

"But there's no point to it," Amy protested. "Sir Cedric is clearly very interested in me. I don't need any other suitors."

"If you're set on him," said Lizzie tartly, jabbing a needle through the lace, "then you'd be best advised to conform to his wishes."

"We are going to the theater tomorrow," Amy pointed out. "That is at his insistence. And if the haute ton are going to swoon at my feet, that will give them ample opportunity."

"That is not the same thing," said Aunt Lizzie, stopping work and looking up. "Think how it would have pleased your dear mother to see you take your proper place."

Amy reflected that there was no weapon too low for Aunt Lizzie. "I will flaunt myself before the ton with pleasure, Aunt, when I am married." She abandoned her work to go and stare out the window.

Nell Claybury entered to catch the last of this.

"It is perfectly understandable, Amy, that Sir Cedric wishes to be seen with you among the fashionable throng. Any man would be proud to have you on his arm, and your gentle birth merely increases the effect."

"And if I do not care to be shown off like Napoleon's Eagles—a prize of war?"

Nell sat to take up Amy's work. "You were admirably honest, my dear, about your purpose in coming here. You should not cavil now."

Amy could feel her face heat. "I am not caviling. He can crow over his victory all he wishes within his own circle."

"But the ton is his circle, too. The walls dividing Society are less high and strong than you seem to imagine. It is almost," Nell added thoughtfully, "as if you are avoiding something. Is there perhaps a scandal attached to your name?"

Amy swallowed. "No. Except, of course, my father losing his money. But there are no unpaid creditors."

Nell looked up. "Then I cannot see how a little mingling with the glittering elite can harm you, Amy, and it seems important to the man you seek to win."

Amy failed to find a response and took refuge in her room.

It was ridiculous, perhaps, to fear the meeting so much. Among the hordes of people gathered for the Season, there was no reason she should encounter Harry Crisp at all. If she did, it would only be a momentary embarrassment. He would surely be as eager to avoid her as she was to avoid him.

Amy shivered. It wasn't that simple. She realized she was twirling something around her finger and looked down. Unconsciously she had opened a drawer and taken out this tuft of wool, the one he had gathered for her from a hedge an eon ago.

This wasn't the first time she had handled it like this, and it was now soiled and twisted into a crude kind of yarn. Impatiently she moved to throw it on the fire, but of course there was no fire in the grate in this warm weather. As she looked for a place to destroy the foolish memento, there was a scratch on the door.

Amy shoved the wool back in the drawer. "Yes?"

A maid entered and presented a card. "There's a young lady calling, miss."

Amy looked. "Good heavens. Clyta! I will be down in a minute."

She found her guest being entertained by Nell in the best reception room, tea already ordered by her kind hostess. As soon as Amy appeared, Mrs. Claybury excused herself.

"Clyta," Amy declared with delight. "Goodness, it must be quite two years since we parted at the doors to Miss Mallory's."

"And promised to write every day," said Clyta, hugging her friend. "I did write. I am sure it was you who stopped, you know."

"You are probably correct," Amy admitted ruefully. Even the cost of a letter had been a consideration, and time to write had been scarce. "Things have been difficult, I'm afraid." She was determined to get her dirty laundry out in the open immediately. But the thought flashed a memory of wringing a blue dress dry and ending up so close to Harry Crisp. Oh, she hated the way her mind played these tricks.

"What do you mean?" prompted Clyta, and Amy realized she had lapsed into silence.

"My father died soon after I left school. We found we were all rolled up."

"Oh," said Clyta. "I'm sorry."

Amy shrugged. "We've managed. But I'm afraid I found I had very little time." She smiled at her friend. "I am delighted to see you again, though. How on earth did you find me?"

"It is a little out of the way," said Clyta, then colored at what could be seen as snobbery. "I . . . er . . . saw you drive by and made inquiries. I simply had to come and call."

It sounded a little strange, but Amy did not feel she could question the story. "So you are doing the Season," she said. "I thought you would have made your curtsy last year."

Clyta blushed. "No. Mama delayed, hoping I would gain more composure, as she puts it. I think now she's decided that rather than becoming more composed, I'm decomposing due to old age. So here I am."

Amy gave Clyta's hand a comforting squeeze and wished she were in a position to help her. Clyta's problem had always been that she was painfully shy with strangers, and yet with her strong, mature looks she did not appear so. She had developed an excellent ability to act a part but not always the part appropriate to the moment.

"I'm sure you are a great success," she said.

"I don't know," said Clyta sadly. "I'm not ambitious. All I want, Amy, is to find a man I can be comfortable with. Someone who'll treat me like Chart or H— Oh well," she said gaily. "One day I'll meet my hero. But Amy, dearest, it would be so much easier if I had your company."

Amy stared and tried to understand this sudden change. For a little while Clyta had been herself; now she was acting the part of the gay Society miss. That probably meant she was unhappy about something.

Amy tried a light tone. "I don't see how it would help to have me acting your shadow."

Clyta giggled. "Well, for one thing, it would attract all the men like honey." Amy let the silence run while Clyta fiddled with her reticule. In the end Clyta said, "It's just that I usually feel like being myself when I'm with you, Amy. I don't know why. I think it's because you're always honest with yourself."

"Am I?" asked Amy, guiltily aware that she'd been acting a part for weeks.

"Yes," said Clyta firmly. "You don't watch people, trying to guess what they want and then trying to be it. It's horrible actually, but I can't seem to help it."

Yes, it is horrible, thought Amy. She took her friend's hand again. "Oh, Clyta, what is it you want of me?"

Clyta gripped Amy's hand. "Will you come to my ball next week?" she said in a rush. "It will be fun if you're there. We can ask your aunt and Mrs. Claybury. I'm sure they'd like it, too. Please say yes. I need you, Amy. And that," she added, with strange intensity, "is the truth."

Amy stared at Clyta. It looked like a conspiracy, but that was ridiculous. There was no connection between Sir Cedric and the Ashbys. "I was not intending to move in such high circles," she demurred.

"Why not?" asked Clyta. "You're entitled to. I'm sure there will be any number of people there you know."

That was what Amy was afraid of. She wanted to ask if Clyta knew Harry Crisp but didn't dare. Then she realized something. "Good Lord. Your brother's Chart, isn't he?"

Clyta nodded, looking scared.

"You only ever used to call him Charteris."

Clyta licked her lips. "That's because Mama insisted. But he prefers to be called Chart. Do you know him?"

"We met once," said Amy dryly. "I suppose he is in Town."

Clyta nodded, and the guilt was clear on her face.

Amy knew then if she went to Clyta's ball she would at least be in the same room as Harry Crisp. Chart Ashby would bring his friend along, and there might be some plan afoot to bring them face-to-face, though why Amy could not imagine. Were they planning revenge by humiliating her in public? She remembered her shift, but surely they wouldn't sink so low as to shame her at Clyta's ball.

And Clyta probably did need her support. It had never been easy for her to make friends. Amy couldn't imagine that Clyta would be part of a malicious plot against her.

Amy thought of Clyta's belief that she was so honest. Perhaps the time had come for honesty. It was ridiculous to be pretending to be a pretty wigeon in order to catch a husband. She couldn't keep it up for the rest of her life. It was equally silly to be hiding for fear of meeting a gentleman she hardly knew.

She would be herself, face down the devil, and by showing that she belonged in the very highest stratas of Society, bring Sir Cedric to the point.

"I will be delighted to attend, Clyta," said Amy.

❧ 10 ❧

CHART WAS CONVINCED his hair was turning gray by the minute. It was close to the time to leave for his sister's ball, and Harry was sitting in his shirtsleeves playing with a doll. The music tinkled and the dancing lady raised her leg and pointed her toe.

"Will you stop fiddling with that damned thing!" he snapped.

Harry looked up with an ironic smile. "Why the heat? Clyta doesn't care whether I attend or not." There was a *ping*, and the dancer's leg went limp.

"Yes, she does. She asked after you particularly."

Harry looked up from the mechanism to raise an unusually cynical brow. "If she's developed a crush on me, I'd best stay away. You were right. We wouldn't suit."

Chart walked over, picked up the automaton, and placed it on the sideboard. "She does not have a crush on you, but she's nervous and wants a horde of handsome young men to do her proud, at least some of them not related. You're coming."

Harry gave a brief laugh and rose. "If it means that much." He went to a mirror and inspected his cravat, rearranging the folds slightly. "I suppose Lucy Frogmorton may be there. I suspect I may end up married to her."

Chart could feel more gray hairs sprouting by the minute.

Clyta's ball was to be held at the magnificent mansion belonging to her uncle, the Duke of Tyne. As the Claybury carriage set them down in front of it, Amy reflected that she might have been hasty in writing off the fortunes of the ton. Some people were obviously still very rich.

"It is a very fine house, isn't it?" said Sir Cedric as he assisted her down. It had turned out that he, too, had an invitation to this event and so he had arranged to escort them. On the whole, Amy was pleased. She would be able to show him she wasn't afraid of moving in high circles, and—should the worst happen—he would form a buffer between herself and Harry Crisp.

Amy kept to her resolution and ceased acting a part. She did not know whether Sir Cedric noticed it or not, but it had certainly not diluted his regard. Amy had no doubt he felt warmly toward her and she waited anxiously for him to address the subject of marriage. The sooner it was settled, the sooner she could go home.

"It is magnificent," she replied. "And with all the windows lit it looks like a fairy palace." Feeling bold, she added, "What is your house like, Sir Cedric?"

"Not nearly so fine as this, I'm afraid, but I think it a pleasant home. Perhaps tomorrow you and your aunt would take tea there."

There, thought Amy with a glow of triumph, that wasn't so hard. "I must ask Aunt Lizzie, but I do not believe we have any engagements."

In fact, as they worked their way up the stairs, she began to think that she might be able to prompt Sir Cedric to speak of marriage tonight. She knew she looked her best, and the startled attention she was garnering from every quarter confirmed it.

On hearing of the invitation, Nell Claybury had insisted on ordering a special dress for Amy, and no protest had been able to dissuade her. The kind woman was so cock-a-hoop to be going to a ball at a ducal mansion that she clearly needed to make some gesture in return. In the end Amy had given in.

They had decided to give the order to Mrs. Littlewood, Nell's normal dressmaker, rather than try a new and more fashionable one. The woman had easily risen to the challenge. They had all worked together to pick a design and adapt it, for, said Mrs. Littlewood shrewdly, looks like Amy's did not need ornamenting and simplicity would serve them better than flounces.

The gown was of cream satin under a tunic of white lace dusted with tiny golden beads. It fell smooth without flounce or fringing. On the very short bodice the beads were arranged in a pattern of leaves, and the same design decorated the puffed sleeves. Golden ribbons were woven through Amy's curls, and around her neck she wore a pretty, delicate golden necklace set with pearls, which Nell Claybury had lent her.

Though she had set out to look her best, as the gasps and whispers marked her progress, Amy began to feel her usual embarrassment.

Nell Claybury leaned forward and murmured, "Goodness, it's just like being in a play, isn't it, dear?"

Amy looked around and decided it was. Everyone was posing and preening, and delivering witty lines which often sounded rehearsed. Her part, it would appear, was fairy princess. So be it. She flashed a grateful smile at Nell, raised her chin, and prepared to enjoy herself.

In the receiving line, Clyta's parents were haughty but pleased to approve of "one of the Lincolnshire de Lacys." Clyta was handsome in pale blue lace and bubbling with excitement and nervousness, which was a dangerous combination. "Just be yourself, dear," Amy whispered before she had to move on.

To Chart Ashby.

He took her hand. "Miss de Lacy."

"Mr. Ashby." Amy tried to read his face and couldn't. He was acting as if they were slight acquaintances. That was true, of course, but was that all? She had the sudden paralyzing image of Harry Crisp saying, "Who? Amy de Lacy? Oh yes. Met her in the Shires somewhere."

She found herself well advanced into the room with no idea how she had come there.

"You are looking faint again, Miss de Lacy," said Sir Cedric with concern. "I do not think crowds agree with you."

Amy plied her ivory fan. "You may be correct. Perhaps we could move closer to the windows."

Harry watched Amy numbly.

A hum in the room had alerted him. It was nothing definite, just a change in the tone of the voices all around. It drew his attention and focused it—focused it on a vision in white and gold floating through the glittering throng and making everyone else look decidedly shabby.

Amethyst de Lacy, smiling, at ease, and looking like a princess.

What a fool he'd been to even imagine she would marry him. She was fit for a king, or at least a duke. He glanced sideways at the Duke of Rowanford—young and eligible.

"Who in God's name is that?" asked Rowanford in a reverent whisper.

"Amethyst de Lacy of Lincolnshire," said Harry coolly.

Rowanford looked at him. "You know her, Harry? Care to introduce me?"

Harry almost laughed, but then he thought, Why not? and led the way over to Amy. She was with her aunt, another older woman, and that damned banker. He wondered cynically what she'd do when she had to choose between a young, wealthy duke and an older, much wealthier banker. This should be amusing.

She was facing away from him, so he had the advantage of surprise. "Miss de Lacy."

She turned quickly, pale, and with huge eyes. He remembered her looking like that in the kitchen at Coppice Farm before he'd set himself out to soothe her. What on earth was she afraid of now with friends, relatives, and the whole of Society at her back? Probably that he'd expose her for the greedy, heartless harpy she was.

"Mr. Crisp," she said faintly. He saw her swallow.

He indicated Rowanford. "Beg leave to present my friend, the Duke of Rowanford, Miss de Lacy." As she extended her hand he added, "Rowanford, Miss de Lacy."

He watched cynically as she chatted and promised the duke the supper dance. She was making no particular play to catch Rowanford's interest, but then she didn't need to. Her damn beauty did it all for her. She'd ensnared Harry dressed in a blanket, and now she had the finest gown a London modiste could provide.

What had happened to her poverty? he wondered cynically. She'd doubtless been borrowing against expectations.

Rowanford dug him in the ribs, "Wits wandering, Harry? You should grab a dance now before the hordes descend."

Harry looked to Amy for any indication of her feelings, but her face was as smooth as the porcelain features of Lady Jane. As well be hung for a sheep as a lamb. "May I have the first waltz, Miss de Lacy?"

Her eyes widened, and he only then realized she could hardly say no. "Of course, Mr. Crisp."

He looked so strange, thought Amy. Pale, not the least like smiling. But he had come over to her. No one had forced him. And why on earth had he asked her for a dance, for a waltz?

She didn't know what it was going to be like to swirl round and round in his arms. She didn't want to think about it.

The music finally began for the first dance, and Sir Cedric led her out into the same set as Clyta, who was partnered by her brother. Sir Cedric rarely danced, but he had claimed "the first dance with the most beautiful woman in the room." Amy told herself that this warm flattery sounded very hopeful and smiled up at him. He was very handsome and distinguished and fit into this company perfectly. There would be no need to blush for her husband.

Then Harry joined them. His partner was the girl he'd been with at the Surrey Institution. She was pretty, elegant, and sparkled with vitality. She said something to Harry and he laughed with honest amusement.

Amy couldn't help it. She was assailed by searing, irrational jealousy. She had to know.

She moved a step closer to Clyta. "Who is the auburn-haired woman?"

Clyta had the tremulous blankness she always had when she was feeling nervous or guilty. "Oh her!" she said with piercing gaiety. "That's Sophie. Lady Randal Ashby. Randal's our cousin, isn't he, Chart?"

"Was last time I thought about it," said Chart dryly. "Calm down, Clyta."

Clyta calmed like a pricked bubble. Really, thought Amy as the music began, a Season could be cruel torment for someone like Clyta. She had the feeling her friend had been doing a little scheming and was nervous about it, but she could hardly task her with it when Clyta was already in a state.

Besides, she and Harry had met and the world had not ended, and Harry was dancing with a safely married lady.

It was only as she curtsied to Sir Cedric that she saw him glance thoughtfully at Harry Crisp. She set out to charm his mind away from the subject.

Amy's next partner was the Duke of Rowanford, who had turned greedy and demanded another dance before the supper one. She smiled to think how delighted Aunt Lizzie would be to see her dance twice with a duke. He was even that rare specimen, a young and handsome duke, with wavy brown hair and rather soulful dark eyes.

"You smile?" he asked. "Why?"

"Because I have finally met a duke," Amy said in her new spirit of honesty. "My family have always been of the opinion that I should marry a duke."

After a startled moment he laughed. When the dance brought them back together he said, "Are you not afraid of being thought bold, Miss de Lacy?"

"Why is that bold? I'll go odds half the women in this room think they should marry a duke."

He grinned. "I'd have to cut myself into tiny pieces. There aren't many of us available."

"That," she pointed out, "is why you are so sought after, your grace."

He laughed again. "You are set on deflating my pride, I

see. Pray tell me, Miss de Lacy, where have you sprung from?"

"Chelsea," she said blithely as she danced off into a new pattern.

As they promenaded afterward he said, "Are you, like Cinderella, going to disappear at midnight, Miss de Lacy?"

"I hardly think so, your grace. But don't expect to see me again at these events. I only came to oblige Clyta Ashby. In fact, I think I should go and speak to her, if we could progress in that direction."

It was as they worked their way toward Clyta that Amy realized she had created great problems for herself this evening. She had promised to be with her friend, but that would throw her in with Chart Ashby, and doubtless Harry Crisp as well. Moreover, this would not allow much opportunity to work a declaration out of Sir Cedric. To make matters worse, the duke seemed inclined to attach himself to her, and Sir Cedric might gain the impression that she was throwing him over for bigger game.

It might, of course, stimulate jealousy, but Amy judged Sir Cedric as too cool and mature to allow himself to be manipulated by that base emotion.

When they arrived at the group which centered on Clyta, Amy saw that Harry's dancing partner, Sophie, was there along with the handsome blond man of the Surrey Institution. She was introduced to Clyta's cousin Lord Randal Ashby, son of the Duke of Tyne, who owned this house.

Was it her imagination the Ashbys looked at her with particular attention?

As she tried to calm Clyta and bolster her confidence, Amy was most uncomfortable herself. These were Harry's friends and they must know of her wretched behavior. What did they think of her?

Where was he?

The music struck up for the first waltz and Harry appeared at her side, face guarded. "This is our dance, I believe, Miss de Lacy."

As she turned to go with him, she saw astonishment of varying degrees on the faces around.

"I am sure there is no need for this dance, sir," she said coolly as he led her onto the floor. "I am quite willing to pretend some sort of indisposition."

His face was a mask of courtesy. "I asked you to partner me and you accepted. There is no need to fuss."

"I could hardly refuse without seeming intolerably rude."

"I would not have thought such considerations would bear heavily upon you, Miss de Lacy."

Amy gasped and would have stalked away except that he grasped her wrist, and that brought her to her senses. Perhaps it was his intention after all to make her an object of scandal, but she would not play into his hands.

She looked at him and smiled. She placed her hand upon his shoulder.

He took her right hand in his left and placed his other at her waist, looking at her as if she were an unexploded bomb. They began to dance.

Perhaps it was the glittering room and the fine company, but the waltz had never been like this before. It had been danced in Lincolnshire—greatly daring—at informal hops and the occasional assembly, but Amy had always preferred the country dances. They were more fun.

Now, spinning in Harry Crisp's arms, surrendering to his direction, trusting to his skill, she felt the magic touch her and knew why so many were still scandalized by it. Such rapturous feelings must be wrong.

She was irresistibly carried back to their short time of harmony—shared laughter, kindness, a kiss—but when she looked up at him, he was a stranger.

She wished the mask would fall and reveal the man she had spent that afternoon with, he in shirtsleeves, she in a blanket. Though there could be no future for them, could they not be friends? Reviewing their path to this bitter point, she had to admit that a great deal of it had been her fault. Her feelings had frightened her, and she had lost control and struck out to drive him away.

She made a decision and forced out the words. "I'm sorry."

"For what?" he asked coolly, not even looking at her. "You dance as beautifully as anyone would expect."

"For being intolerably rude," she persisted. "If that is how you see it."

He glanced down and raised a brow. "Is not that how you see it?"

Amy kept a hold on her temper. "Perhaps. But chiefly, I was being honest," she said.

"So was I."

"When?" she asked, confused.

"When I called you a bitch." He smiled and executed a particularly dizzy turn.

Amy gasped and tried to pull out of his arms, but he was too strong for her. "Going to hit me again?" he asked through a tight smile. "Not here, you're not."

"I wouldn't put myself to the trouble," snapped Amy, giving up the struggle and refusing to look at him. "Your manners are beyond correction."

"Was that what you were trying to do? You might try to teach by example the next time."

"There will be no next time."

"Ah, no," he said. "Both Forbes and Rowanford have excellent manners, I'm sure. I think I'll set up a book on which one you'll pick. Are you willing to give up a few hundred thousand in ready cash for a coronet, or is it really just the money that counts?"

Amy refused to speak to him, though she remembered to keep a small, tight smile on her face.

"Of course Rowanford also has the advantage of being childless," he carried on. "Sir Cedric's hopeful offspring will doubtless cut up rough at seeing the family fortune trickling through your fingers. Have you got into it already? Such fine feathers, and a very pretty necklace."

The music ended, thank God. Amy would have walked away, but he took a grip on her arm, which she couldn't break, and said, "I will, of course, escort you to your aunt."

As they approached Aunt Lizzie, Amy said, "You understand, of course, that I will never agree to dance with you again, Mr. Crisp."

His smile was chilly as he bowed. "My dear Amethyst, you will never be asked."

With willpower she had never before been aware of, Amy smiled as he walked away, and as she took a seat by her aunt.

"I was never so surprised!" declared Lizzie. "Fancy you standing up with him and acting as if you were nothing but casual acquaintances."

"That is all we are," said Amy, her jaw aching with the smile.

"With a proposal and a red face between you," said Lizzie skeptically. "Oh well, I never did think to understand you, Amethyst. Even in the cradle you were contrary. Now, what about that duke?"

"What about Sir Cedric?" countered Amy, looking around.

She was in an excellent mood to bring the man to the point.

"He was dancing with Nell. Really, Amethyst. You *can't* turn your nose up at a duke. He's warm enough—I've made inquiries. Think what it would be for your sisters and Jasper to be related to a duke."

Oh heavens, thought Amy. She'd never thought of the power of connections. Was it her duty to weigh title against cash just as Harry Crisp had implied? She had no time to consider it, for her next partner came to claim her, and after that was the supper dance.

She knew the fact that the duke was standing up with her for the second time was being noticed. She supposed he was the catch of the Season and she really should make some effort to reel him in. She even liked him, for he seemed thoroughly pleasant for such an exalted personage.

She spent most of the dance pondering her reluctance to try to snare Rowanford. She decided it was that it wouldn't be fair to cheat such a man out of the warmth he deserved, and she felt no particular warmth for him. Sir Cedric was a simpler case and would be content with what she had to offer.

Having made up her mind, Amy was anxious to be back in her prospective husband's company.

When she and Rowanford entered the supper room, however, Clyta noisily summoned them over to her table, and Amy felt obliged to go. This was, after all, why she was here. She spotted Sir Cedric at another table with Clyta's parents, Nell, Lizzie, and another gentleman. She gave a little wave and told herself she wished she were at that table. Honesty compelled her to admit, however, that such a middle-aged group looked extremely dull. It was a little daunting to think that such groupings would be her natural setting as Lady Forbes.

Clyta's supper partner was Harry, and he was sitting at the head of the small oval table. Chart Ashby was there with a dark-haired beauty who was introduced as Lucy Frogmorton. Amy and Rowanford took the two vacant seats, and Amy found herself between the duke and Chart but directly opposite Harry.

She immediately turned her attention away to her right side. "Do you come to London every year, Mr. Ashby?" she asked as she forked a morsel of tender poached salmon.

"A week or two, perhaps, Miss de Lacy," he said with bland courtesy. "This year I'm fixed here for the Season, helping Harry to choose a wife."

Amy found the salmon stuck in her throat so that she feared she would choke. She managed to get it down and took a quick drink of wine to help it. "Er . . . that should not be difficult," she said, hoping she sounded blasé.

"No," he said with a slanting look at her. "What woman would refuse him?"

Amy swallowed against a dry throat. This man disliked her for what she had done to his friend.

After a moment anger came to her rescue. What had she done, after all? On only a few hours' acquaintance, the man had had the effrontery to propose marriage and then not take no for an answer. He had been abominably rude and she had reacted to that.

"Tastes vary, Mr. Ashby," she said coolly. "Otherwise all this strutting and preening would not be necessary. We could all just draw lots."

"And are you strutting or preening, Miss de Lacy?" he asked, but she thought she saw a glint of reluctant admiration in his eyes.

"Oh, both. And you?"

"I'm not on the lookout for a wife, so I don't have to

bother. I'm merely protecting my friend from scheming har-pies. May I help you to some sauce, Miss de Lacy?"

Amy prayed she wasn't blushing, but feared she was. She refused the sauce, then asked sweetly, "Does he need protec-tion? I would have thought Mr. Crisp able to stand up for himself."

"No man is impervious to all attacks, I fear."

"Of what do you speak, Ashby?" asked the duke, turning away from Clyta. "It almost sounds like war. Not a subject for supper."

Amy turned gladly to her left, relieved to have the con-frontation ended. She wondered briefly whether the conver-sation could be overheard from the other end of the table and what Harry Crisp was making of it. "Love and war are closely related, your grace," she said.

"So you were speaking of love," said the duke, and Amy was startled. *Had* she been speaking of love? "I hope you're wrong," he continued. "I hope to marry for love but fancy a peaceful life."

"Then don't marry Amy," said Clyta loudly. "She's always planning something or other."

Amy stared at her friend, hurt, but then realized the words had been innocent. It was true that at school she'd thought up some interesting pranks and adventures. A quick glance around the table showed her that Chart and Harry had taken it wrongly. "What are you suggesting, Clyta?" she asked lightly.

"Well, I swear," said Clyta, unaware of undercurrents, "we would all have been perfectly content with a simple picnic at Lord Forster's if you hadn't conceived the notion to invade his orchard and have an apple fight."

Amy couldn't help but grin at the memory. "They were only windfalls."

"But Miss Lindsay had the vapors and Miss Mallory was not amused. And," went on Clyta, "what about the night you climbed out of your room down a rope of sheets, for a dare?"

"I wanted to see if it could be done," said Amy, lost in memory.

"Planning an elopement, perhaps?" asked Harry dryly.

Amy came back to reality with a bump.

"Oh no," said Clyta. "That was Chloe." She was referring to her older sister.

"Chloe eloped from home, not school," said Chart pointedly, "and there was no need of ropes. Stop waving our dirty linen in public, Clyta."

She looked abashed but said, "I don't consider Chloe dirty linen, Chart. And it all worked out in the end. Oh!"

It was clear to Amy at least that Chart had just kicked his sister under the table. It seemed a bit nonsensical. The whole world knew Chloe Ashby had eloped at seventeen with a scoundrel who broke his neck in a driving accident. She had since made a wiser, better marriage.

The duke said to Amy, "So you are a prankster, Miss de Lacy."

"I have outgrown such foolishness, your grace."

He smiled. "What a shame."

"Oh, don't worry, Rowanford," said Harry smiling coolly at Amy. "Pranksters probably grow up to be full-fledged adventurers. Or, I suppose, adventuresses."

"Oh no," said Miss Frogmorton blandly. "You cannot mean that, Mr. Crisp. An adventuress is not a proper thing to call a lady."

"Of course, Miss Frogmorton," said Harry. "You are quite correct." His eyes clashed with Amy's for a moment before he turned to address some remark to Miss Frogmorton.

Amy saw how very warmly the young woman smiled at

him, how she lowered her lashes and peeped up at him, and how he laid a hand over hers for a moment, summoning a convenient and very becoming blush. Amy's hand hurt, and she realized her grip was bruisingly tight on her fork. She relaxed it and wrenched her attention away.

Clyta was talking with great animation to the duke. Amy was not sure this boded well—heaven knows what she was saying—but it forced her to turn warily back to Chart Ashby.

"This is a lovely house," she said. "Does the duke entertain here often?"

"Very rarely," he said. "My uncle is in frail health and my cousin, the Marquess of Chelmly, has little taste for London. He stays here when he comes to town on business but doesn't entertain."

"It seems a shame," said Amy, meaning that the mansion was so rarely used.

"That he doesn't like London?" queried Chart. "I suppose it does disappoint you that he is not accessible. But you have to admit, being prime quarry in this jungle is enough to put anyone off. Rowanford," he said across the table, "do you ever feel like donning armor before venturing to a Society function? Some of these young ladies would stop at nothing to squeeze an offer of marriage out of you."

The conversation swirled off into some of the more outlandish tricks attempted by desperate young ladies. When Rowanford described one hopeful's maneuver of having her coach break down at his gates, Amy could feel her face heat. She looked up and her eyes were trapped by Harry Crisp's; she seemed to be unable to do anything about it. He looked puzzled rather than angry.

Amy forced herself to look away, and she saw that Clyta looked close to tears.

Why? Surely Clyta couldn't realize how uncomfortable this topic made Amy. Though Amy was very fond of her friend, she did not think Clyta particularly perceptive.

Then Amy saw the way Clyta was looking at Rowanford and had a flash of inspiration. Clyta loved him. Doubtless she was hunting him in her own fashion and would assume all this laughter was addressed at her, even though she would never think of using these conniving tricks.

No wonder Clyta had reacted so stridently to the idea that Amy might be a contender for the duke's hand. She was doubtless wishing she'd never invited Amy to the ball.

Amy felt the familiar sickness creep over her, the disgust at her own looks and the effect they could have on both women and men. Unlike some of the other girls at school, Clyta had never minded being with Amy, for she was good-looking herself, of unassailably high rank, and had never been given to envy. Now it was different. Now there was something Clyta wanted, and Amy might be the enemy.

As soon as she saw the opportunity, Amy deflected the conversation into less painful paths. She saw Harry Crisp note her maneuver but shrugged it off. To Hades with him, she thought impatiently. It was Clyta's feelings that were important.

After the meal, she went with Clyta to the ladies' withdrawing room, wondering how to set her friend's mind at rest without revealing that she knew her secret.

Clyta's hair was losing some of the blue ribbons wound in it, and a maid set about repairs.

"You're a great success, Clyta," Amy said. "That gown is very becoming."

"Mama has excellent taste," said Clyta flatly.

"You will soon have a procession of suitors and be prostrated by the effort of choosing between them."

The joking tone got through to Clyta and she smiled a little. "More likely you, I would think, Amy."

"Me?" said Amy, pleased to have worked an opening. "Oh, I doubt it. After all, I haven't a penny to my name, and I don't intend to be coming to more of these events. Besides," she said, leaning close and lowering her voice, "I have great hopes of an offer from Sir Cedric."

Clyta stared. "But he's old enough to be your father!"

Amy tried to look enchanted with her fate. "I like a mature man."

The maid finished and they left the room to return to the ballroom. In the corridor, Clyta stopped and hesitantly asked, "Do you mean that if someone younger were to offer for you—someone like Rowanford, for example—you would turn him down?"

Heavens, thought Amy, Clyta was guileless as a baby. Amy feared for her in this silken jungle. Unfortunately she couldn't imagine her winning her heart's desire, even without competition, but all she could do was make sure that competition was not herself. "The duke wouldn't offer for a penniless creature such as I," she said briskly, "and he would probably look for higher birth, too. It seems to me that dukes tend to marry into other ducal families."

"Do you think so?" asked Clyta, brightening. "But if he did offer?" she persisted. "After all, there were the Gunning sisters."

"If Rowanford were to offer," said Amy firmly, "I would not accept." They entered the ballroom, where selections from *Così fan tutte* were being sung by part of the company from the Royal Opera. Amy leaned close to Clyta's ear. "If you don't mind, Clyta, I would like to join Sir Cedric over there."

Clyta turned a brilliant smile on her. "Of course not, dearest." She even squeezed her hand. "Good luck."

As Amy wove her way across the room, she tried to think of ways to help Clyta snare the Duke of Rowanford, and failed. Clyta had her fair share of the family's handsome looks, and when at ease and natural she was possessed of an innocent charm, but she was not showing at all well in Society. Even if the duke were looking for a bride—and he was on the young side, being surely of an age with Chart Ashby and Harry Crisp—there was little reason for his choice to fall on Clyta.

And yet Chart Ashby had said that Harry Crisp was looking for a bride. Amy stopped dead.

He'd produced that abrupt offer after the slightest of acquaintance. Had he just been trying to get a bride with as little trouble as possible? And for that he'd put her through this torture of self-recrimination and exposed her to the taunting of his friends?

She wished she had the rejecting of him to do all over again!

She saw Nell, Lizzie, and Sir Cedric and eased in next to them. Sir Cedric's welcoming smile did seem very warm and admiring. Amy smiled back as brilliantly as she knew how. *Ask me, Sir Cedric. Ask me now. Then I can go home and never see Harry Crisp again, at least not until I'm safely married.*

Sir Cedric was kind and attentive for the remainder of the ball, but he said nothing particular. Amy pinned her hopes on tomorrow's visit to his home.

❧ 11 ❧

SIR CEDRIC'S HOUSE was very fine. It was new, with snowy white stucco, large, gleaming windows, and a fine garden. He invited his guests to stroll with him down the length of the garden to the orchard, but only Amy accepted. Lizzie and Nell preferred to rest on chairs on the lawn close to the house.

As Amy and Sir Cedric passed a yew hedge so they were out of sight of her chaperons, her heart began to beat faster. Was this the moment?

"How lovely this is," she said.

"I do not keep up a country property, Miss de Lacy, having little time for it, and so I like to have the country here in London."

"One could almost think oneself in the country, Sir Cedric." Amy felt she was gushing but the comment was true. The large garden, with flowers, fruit trees, and vegetables, was surrounded by a high wall, which cut out the bustle of the city. The place seemed extraordinarily full of bees and butterflies, as if they recognized the haven it represented.

"I think you miss the country, my dear."

"Yes," said Amy, only then realizing that this wasn't the right answer for someone who had just admitted that he rarely went there. She went on quickly, "But that is largely because I have always lived in the country."

"So you are enjoying London?"

"Oh yes. There are so many new things to see and do."

"And when you have done them all?" he asked.

Amy felt rather as if she were being interrogated, but she smiled at him. "Was it not Dr. Johnson who said, 'When a man is tired of London, he is tired of life'? I assure you I am not tired of life yet, Sir Cedric."

He laughed, "I should hope not, young lady. You have your life spread before you like a magic carpet. You are made for balls and other festivities. You should enjoy them to the full while you are here."

That "while you are here" sounded ominous. "But I expect to be here for a long time," she said firmly.

He made no response, but changed direction so they were returning to the house. Amy felt desperate. This was surely the point at which a true fortune hunter would act to save the day. She reviewed the stories told the night before but couldn't bring herself to use any of the techniques described. She didn't believe she could swoon into his arms, and she would die rather than rip her clothing and cry rape.

She made one try. "You must be lonely living in this big house all by yourself, Sir Cedric."

"But I don't," he responded. "My oldest son and his family live here with me. It will, after all, be his one day. I hope . . . ah, yes." They passed back through the yew hedge, and Amy saw that her chaperons had been joined by a family.

A severe-looking man in the knee breeches commonly

worn for business sat by a quiet, pleasant-looking woman who was clearly expecting another child. A toddler and a boy of about five played nearby under the eye of a nursemaid.

Amy was introduced to Edwin Forbes and his wife, Susan. Mrs. Forbes seemed pleasant enough, but her husband was chilly. It might just be his nature, for he had a cool demeanor, but Amy suspected he disliked his father's association with her, and with reason.

Amy looked guiltily at the two charming children and felt as if she were planning to steal the bread from their mouths. It did no good to remind herself that Sir Cedric was reputed to be enormously rich; anything she gained for her family would be taken from his.

But she must. She had no choice. She could not go home empty-handed.

She thought briefly of the Duke of Rowanford. He was wealthy enough and free of entanglements. But even if he could be brought to the point, he wanted to marry for love. Nor could she contemplate stealing Clyta's beloved, even if she could find no way to help her friend to gain him. Better he marry another entirely.

Amy tried to be gay and charming as the tea progressed, but the effort exhausted her and she subsided into silence, giving thanks for Nell Claybury, who filled the gap with effortlessly pleasant chatter.

As she parted from Sir Cedric at the coach, Amy looked anxiously for some indication of his feeling. His smile was very kind, and he squeezed her hand slightly before releasing it. She forced herself to relax. Just because she felt this pressing urgency was no reason for him to feel it. Indeed, he would doubtless believe it was too soon to be speaking. He had only known her for a fortnight and not everyone, she thought waspishly, was as crass as Harry Crisp.

"Sir Cedric is such a charming man, isn't he?" said Nell as they headed back to Chelsea. "His wife was a lovely woman, so warm and generous."

"How long ago did she die?" Amy asked.

Nell wrinkled her brow in thought. "It must be a few years. Before my Bertie, of that I'm sure. It was a long illness, I'm afraid. It must have been very difficult for them all. It is time he married again." She looked at Amy thoughtfully.

On their return to New Street, Amy found a letter from Beryl and a note from Clyta.

Beryl wrote:

Dearest Amy,

We are so pleased to hear of your adventures, and you mustn't feel guilty for enjoying yourself. I am sure we will all have our turn at dissipation once you are married. Nor must you be in a hurry about such an important decision. You must be sure to choose the man who will truly make you happy.

Heavens. Beryl seemed to think they were lining up at the door.

We are all well and, yes, we are remembering to water the vegetables and I have sown another crop of peas and beans. I laugh to think of you at a grand ball worrying about whether we have earthed up the potatoes. I am sure your conversation is extraordinary, but will doubtless charm an agriculturally minded gentleman!

Mr. Staverley invited us over again to consider his plans for the acolyte's cell, for we are convinced that is what it is. He has ordered a great many books on the subject and is in daily expectation of a visit from Sir Arnold Foulks-Hamilton, the antiquarian, who will surely be able to give a definitive assessment. I fear poor Mr. Staverley will be upset if the building does not prove to be monastic, but I am convinced it must be.

He was most disappointed that you were away. I took Jassy for convention's sake but it did not serve, for she was bored and restless, so I think I will go alone next time. Do you think that too bold? I told him a little of your triumphs and I am sure it piqued his interest. So if your London beaux are not to your liking perhaps you should give Mr. Staverley another chance. I am convinced he is shy. Though he does not advertise the fact I believe he was born a trademan's son and has made himself. I think the better of him for it.

The only problem I have to relate is that the pig seems very out of sorts whenever either I or Jassy feed him. (It does not surprise me that he misses you as much as we all do.) He eventually settles to his feed but there is a great deal of squealing at first, as if he is in pain. Do you have any advice?

Wave at the tsar for us, dearest.

Your loving sister, Beryl.

Amy chuckled, rather misty eyed. She'd go odds they wouldn't earth up the potatoes high enough, especially if Beryl had her head in a book on medieval architecture. She feared Mr. Staverley was taking advantage of Beryl's generous nature but it was providing diversion, which was something.

As for poor Augustus . . .

Amy sat at the writing desk and gave a cheerful account of her activities, especially Clyta's ball, for Beryl would like that. She made no mention of Harry Crisp, and only passing reference to Sir Cedric. She wanted Beryl to be prepared for the news when it came, but did not want to raise her hopes too high in case nothing came of it.

She paused and worried the end of the quill with her teeth. It *must*. It *must*.

She briskly dipped the pen in the well. "As for Augustus," she wrote, "I fear he may have a delicate digestion. I find a whole apple or carrot with his food seems to stimulate his system. Failing that, a large hunk of stale bread or even cake if available. This may seem indulgent, but I fear it is necessary if he is to fatten up adequately for" —Amy had to brace herself to write the words—"slaughtering day."

A tear rolled down her cheek. She only just whipped the paper away before it fell. More splashed to the desk, one after the other. She gulped and swallowed them, then wiped at her eyes. She *couldn't* be weeping over a pig!

But she wasn't. She was weeping over herself, for her own slaughtering day approached.

She forced herself to contemplate roast pork, plump sausages, crunchy-crust pie. That, however, reminded her of the Melton pie she had shared in the kitchen of Coppice Farm, with Harry Crisp sitting across from her, smiling, and confessing that he wasn't truly mad about hunting.

He had talked to her easily and honestly. She had never really been honest with him, except when she had told him she would marry for money. This was tragic, when he was the one person with whom she might be able to share her thoughts.

Oh, damnation! Amy blew her nose, sealed the letter, and picked up Clyta's, praying it was a cheerful message.

Dear Amy,

We are planning a jaunt to Lord Templemore's estate, Maiden Hall. (I overheard my mother comment that a less appropriate name for his residence was hard to imagine. My father was unwise enough to say that he didn't doubt any number of maidens had passed through the door. You can imagine the fireworks! I was very nearly forbidden to go, but Chart and Randal both weighed in to assure Mama he is a reformed man now that he is married. I am a little disappointed. Gossip has always painted a very intriguing picture and I saw him at Randal's wedding. Quel beau! I could imagine his fatal attraction.)

We very much want you to join us. Rowanford says he is going to call and ask you, and will provide a mount. Please say yes, otherwise I'm not sure he will join the party.

I know I gave myself away last night, dear friend. I fear I am no hand at dissembling. I doubt I have a chance to attach his interest, but I must make a push. I fear he is too used to regarding me as an awkward younger sister, just like all Chart's friends.

I do show well on a horse, though.

In case you have not brought a habit to Town, I have had Melrose take up the hem on my spare one and sent it over, along with a spare pair of boots. We always were of a size, except for a couple of inches of height.

Please, please, please agree, Amy.

Your dearest friend,
Clyta.

Amy sighed.

"Bad news, dear?" asked Nell Claybury as she entered. Amy feared her tears had left a mark.

"Not really," she said with a smile. "It is just Clyta Ashby asking me to join a riding party. Or at least, forewarning me that Rowanford is going to invite me."

Nell looked unconvinced that this was the whole story but said, "That is wonderful, Amy. Just what you need."

"I told you I have no wish to move in high circles," Amy said. "And I may have other invitations."

"If you mean Sir Cedric," said Nell, causing Amy to blush, "did you not hear him say that he will be out of Town for a few days?"

That must have been while she was daydreaming. Amy felt a mixture of frustration and relief at the news.

"So there is no reason," Nell continued, "for you not to enjoy yourself. What harm can it do if you spend a pleasant afternoon with your friends?"

None at all, thought Amy, except that she feared Harry Crisp would be one of the group.

But she wanted to go. It was over two years since she had ridden a decent horse. Why the devil should she let Harry Crisp keep her from such a treat? He could stay home if the situation bothered him.

"Lord save us!" declared Nell, startling Amy out of her thoughts. "Do you mean the Duke of Rowanford is going to come *here*?"

"I think so," said Amy. To her amazement, sensible Nell Claybury was transformed before her eyes into a bundle of anticipation and nerves, dashing around to make sure every corner of the house was perfect, and lamenting the fact that she did not keep a butler who would be knowledgeable about wines.

In the end she sent the footman to her friend, Jerome Irons, the wine merchant, begging him to send over a selection of fine wines suitable for immediate drinking. Within half an hour four clerks arrived bearing the bottles with great care, so as to avoid disturbing them, and left them along with careful instructions for their correct handling.

"Bertie always looked after the wines," said Nell nervously. "I have no palate at all—the cheapest wine tastes as good as the most expensive, so I don't bother myself overmuch. Am I acting the fool?" she asked ruefully.

Amy smiled. "Not at all. A duke is a duke, after all. I just hope you don't mind him coming here. I'm causing you a great deal of bother."

"Not a bit of it," said Nell. "I was bored to death before you came. I'm having a wonderful time."

And indeed, thought Amy, that was surely the truth. Nell was looking brighter and younger day by day. Amy told her so, adding, "I expect we will have your suitors beating down the door as well as mine." She was amused when Nell blushed, and wondered just who the promising gentleman might be.

Francis, the footman, looked puffed up with pride when he ushered the duke into Nell's drawing room, and the maid who helped bring in the tea tray appeared ready to drop it with nerves. Aunt Lizzie had the complacent look of one who says to herself, "I told you so."

Rowanford must be aware of the effect he was having— Amy wondered if he found it tiresome to be set apart so young merely by a title—but he put on no airs and graces. He soon had Nell at her ease. He was a thoroughly pleasant man.

Again the thought came to Amy that she could surely induce the appropriate degree of warmth for him in her heart if she tried, and she certainly wasn't above the idea that marrying the duke would be a glorious triumph. But then she remembered Clyta. It wouldn't do. And the simple fact was that it might be possible to make oneself fall in love, but only when the heart was free.

Amy was having to accept that her heart was not free.

Rowanford turned to her and delivered the expected invitation. Amy hesitated. Her acceptance might encourage him, and she knew she was going to be thrown together with Harry. Perhaps it might be wiser to say no.

On the other hand, she wanted to go, and perhaps she could find a way to promote Clyta's cause. Sir Cedric would be out of town, so she needn't feel guilty.

The old saying came to mind—While the cat's away, the mice will play. That wasn't the right sort of thing to think at all.

Then she recalled Nell saying, "So there is no reason for you not to enjoy yourself," as if she did not expect Amy to have true pleasure with Sir Cedric. Amy looked at Nell with dismay. That was nonsense, surely.

"Amy, dear," said Nell. "Are you all right?"

Amy collected her wits. "I'm sorry." She turned to Rowanford. "That is very kind of you, your grace. If you can provide the mount, I will be delighted to join the party. But please make the horse a gentle one. I am somewhat out of practice."

His smile was exceedingly warm. "Don't worry, Miss de Lacy. I will take the greatest care of you."

As he left, Amy realized he had taken her confusion as being the result of her feelings at receiving such a flattering invitation. He might be a thoroughly pleasant man, but he was a duke. He had apparently inherited during his school days, so it was not surprising that he have a high opinion of his own importance.

She feared she had paved the way for yet further complications in her life.

Two days later, Amy waited the arrival of the party, dressed in Clyta's rich red habit, and tremulous with the hope that Harry Crisp would be present.

It was stupid, it was wrong, but she was rapidly losing control of her feelings. She was glad Sir Cedric was away, as if she had been let out of prison. She wanted to see Harry and be with him as happily and warmly as they had been in the farm kitchen.

She knew that was impossible, but she would see him. At least she would see him.

It was Rowanford who came to the door, and who tossed Amy into the saddle of the rather solid gray he had brought for her. She gave a general, cheery greeting, her eyes passing over Harry without pause, but catching an impression she held in her heart. She hadn't clearly noted who else was present.

As they set out, she was aware of him riding behind, but as her feelings steadied, she took in the party. Harry was behind, she knew, riding with that dark-haired girl from Clyta's ball—Lucy Frogmorton.

He was going to marry her. It must be so if he was singling her out in such a fashion. She shouldn't begrudge him his happiness, but she did.

Ahead in the lead were Lord Randal and his wife, behind them Chart and Clyta. Clyta waved back cheerfully.

Amy remembered her purpose. "Clyta and I were great friends at school," she said to the duke. "She has a wonderfully warm heart."

"Yes," he said carelessly. "A pretty good sort. Doesn't make a fuss over things."

"And very pretty," Amy continued. "I'm sure she'll make an excellent match." Was she laying it on a bit thick? It was clear, however, that she would need a bludgeon to make an impression upon his mind.

"Clyta?" he said, looking at the subject of the conversation. "She's got a fine seat. All the Ashbys are bruising riders. How do you find your mount, Miss de Lacy?"

Amy found it a slug. It was clear Rowanford had taken her caution too seriously. This horse would be ideal for a non-equestrian grandmother. "I feel very safe," she said.

"Excellent. I shall take good care of you, Miss de Lacy. Have no fear."

Amy sighed and wished there was a convenient piece of furniture to heft to prove she was not as fragile as she appeared.

It was not too bad as long as they were on the city streets, but they were soon in countryside and the pace began to quicken. Amy's mount quickened, but not nearly as much as the others. This was made worse by the duke saying that they must hold back for Miss de Lacy's sake, as if she were scared to canter.

In the end, as when she had returned home from the Coneybears, the rest of the party took side trips while she ambled along, trying to pretend she was content. Even Rowanford abandoned her at times, though someone always kept her company.

She suddenly found Lord Randal by her side. "Is this pace really the best you can do?"

There was something in his eyes that brought out an honest answer. "It is the best this horse can do. But don't say anything. The duke will be hurt."

He grinned. "I am an authority on dukes. A duke's self-esteem can only be dented by a grenade." He put two fingers in his mouth like a barrow-boy and whistled. His wife waved and rode back.

"You," he said as soon as she arrived, "are in need of a rest."

"Hardly," she replied.

He ignored this. "Miss de Lacy has kindly agreed to let you borrow this placid, gentle beast for a while. I'm sure you are grateful."

"Oh no," Amy protested, but was overridden.

"How kind," said Sophie. "I'm sure I am in need of a rest.

Married life," she said faintly, with a sliding look at her husband, "is *so* exhausting."

He was fighting laughter as he dismounted and assisted them in the exchange, adjusting the stirrup leathers. By this time the rest of the party had gathered.

"Is something the matter?" Rowanford asked.

"Sophie needs a rest," said Randal, causing looks of astonishment from all except the duke, "and Miss de Lacy has agreed it would do her good to be a bit more venturesome. Perhaps you could stay with Sophie for a little while, Rowanford, while I see how Miss de Lacy does."

He gave the duke no chance to object but led the way into a piece of light woodland. Amy happily followed. Lady Randal's black Thoroughbred was a marvelous piece of horseflesh. They were soon traveling the wide bridle paths at a canter.

He grinned at her. "All right?"

"Of course! I only meant I was a little out of practice, not that I was unable to ride entirely."

There was a log lying across the path ahead. "Game?" he asked.

Amy nodded and they both sailed over it. She laughed.

He slowed his mount down. "We mustn't tire them. There's a way to go. If we head this way it should bring us back to the road." As the pace steadied he said, "You ride well."

Amy looked at him. "I was raised in the Shires, Lord Randal."

He laughed. "I suppose you were. And the Belvoir used to meet at Stonycourt, didn't it? I remember attending there."

Amy nodded. "In better days."

They rode on, hooves muffled by the soft leaf mold, seeming alone among the trees in heavy green leaf.

Suddenly he spoke. "There are more important things in life than money, you know."

Amy was shocked by the attack. "There speaks someone who has never been without."

"True," he acknowledged. "But my comment is still valid. No one can survive without food and shelter, but I would give up almost everything for Sophie."

Amy knew what he was saying, and it was unfair, but she couldn't say so. "We are all different, I suppose, my lord."

They had come to the road, and the party was some way behind.

"I wonder," he said, then called to the others.

❧ 12 ❧

THEY SPEEDED UP and soon the party was all together again. Amy insisted on changing horses and soon found herself partnered with the duke.

"I am sorry the horse is too slow for you," he said stiffly.

Amy was about to be conciliatory when she realized that she might serve Clyta's case better if she could keep his feathers ruffled. "It is a little placid, your grace," she said. "I was raised in hunting country and am used to spirited mounts."

He turned distinctly cool. "Perhaps Templemore will be able to offer you an exchange for the return." At the earliest opportunity he jumped his gray into a nearby meadow for a gallop. Randal and Sophie were already gone. Chart and Miss Frogmorton were ahead. When Clyta and Harry moved to follow the duke, Amy saw her chance and called out, "Mr. Crisp!"

He turned, startled, then waved Clyta on and came back.

Clyta flashed Amy a grateful smile and set off after the duke. Amy had acted on impulse, but now she was faced with the problem of what to say to her rejected suitor.

"Yes, Miss de Lacy," he said warily as his horse came alongside hers.

Amy badly wanted him to smile at her. "I wish we could put an end to the ill feelings between us, sir."

He raised his brows. "Ill feelings?" he queried. "I would say we disliked one another intensely."

Amy swallowed and stared between her horse's ears. "I don't dislike you."

When she risked a look at him, he seemed sober. "Don't you? You're very tolerant of insults then."

"You insulted me and I hit you. That should wipe the slate clean."

He appeared skeptical. "What's the matter? Are all your other suitors failing you, Miss de Lacy? You have just mishandled Rowanford, but don't despair. You can doubtless get him back with a smile or two."

"I don't want Rowanford," said Amy sharply, "and if you were to ask me again to marry you I would again say no. I do have thoughts other than marital!" She moderated her tone. "I just wish we could be more at ease."

"Why?"

Amy looked away. It was an excellent question. "I don't know."

They rode for a while in silence, then he said, "So it's to be the banker. You surprise me. Rowanford's nearly as rich, and there is no comparison in other respects."

"Sir Cedric is an estimable man."

"Yes," he said dryly. "He'd make you an excellent father."

Amy looked at him. "It is not unusual for there to be a disparity of ages in marriage."

"But not desirable. It will be a foolish match. He's not an old man in need of an heir, and I doubt he wants a new young family to add to his grown one. What have you in common? Ah, I forgot," he said with what could almost be a touch of humor, "you share an interest in steam engines."

Amy's lips twitched in response. "I'm afraid not." He *was* teasing her. Her heart swelled in response, and she only wanted to keep him here beside her in harmony. "Do you think there is anything in it?"

"Steam?" he said. "Assuredly. Steam pumps have been in use in mining for decades, and now steam carriages on rails haul coal at a number of mines. Steam boats are widely used in the Americas, and there is one on the Clyde, I believe. You must know this, however," he said with a distinctly humorous glance at her. "You were at Mr. Boyd's lecture."

Amy bit her lip. "I was present, yes. I did think," she added hurriedly, "that the powerful effect of steam was clearly demonstrated. I wondered if it could be put to domestic use."

"Cleaning, washing, and such like?" he asked, intrigued. "I suppose a steam mechanism could move a scrubbing brush backward and forward, or agitate washing. But steam engines are too large."

"Could they not be made smaller?"

"It should be looked into. It is a dangerous notion," he pointed out with a smile. "If machines do the cleaning, the servants will be idle, and you know what the devil does with idle hands."

Amy shared his amusement, but then had a disquieting thought. Their harmony felt as fragile as a cobweb, and she hated to break it with one of her gloomy, sensible predictions but she could not help it. "More dangerous than that," she said. "Would it not be like the new agricultural machines, and the power looms, which are throwing people out of work? If machines take over all the household work, what would the servants do? The poverty would be terrible."

He was not disgusted but nodded thoughtfully. "Good

point. Perhaps we'd better not share our inspiration with the world, then. Poverty creates all kinds of havoc."

Amy felt the heat in her cheeks, but she did not look away. Did that refer to her and did he perhaps understand her predicament? "Poverty is terrible," she agreed. "It strips away dignity and leaves no time and energy for pleasure."

"Employment doesn't leave much time and energy for pleasure either," he pointed out. "Nor does it necessarily preclude poverty. Perhaps our machines would be useful after all if they made the servants' lives easier."

Amy was confused. Perhaps he hadn't been referring to her lack of money. Whatever his motives, she was entranced to find that he did not shy away from a serious topic, or appear shocked to find she had some thoughts of her own. "Some people expect their servants to work morn till night," she said. "If machines could do some of the work, they would simply hire fewer and expect more of the ones that remained."

"Is that what you would do?"

"No," said Amy with a sigh. "I would love to have the money to hire ample staff, and clothe and feed them well, and give them generous days off." She looked at him frankly. "A taste of menial labor would make us all better masters and mistresses."

He reached down to take her rein and stop her horse. "Miss de Lacy," he said somberly, "if you had accepted my offer you would have been mistress of a handsome estate, with yet greater to come in time. I would happily have provided ample funds for your generous rule. Did this not occur to you?"

"No," said Amy honestly, for such thoughts had not come into it that day. Had she thought at all?

"And now it has been pointed out?" he asked carefully.

Amy's heart constricted painfully. Was it all to do again?

Nothing had really changed except now her fortune was within grasp, not hypothetical. "Now," she said woodenly, "I am going to marry Sir Cedric."

"My felicitations." He dropped her reins and set his horse in motion again.

Amy held her horse back and let him go. She felt sick. After all that had gone before he would have asked her again, given the smallest encouragement. His feelings perhaps ran as deep as hers and it could not be. Not when Sir Cedric and his millions were as good as hers.

But the thought that she was hurting Harry as much as she was hurting herself was close to unbearable. If there had been any sense to turning back and fleeing the rest of the day she would have done it, but Lord Randal was already riding back to see why she was just sitting there. She saw the others turn in some gates. At least they had arrived. She kicked her sluggard mount into a trot and followed.

Maiden Hall was an old house, a timbered Elizabethan sprawl in which few of the verticals or horizontals were straight. Riotously flowering borders surrounded it, backed by tall hollyhocks and delphiniums, and old-fashioned roses scrambled over the uneven surfaces on trellises.

The whole house seemed organic, growing out of the earth. It was beautiful and looked nothing like the home of a gazetted rake.

The rake himself lived up to Amy's expectations, however, when he came out to greet his guests. Tall, dark, handsome, and dressed with devastating informality in an open-necked shirt, sleeves rolled up to expose his arms like a laborer. No one could fail to be aware of a lithe body beneath the slight amount of clothing, and there was a wicked gleam in his eye even if he was supposed to have been tamed by matrimony.

Amy found it difficult to believe that the very ordinary woman by his side had achieved such a miracle. Lady Templemore was short and her gown was a simple green muslin. Her face was close to plain and her brown hair was gathered into a simple knot at the back.

But then she smiled at her guests and was beautiful. When she turned to her husband with a comment, she was dazzling, and the look in his eye showed he was tamed indeed, if devotion so heated could be called tame at all.

Amy looked over at Harry Crisp, who had dismounted to greet the Templemores. He would look at her like that, given the slightest encouragement. She'd seen the pale trace of it in his eyes that day in the kitchen, and the same, tightly controlled, just a little while ago. Perhaps he felt her eyes on his, for he turned, and after a hesitation came to assist her.

His eyes were shielded but could not hide his feelings. His hands burned at her waist as he lowered her. They lingered there far longer than necessary.

"I'm sorry," Amy said helplessly. "Oh dear. Why do I keep apologizing to you?"

He sighed with bleak humor. "Perhaps because you are constantly at fault? I wonder what sins I committed in some previous existence to have encountered you, dear Amethyst."

She placed a hand on his arm. "Don't call me that, please."

He moved away, then held out his arm. "Come and be introduced to your hosts. You have something in common with Ver. He doesn't like his name either."

Amy was introduced to Lord and Lady Templemore, but when she made her curtsy and attempted to address them as such found Harry's words were true.

"If you wish to be invited here again," the viscount said

with a smile, "you will address me as Ver, and Emily as Emily. Outrageous, I know, but I have always been so and make it my practice to infect everyone I meet. So you won't feel uncomfortable, we will address you as Amy. Unless," he added with a distinctly wicked look, "you prefer Amethyst?"

Now, how did he even know her real name? Amy cast an alarmed look at Harry. Did the whole world know everything?

"You forget, Amy," said Verderan, offering an arm to lead her into the house, "Harry was staying at my hunting box when you had your contretemps with him."

Amy allowed herself to be led in, feeling as if she were being taken to court. Had she walked into a trap? It would not surprise her to find herself sat down and interrogated by all the friends of the man she was treating so cruelly.

Instead she was given into the hands of a maid, who showed her where she could take off her hat and refresh herself. The other women soon joined her.

Clyta took the opportunity to whisper, "Thank you. We rode together and he complimented my riding. I fear you offended Rowanford, though, by seeming dissatisfied with your mount."

"Indeed you did," said Miss Frogmorton snappily as she pushed at her perfect, glossy curls. Amy wondered if she was beginning to sense some threat to her pursuit of Harry. "You would do better to learn a little decorum, Miss de Lacy, especially when having to admit to an address in *Chelsea*."

"I know all about decorum," said Amy coolly, "but I don't care a fig if I offend the duke."

Miss Frogmorton sneered. "Yes, my mother said you were on the catch for that rich old banker. Doubtless the best you can hope for from *Chelsea*. I think I begin to understand what Mr. Crisp meant about adventuresses."

She swept out before Clyta could get out a heated rebuttal. Amy merely stood tight lipped.

"Why, that cat!" Clyta exploded.

"Not at all," said Amy. "It is perfectly true."

"No, it isn't. You could have the duke if you made a push, and that's more than Lucy Frogmorton could."

Amy smiled and hugged her friend. "I always did love your loyalty, Clyta."

Sophie came in and ran a comb through auburn curls, "Miss Frogmorton looked as if she had just slain a dragon," she remarked.

"Just been rude you mean," said Clyta. "She was sneering at Amy just because she is living in Chelsea."

"It seemed a very pleasant part of Town," said Sophie lightly. "Perhaps Randal and I should move there and bring it into fashion." She assessed Amy. "It must be difficult being so uncomfortably beautiful." Without giving Amy a chance to comment, she linked arms with her. "Come along. Emily and I are completely secure in our husbands' affections and Clyta is your friend. The only envy you need fear here is from the green frog."

All three were giggling as they left the room.

After an ample luncheon, everyone walked out to explore the grounds of Maiden Hall. Amy found herself on the left arm of her host, with Sophie on his right. Emily balanced this by giving an arm each to Randal and Chart, while Clyta walked with Harry, and Lucy Frogmorton clung to the arm of the duke, looking extremely pleased with herself.

It was clear that Lucy had begun to aim higher than the future Lord Thoresby. Really, thought Amy, the girl was shameful. She cared nothing for feelings but was just out for the best catch she could land.

And how's that for a case of the pot calling the kettle black? Amy asked herself, but then reminded herself that she was seeking the greatest fortune for her family's sake, not her own.

"Despite what people think," said Verderan as they strolled between old yew hedges, "I did not name the place when I bought it. The name is ancient."

"But," asked Sophie naughtily, "didn't it add to the attractions just a little bit?"

"I still think Randal should beat you daily," he replied, with a look at Sophie which told Amy he was tamed in much the way a pet tiger is tamed—which is to say, not very much.

They had come to the end of the path and walked out into a meadow. Emily had brought some salt to feed the fallow deer which wandered beneath the nearby trees. She passed it out and the deer, for whom this was a familiar treat, pricked their way delicately to lip the food from their hands.

Amy offered some to a shy fawn and laughed with delight when it took it.

"And do you see just a piece of venison?"

Amy jerked round to face Harry. "Don't be horrible!"

"In what way is it different from the charming lamb?"

"Its mother is prettier."

He frowned slightly.

"Now what have I said?" Amy asked.

He grinned. "I've just remembered what Lucy Frogmorton's mother looks like."

Amy bit her lip and said, "Appearances are not everything, sir."

"True. But the woman also has a sheep's mind."

Amy gave him a reproving look. "Are you suggesting the deer are the epitome of intellectual wit? You are being deceived by appearances again."

He started as if suddenly brought back to himself. "So I am," he said and walked away.

Amy looked around and discovered Lord Randal had decided to emulate his friend and shed a great deal of clothing. As he was equally as handsome as Lord Templemore the effect was dramatic. Before her startled eyes Harry and Chart followed suit, shedding jackets and stocks and opening shirts to the breeze.

Neither had the lithe elegance of the older men but they were well built. Amy remembered thinking that she had never seen more of Harry's body than his face and hands, and she wished it had stayed that way.

The open shirt showed a glimpse of tawny curls on his chest, and there was a soft glint of them on his forearms. Amy discovered the desire to run her hand along those muscular arms was almost overpowering. She dragged her eyes away.

She stared over at Lord Templemore, who was laughing and looked a very Lucifer indeed. He had said, "I make it my practice to infect everyone I meet," and he'd been telling no less than the truth. A cricket ball had appeared from somewhere and he threw it hard and long to Chart, who caught it and threw it back. The man's body as he reached up to catch it was that of a Thoroughbred, a hunting cat, sinuously graceful, dangerous.

He was not tamed at all. He was wicked, this place was wicked, and they were all being infected by it.

To prove Amy's point, Sophie shed the jacket of her habit, and pulled off her boots and stockings so she could join the game barefoot. Clyta giggled and followed suit.

"Oh dear," said Lucy Frogmorton looking aghast. "My mother . . ."

What they needed here, thought Amy, was a proper chaperon. Sophie, married lady though she was, was clearly no use. Lady Templemore was watching without a trace of unease. She came over to Amy and Lucy and said, "Don't you care to act like children? Very wise. Come and sit with me in the shade."

Amy trailed along but resentment grew in her. Where was it written she could not join in this madness if she wanted to? A servant had brought cricket bats, and a game of sorts was taking place, though the rules were not ones that the Marylebone Cricket Club would recognize. Chart was currently chasing Lord Randal about with the ball.

The men's shirts were beginning to stick to their heated bodies. So were the lawn bodices of Sophie's and Clyta's habits. Sophie had somehow pinned her skirt up so that it did not trail on the ground. A great deal of leg was exposed.

Lucy sat stiffly on a blanket in the shade of an oak and stared into the harmless distance. Lady Templemore was waiting for Amy.

"Why aren't you joining in?" Amy asked her.

"I'm increasing," Lady Templemore replied frankly. "I doubt one has to be as careful as they say, but Ver worries if I'm likely to fall or be hit." She gave a wistful sigh. "It's the very devil."

"Increasing?" asked Amy with a blush.

"Love," said the older woman. She looked shrewdly at Amy. "Why don't you join in? The sides are uneven."

Amy found she had her jacket, boots, and stockings off without conscious thought. She looked at her bare feet and remembered her time in Harry's kitchen. This was very, very dangerous, and if she had a particle of common sense she would dress again and watch the horizon with Lucy Frogmorton until sanity returned.

Common sense had deserted her.

"Here," said Lady Templemore and took a long pin from

the etui which hung from her belt. "One learns to be prepared for anything," she commented. "It will be safer if your skirts don't trail." She went off to hitch up Clyta's skirts.

Amy did her best to pin up her skirts without revealing much leg. It proved impossible.

"This is terrible!" exclaimed Lucy, glaring at her. "My mother did question visiting such a place, but Mr. Crisp, and the duke . . ."

"Since you're here," said Amy, "don't you think you might as well join in? It can't do any harm."

Lucy stared at her. "It is as good as an orgy!"

Amy laughed as she went off to join in, but she thought Lucy made more sense than she knew. It wasn't an orgy and there was no chance that any true impropriety would take place, but it was wild and uncivilized. The laws of Society had been blown away as a brisk breeze dispels fog, and all sorts of outrageous things could happen.

There were no formal teams. Clyta and the duke were at bat and the rest were fielding. Lord Templemore placed Amy in right field a safe distance from the batters.

"I'm not afraid of a cricket ball, Lord Templemore," she said to him.

"Humor me," he replied. "Beauty such as yours should be preserved for a few years longer. And remember, it's Ver. You do want to be invited back, don't you?"

His shirt clung to him. His dark hair curled more madly than before and clung damply to his bare neck. Amy felt a dizziness that was nothing to do with him, except that he was bringing to life feelings she had thought not for her. "I don't know," she said, then added, "Beauty is dangerous."

"You want to be invited back," he said firmly. "And beauty is a weapon. If you can't get rid of it, the least you can do is learn to use it appropriately."

Amy shivered as he walked away. She pushed her hands through her hair and felt that it, too, was damp. It doubtless had the same wildness as his. She looked down. Her bodice was already clinging to her breasts.

She looked toward Harry, who was stationed not far away. As if drawn he walked over to her.

"Do you know how to play?" he asked. His neck was so strong and brown and his chest was smoothly muscled.

"Yes," she said. "I'm quite good, actually, and I have a strong throwing arm."

He grinned, and his eyes were darker than usual. "I know that."

Amy felt herself heat up even more. "I am sorry for that."

"I'm not."

Amy thought it much wiser to turn her attention back to the game, though she was aware that he stayed by her instead of returning to his place. Sir Cedric, she reminded herself desperately. Sir Cedric and all the money they needed for Stonycourt, and horses, and luxuries, and dowries.

The ball came her way. She stopped it, but as she began to throw she realized her fashionable habit had sleeves too tight to allow a good throwing movement. With a muttered, "Drat," she tossed it to Harry and let him hurl it back to the bowler.

"I have a penknife in my pocket," he said. "I could cut your sleeves off. You have lovely arms, as I remember."

"I am lovely everywhere," she said tartly, using her beauty as a weapon, as Lord Templemore had suggested.

It did not drive Harry away. "I don't doubt it," he said. "I hope one day to have the evidence of my own eyes."

Amy stared at him. "You won't."

"Won't I?" he asked gently. "I wonder. I have decided to fight for you, Amethyst. You're everything I want in a wife—mind, body, and soul. And you're not indifferent. I knew it at

Coppice Farm, and since then I've seen your eyes travel my body just as mine have traveled yours. You deserve better than an old man in your bed."

Amy turned away and closed her eyes. "Don't."

His voice could not be shut out. "I won't let you do this to yourself. I'm going to woo you, seduce you. If necessary, I'll abduct you."

Amy looked at him again. "You'd hang."

He smiled with hot, ravishing confidence. "Would you say you're sorry?"

The ball came their way again and he fielded it. Amy could no more have handled the ball than she could fly. "You're mad," she said dazedly. "I'm going to marry Sir Cedric."

"No, you're not. You're going to marry someone you love. I hope that will be me."

Amy didn't know what to say in the face of such madness.

"If you're afraid of your family," he said gently, "I will protect you, Amy."

At last she found anger of sorts. "Of course I'm not afraid of my family. I love my family. Go away. How many times must I tell you I am perfectly happy with my situation?"

When she glanced around he had gone back to his place, but she felt no reassurance, especially when she had to force her eyes not to feast on him. He wanted her to marry for love, even if it was not himself. That was love speaking. And she wanted him to marry for love, because she loved him.

And they were both condemned to something much, much less.

❧ 13 ❧

A BREAK WAS CALLED for shade and lemonade. Everyone collapsed beneath the oak in shameless abandon. Lucy Frogmorton lowered her gaze from the horizon only when Rowanford sat beside her.

Amy frowned at this. She hadn't driven him off just to see him fall into Lucy's greedy paws. She looked at Clyta, who was laughing at something Lord Templemore had said to her, something slightly naughty, Amy would guess. It had the effect of making Clyta look magnificent. Relaxed among friends in the country, Clyta was at her best.

With determination, Amy sat beside the duke and was pleased to hear that Lucy was complaining about the lack of decorum. The duke did not look as if he enjoyed the topic, and he turned away readily enough when Amy broke into the conversation.

"I do hope you weren't offended over the horse, your grace," she said in her best demure manner. "I feel so touched that you wanted to take care of me, and it is a long time since I last rode a spirited animal."

He preened a little. "Not at all, Miss de Lacy. I will certainly know better another time. And you mustn't be 'your gracing' me as if we were strangers."

"You're very kind. I did used to be a good rider, but I was never as good as Clyta."

He looked over at Clyta as she had intended. "No, she's a wonderful horsewoman."

Clyta laughed again. Her heavy dark hair was escaping its pins and she was beginning to look wanton, but in this situation it might work to her advantage. "She's enjoying herself," Amy said softly, trying to keep his attention fixed to Clyta. "She much prefers the country to London."

"Oh," said the duke, his eyes fixed where Amy wanted them as if glued.

"It is her duty, I suppose, as a duke's granddaughter to do a Season," Amy persevered, feeling like the serpent in the Garden of Eden. "I'm sure she'll marry well—don't you think, Duke? I know any number of eligible men are already interested." She leaned closer to his ear. "Don't you think her very handsome?"

By some act of Providence, Chart chose that moment to tease his sister so she pounced on him for a minor tussle. Her hair came down completely and a great deal of her shapely legs was revealed before Chart realized this and established some control.

"My, my," said Rowanford in the tones of a man who has had a revelation.

"Oh dear," said Amy briskly, leaping to her feet. "If Chart's going to tease, I think we should go and rescue Clyta. Brothers can be horrible," she added, whose only brother had never given her that kind of trouble at all.

Like a puppet, the duke got to his feet and followed. Amy settled him by Clyta, then drew Chart off. When she looked back and saw Clyta laughing and joking with the duke without a trace of shyness, and Rowanford leaning closer, bewitched, she felt she had done a fine piece of work. It might not amount to anything but it was a start, and in the hedonistic atmosphere of Maiden Hall anything could happen.

She glanced back at Lucy and received a glare of dislike. She felt no ill will toward the young woman and would have tried a little matchmaking on her behalf if she could, but Lucy couldn't have Rowanford because Clyta wanted him, and she couldn't have Chart or Harry because they both deserved a warmer heart.

Amy wasn't aware that Lord Templemore had disappeared until he came back. "I have arranged a little entertainment," he said with a twinkle in his eyes.

Amy immediately felt alarm and anticipation. What now?

"Not the maze," said Lord Randal with a grin.

"The maze," said Lord Templemore.

"Do you really have a maze?" asked Clyta, bouncing to her feet, then leaning down to pull Rowanford up. Amy winced, but the duke didn't seem to mind at all.

"I really do. A genuine Elizabethan maze that took a devilish amount of work to shape up again. Come and see."

The ladies resumed their stockings and boots, but that was the only gesture toward resuming propriety before they walked around the house. Amy was pleased to see the duke staying close to Clyta. She wondered why Lord Randal had seemed so amused at the thought of the maze. It sounded interesting, but no more than that.

They were walking along a tall, dense box hedge when Lord Templemore stopped by a narrow gap. Amy realized the hedge was part of the maze. It was at least eight feet high and impenetrable and stretched quite a distance in either direction. The narrow gap led to a path between more dense hedges. Amy suddenly felt nervous.

"There are four entrances—or exits," said their host, "and a central square with some statues. I've left two prizes in the center, one for the first lady, one for the first gentleman. They are to be given to the partner of their choice." It was clear from the glint in his eye that he knew that could open some mischievous pathways.

"I think the ladies should go in first," he said. "Who will volunteer?"

Clyta stepped forward. "I will. But what if we can't find our way out?"

"Someone will rescue you before dark, I promise."

With a flitting, teasing look at the duke, Clyta slipped through the gap and moved out of sight. Rowanford made as if to follow, but Lord Templemore stopped him.

"On to the next entrance," he said and led the way. It was some distance to the corner, and then Amy could see the dimensions more clearly. "This is enormous," she said.

"Yes," agreed Lord Templemore. "Are you game to go next?"

There seemed no point in refusing, so Amy slipped between the trimmed box and into the maze. The outer path went forward the length of the maze, cut by a number of gaps leading inward. Amy listened, but it was quiet now. She couldn't even hear the voices of the others. It was as if she were alone in the narrow green world, and she poked her head back out to assure herself that the real world was still there.

Then she stiffened her nerve and took the next gap.

Sometimes the paths became dead ends, sometimes they went in circles. She tried to carry some plan of where she had been but found it impossible. She encountered no one, and a fear that she was stuck in the maze began to grow in her. She imagined the others back at the house having tea and laughing at the joke they had played to trap her here.

She began to hurry, then run, plunging always through the first gap she came to. She heard a noise through the hedge. "Hello!" she cried. "Who's there?"

"Miss de Lacy?" It was Lucy Frogmorton. "Oh, this is horrible. How can I get to your side?"

Amy came to her senses. She wouldn't be as much of a ninny as Lucy. "I don't know," she called. "Don't worry. Just wander around. You'll either get out, or to the middle sooner or later."

"I want to get out now!" Lucy demanded.

"Scream then," recommended Amy and headed away from the voice. She didn't hear any screaming, so Lucy must have decided not to make a fool of herself. Amy took her own advice and wandered. If she began to feel trapped, she looked up at the blue sky. Whenever she heard a sound she called out, and she made contact with Clyta and Chart that way, though she never saw them.

She was amused to find small grottoes here and there in dead ends. They were furnished with benches and a certain amount of screening. In view of her host's rakish reputation she could imagine their purpose.

She found her mind dwelling on the kind of parties that had doubtless been held here in his bachelor days, with ladies and gentlemen finding and losing each other in these dark green passageways, feeling alone together here, apart from the world and all the burdens of responsibility and correct behavior.

She wondered if Lord Templemore wandered here with his wife to stop and share kisses in a secret corner. She could imagine it. It was perhaps improper to dwell on such things but she couldn't help it. She could imagine Lord Randal and Sophie enjoying the same pleasure.

There would be none of that for her. No teasing romps, no romantic trysts. Amy allowed her mind in a direction she had never permitted it before. She knew, in general terms, what marriage involved. She imagined her marriage bed when Sir Cedric joined her. He would kiss her, and then do what he had to do. She supposed he would enjoy it, for men apparently did, but it was hard to imagine any enjoyment for herself. It was equally hard to imagine Sir Cedric looking at her with the hunger she had seen in other eyes today.

Having opened her mind to these thoughts, they could not be shut out. She saw new dimensions to the world around her. She had thought Lord Templemore's gaze at his wife heated, but now she recognized hunger. It was decently controlled by maturity, civilization, and, she supposed, the expectation of satisfaction, but it was hunger all the same. She remembered the way Sophie had said, "Married life is so exhausting," and the gleam in her husband's eye. Hunger again.

And maybe there had been just a little hunger in Rowanford's eyes when he looked at Clyta. Amy certainly hoped so.

It had been there in Harry's and, she suspected, in her own. She sighed. Was she to go hungry all her life?

She turned a corner and came face-to-face with Harry.

"Ah, another human being," he said lightly, but his eyes were hungry.

Amy swallowed. "Just what I was thinking."

It was silent and shadowed and cool. She walked toward him and put her hands on his broad shoulders. "I'd like you please to kiss me, just once."

His arms came to rest at her waist, and his breathing was suddenly unsteady. "Why just once?"

She rested her head against his warm shoulder and heard

the pounding of his heart. She watched as her hand slid down his damp neck to play among the curls on his chest. "Well, maybe twice."

His hand came up to cover hers against his skin, holding it still for a moment. Then he grasped it, moved apart from her, and set off back the way he had come, pulling her behind him.

"Where are we going?" she demanded. "Don't you want to kiss me?"

"Yes, I want to kiss you," he said and turned a corner that led to a grotto. He sat on the bench and drew her down beside him. His eyes were dark and dangerous, and Amy knew she was in peril, delicious peril.

He drew her against him with a relentless arm, guided her head with his other hand, and kissed her. It was not the gentle, questing kiss they had shared before, but hotly demanding and not a little angry. Amy surrendered to it. She, too, was hungry and angry and hot.

She pressed herself closer and held him tighter, sliding her hands beneath his shirt to feel his heated skin. She tasted him and swirled within a mad, heated passion, a hunger that was not appeased but grew and grew.

"God," he groaned and tore his lips from hers.

Amy made a faint protest, then came to herself and stared at him, dazed. She had somehow come to be on his lap, and his shirt looked as if she had half torn it off his body. "I'm terribly hard on buttons," she wailed and burst into tears.

He held her and stroked her and murmured to her. He held her tight and close as no one had held her before. Amy wept for Stonycourt, which would never be as it once was; for Beryl who would only be an aunt, never a mother; for Jassy, who would not marry well; for Jasper, who wouldn't have a string of hunters and host the Belvoir; and for herself, who wouldn't have any joy either because she wouldn't be happy if none of the others could be.

The sobs faded to gulps and then to numb silence. Amy clung close, filling her senses with the feel of his body and the scent of his skin, something to take with her and remember.

"You take buttons very seriously," he said shakily. His hand cradled her head, his fingers sending a message of comfort.

Amy sniffed. "You have to when you're poor."

He pushed her away. "There's no need for you to be poor, Amy. I can take care of you."

Amy shook her head. "Can you provide dowries for Jassy and Beryl?"

"Something, at least."

"Something isn't enough." She looked up at him. "I don't have a dowry, you know."

"I guessed. It doesn't matter." He looked impatient. "Isn't it a bit arrogant for you to assume that your sisters can't find love without money to sweeten the pot?"

Amy pushed away sharply. "That's a horrid thing to say!"

"It's what you're saying."

"No it isn't!" She jumped off his lap entirely. "It's just that that's the way of the world. At least they need decent clothes."

"I fell in love with you in a blanket."

Amy's anger escaped her. "Oh, don't."

"Don't what?"

"Don't say you love me."

"But I do."

"So do I." She clapped her hand over her mouth to call back the error.

He grasped her shoulders and pulled her closer. "Then you cannot marry anyone else."

"I love my family, too."

"Do they love you?" he asked in exasperation.

"Of course they do!"

"Then they won't want you to marry where you don't love, Amy. Why are you doing this?"

"They won't know. They *mustn't* know."

"Of course they'll know." He gave her a little shake. "Have some sense!"

"Stop shouting at me!"

"I feel like strangling you! If I had any sense I'd take you here and now in this damned bower and then you'd *have* to marry me."

They stared at each other and Amy knew it was temptation which wove through the heated air. She'd have to marry him, and she wanted him, now. Hunger. She hadn't recognized it before.

She backed away.

"Amy," he said and held out a hand.

She turned and fled.

She did not look, just ran, gasping. She collided with a hard body. Hands grasped and steadied her.

"Miss de Lacy," said Lord Randal. "Are you all right?"

Amy collapsed against him, heart thudding. "No."

He held her for a moment, then pushed her gently away so he could look at her. He was very sober for one so light-hearted. "What has happened?"

Amy took a deep breath. She knew what he thought. "If I said Harry and I had . . . committed an indiscretion, you'd say we had to get married, wouldn't you?"

"The world would."

"You wouldn't?"

His earlier somberness had gone and he looked, if anything, amused. "It would depend, I suppose, on the indiscretion, the consequences, and the feelings you share."

She might have known she'd get no sane answers from these people. They were all mad. Amy turned away. "Nothing happened," she said flatly.

"That is a lie."

She turned sharply, guiltily. "What do you mean?"

He just smiled, shook his head, and gently rearranged her bodice. "Let me escort you out of here."

She went willingly. Perhaps once out of the strange world of narrow green paths she could find sanity again.

In a little while he said, "This wasn't planned, Miss de Lacy."

"What wasn't?"

"Today. I admit we connived a little to bring you and Harry together at the ball. We all thought you'd both be better to get one another out of your systems. But today, well it was Rowanford's idea to invite you, and he was supported by Clyta. Now I think I see why. I noted the way you've tried to help her. Thank you."

"She's my friend. She'd do as much for me."

"We all would," he said gently.

Amy looked at him in surprise and swallowed tears. It was all too much. "I am an unscrupulous fortune hunter, Lord Randal. Your kindness is misguided."

He smiled with amazing sweetness. "I don't think so."

They had reached an exit, and they passed out into open spaces and clean air. Amy shuddered as reality invaded and cooled her senses, opening the way for the enormity of what had happened. Lady Templemore was nearby and she hurried over.

Lord Randal spoke first. "I think Miss de Lacy would appreciate returning to the house, Emily, for some peace and a cup of tea."

"Of course. Miss Frogmorton is already there with a cool

cloth on her head. The maze does not usually have such a dramatic effect."

"Are the others still inside?" he asked.

"I think so."

"Then I had best go and find Sophie. I'm sure the rest will manage with ease."

"Do you imply Sophie will be having the vapors?" queried Lady Templemore skeptically.

"Of course not," he said with a smile. "I just miss her."

With that he disappeared back into the maze, and Amy followed her hostess toward the house.

"You look a little pale, dear. I do hope it wasn't the maze. It can upset some people. I confess at first I found it strange, but now I like it. It's like entering a separate world."

"Yes, it is," said Amy, adding to herself, An extremely dangerous one.

Amy took tea with Lucy and Lady Templemore, and the others gradually drifted in to join them. Everyone else seemed to have had a merry time, and Clyta and the duke had clearly had some satisfactory encounter there. They both looked dazed but happy. Clyta had found the ladies' prize—a silver fob—and given it to Rowanford without hesitation.

Harry came in last. He had already resumed proper dress and looked sober. He had found the gentlemen's prize, perhaps because none of the others had bothered to look. He considered the ladies thoughtfully, then presented it to his hostess.

She unwrapped the small package to reveal a gold frog brooch with green eyes, which were presumably emeralds. It was a valuable piece but very ugly.

Lady Templemore laughed at her husband. "What a wonderful way of trying to get rid of it, Ver, but you see, it simply won't go away."

"We'll try again," he said with a grin. He explained, "It was given Emily by an eccentric Italian acquaintance of mine, and she's afraid she'll give birth to frogs if she wears it."

The lady protested and there was considerable banter. Lucy looked as if she'd like to faint, and Amy was shocked at the casual way Lord Templemore referred to his wife's condition. No one else appeared to be.

Sophie said, "I think you should give the frog to Lucy."

Everyone looked at her for an explanation. "It would suit her—because of her name, of course," she added blithely. "And she'd be doing the world a favor. Bad enough having little Verderans without them having green skin and bulging eyes."

Lucy took the piece in a daze, clearly at a loss, and then they all prepared to depart.

Lord Templemore offered Amy another mount but she refused. The fewer high spirits there were today the better.

The ride home was uneventful. Everyone was content with a leisurely pace, satiated almost with excitement. The duke rode happily with Clyta, but the other couples were arranged for tact. Amy was partnered with Chart, who kept conversation light and impersonal, Sophie rode with Harry, and Lord Randal was using his considerable charm to soothe Lucy Frogmorton before she was returned to her mama.

Amy saw Harry look back at her with intensity once or twice, but he made no move to speak to her.

When they arrived back in New Street, however, it was he who came to assist Amy from her horse.

He kept his hands on her waist a moment longer than necessary. "I meant what I said."

"So did I. Please don't make things more difficult for me."

"So you admit they are difficult."

Amy pulled herself out of his hands and summoned a

smile for the whole company as she thanked them. Then there was only the matter of giving a light account of her day to Nell and her aunt before she could find refuge in her room.

It seemed as if she had come out of a dream. It couldn't have been real—the barefoot romping, the passion, the kiss. But one thing remained. She did not want an old man in her bed.

Amy claimed to have developed a headache from too much sun and kept to her room the next day. Both Lord and Lady Randal, and Harry Crisp came to call on her separately and were sent away.

Amy tussled with what was right.

She was quite certain that she must not marry Harry. The pleasure to be found in that was too great when there would be so little for her family. But would it be a better thing for them all to suffer the straitened circumstances which they deserved—by inheritance if not from personal responsibility—or for her to marry Sir Cedric?

Amy was still willing to marry Sir Cedric and do her best to make him a good wife, but she knew now what she would be missing and how little she had to offer. Such an old man would not want passion, of course, but he would expect some warmth. Did she have that for him?

And, of course, Amy would have to give him what devotion she could under the eyes of his chilly son and saddened daughter-in-law, even as she grabbed as much of his money as she could get her hands on so it would all be worthwhile.

Amy's headache became a grim reality.

❧ 14 ❧

S HE KEPT TO HER ROOM THE NEXT DAY, too. Nell and Lizzie both fussed over her and discussed whether to send for the doctor. Amy assured them that was not necessary.

"Sir Cedric is expected back today," said Nell. "Will you not want to see him?"

"No," said Amy, a little more forcefully than she intended. "I mean . . . I really wouldn't be good company today. Apologize for me, please."

Lizzie came up with a tea tray in the afternoon and coaxed Amy into taking a little. "Been overdoing it, I suppose. But you must get your looks back before Sir Cedric cools down, dear. Most anxious to see you, he was. He seemed to want someone to go for a drive with him, so Nell went."

Get her looks back. Amy sat up and studied her reflection in the mirror. Good heavens, her beauty was fading. It was the pallor and the dark smudges beneath her eyes which were doing it. Perhaps she wouldn't have any choice as to whether to remain a spinster or not.

"And no sign of that duke," said Lizzie, "so it will have to be the banker, I suppose."

"If the worse comes to the worse," said Amy, "it won't be so bad to carry on as we were. In just a few years we'll be able to live in modest comfort."

"What!" exclaimed Lizzie. "Back at Stonycourt, living on potatoes, mutton, and chamomile tea. You must be mad!"

Amy retreated. "It's just that he hasn't offered for me, Aunt Lizzie, and there doesn't seem to be anyone else."

"How can he offer for you if you mope up here? Drink your tea and get well." When she left with the tray she said, "Oh, that Mr. Crisp was here again. Some people won't be put off, will they? He left something for you. I'll have the footman bring it up."

Amy found her energy had returned with a jolt and sat up in bed. The footman, escorted by Aunt Lizzie, carried in a medium-sized box and placed it on the bed. When he had gone Amy opened it with some anxiety. He had said he intended to woo her. What on earth would it be?

The crate contained an item swathed in cloth and surrounded by padding. When the bundled object was unwrapped it proved to be Lady Jane.

"Pretty," said Lizzie as Amy lifted it out gently. "Though what he thinks he's about sending you gifts I don't know. I would have thought you'd shown him what you thought of him clearly enough."

Amy ignored this and turned the key. The music started, the sweet tinkling tune carrying her straight back to Coppice Farm. Lady Jane turned her head gracefully, then began to lift her leg. There was a *ping* and the leg fell limp again, though the music played on.

"Why, it doesn't even work!" exclaimed Lizzie. "I'll have

Simon come and get it. Mr. Crisp can have his gift straight back."

"No," said Amy. "It's pretty and the music box works."

With a sniff, Lizzie left.

When she was alone Amy picked up the note that had been in the box and opened it. She had never seen his handwriting before. It was dark and a little wild.

Darling Amy,

I hope you will take Lady Jane. She means a lot to both of us, as a memory of that time in my kitchen with your clothes abandoned in the corner and us sharing such delights. Of course, I hope we will one day be reunited, you, me, and Lady Jane.

I cannot doubt that, when I think of our passion yesterday. I remember you throwing off your stockings, so eager were you. My skin still bears the marks of your nails, my mind the memory of your desire.

You are the only one I desire. I long to see you nestled in my blanket once again.

Harry

After a shocked moment, Amy collapsed in laughter. The cunning rogue. Not an untrue word in it and if anyone saw it she'd be at the altar with him in the twinkling of an eye.

There was more on the back.

Lady Jane is, I'm afraid, irreparable. I still think her worthy of care. Not everything can be put back together as it was.

Your loving Harry

That was a direct reference to her purpose, but he was wrong. Many things could be put right, and as he had proved with the automaton, it was often worth the effort.

Amy looked at the note. She should destroy it, but the temptation was very strong to leave it around and let fate take its course. Aunt Lizzie was certainly not above reading someone else's correspondence. In the end she slipped it between the pages of her book. It was Adam Smith's *The Wealth of Nations,* and she didn't think Lizzie would pick that up.

What on earth would he try next? She couldn't let him get away with this. She had to make her own decisions and stick to them.,

Amy got out of bed and went to the window. Was she going to marry Sir Cedric or not?

Presumably he was mainly interested in her beauty, since they had so little else in common. She could offer him that, as long as she didn't allow misery to fade it. It would be an honest bargain—youth and beauty for money.

That sounded despicable.

Amy straightened her shoulders. It was the way of the world. The family had spent so much money to send her to London that it would be wicked to turn her back on triumph when it was to hand. Moreover, she ruthlessly acknowledged that she had no real expectation of going back home to live in poverty. If she didn't marry Sir Cedric, she would doubtless be won over by Harry one of these days. She would end up with everything she had ever wanted, while her family had nothing.

Amy resolutely spent an hour walking in the garden to bring some color to her cheeks, but she made sure she was to be denied to all callers. She could not bear to see Harry. She went down to dinner that night.

Nell seemed to be in a fidgety mood, and chattered of this and that. She did not mention her drive with Sir Cedric, so nothing of significance could have been said. Anyway,

Amy supposed he would approach Aunt Lizzie for permission to pay his addresses, not Nell.

"Tell me, Amy," said Nell, who had only picked at her roast chicken, "what of the duke? He seemed a very charming young man."

"He's pleasant as dukes go," said Amy. "I hope I've tied him up with Clyta Ashby. She's madly in love with him."

"Oh," said Nell. "I thought you would make a lovely duchess."

"Indeed she would," said Lizzie. "It would have been a triumph to warm her mother's heart. But no, she has to push him off on her friend and settle for a mere knight." She helped herself to more peas.

"Oh dear," said Nell faintly, then she jumped to her feet. "Look at the time. I am expected at Fanny Bamford's. I did promise to go early and help with her soirée. She always worries so. Do please excuse me."

"I must say," said Lizzie staring at the door, "Nell is behaving most strangely. She used to be a very sensible woman."

Amy smiled. "I think she's in love, Aunt."

"In love? Nonsense. Not at her age. Are you finished? Ring for the sweet. It's apricot soufflé."

Amy did as she was requested, reflecting that she would once have thought Nell too old for love, but no longer. The hunger that was love had nothing to do with age.

By the next day Amy had regained some of her detachment and all of her resolve. If Sir Cedric truly wished to marry her, she would agree. She would be honest, though. She would tell him that she could offer nothing but friendship and genuine regard. After some consideration she decided she wouldn't tell him she loved another; he would doubtless be as romantical as all the rest and insist that she sacrifice all for love.

She would also explain the financial commitment she required from him. If after all this he still wanted her, she would accept.

Amy sat in her room, awaiting the news that he had called, aware of a secret hope that all her cavils and demands would be too much for him.

The ormolu clock ticked away the afternoon. What if he didn't come? If he truly wanted to see her, he would come.

Amy thought she heard something and went to her window. His carriage!

She rushed to the mirror and checked her appearance. She was improved. Not in full bloom, but well enough, surely, and the blue sprig muslin she was wearing was her most becoming. She generally maided herself, but today she had requested Nell's maid to weave some ribbons through her curls, and the effect was pleasing.

Amy went to the door and hovered, waiting for the summons, hands clasped anxiously.

The clock ticked on. What was happening?

Of course, he would have asked to speak to Aunt Lizzie first. But Aunt Lizzie had gone to the British Museum with a friend, Mrs. Fellows. Perhaps he was speaking to Nell instead.

Amy paced the room, glancing at the monotonous clock. It must have been quite twenty minutes.

She stopped dead. What if the foolish maid had forgotten that she was home to Sir Cedric? Amy hadn't seen Nell to tell her she was receiving guests. Sir Cedric could this very minute be leaving.

Amy couldn't bear another day of this waiting. She ran out into the corridor and down the stairs. She slowed in relief when she saw the empty hall. At least he wasn't leaving yet.

The drawing room was open; the room was empty. They must be in the morning room.

Amy hesitated. She didn't want to barge in like an over-eager hussy, but it wouldn't take this long for Nell to give him permission to make his offer. They must think she was still unwell.

Amy walked up to the door. She raised her hand to knock, but that was silly. This was a public room. She turned the handle, walked in, and stopped dead.

The couple didn't notice her for a moment, which wasn't surprising since Nell was on Sir Cedric's lap and they were kissing with passionate abandon. Perhaps Amy made a sound, for they broke apart and stared at her with horror.

In a flash Nell was up and rearranging her gown. Sir Cedric was on his feet twitching at his disarranged cravat.

Amy backed away.

"Amy, dear, don't go," said Nell. "Let us explain."

"There's nothing to explain," said Amy numbly. "I'm . . . I'm very happy for you. I'm sorry I interrupted."

Nell grasped her hand and wouldn't let her flee. "You must come and talk, dear. We can't pretend nothing has happened here. Cedric and I have been feeling dreadful ever since we realized."

Amy found herself sitting down, with Nell and Sir Cedric facing her like guilty children. "Really," she said. "It's nothing to do with me."

"Yes it is," said Sir Cedric firmly, for all that he looked like a raw stripling. "I paid you particular attentions, Miss de Lacy. I was greatly attracted to your beauty, but also by your inner qualities. You have courage, honesty, and wit. I thought we could make a comfortable match of it to both our benefits." He looked to his side and took Nell's hand in his. "My feelings for Nell took me quite by surprise."

Amy was aware that this was a disaster, but she couldn't help delight in their love. "I'm glad," she said. "I truly am."

Nell smiled mistily. "Oh, Amy. You really are amazing. You mean it, don't you?"

"Yes. You both deserve to love and be loved. Everyone does." Amy sighed and rose. "It is probably time for Lizzie and me to return home."

"Lizzie has been offered a home with a friend, Dorothy Fellows," said Nell apologetically. "I think she will prefer to stay in London."

Amy felt as if this was abandonment, which was ridiculous. "Well, that's one less mouth to feed," she said.

She tried to make the door again, but Sir Cedric put himself between her and it. "Miss de Lacy—Amy—I will not let you run away. There are matters to be discussed. Though there is no longer any question of a marriage between us, I do feel very fond of you, as if you were a daughter. I have considered how best to help you—"

"No!" said Amy. "You must not. We are not a charity case."

"You cannot refuse to let me help you."

"I can and do. We will manage for ourselves."

"My dear child, you were willing to sacrifice yourself—for that is what it amounted to—for the sake of your family. Can you not let go of a scrap of your pride?"

Amy was trying to find an answer to this when a commotion erupted outside. "That sounds like Jasper," Amy said in amazement and headed for the door. This time no one stopped her.

Nell's hall was full of people.

"Amy!" cried Jassy, running into her arms. "Isn't this a wonderful surprise?"

Amy hugged her younger sister and looked over at a smiling Beryl. A Beryl who was arm in arm with a frowning Mr. Staverley.

"What on earth has happened?" Amy asked.

"We've come to London for the Season," Jasper announced, then looked over Amy's shoulder. "Good afternoon, ma'am, sir. Sorry for the disturbance. Girls are always a bit overly excitable."

Reminded of her manners, a dazed Amy introduced her family to Nell and Sir Cedric. She still didn't understand why Mr. Staverley was here, especially as he looked so cross about it. "But you can't stay here," she told everyone. "Mrs. Claybury doesn't have room."

There was a gabble of explanation, which Amy could not follow, then Nell's voice cut through. "That is unfortunately true, but at least you must all come in for tea." Within moments everyone was settled in the drawing room and the tea tray had been ordered.

"Now," said Amy, "will someone please explain what you're up to. This is madness. Where are you all to stay?"

"Owen's hired a house," declared Jasper. "Montague Street. Very handsome."

"But you can't stay there with him," Amy said blankly.

"Can," said Staverley. "Though we're in a hotel for tonight. Your sister and me, we're to be married. Tomorrow. Special license. Wanted to do it back home but she wouldn't hear of it without her favorite sister, so here we are. Honeymoon in London. Bound to be plenty of excitement for the younger ones with the victory celebrations." By the end of this speech, his frown had lifted a little and he merely looked flustered. He took Beryl's hand and they smiled at each other. For the first time, Amy noticed the handsome diamond on her sister's hand.

Amy was speechless. She heard Sir Cedric and Nell say all that was proper and tried to summon the right words herself, but Beryl was sacrificing herself because Amy had failed.

"Amy, dear, aren't you happy for me?"

Beryl had come to sit beside her. "Are you happy?" Amy asked.

Beryl smiled. "Of course I am, dearest. You don't mind, do you? I know you didn't take a great liking to Owen, but I'm sure you'll come to see his qualities as I do."

"Well, he's rich," said Amy.

"Amy, dear," said Beryl with a slight frown, "you know I would never marry for money alone. Owen and I are very fond of each other. Very fond." Beryl looked over at monkey-ish Owen Staverley with warm devotion. He caught her eye and looked away, reddening. Hunger.

Amy became aware her mouth was hanging open and closed it.

"You mustn't mind his manner," Beryl said quietly. "He's just shy, you see, and hides it with a frown. He feels ill at ease until he knows people well. But he's the soul of generosity. He's settled a handsome amount on Jassy and put money into the estate, so by the time Jasper achieves his majority the estate should be debt free."

"He must have put in a great deal of money," said Amy, startled.

"Yes, but he said it was made easier because someone had recently done something with the debts. I don't understand it, but you may. They've been bought up, I think, and the interest reduced to a mere nothing. Perhaps it was something Uncle Cuthbert arranged."

Amy looked over at Sir Cedric, who was clearly attending to this conversation. He looked rueful and winked.

Her stunned amazement was beginning to fade, and facts were beginning to settle and sort in her mind. There was a chance that it was all going to be all right. Could she dare believe it?

More arrivals. Amy looked up to see Harry, Randal, and

Sophie at the door. Numbly awaiting what was to come next, Amy made a fresh round of introductions. Nell ordered more cups and tea.

Randal and Sophie sat. Harry remained standing.

"I have come," he said loudly, "to ask Miss de Lacy to marry me."

"You can't," said Amy pleasantly. "She's going to marry Mr. Staverley."

Harry looked startled, but then laughed. "I have come to ask Miss Amethyst de Lacy to marry me. Will you, Amy?"

Amy considered him. "I would have thought after last time that you'd have realized I don't much care for such blunt proposals."

"After last time," he said bluntly, "and all that's gone in between, I'm not sure it's worth making a long speech of it."

He seemed quite unconscious of their fascinated audience. Not so Amy, particularly if he intended a review of their encounters. She stood. "Perhaps we can continue this discussion in private."

He stopped her before she reached the door and wrapped an imprisoning arm around her. "Oh no, I may need witnesses."

"What on earth are you talking about?" But Amy relaxed against his body and laid her head on his shoulder.

He leaned close to her ear, which was enough in itself to make her begin to lose her hold on her senses. "That note should have given you a hint," he whispered. "I'll stop at nothing, wench. It's up my sleeve."

"What is?" she murmured, fighting giggles. Everyone was staring at them as if they'd gone mad.

"Your shift," he whispered, warm and soft against her ear. "Shall I pull it out and wave it before the company, or do you surrender gracefully?"

Amy was very tempted to call his bluff. When had she become such a wicked, reckless woman? But she surrendered, if not very gracefully. "I'll probably accept you," she said clearly, "if you mange to make a handsome proposal."

He looked startled, then blindingly happy. She realized that he knew nothing of what had transpired today but had truly come to force her hand by any means possible.

He went dramatically to one knee. "My dearest Amethyst, precious jewel of my heart, I can imagine no joy in life if you are not by my side. In my eyes you are perfect. I adore you. Give me the right to love and cherish you forever."

He was acting the fool, but his eyes told her every exaggerated word was true.

Amy gave her hand and drew him to his feet, fighting tears. "I think you should know I would have married Sir Cedric if he'd asked me. He's going to marry Nell instead."

"Congratulations, sir," said Harry to the banker. "No you wouldn't," he said to Amy. "Why do you think I came armed?"

"You really would?" she asked.

"I really would. That's why I brought Randal. He'd force us to the altar if no one else did."

"I haven't the faintest idea what he's talking about," said Randal. "But I would point out that you haven't answered, Amy, and the tea tray is behind you."

Amy and Harry stepped out of the doorway to allow the maid to bring in the tea.

"Well?" said Harry.

"I'm scared," said Amy.

"What on earth of? Of me?"

"No, no, never of you. I'm scared this will all be a dream."

He gathered her into his arms, despite the crowded room.

"I'll make it a dream that will last your whole life long. Say yes, darling."

"Yes, darling."

As Harry kissed Amy, Beryl beamed at her betrothed and said, "Do you know, Owen, dear, you are joining the most fortunate family in the world."

DEIRDRE
AND DON JUAN

1

THE NEWS OF HIS WIFE'S DEATH caught the Earl of Everdon in his mistress's bed. He knew most of the world would consider this unremarkable for a man generally known as Don Juan, but he could only see it as a social solecism. Even as he read the disturbing letter, he directed a few choice epithets toward his thick-skulled secretary. What had possessed young Morrow to send it here?

After all, he'd not clapped eyes on his wife for close to ten years, so this travel-stained record of Genie's demise could surely have waited until he returned home.

Noblesse obliged, however, and he detached himself from Barbara Vayne's demanding fingers, swung out of bed, and began to pull on his clothes.

He was a tall, handsome man of thirty, who had inherited a distinctly Latin cast to his features from his Spanish mother. His skin had a yearlong darkness unusual in England; his eyes were a deep velvet brown under smooth, heavy lids; his brows and lashes were richly dark. His hair, however, had been touched by his English heritage, and showed sherry gold lights in the afternoon sun. This merely served to emphasize the darker cast of his skin.

"Don, what's the matter?" his abandoned lover demanded plaintively, pouting her lush lips.

He fastened his pantaloons. "A family crisis."

Barbara threw off the covers and arched. "Something more important than this?"

He tried never to be unkind to a woman, so he paid her the homage of a hot, regretful look, but didn't halt his dressing. His mind was on other things.

There were disturbing aspects to this situation.

Ten years of freedom were over.

He had married Iphegenia Brandon when only twenty, and just down from Cambridge. In retrospect, it had not been wise, and the subsequent disasters had been excruciatingly embarrassing, but he had grown accustomed. In time, he had even discovered that there were advantages to being an abandoned husband.

For the past ten years the Matchmaking Mamas had regretfully ignored him. He had been able to behave with remarkable rashness without any possibility of being forced to the altar. His only brother's death the year before had caused him to investigate the possibility of divorce, but he had intended to select a bride with great care well before he was known to be available.

Now, however, he was fair prey in the matrimonial hunt. Absurd though it was, once this news broke, even someone like Barbara—the wanton widow of a highly disreputable infantry captain—might think she had a chance of getting Lord Everdon to the altar.

He didn't neglect the courtesy of a heated farewell kiss,

but he first imprisoned Barbara's hands above her head, just to be sure he escaped her bedroom safely.

Then Mark Juan Carlos Renfrew, Earl of Everdon and lord of a score of minor properties, walked through the streets of Mayfair feeling vulnerable for the first time in his adult life.

During the walk his wariness turned to irritation, and the irritation found a focus. When he arrived at his Marlborough Square mansion, he stalked into his secretary's study and tossed the letter on David Morrow's desk. "Preaching, I'll abide, but not outright malice. You are dismissed."

The young man was already on his feet. Now he wavered, sheet white. "I'm *what* . . . ?"

"You heard me. I will give you an adequate reference as to the conscientiousness of your work."

"But . . . but *why*, my lord?"

Everdon was arrested. Young Morrow was nothing if not honest, and his bewilderment rang true. "Why did you send that letter over to Barbara's house?"

"But . . . but your wife, my lord. She's *dead*!"

"Six months ago, according to that Greek priest."

"But even so . . . you would want to know . . . You wouldn't want, at such a moment . . ." The young man flushed red with embarrassment.

Everdon swore with exasperation. "David, my beloved Genie ran off with an Italian diplomat nearly ten years ago, within six months of our ill-judged and juvenile marriage. She has since worked her way through the best—or worst—part of the European nobility. Why the devil should I care that she's finally met her end?"

But Everdon did care, and knew his untypical foul mood was a direct consequence of that distant death.

Young Morrow's lips quivered slightly, but he stiffened his spine. "I am sorry for so misjudging the situation, my lord. I will just collect my possessions—"

"Stubble it," said Everdon curtly, fairness reasserting itself. As the fourth son of an impoverished family, David Morrow had his way to make in the world, and he was an excellent employee. It wasn't the lad's fault that he was as prissy as a cloistered nun. It amused Everdon to surround himself with righteousness.

"I apologize for misjudging you." Everdon smiled, deliberately using his charm to soothe. "Sit down and get on with your work, David. But if you're researching that matter of the relief of debtors for me, remember my interest as always is pragmatic, not moral or sanctimonious. Give me facts and figures, not sermons."

The secretary sat with a thump, relief flooding his round face. "Thank you, my lord. Of course, my lord . . ."

Everdon waved away gratitude. "As you see, I am decidedly out of curl."

"Er . . . because of your wife, my lord?"

Everdon's smile became twisted. "You could put it that way. I'm out of curl because I'm going to have to choose my next wife in a devil of a hurry."

Upon leaving his secretary, Everdon went straight to his mother's suite.

Lucetta, Dowager Countess of Everdon, was a handsome woman whose strong-boned face clearly showed her Spanish heritage. Though she was fifty, her black hair held no touch of gray, and her fine dark eyes could still flash with emotion. She was, however, afflicted with a hip disease that made even walking painful, and she largely kept to her rooms, receiving guests and engaging in her passion—embroidery. Everdon kissed her cheek, then surveyed her latest piece, an exquisite working of purple pansies on gossamer silk.

"That is very beautiful, Mother, but I can hardly see it as a chairback." He spoke Spanish, as he always did when alone with his mother.

She chuckled. "Assuredly not, my dear. In truth, I am not sure what I shall do with it. Lady Deirdre has infected me with this notion of needlework for its own sake. I suppose if nothing else occurs, it will make a panel for a gown."

He shook his head. "The lady does not exist who is worthy of such ornamentation."

"What nonsense you speak, Marco. It is just embroidery. Poor women do work as fine for pennies to ornament our society blossoms."

"I disagree." He studied the work in her frame. "That is a special piece. It's the difference between a portrait by Lawrence, and one by an itinerant artist. Lady Deirdre has a case to make. When it is finished, I shall have that work framed."

Lucetta studied her son, her only child now his younger brother was dead, killed at Vittoria. She sensed an unusual uneasiness in him. "What brings you here today, Marco?"

He glanced up, and his long-lashed dark eyes reminded her poignantly of her brother at the same age, and in a scrape. She knew she really shouldn't blame Marco for his philandering when he had inherited her family's devastating charms, but she did. Or at least, she worried.

He evaded her question. "Do I need an excuse to visit you, *Madrecita?*"

"Of course not, but it is rare to see you in the afternoon. There are so many competing attractions."

A faint color rose in his cheeks. Beneath the olive skin many would not have noticed it, but she was accustomed to reading such things. "Well?" she demanded.

He looked down at a glossy boot. "Genie's dead."

Lucetta's needle paused for a moment. "At last," she said.

"Mother!"

She continued setting stitches. "Am I supposed to feign grief? I am not sorry. I am not surprised. I can even guess the cause of her death."

"Mother, really . . ."

"You English are so mealymouthed. She was a wretched young woman, and doubtless died miserably of the pox. Her suffering may save her immortal soul."

"Hardly the sentiment of a good English Protestant," he pointed out.

"I became a Protestant for your father. I reverted to the true faith when he died, as you know." She fixed him with a direct look. "This is good. Now you can marry again."

"That is my duty," he said bleakly.

Lucetta's face softened. "Not all women are as Iphegenia was, dearest one. And you are much wiser now." She sighed. "I have blamed myself most deeply."

He moved restlessly to a window overlooking the extensive gardens of his mansion. "It wasn't your fault, love. I was mad for her."

"But you were young, Marco. Not yet twenty. It was my duty as your mother to be wise for you."

Lucetta abandoned her work before she made a botch of it. It was time for truth. "I saw your grandfather and uncles in you, you see. Women came to them so easily, they could not resist. It caused great problems. Genie was so beautiful, so passionate. When you loved her, I thought she might satisfy you and keep you safe."

He turned to face her. "And instead, I failed to satisfy her."

"No man could satisfy her. She proved that over and again."

He said nothing—he never had on this subject—but she read old anguish in his face. "Do you still feel tenderly toward her, Marco?"

He turned again, hiding from her. "Feel for her? I can hardly remember her. I remember how I felt . . ." His voice turned brisk. "Never fear. I know I must marry. With Richard gone, and Cousin Ian ailing, I have no choice. I can hardly leave the earldom to Kevin, fond though I am of him. I must get an heir. It is merely a matter of finding the right woman."

"That should not be difficult. You will be the prize of the Marriage Mart." Lucetta saw him wince and struggled to keep a straight face. As she took up her needle again, she thought that the next weeks could be amusing. She was determined, however, that this time her son would make a good marriage. He probably wouldn't believe it, but he was capable of making the right woman a wonderful husband.

"I suppose I shall have to see what is still available this late in the Season," he said. "At least I'm not looking for a Belle or an heiress. Just someone quiet, plain, and content to stay at home."

Lucetta's needle froze. "Quiet? Plain? That is hardly to your taste."

"It is in wives," he said crisply. "I am hoping you have a candidate in mind."

"I will have nothing to do with such foolishness," she stated. "You will join the social whirl and find someone who appeals to you."

"I am recently bereaved," he said piously.

His mother spat a Spanish opinion of that excuse. "Six months bereaved."

Everdon leaned against a wall, arms folded. "Very well, the truth. It's too dangerous out there. I intend to be in control of this selection."

"Foolish boy. Are you afraid of the Matchmaking Mamas?"

His grin was disarming. "Terrified. I've worn the armor of my marriage for so long, I feel naked without it." He put on a most beguiling smile. "If you love me, *mama mia*, you will find me a safe candidate. You can't persuade me you don't know every one of this year's crop."

Lucetta placed a careful stitch. "Maud Tiverton, then."

"Maud Tiverton! She looks like a cross between Torquemada and a pug."

Lucetta smiled sweetly at him. "At least you could be sure no man would steal her from under your nose."

This time anyone would have seen the color in his cheeks. He made no defense or denial.

"Oh, my dear," said Lucetta seriously. "This is no way to choose your companion in life. Give it time."

He shook his head. "Life can be chancy—look at Richard and Ian. I know my duty." He twisted his gold signet ring. "Since Ian fell sick and recovery became unlikely, I'd even made moves to obtain a divorce, though I hate the thought of a public airing of Genie's behavior. I know the distress it would cause her parents . . ."

"At least that is no longer necessary," said Lucetta gently.

"True. And I'd be a fool to waste the last weeks of the Season. What better time to find a bride? If you won't help, I will just have to pick one blindfolded." He shrugged. "Marriage is a mere lottery anyway. If one doesn't spend too long anguishing over the ticket, there's less pain if it turns out a loser."

Lucetta rested her hands on her frame and considered him with a frown. She could tell he was in earnest and would do this foolish thing. "Very well, then. If that is how it is, I think you should marry Deirdre."

"Deirdre Stowe?" he said blankly.

"Lady Deirdre Stowe, daughter of the Earl of Harby. My young friend, whom you have met here now and again. That Deirdre."

"Why?"

"Why not?" she asked briskly. "Is not one lottery ticket as good as another? She is wellborn and well-bred. Her portion is comfortable. She is composed, but not weak. She will be well able to run your households and raise your children. It does, however, seem highly unlikely that some man will try to filch her from you—men being shortsighted in these matters—and even less likely that she would dream of being filched. Furthermore," she added tartly, "I have more concern for my comfort than you have for yours, and I like her."

He shrugged. "The best argument of all. Consider it done."

Her eyes flashed angrily. "Does it not occur to you, you wretch, that she might refuse you?"

He quirked a brow. "No. Will she?"

She glared at him but then sighed and shook her head. "It is unlikely, I fear. It would do you good to be refused for once. One reason I suggested Deirdre—and I am beginning to regret it—is that she is having a miserable time. She doesn't speak of it, but I am sure she is a wallflower."

"Men probably just don't notice her," Everdon pointed out. "She's so thin and wishy-washy, *I* hardly notice her when she's here in the room." He looked around, in the pretense that the young lady might in fact be present.

Lucetta shook her head. "It will not do, will it? I will try to think of someone more suitable."

"Nonsense. She is ideal. I believe the Ashbys are holding a soirée tonight. Will she be there?"

"It is likely. Her mother drags her everywhere, firmly

convinced that one day a miracle will happen, and Deirdre will turn into a Toast before everyone's eyes."

He grinned. "And so she will. She is about to sweep Don Juan off his feet."

Lucetta focused on him the full force of a maternal look. "Marco, I warn you: hurt Deirdre and you will pray for the fires of hell."

That evening Lord Everdon commanded his valet to produce his dark evening clothes and kid slippers, a sure sign that he was intent on Polite Society and not debauchery. Joseph Bing's conscience could for once be at ease as he used his considerable skills to turn his employer out to perfection.

Joseph's conscience had frequently been troubled since he had been saved and become a follower of John Wesley.

He told his friends at the Chapel that he only kept his post with the earl because his employer indulgently allowed him plenty of free time to attend to Chapel business, and the whole of Sunday off. The truth was that he was very fond of Everdon, whom he'd served since his Cambridge days. He found professional satisfaction in valeting such a fine figure of a man, and he hoped to save him from perdition.

The perils Joseph feared were twofold. On the one hand, the earl was clearly given over to fornication of the most blatant kind. That placed him in risk of damnation. The far greater danger, however, was that he would have a sudden religious experience and follow his mother into the maw of papacy.

Joseph Bing was determined to prevent that fate, and to somehow wean the earl from his fondness for loose women. He could hardly hope Everdon would ever join the Wesleyan fraternity, but a virtuous lifestyle and a sober adherence to the Church of England would make Joseph a very happy man.

As Joseph finished shaving his master's smooth, brown skin, the earl said, "Has the news somehow escaped, Joseph? I am a widower. You may felicitate me."

Joseph gave thanks he had put down the razor before that disconcerting announcement. "Congratulations, my lord," he said, though it hardly seemed proper. He remembered sadly the beautiful, willful Iphegenia, and the brief fury of youthful passion that had been that ill-fated marriage. In the aftermath he had feared for the young earl's sanity. It was a miracle really that it had merely turned him to vice . . .

"You needn't sound so squeamish," said Everdon as he stood and shrugged off the cloth that protected his shirt. "Genie died six months ago." He deftly tied a cravat, then allowed Joseph to ease on his brocade waistcoat and plain, elegant jacket. "I merely forewarn you of possible changes. I intend to marry again."

"That is good news, milord," said Joseph as he smoothed the cloth over broad shoulders. His joy was honest. That's what the earl needed—the love of a good woman.

But would he choose one?

"I'm glad you think so. Time will tell." Everdon surveyed himself in the mirror. "The pearl, I think." When the valet brought the pearl pin, Everdon said, "And how are matters at the Chapel?"

Joseph had thought at one time that his master mocked him when he said such things, but it appeared not to be the case. "Very well, thank you, milord. Your support for our school is much appreciated."

Everdon deftly adjusted his cravat and fixed the pin. "Have you ever thought of providing a refuge for unfortunate women?"

Joseph glanced at his employer. What lay behind this? He cleared his throat. "You would perhaps mean streetwalkers, my lord?"

"And others too unsavory to be helped by the tight-lipped brigade. There must be many women who make unfortunate choices and come to regret them. What becomes of them?"

Joseph foresaw trouble with some of the Chapel members, but he was a true seeker after good. "I believe our Savior would want us to help such women, as He helped Mary Magdalene."

"So do I. I will be most generous in my support of such a project." Everdon swung on his cloak. "I dislike seeing any woman in distress."

It was said in his usual flippant manner, but Joseph detected some deeper meaning behind it. Did Lord Everdon have a particular woman in mind? Well, if housing one of the earl's old loves was the price of helping hundreds, it was a small price to pay.

Everdon took his hat and gloves from Joseph. "The news of my widowing is not to be made public just yet, Joseph. I prefer not to create a stir. To be more precise," he added with a flickering smile, "I do not want to alert the hunt. Now I go to pick a lottery ticket. Wish me luck, but don't wait up."

As Joseph tidied the room, he muttered, "The nonsense he do talk. Now, why would he want a lottery ticket, rich as he is?"

The Ashby soirée was being hosted by Lord and Lady Randal Ashby, dashing leaders of Society, in the mansion of Lord Randal's father, the Duke of Tyne. Everdon had learned from his invitation that it was in honor of Randal's cousin, Harry Crisp, and his promised bride, Miss Amy de Lacy. He knew Harry slightly, but not the girl; he was not in the habit of attending the more formal social affairs.

The event was well under way when Everdon arrived, and he had to search out his host and hostess.

"Lord Everdon, we're honored," said Sophie Ashby, affecting satirical amazement, but she smiled warmly as he kissed her hand. They were well acquainted, for Randal did not hesitate to bring his wife to more racy entertainments.

She was a vivacious young woman with something of a gamine appearance, but a sweetly curved figure. Everdon had a taste for curves in his women. He thought of thin Deirdre Stowe, and suffered a pang of doubt.

He gave Sophie a genuinely admiring smile. "I thought I'd see how the polite world went along."

"Being more familiar with the impolite?" she queried with a twinkle of humor.

He laughed. He also admired a woman who could bandy words. "They christened me Don Juan in my school days, and my fate was sealed."

Lord Randal remarked, "I earned the nickname of the Bright Angel. I managed to outgrow it, Don."

"Did you indeed? Yet I detect a glitter still, and the touch of the wicked that was behind the name."

"How true," said Sophie with a teasing look at her handsome blond husband. Randal's response was a glance of heated yet discreet intimacy.

Everdon realized with a pang that he'd shared something similar once with Genie, who hadn't really loved him, and was dead . . .

"So," Randal was asking, "why are you here, Don? I assure you, this evening ain't about to become exciting. All the ancient family connections are here, for a start."

"I merely thought to see how the ton is enduring the dying days of this summer of excitement."

"We cannot always have visiting kings and emperors to amuse us," Sophie pointed out.

"I'd have thought everyone would be relieved to have a little peace and quiet after endless parades and displays."

"Do I detect a jaded tone?" asked Lord Randal. "You have to confess, Don, it was a livelier Season than we've seen in years. And as a bonus, we are now permitted to dance the waltz without censure."

Everdon grinned. "That doubtless takes all the thrill out of it."

"I fear you are right," said Sophie, "though I have a marked partiality for the dance, wicked or no. And you," she said to Everdon, "are very skilled at it."

"That," pointed out her husband, "if you didn't recognize it, was a hint."

"I'm positively bruised by the force of it. Do I gather you won't dance with your wife, Randal?"

"Of course he will," said Sophie, "but as hosts, we have to attend to the needs of our guests. We are to have three waltzes, and he can't dance every one with me."

Everdon kissed her hand and held it to his heart. "If you were mine, enchanting one, I would dance every waltz with you, host or no."

Sophie gurgled with laughter. "Are you trying to seduce me under Randal's very nose?"

Everdon smiled into her eyes. "Only if you are willing, *querida.*"

Sophie looked rather startled. "But you never entangle yourself with happily married women."

"Perhaps I am just more discreet with them . . ."

Randal removed his wife from Everdon's grasp. "How is it no one has shot you, Don?"

Everdon took time for a pinch of snuff. "Perhaps because I'm a crack shot, old boy."

Randal smiled, but there was an edge on it. "I'm better."

Everdon laughed and dropped his pose. "Don't raise your hackles. I'm a charitable foundation, don't you know? I only interest myself with unhappy women, and Sophie appears to be entirely happy, alas."

"Yes, I am," said Sophie with a playful flutter of her fan. "What a shame . . ."

Her husband groaned. "I'm sure there are a great number of unhappy women in this room, Sophie. Why not steer the charitable foundation in their direction."

Sophie looked at Everdon. "Well, my lord?"

He bowed, hand on heart. "'Tis my very purpose in coming. I am corrupted by my mother's Romish beliefs and fear for my immortal soul. I am here to do reparation for my many sins. Lead me to the most deserving cases!"

Sophie chuckled but said, "I warn you, I am taking you at your word, Don. Come along."

She led him toward the room set aside for dancing. En route she pointed out the guests of honor—a tawny-haired young man and a breathtakingly beautiful young blonde.

"Now, how did *she* escape my notice?" Everdon murmured.

Sophie's lips twitched. "She hid herself in Chelsea. But she was strictly interested in marriage anyway, so would have had no time for you, Don."

Everdon kept his smile to himself. "Are there many unclaimed hopefuls this year?"

"The usual number, I suppose. I find it rather depressing. Now, let me find you a suitable hair shirt . . ."

Everdon quickly said, "Not Maud Tiverton. Please."

Sophie grinned. "She would wipe away any number of sins, but she is not here."

A set was already in progress, and so the wallflowers were obvious. Most were chattering to friends or chaperons, trying to pretend that this conversation was what they had come for. A few did not hesitate to look bored. One of these was Lady Deirdre Stowe. She sat by her mother, hands in lap, a vacant expression on her plain face.

Everdon had encountered Lady Deirdre any number of times in his mother's rooms, for the two women's interest in embroidery spanned the difference in age, but she had made little impression on him. On his way here he had tried to summon up a picture of her. He knew she was of medium height, and thin. He rather thought her hair was brown. He knew her voice neither appealed nor offended.

Now he studied her more closely. Some effort had been made to pretty her up for the evening, but if anything, it had made matters worse. A fussy pink dress overwhelmed her without disguising her thinness. A confection of curls pulled the hair from her face, emphasizing its angular length and pallor and an unfortunately heavy nose. That hair could not really be called brown, being more the color of weak milky tea.

She was plain, and close to being ugly.

He wasn't repulsed. He experienced instead a spurt of pity, and rejoiced that he was going to brighten her life. He would surely be rewarded by gratitude at the very least.

"It seems a shame to disturb one of those interesting conversations," he said. "Isn't that Lady Deirdre Stowe over there? She's a friend of my mother's. Why not present me to her as a partner."

Sophie Ashby, no fool, gave him a shrewd look. "I remind myself that you have never been known to toy with vulnerable hearts . . . Certainly. Lady Deirdre deserves a few more dances."

Lady Harby looked up hopefully as they approached. A flicker of disappointment crossed her plumply amiable face when she saw that Lady Randal had a married man in tow, but then she smiled. When Everdon was presented to her daughter as a partner for the next set, she made no objection.

He took a seat next to Deirdre until the new dance started. Lady Deirdre looked faintly surprised at the turn of events, but not excited. He wondered if she was capable of excitement. He reminded himself that it didn't matter. He intended that she stay quietly in the country, setting stitches and rearing children, while he sought excitement elsewhere.

He addressed a few conventional remarks to her—about the weather, and the recent excitement of the victory celebrations. She replied, but without animation.

He tried a new tack.

"I have seen the work my mother has in hand, Lady Deirdre. It is remarkable. I understand you are encouraging her to see her skills as art. I think you are correct."

At last there was a spark of interest in her gray-blue eyes. "Thank you. I do believe people can be artists with the needle as well as with the brush."

"Needle-painting, is it not called? I have seen the needlework renderings of Old Masters by Mrs. Knowles and Mrs. Linwood. They are very cleverly executed. Is this the kind of work you do, Lady Deirdre?"

Her animation faded. "No, not really."

He was intrigued. "What, then, do you do?"

She looked down self-consciously, and her voice was muffled as she replied, "I create original designs, my lord. Most people do not admire my efforts."

"Why not?" Everdon recognized with resignation that the

usual was happening. As soon as he met a sad woman, he felt a compulsion to make her happier in some way. He was distracted by wondering whether the urge would have taken him with Maud Tiverton, a woman whose nature was as ugly as her form.

His companion had said something. "I beg your pardon. The music drowned your words."

She looked dubious, for where they sat, the music was not particularly loud, but she repeated, "I use my needle to create pictures of things other than flowers."

"Surely that is not so unusual. Tapestries have formed scenes of landscapes, people, architecture . . ."

His interest had broken her reserve a little. "My work is not exactly tapestry. I use a variety of stitches." She hesitated, then added, "I am experimenting with the style of Mr. Turner."

Everdon had to admit he had difficulty envisioning embroidery in that sweeping, messy style. He was not an admirer of Mr. Turner's paintings. He made the polite response. "I hope to see an example of your work one day, Lady Deirdre."

Again a dubious look, but she replied conventionally. "I would be honored by your opinion, my lord. I understand you are a patron of the arts."

"I buy what I like, particularly if it is by a young artist. I like to surround myself with beauty, and I hope I occasionally support a struggling new artist who will one day become someone great. See, Lady Deirdre, the set is over. Why don't we walk as we wait for the next one to form?"

She rose without complaint, and he thought she must be glad to leave her station. He wondered if there were any men here he could encourage to dance with her. He had no intention of making her remarkable by dancing with her more than once, but had no desire to see her back in her tedium.

He saw the young Duke of Rowanford talking to another of Randal's cousins, Chart Ashby, and a striking, dark-haired young woman. What a remarkable number of handsome ladies there were in Society when one stopped to look. He steered their way. The men were known to him, and handsome and highborn enough to be flattering dancing partners.

Rowanford raised his brows in surprise. "Hello, Don. Don't often see you at these affairs."

"'No pleasure endures unseasoned by variety,'" quoted Everdon. "Lady Deirdre, do you know Rowanford and Mr. Ashby?" He performed the introductions and discovered that the handsome girl was Clytemnestra Ashby, Chart's sister. If he was any judge of such matters, and he was, an announcement concerning her and Rowanford would appear any day. Another promising bud snatched from his reaching fingers . . .

But this was only a humorous thought. He knew he had settled on Deirdre Stowe.

"Lady Deirdre is a dear friend of my mother's," he said. "They share an interest, nay, a passion, for the art of embroidery."

He saw Deirdre register the word "art" with pleasure, and the men take in his message that he wanted them to be kind to her. They both requested dances, and Lady Deirdre, flustered, accepted. After a few moments' chat, the music started and he led her into the set.

At the beginning she danced rather stiffly, but Everdon soon suspected that Lady Deirdre Stowe could be a beautiful dancer. He set himself to draw out her talent by distracting her from self-consciousness. Then, when they were together, he subtly urged her into more fluent movement. Slowly she was transformed. She surrendered to the music. She became light on her feet and moved the whole of her body in a supple way most pleasing to the eye. At the end of the dance he was rewarded by an unself-conscious, delighted smile, and noted that the healthy flush of exercise improved her looks considerably.

"That was most enjoyable, Lord Everdon," she said, "You are a skillful partner."

"You are a natural dancer, Lady Deirdre."

She demurred but did not make extreme denials. She was, he thought with approval, a young woman of admirable common sense.

He noted that others had seen her performance, and that when Rowanford claimed the next set, it was with genuine enthusiasm.

Everdon moved on, content with the first moves of the game. He was already thinking of Deirdre Stowe as his own, and planning her welfare and improvement. With a simpler, lighter gown and a more natural hairstyle, she would do quite well in any circle. He had no problem with her behavior at all except for a certain diffidence, which would surely fade when she found herself mistress of her own establishment, secure and valued.

He didn't want to mark Lady Deirdre out with his attentions, and so he had Sophie present him to two other young ladies. It soon became clear to him why they were languishing unwanted. One chattered nonsense in a way bound to drive a man to drink; the other had a hard, bony angularity of body that was most unappealing, especially as he suspected it came out of an anxious temperament that approached the insane. It was quite different from Lady Deirdre's delicate thinness.

His instinct to help twitched in both cases, but he suppressed it.

When he finished the third set, he moved apart to observe the scene, while talking with Randal and Sophie. He smiled wryly when he saw Deirdre taken out for another set by a gentleman unprompted by him. It would be ironic if she found a rival suitor through his meddling. She did look rather more appealing than she had when sitting steeped in tedium.

Success breeds success.

"Pray, why are you staring at Lady Deirdre?" asked Sophie.

Everdon turned to her. "My mother asked me to see if I could liven the last weeks of her Season."

"You've certainly enlivened this evening. If you weren't a married man, I'd wonder about your intentions."

Everdon hoped he didn't show how that had found a mark. "I suppose she would make a tolerable wife, if a man were looking for such."

Sophie wrinkled her brow. "Tolerable? How dull. But I'm afraid people like Lady Deirdre do not show well in London. She doubtless will do better at home now she's spread her wings. Lady Harby, however, has a bee in her bonnet about good matches. She's married the three older girls brilliantly and is determined to do the same for the last. Foolishness, of course."

Everdon glanced at her. "You don't think Lady Deirdre can make a brilliant match?"

Sophie was taken aback. "You're pushing me into sounding mean-spirited, but no, I don't. She simply has no remarkable feature and is rather plain."

"Oh, you are doubtless correct," Everdon said amiably, and took his leave.

❧ 2 ❧

EVERDON CONSIDERED MATTERS CAREFULLY, and decided there was little point in delaying before making his offer. To woo Lady Deirdre might raise expectations beyond those he felt able to fulfill, and besides, he couldn't woo her publicly without revealing his widowed status. He would much prefer to be spoken for when that news broke.

He duly presented himself at the Harbys' hired house the next day, and was soon closeted with the earl. Lord Harby didn't hide his surprise and delight at the turn of events.

"Wife dead, hey?" said Harby, a plain country man who would never leave his acres if he had the choice. "And six months ago, too. Well, if you're for making a sensible match, you won't do better than Deirdre. Very sound head on her shoulders, has Deirdre."

"So I think, my lord. You have no objection, then, to my pressing my suit?"

"Objection?" said the earl, rubbing his hands. "Not at all.

Delighted. That'll be the last of 'em, and with any luck, I'll never have to join this circus again. Worse than usual this year, with foreigners all over the place, and the ragtag of the world come to gawk. Fêtes in the park, indeed . . . But come now, let's just get business out of the way."

Lord Harby had a sound head on his shoulders, too, and the experience of marrying off three daughters already. Settlements were soon outlined and agreed to that would ensure his youngest daughter's security. Everdon agreed to everything without debate.

"Excellent, excellent." Lord Harby poured them both wine, and they toasted the coming union. Then he sent for his wife.

Lady Harby came close to palpitations when she realized what was afoot. "Oh my, oh lud! Didn't I *tell* you, my dear Harby, that someone suitable would see the worth of our lamb? I *knew* it must be so. Oh, I am so happy. Four daughters all well set in life!"

Then, disconcertingly, the fluttery manner dropped away and she fixed Everdon with eyes that were no longer vague. "I must say something, however . . ."

"Now, my dear . . ." Lord Harby interrupted uneasily.

"No, Harby, I will have my say." She remained a plump woman dressed in a very silly manner, but there was nothing silly in her expression. "Lord Everdon, I am a plain woman, and stand no nonsense where my chicks are concerned. You are known as Don Juan, and not without reason."

Everdon stiffened under this attack, for he had not expected it. "Indeed," he said rather coolly. "Such a sobriquet is to be expected when I have a Spanish mother and foreign names."

Lady Harby sniffed. "That has nothing to do with it, as all the world knows. You name comes from that lewd Spanish poem, and is well deserved. Don't seek to flummery me, young man, for I'll not have it."

Everdon was strongly tempted to say that she could keep her damned daughter if that was her mood, but along with the outrage came some admiration. If daughters turned out like their mothers, he was pleased to find some backbone in the stable.

"You refer to my many lovers," he said frankly.

Red flags appeared in Lady Harby's cheeks, but frankness did not deter her. "I do. And I tell you straight, I won't have my daughter made unhappy by scandalous gossip."

Everdon took a calculated pinch of snuff, then dusted his fingers. "As I wouldn't want my wife to be made unhappy by scandalous gossip, Lady Harby, I think we are in complete agreement. May I see Deirdre now and put my case to her?"

Lady Harby looked as if she would say more, but her husband stepped in quickly. "I'm sure Everdon will do all that is proper, my dear. Come along, my lord. Deirdre will be in her little room at her stitchery. One thing's for sure, you'll never lack for a good chairback or a neatly sewn pair of slippers . . ."

It was not to be quite so easy. A hissing conversation developed between the parents, of which Everdon pretended polite ignorance. He heard Lord Harby mutter, "She'll look well enough, Lady Harby. Looks better before you get your hands on her, in my opinion!"

Then Everdon was shepherded across the hall to a small but pleasant room with excellent light where Lady Deirdre Stowe sat working at an embroidery frame. He gained an immediate impression that Lord Harby was right—she looked better unfussed-over. Her plain white muslin, and her hair looped carelessly on her head with tendrils escaping, became her much better than elaborate styles. It still didn't make her anything but a very plain young woman.

She looked up, surprised. "Father? Mother? Why, Lord Everdon, how pleasant to see you."

His lips twitched. Despite her polite words, Lady Deirdre was clearly put out by the interruption.

Lord Harby rubbed his hands nervously. "Good morning, Deirdre. Here's Everdon come to see you."

She stood. "How kind. You have a message from your mother, my lord?"

Everdon heard the door close behind the retreating parents, and saw her eyes widen. She was naturally pale, but he would swear she grew paler. Shock. Better get on with it.

"Lady Deirdre, I think you have guessed my purpose. I wish to make you an offer of marriage. I have your parents' blessing, but it is your consent that counts. You may think we do not know one another very well, but I have observed you, and I am sure you are everything I wish for in my life's companion."

Her mouth worked, and then she said, "But you are already married!" It sounded strangely like a cry of relief.

"My wife is dead. She died some time ago, though the news is recent."

Deirdre Stowe sat back upon her chair with a thump. How could this be happening when she'd thought everything safe? How could this stupid man be ruining her life like this? She wanted to rage at him, but sought some more subtle approach.

"Even if your wife died some time ago, my lord, it would cause a deal of talk for you to marry again so soon after the news becomes known."

"Talk doesn't bother me. If it bothers you, Lady Deirdre, the wedding can be delayed for some months."

The sense of imminent danger retreated, and Deirdre took a deep breath to steady her whirling head. There had to be a way out of this. She looked up at him, looked closely at him for the first time.

She'd seen the Earl of Everdon occasionally during her visits to his mother, but not very often. As she had considered him of no consequence in her life, she had not studied him, though she had to admit that his reputation had always fascinated her.

What made a man irresistible to women?

He was, she supposed, very handsome. His parts were well formed and put together perfectly, but his claim to attractiveness must also come from less definable things, she thought—his ease in movement, and an expressiveness in his features. Even now she could detect the ghosts of humor, warmth, and something else remarkable that she could not pinpoint.

Whatever it was, she wanted no part of it.

She raised her chin. "I cannot imagine how you can think you know me well enough to propose this step, my lord."

"You will allow me to know my own mind, Lady Deirdre. I know enough."

"How, pray?"

His brow raised at this bluntness. "My mother speaks often of you."

"And that is a basis for marriage? I confess, my lord, I am shocked."

He came toward her, dark eyes far too knowing. "And not pleased, I think. Why?"

His arrogance snapped her patience. "Why on earth *should* I be pleased?"

"Lady Deirdre," he said with an edge, "let us not fall to squabbling. If you do not want me, you have merely to say so."

"Oh, have I? And how do I explain that to my parents?"

He sat in a nearby chair and crossed one elegant leg over

the other. "You could practice by explaining it to me. I believe I have a right to that, at least."

He looked so completely at home that it offended Deirdre almost as much as his proposal. This was her private place, and he was invading it. "You have no right to anything," she retorted, "but I will tell you, my lord. I am pledged to another."

"*What?*" His surprise rang sharp enough to be insulting, but he covered it by quickly adding, "But your parents . . ."

"They do not approve."

He studied her for a long moment, and she knew he did not believe her. She wanted to poke him with a bodkin.

"Then marry me," he said lightly. "I won't hold it against you."

The sound that escaped was close to a snarl. "*I* would hold it against you, you oaf. I *want* to marry Howard. I will be *permitted* to marry Howard, but only if no better offer comes along during this Season." She glared at him. "I was so *close!*"

Everdon stared at her. No woman had ever called him an oaf. How the devil had a perfectly simple plan gone so awry? He rose to his feet. "There is no need for this unseemly heat, Lady Deirdre," he said icily. "I withdraw my offer. Marry your Howard with my blessing."

She, too, jumped to her feet. "If only I could! If you had had the courtesy to sound me out before speaking to my parents, we could have avoided this. But by my given word I am not allowed to refuse a suitable offer." She paused and eyed him in a way that reminded him forcibly of her mother. "I could object to your loose reputation . . ."

"*Loose!* Lady Deirdre, you go too far."

"Are you denying you've bedded more women than the Regent's drunk bottles of claret?"

He wanted to lay violent hands on her. Another first. "How would I know?" he snapped. "I don't count my women any more than Prinny counts his bottles."

"Both probably mean as much to the user."

He grabbed her bony shoulders. "*Shut up.*"

Deirdre shut up.

Such anger and peril emanated from him that she couldn't have spoken to save her life. His lips were tight and a muscle twitched from the tension in his jaw. His hands were hot on her shoulders, their power just short of pain. She saw him swallow before he spoke.

"Lady Deirdre, I no longer have the slightest desire to take you to wife. I have, however, made my offer to your parents and agreed to the marriage settlements. The only way out is for you to refuse."

"I can't," she squeaked, then swallowed in order to do better. "I gave my word."

He suddenly let her go. Her shoulders felt bruised and her nerves were quivering. She collapsed back into her chair.

He paced for a moment, then spun to face her. "As you said, you could point out my intolerable reputation."

"If my parents were going to balk at that, you wouldn't have come this far, would you? Father will accept almost any offer that gets me off his hands, and Mother is rather a cynic about men." Deirdre summoned a sneer. "She has been known to say, my lord, that the advantage of a rake is that a woman knows the truth, whereas other men merely conceal their behavior."

His lips curled, too. "A charming philosophy."

"Are you saying it's untrue? Among the haut ton, at least?"

"I refuse to discuss such a matter. You mind is soiled

enough as it is. I repeat, Lady Deirdre, how do we escape this entanglement?"

This was growing worse by the moment, and Deirdre felt perilously close to tears. "I don't know." She heard a betraying waver in her voice.

He stalked over to the empty fireplace, and one hand formed a very daunting fist. Deirdre watched that fist nervously. She had little experience of men other than Howard and her brothers, and none of them had ever been violent around her.

Then the anger seemed to fall away, and the fist became a hand again, looking more fit for gentleness than violence.

He turned to her. "Then the only thing is to go through with it." He laughed dryly. "Oh, don't look so despairing, Lady Deirdre. I mean go through with the betrothal, not the marriage. We will become engaged to marry, but in view of my peculiar situation, no announcement will be made just yet."

"But, my lord, how will we escape marriage? We cannot put it off indefinitely, and I, for one, do not wish to. I had hoped to marry Howard this autumn."

He brushed aside her fears. "I'm sure I can soon manage to behave in such a way that even your tolerant parents will be happy to allow you to terminate the arrangement."

Deirdre's mind skittered around outrageous possibilities. "What on earth will you do?"

He raised a brow. "Is your mother truly so hard to shock? I will leave it, then, to the inspiration of the moment." A devilish look entered his eyes. "Do you have a pretty maid, Lady Deirdre?"

"No," snapped Deirdre, deeply shocked. "She's forty, and rather sullen."

"Pity, I'll—"

A knock at the door interrupted them. His wicked air dropped from him and he came swiftly over to her side. He pulled a ring out of his pocket, and by the time her parents peeped coyly into the room, he was slipping it onto her finger.

Deirdre was numb with surprise, as much at the chameleon change in him as at his action. Her astonishment was complete when he smiled tenderly and tilted her chin for a kiss.

Deirdre stared into his deep brown eyes, wondering what was the true face of the Earl of Everdon, and aware that she was responding to the meaningless touch of his lips against hers. She immediately armed herself against such a response. She must remember that a Don Juan would be bound to have a powerful attractive force. It meant nothing.

He let her go. She looked down at the diamond on her finger, knowing she had red blotches in her cheeks. She didn't blush prettily as some women did, but just developed two farcical red stains on her pale skin.

Deirdre was not in the habit of repining over her looks, but at this moment she wished quite desperately that she were pretty. Perhaps then she would know how to handle this muddle with more grace.

Then she realized plans were being made. She put aside her useless musings and paid attention.

"No need to hang around here anymore," said her father with patent relief. "We can get back to Missinger."

Lord Everdon cast Deirdre a tender look. How could he, the wretch? "But you will be depriving me of Deirdre's presence, my lord, and depriving Deirdre of the rest of her Season. It looks to extend well into the summer this year, what with victory pageants and celebrations . . ."

Lord Harby gave a visible shudder. "London's a hotbed of

vice and disease," he said, "and all these crowds make it worse. Best to be back in the pure country air, say I. Thing to do is for you to come along, Everdon! Fine chance for you and Deirdre to become better acquainted, and plan your future."

Everdon slanted another look at Deirdre, one that made her shiver with its deceptive longing. "If you insist in taking Deirdre away, my lord, I must assuredly follow. First, however, I must escort my mother to Everdon Park."

Deirdre spoke up then. "Would Lady Everdon care to visit Missinger, my lord? I would be delighted to have her come with us, especially as she is to be my mama." Lucetta, she was thinking, would be a bulwark against this trickster.

"How charming," fluttered Lady Harby with a sigh and a simper. "I, too, would be delighted of the opportunity to become better acquainted with your mother, Everdon."

"I will ask her," said Everdon. "I anticipate no difficulty." He smiled at Deirdre as if she really were the love of his life. "She is already very fond of you, my dear." He kissed Deirdre's hand tenderly before taking his leave.

She didn't know how a man could act a lie so shamelessly.

Deirdre wanted to return to her needlework but had to suffer her mother's excited chatter. Lady Harby was in ecstasies about this unlooked-for success, and busily planning the wedding that would never be. Seeing that her mother was set for a long chat, Deirdre took up her work again and let the words wash over her.

"I knew you could do much better than that Howard Dunstable," said Lady Harby. "How any daughter of mine could be such a wigeon, I'll never know. A hundred a year and no prospects! He would never have made you a good husband, I know it."

And Everdon would? thought Deirdre. How money and title could blind. Howard Dunstable had little money, but he was involved in meaningful, important work, not a search for new debauchery. And Howard needed her.

Deirdre knew Howard would be lonely just now with her here in London. He was probably not eating well, or remembering to change if he was caught in a shower. As a mathematician, he frequently lost track of reality among the numbers in his head.

When Lady Harby began to wind down, Deirdre looked up from her needlework and said, "You must know, Mama, that I do not want this marriage."

Lady Harby was not at all disconcerted. "Yes, of course I know, dear. You still want that Dunstable. But you gave your word, and I'll see you keep it. Trust me in this, Deirdre. Everdon will make you a far better husband than that other one. I'm not willing to let you make a tangle of your life through sheer stubbornness."

"It is not stubbornness, Mama. I *love* Howard."

Lady Harby snorted. "You don't know what love is. I suppose he makes you feel needed. Men sometimes do that. There's nothing wrong with being needed, dear, but there has to be more than that to make a good marriage. Respect, for one thing."

"I *do* respect Howard!"

"Do you? For what?"

"He has a brilliant mind."

"Very likely," said Lady Harby, unimpressed.

Deirdre wished her mother were as foolish as she often appeared. Nothing escaped her at all. "Am I supposed to respect Everdon? He's a worthless rake."

"He is not worthless. He's very rich." Lady Harby overrode Deirdre's scathing comment. "He's also more than that, dear.

He's a man who runs his properties well, and speaks intelligently in Parliament from time to time. He's not even a rake in the true sense of the word. Harby assures me he don't gamble or drink to excess. He just likes women. If you do your part, he won't stray much, and I'd judge that he'll always be discreet."

Now it was Deirdre's turn to snort. "How can he be discreet when he's labeled Don Juan? No one will ever believe he's not going from bed to bed, no matter how he behaves!"

"We'll see." But this was a distinctly weak response.

Deirdre pounced on her mother's point of vulnerability. "Mama, I don't want to marry a man who'll go from bed to bed. If he behaves badly before the wedding, will you let me break the engagement?"

Lady Harby looked at Deirdre searchingly, but then she nodded. "Yes, I will, dear. If he's rogue enough to behave badly before you're even wed, I'll admit you're right about him. I'll even let you marry your silly Howard." She rose and smiled confidently. "But it won't come to that, you'll see, which is the only reason I make the promise. Everdon is far too much of a gentleman to embarrass you in that way, so playing silly games to turn him off won't get you anywhere, young lady."

Deirdre fought not to show her glee. "I wouldn't know how to play silly games, Mama."

"Every girl knows. They come into them like they come into talking and walking. Just remember, you'll be under my eye, so no tricks. September," she said with a brisk nod. "We'll have the wedding in September." With that, she bustled off.

As soon as her mother left, Deirdre let out a muted whoop of delight. It was all set! Lord Everdon was as eager to escape this engagement as she, and surely he knew just what to do to disgust her mother. She was even naughtily intrigued as to what the wretch would do. Deirdre giggled at the thought of him trying to seduce Agatha Tremsham, her dresser.

She supposed he'd find a willing dairymaid, or one of the country lasses, and be indiscreet about it.

Then the engagement would be over, and Deirdre would have her mother's permission to marry Howard. She leapt up and did a little dance through the sunbeams. She couldn't wait to tell Howard how perfectly it had all turned out.

Then she halted, thoughtful. Affairs were going to be a little awkward for the next few weeks. She and Everdon would be at Missinger playing the happy couple, while Howard was down in the village feeling neglected . . .

But, she told herself, they could regard it as merely a short trial before total happiness. Thank goodness Howard was not of a jealous nature. He would understand immediately that this was the only path to their wedded bliss, and by summer's end they would be married.

Deirdre settled back to her needlework—a picture of fish underwater done on many layers of gauze. Everything, she thought, was turning out perfectly, and she counted off the blessings in her mind to prove it.

One, if they were to leave London soon, there would be no more excruciating balls and soirées to sit through.

Two, Lucetta would be coming with them, which would mean that Deirdre could continue the only true pleasure she had found in London—her friendship with Lady Everdon.

Three, Lady Harby would keep her word and allow Deirdre to break her engagement and marry Howard.

She nodded. There could even be a September wedding, but not the one her mother planned.

She would not, Deirdre decided with a grin, let Lord Everdon know what a good turn he had served her.

Over dinner and after, Deirdre had to endure yet more excited discussion of her future as Countess of Everdon, but at least she wasn't dragged out to Almack's. She smiled, and let her mother chatter.

When she went to bed, she took off the meaningless diamond ring and tucked it away in her jewel box. If the engagement was not to be announced, she could not be expected to wear it in public.

She climbed into bed, intending to enjoy the planning of her future with Howard. Instead, she found her mind determinedly fixed upon her unlikely betrothed.

Why would any woman want to marry a man with such a notorious reputation?

She supposed the fact that Everdon was an earl would count with some women, and his looks would carry weight with others. Even she had to confess that he had lovely hands. She toyed with the idea of stitching a picture of them—long-fingered, strong, deft . . .

Then she remembered them tight on her shoulders and forming purposeful fists, and shuddered. The man was clearly a bully.

She forced her mind to turn to Howard, who was also very handsome. Howard, however, was a gentle and pure-living man.

Everdon was the complete antithesis. Despite his outrage when she spoke of it, he made no secret of the fact that he went from bed to bed. Some of his lovers were known, some merely rumored. Some, she supposed, were kept discreetly private. She wondered waspishly if he truly was so irresistible when he never stayed with any woman long. Even his wife, it was said, had given up on him after a mere six months.

Perhaps that was it, she thought with a chuckle. He couldn't keep a woman longer than a six-month and thus had to work on quantity. Deirdre covered her mouth. Oh, dear, what with her mother, her friend Anna, and Lucetta, she had developed a rather bold turn of mind. Now, see the consequences. When she'd lost her temper with Everdon, she had said the most outrageous things.

She chuckled again at the memory of his shock and anger. Served the conceited wretch right.

Deirdre rolled over and snuggled down in bed.

Everything was finally going to be perfect.

Everdon decided not to enlighten his mother immediately as to the true state of affairs. She clearly favored a match with Lady Deirdre, and if he told her it was all a sham, soon to be ended, she might try to hold them to it. However, when he broke the news that he was engaged to marry Lady Deirdre, he was surprised by her lack of delight.

"I thought you'd be ecstatic," he said.

"I will be pleased if you deal well together, dear."

"I suppose we will." At her silence, he became impatient. "You suggested her, remember? You can hardly expect me to be in quivers of delight. I scarcely know the girl."

"Quite so."

He swore, but under his breath. "I told you, Mama. It's a lottery. Time will show whether I win or lose. By the way, no announcement will be made as yet. It would be a little crass to announce my widowing and my engagement in the same news sheet, and I must post down to tell Genie's family before making her death public."

At that, Lucetta looked up with concern. "Must you tell them in person, dearest? It will not be a pleasant mission. They have always held you to blame, unfair though that is."

"It is something to be done in person, Mama. I doubt they'll shoot me. After that, I am invited to visit Missinger and continue my wooing of Lady Deirdre. She asked that you come, too, if you feel up to it."

The dowager's eyes glinted with interest. "Clever girl. I would be delighted."

He looked at her warily. "Why clever?"

The dowager merely smiled with all the enigmatic quality of the Sphinx. "You will see."

Everdon sincerely hoped not, and took himself off to his club. He was distinctly uneasy.

He would have been hard put to say what he thought of his strange betrothal. It would delay his plans for his real marriage, which was unfortunate, but on the other hand, it could be amusing to spar with Lady Deirdre for a month or so.

Surprising what she concealed beneath that dull surface. She was something of a termagant when roused. He supposed he should have realized his mother would not have grown so close to a tepid miss, no matter how strong her interest in needlework. He'd rather like to be a fly on the wall at one of their stitchery sessions, especially if they came around to discussing him.

The thought of Deirdre and his mother conspiring together in the intimacy of a country house did give him pause, however. Perhaps he would be wiser to alert the dowager to the true state of affairs. Otherwise, she might exert herself in his and Deirdre's interest to such good effect that they found themselves shackled for life.

He chuckled at the thought. He would be as content to marry Lady Deirdre now as he had been yesterday, for her lively reaction to his offer had increased rather than diminished her appeal, but he had no intention of taking a reluctant bride. Let her go to her Howard.

Simply to torment her, however, he sent around a note inviting her to drive with him the next afternoon.

• • •

Deirdre received the invitation in the spirit in which it had been sent, and planned the outing much like a general approaching an enemy force.

Lady Harby had deplorable taste. In every other respect, Deirdre admired her mother, but it was a simple fact that the lady had no sense of color or design, particularly when it came to clothing. Even in the schoolroom, the Stowe girls had subtly conspired to deflect their mother from the worst choices. When it came to their come-outs, they had been more forceful, despite their mother's complaints that they all liked to dress so dull. Only Deirdre, with her plan in mind, had allowed Lady Harby free rein.

She had been fairly certain that she could survive a London Season unbetrothed, for she harbored no illusion as to her physical charms, and was intent on behaving as dully as possible. She had made certain of her unpopularity, however, by allowing her mother to choose all her outfits. She now possessed the most ghastly wardrobe in London, probably in all England.

For her drive, Deirdre surveyed her weapons. The green, she thought gleefully. It had to be the green.

She had never actually brought herself to wear this outfit, but clearly remembered the modiste's rather strangled expression when it was ordered. Madame d'Esterville had not been about to object to any part of such a lavish order, but she clearly hoped no one would ever know whence it came.

The walking dress was a striking lime green, bold but unexceptionable in itself, though far too strong a color for Deirdre. Lady Harby had considered it plain, however, and ordered it trimmed with green and white satin puffs, most particularly over the bust to conceal Deirdre's lack of endowments. The striped puffs drew the eye most forcibly to that part of her anatomy, and gave her the appearance of one of those exotic birds that inflated its chest in the search for a mate.

Still unhappy, Lady Harby had then commanded the addition of canary yellow mull muslin flounces and collar, and purchased accessories to match.

Agatha Tremsham helped Deirdre into the outfit but said faintly, "Are you sure, milady?"

"Oh yes," said Deirdre. "I must look my best for Lord Everdon, mustn't I?"

Agatha said nothing. She had been hired at the beginning of the Season, and clearly was resigned to the fact that Deirdre had inherited her mother's taste in clothes.

Deirdre surveyed the complete effect in the mirror. The straw bonnet lined with green and white stripes served admirably to turn her pallor to a sickly green. A green and white striped parasol lined with yellow augmented the effect.

She put on the yellow slippers and mittens, and nodded. "Perfect," she said.

Agatha staggered off, muttering.

When Deirdre walked into the reception room to join Lord Everdon, she enjoyed the glazed look that came over his face, but a second later she saw him recognize exactly what she was about.

Humor glinted in his eyes as he kissed her hand. "My dear Lady Deirdre, I am speechless. I fear I do not do you justice, though. In future, I must try to match you in sartorial brilliance."

She threw him a startled look. Surely he wouldn't really start going abroad in lurid colors?

As he led her to his carriage, he mused, "I'm sure my cousin Kevin has something suitable. Do you know Kevin Renfrew? He has recently acquired the sobriquet of the

Daffodil Dandy. It suits him admirably in view of his habit of always dressing in yellow. What a pair you two would make . . ."

Deirdre allowed him to settle her in his phaeton—a very handsome equipage but not, she noted gratefully, excessively high. "Always in yellow?" she queried. "How dull. I prefer to use the full range of the palette. Next time we go on an outing, I must wear my pink and purple for you, my lord."

He settled into his seat, nodded to his groom, and gave the horses the office to go. "I see I shall have to exert myself, Lady Deirdre. Perhaps I should aim for the name the Rainbow Dandy."

Deirdre found herself unwillingly amused and let a smile escape. Now they were alone, she said, "Pray, don't be foolish, my lord. I wore this outfit to punish you a little, as you well know. You have no cause to punish me."

"Have I not?" he responded. "But if you had not been so cleverly outwitting your mama, I would never have taken the fateful step of offering you my name. I could happily have been planning my life with Maud Tiverton."

"Maud . . . !" Her eyes met his teasing ones and she laughed. "You truly are a rascal, my lord."

His eyes reflected her amusement. "And you are a minx. Tell me about your Howard."

He turned the team of matched chestnuts smoothly into the park, but took one of the less-traveled roads. Deirdre felt a frisson of alarm at finding herself alone in the power of Don Juan, but her common sense soon returned. She was the last woman in the world he would try to seduce.

She did not, however, intend to discuss personal matters with him. She looked around instead. "How sad it is to see the state of the park this summer. One would think a herd of cattle had stampeded through it again and again."

"So it has, after a fashion, but a herd of people, not cattle. There were estimated to be a hundred and fifty thousand people here on one day in May to watch the tsar and the king of Prussia ride by. Were you not one of them?"

"No. I can see no appeal in standing in the sun to watch men ride by."

"How dauntingly unromantic you are, to be sure."

Deirdre met his gaze. "Quite." But the effect of those beautiful eyes twinkling with humor almost made a liar of her.

She turned away to frown at the battered remnants of grass and shrubs. "I think it a shame to permit this kind of destruction in any cause."

"Even in celebration of peace?" he asked. "I have no doubt battlefields fare worse. And how can it be stopped? Anyway, I fear that peace—welcome as it is—will mean hard times for the poor, so let them have their moment." He guided the phaeton down toward the deer pound, where the evidence of mass invasion was less obvious. "Now," he repeated, "tell me all about your Howard."

Deirdre did not reply.

At her silence, he glanced over. "There must be something about your devoted admirer that is of interest."

Deirdre looked down at her yellow mittens. "I'm not sure I wish to speak of him to you, my lord."

"Why not? I'm hardly a rival for your hand. I've bowed out, remember?"

Still, Deirdre felt reluctant. No one had encouraged her to talk about Howard. Her mother always became scathing, and Eunice—her sister who lived close by—could not conceal that she failed to appreciate his charms. Even her dearest friend, Anna Treese, had not been able to enter into her feelings.

Lord Everdon would be the least sympathetic of all.

"He is a scholar," she said reluctantly. "A mathematician. He is working on some new calculation which will have great importance."

"Refining the dimensions of the earth by another inch or so, I suppose."

Deirdre raised her chin. "I knew you would sneer. We will talk of something else, if you please."

"I'm sorry," he said with apparent sincerity. "I know little of mathematics. Perhaps during my stay at Missinger I will meet your suitor and have the opportunity to learn."

"That seems unlikely, my lord. My parents do not invite Howard to the house, and in any case, he is far too busy for idle socializing. Anyway, I fear his work would be beyond you." Then she realized that was a trifle rude and glanced at him.

His brows rose but he only said, "Do *you* understand his work, Lady Deirdre?"

Deirdre felt the splotches grow in her cheeks. "Not exactly. He does try to explain, but I have little background with figures other than household accounts."

"What do you speak of, then?"

Deirdre felt as if she were being interrogated, but she wanted to convince at least one person of how perfect her life with Howard would be. "We plan our life together. He inherited a charming cottage in the village. We will live there, at least at first. It will need a few changes . . ." She racked her brain for more. "I remind him of things, for he is inclined to forget . . ."

Deirdre sighed. It was impossible to describe her time with Howard and convey the truth of it. How could she convince someone like Lord Everdon of her contentment with just sitting and sewing while Howard worked on his calculations? Of how happy she was to walk with him as he spoke of his latest problem, even if she didn't understand it . . .

She stopped trying, and he did not press her. Deirdre relaxed a little and set to enjoying the scenery.

This part of the park was scarcely damaged, and with its spreading trees and deer pound in the distance, could well be the country, so uncivilized did it appear. The leaves were heavy with summer green and formed a barrier to the bustling city. At this time of day, it was largely deserted.

Then Lord Everdon spoke again. "It must be quite delightful for Howard to have someone like you to take care of him, Lady Deirdre. How does he care for you?"

"Of course he cares for me!"

"That is not what I asked."

Deirdre turned to face him. "You have no right to ask me anything."

He stopped the horses, holding them in check with one negligent hand. "Do I not? You wear my ring, Lady Deirdre." He glanced at her gloved hand, which clearly held no rings. "Somewhere."

"It is in my jewel box at home, my lord. Without an announcement, I cannot wear it even if I would."

"Figuratively speaking, you wear my ring," he said firmly. "That gives me some responsibilities."

"It gives you nothing. This engagement is a farce, my lord, and I insist you treat me entirely as a stranger."

"Oh, I think not." He trapped her head with a hand curled around her neck and seared her with a slanting kiss.

It was over before Deirdre had time to react, other than to grow very hot. She scrubbed at her mouth. "How dare you, sir!"

"Don't be foolish. I dare a great deal more than that, but I'm unlikely to go much further without encouragement."

"Which you will never receive," she said hotly. "I give you

fair warning, Lord Everdon. Do that again and I'll slap your face!"

A light flickered in his eyes. "You should never warn the enemy. Now I have only to capture your hands before assaulting you."

Deirdre's eyes didn't waver from his. "Then I will wait until I am free. I mean what I say, my lord. Kiss me again and I will hit you with all the power in my arm at the first occasion, even if it takes decades!"

He burst out laughing. "I am entranced! Imagine us, two decrepit specimens lingering at Bath, when you see your opportunity at last. You totter over to my side and tip me out of my Bath chair with a strong right."

Despite her fury, a laugh escaped Deirdre. "I would not have to wait that long, I assure you."

"Of course not." He started the horses again. "I promise when next I kiss you, I'll wait for the retaliation."

A shiver passed down Deirdre's spine. "You won't kiss me again."

"Won't I?"

"If you don't give me your word not to kiss me again, I will never be alone with you."

"Won't that be a little hard to manage with your mother insisting on us behaving as a properly engaged couple?"

"And you would take advantage of that fact?" Deirdre protested.

"I'm sure I will find it irresistible."

Deirdre's hands fisted with anger. "You, sir, are an unmitigated cad!"

Infuriatingly, he smiled at her. "Oh, there, must be a mitigating factor somewhere . . ."

She swung at him. He swayed aside and she missed. "You'll have to practice your technique, Deirdre."

They were coming up to a group of riders. Deirdre suppressed the urge to do just that. She put her clenched fists firmly in her lap and looked ahead, struggling to understand how this man could have driven her to attempt violence. She could still feel the power of the desire to do him injury vibrating through her, and she knew he had done it deliberately. He had goaded her for his amusement.

How the devil was she going to survive the next few weeks and remain sane?

3

DEIRDRE REPEATED THAT PLEA TO HER FRIEND, Anna Treese, as soon as she was back home in Somerset. Anna's family owned the adjacent estate, Starling Hall, which lay but a two-mile walk from Missinger. Deirdre had rushed over there the morning after her return.

"How will you survive?" repeated Anna, a pretty, dimpled brunette. "What is so terrible about flirting with a Don Juan? Especially as you will get your Howard in the end."

Deirdre caught the sour note in the last sentence. Anna had never made any bones about the fact that she considered Howard a poor candidate for a husband.

"*You* might not mind it," Deirdre pointed out, cradling her teacup. "You've vast experience with flirting, and you've always enjoyed it. I haven't. Compare it to riding, which you do little of. How would you like to be forced to ride a fiery stallion?"

Anna giggled, then hastily steadied her cup. "What a comparison to make!"

Deirdre blushed hot red. "Anna, really!"

"Well, I can't help but have a saucy mind. It's my brothers. They will talk in front of me. And the books they leave lying around . . ."

"You don't have to read them," Deirdre pointed out severely.

"But they're so informative. Have another scone, dear." She took one for herself. "As for your comparison, *I* am not anticipating a life in the saddle. If I were, I suspect I would learn to like riding the best."

"Well, I am not . . ." Deirdre trailed off.

"Anticipating life with a man? Of course you are."

"Howard *is* the best," Deirdre said firmly.

"Really? In what way?"

Why, thought Deirdre, do I always have to justify Howard? "He has a fine mind."

"That won't keep you warm on a cold night."

Deirdre blushed. "He needs me."

Anna shook her head. "Old Tom needs you more. Why not marry him?"

As Old Tom was a lackwit much given to the bottle, this was true and completely irrelevant. "Old Tom is not handsome, whereas Howard is. I'm sure *that* argument carries weight with you."

"More handsome than Lord Everdon?" Anna asked as she topped up their cups.

"In my eyes," said Deirdre firmly. Thank heavens Howard *was* good-looking since that was all anyone seemed to care about.

"Your Howard is well enough," said Anna, adding surprisingly, "though looks are not so important in my mind. I'll grant that Mr. Dunstable has height, and a noble profile, and that his wavy blond hair is very becoming. There's something missing, though, for me at least. I'd rather spend time with Arthur Kealey. He still has spots, poor lad, but he's fun and has a kind heart."

"Has Arthur won your heart, then?" teased Deirdre, deliberately changing the subject. "You always rub along so well."

"Oh no," said Anna practically. "It may just be that he's too young as yet, or that he's not the one. I'm in no hurry. We're all just eighteen," she said, adding pointedly, "None of us need rush into matrimony yet."

"But," said Deirdre triumphantly, "Howard clearly *is* the one for me, for I *want* to rush into matrimony. And it would all be settled now," she added darkly, "if not for Lord Everdon."

"But he's promised to sort it out."

Deirdre put down her empty cup with slightly unsteady hands. "That means he will be coming here, though."

Anna licked crumbs from her fingers and grinned. "Don Juan in Missinger. I can hardly wait."

Deirdre would have willingly waited an eternity for her next encounter with Don Juan, but she knew that could not be. As it was, she spent a great deal of time planning how to limit their encounters to safe locales.

Don Juan, however, caught her in the open, far from cover. So much for careful planning.

Deirdre was strolling down the drive, returning from a flower-gathering expedition, when she heard coach wheels on the gravel. She turned to see a handsome traveling chariot bowling toward her. If she possessed a deeply suspicious nature, she would think Lord Everdon had hovered by the gates all day waiting for just such an opportunity.

The carriage stopped. He opened the door. "May I take you up to the house, Lady Deirdre?"

"Thank you, my lord, but no. I am enjoying the walk."

He leapt down, an image of country perfection in buckskins and top boots, and a great deal more handsome than she remembered. "A stroll after hours in a carriage sounds delightful." He commanded the carriage to go on, then came to her side, a twinkle in his deep brown eyes. "You really should try to look pleased to see me, you know."

Deirdre glared at him. She hadn't seen him since that drive, for she and her family had left London for Missinger the next day, carrying the dowager with them. He had set off for Northamptonshire to inform Sir Bertram and Lady Brandon of their daughter's demise.

The news of his wife's death had appeared in the papers a few days later.

"I am not pleased to see you," she said flatly, wanting to make the situation absolutely clear.

She set off purposefully toward the house, a good mile away. As she went, she considered tactics. If the underhanded wretch tried to kiss her here, she'd either have to put up with it, or drop her armful of flowers to retaliate. She'd be able to retaliate, she was sure. She had sought advice from Margery Noons, one of the dairymaids. She'd once seen Margery lay out one of the stable lads with a mighty blow.

"You got to swing into it good, milady," the girl advised. "Think like you want to knock their block right off their shoulders."

Deirdre was quite prepared to do just that, but she'd rather it be sometime when she didn't have a mass of carefully selected blossoms in her hands.

"An interesting collection of blooms there," Everdon said amiably. "Let me guess. You have decided to embroider plants after all, and intend a novel assembly of wildflowers."

How did he know that? "I never said I refused to use plant designs."

"Wildflowers after the style of Mr. Turner," he mused. "I look forward to seeing the end result."

Deirdre pounced on that. "You will be gone by then, my lord."

"Alas, it is quite likely. Will you send it to me as a parting gift?"

She glanced at him, startled. "Why should I?"

His smile had a lazy kind of power. "I am going to have to exert myself to free you, Lady Deirdre. Do I not deserve a reward?"

"That depends," she said pointedly, "on how you behave in the meantime."

"Ah," he said with twitching lips. "You mean the kisses."

Alarm shot through her. "I warned you, sir . . ."

He raised his brows. "I thought you would have noted my restraint, Lady Deirdre. I am quite aware that you are under a handicap at the moment, and thus have not attacked. I need no such advantages."

Deirdre could think of no suitable response, and speeded up her pace.

Having much longer legs, he kept up with her without difficulty. "This is a charming property," he said, "and the land about seems to be in excellent heart. I understand your father is very well informed on agricultural matters . . ." He kept up an effortless monologue on agriculture all the way to the house.

Deirdre was relieved not to have to bandy words with him. It was only when they arrived at the house that she realized he had been talking sense. He seemed to know his crops and cattle, and could not be entirely a social butterfly.

His monologue had also allowed her to recover her equilibrium and good manners. She turned to face him. "Here we are, my lord. Welcome to Missinger. I see my parents waiting to greet you. I am a little untidy, however, and need to put these blooms into water, so I will leave you here and use a side entrance."

He made no attempt to stay her, but bowed. "Until later, Deirdre."

Deirdre made herself walk away calmly.

A few minutes later, while she arranged the flowers, she talked herself into sense. "I knew he was coming," she muttered as she snipped stems. "I knew he'd be up to mischief." She worked the pump to fill three vases with water. "Heaven knows why he teases me so. I suppose he just can't help himself." She pushed the poor flowers into their vases rather roughly. "Despite what he says, I needn't be alone with him much."

She washed her hands, glaring at the fragile blossoms. "And if he tries to kiss me," she told them, "I *will* try to knock his block off."

What worried Deirdre, however, was not so much the fact that he would try to kiss her again—it had become a kind of challenge, she saw that—but the alarming response she felt to the prospect. She wouldn't say the challenge was pleasant, but it was *unignorable*.

When she'd explained her strange situation to Howard—and he hadn't seemed to mind—she had tried to get him to kiss her, to substitute one experience for the other. He had not complied. In fact, he'd been rather shocked, and accused her of coming back from London with some very peculiar notions.

He was right, she told herself firmly. Libertines like Everdon might kiss women without a care in the world. Good, decent people waited at least until they were properly betrothed, and probably until they were married.

She rang for a footman, and ordered the flowers taken to her workroom, then went up to her bedroom to change.

The question was, what to wear?

She still had all her London gowns, but having been free of them for a week, she really couldn't face the prospect of wearing them again. Anyway, her two brothers would tease her unmercifully if she did. Consequently she let Agatha choose, and ended up in a very ordinary, but becoming, cream muslin sprigged with rosebuds. Then the maid looped her hair back with a ribbon.

When she joined her family in the drawing room, Deirdre knew she looked as well as possible, and better than Everdon had ever seen her.

She found him instantly, safely talking to her mother and the dowager. Her father was part of the same group in body, but could not be said to be so in spirit, as he was absorbed in Poulter's *Treatise on Agricultural Management*. Deirdre's two brothers were some way from their elders, joking together and lounging their lanky bodies in a very sloppy way. She joined them.

Her older brother, Viscount Ripon—generally called Rip—greeted her with, "Ain't you going to sit by your beau, Dee? Most women can't keep their hands off him." Rip was a handsome, dashing blond, and just now his grin came perilously close to a leer.

She smiled tightly. "I'm sure he's a reformed character now, Rip."

"Don't know as they ever reform," said her younger brother, Henry. At just seventeen, nearly two years younger than Deirdre, various bits of him had still to catch up to the rest. He showed every sign of following the Stowe tradition, however, and being a danger to the opposite sex. Deirdre knew herself to be the sparrow in a family of showy birds.

Henry was always trying to emulate his older brother, so he essayed a leer, too. "Everdon's strong meat for a little squab like you, Dee, but I'm sure he'll know how to please any lady. Do you think he'd give me a few pointers?"

Deirdre forced a smile. "I suspect he'd give you a facer if you asked."

She felt her tormentor coming before she really saw him, and experienced no surprise when he sat beside her on the sofa. "What a pleasant house Missinger is," he said smoothly to the three of them. If he'd overheard the conversation, he wasn't going to make an issue of it. "Just large enough to be commodious, but small enough to be comfortable. A real home."

That led them safely into a discussion of the house. Deirdre noted how Everdon continued to steer the conversation—to the local landscape, and then into the sporting opportunities in the area. His sophistication and elegant manners made Rip seem almost as callow as Henry. Soon both her brothers were behaving like wide-eyed acolytes and eagerly offering to take him on any number of sporting outings.

When he accepted, she glanced at him in surprise. She'd thought he would devote his time to tormenting her.

His dark eyes twinkled with humor. "You look disappointed, Deirdre. Do you not approve of the chase? Or do you think I should be hunting some other prey?"

"No, please," she said hastily. "I'm sure you will be well suited with blood sports."

"Dee's a bit squeamish about such things," said Rip. "Never have managed to get her out with the hunt, though she's a pretty good rider. Only weighs a feather, of course, but surprisingly strong."

"Really?" said Everdon. "Swings a good right, does she?"

Deirdre choked back a protest, and Henry rolled with

laughter. "Not of a pugilistic nature, Dee ain't. Anyway, no female can give more than a tickle."

Everdon focused on him. "I wouldn't take that as a rule of life, Mr. Stowe."

"Oh, really?" Henry sat up, clearly intending to pursue this interesting line of discussion, but Everdon smoothly overrode him.

"If you enjoy riding, Deirdre, I hope you will take me about the estate one day."

Not if she could help it. "If you want a tour, my lord, Father is the one for that. I can't tell a turnip from a mangel-wurzel."

"You can introduce me to the beauties of nature." His voice slid over her deep and soft, as if he spoke of intimate secrets.

Deirdre was infuriatingly aware of her brothers taking all this in, including her blush. If she continued to protest, they'd remark it, and doubtless comment on it in front of her mother.

"Very well," she agreed ungraciously, but carefully did not specify the day. "Now I wish to speak to your mother. Excuse me, my lord."

He made no objection to her escape.

For dinner that night, Deirdre wore a cerulean blue gown that became her as well as anything. This wasn't by choice, but because her mother had commanded her to put on something particularly pretty. She knew Lady Harby would be content—delighted even—if she were to choose the pink, or the amazing confection of white lace and roses made for her first ball, but she simply couldn't. Her blue, though a year old, still looked well enough.

She rather thought, anyway, that it would be pointless to

try to turn Everdon off with tastelessness. He'd kissed her in the green, for heaven's sake, and if that hadn't deterred him, nothing would. The man was clearly set on tormenting her regardless of what she wore.

Perhaps he *was* punishing her. She frowned at her own reflection as Agatha arranged her hair. It would hardly be fair, for he was as much to blame as she for the pickle they were in.

But why would she expect him to be fair?

Strangely, she did.

She added her pearls and went down to dinner prepared for battle, but the meal passed without incident or innuendo.

He had been correct, she thought, in describing Missinger as a home. She was so accustomed that she had not noted it, but here elegance and comfort were pleasingly balanced, and the intention was always that people be at ease. She had been fortunate to be raised here.

She looked fondly at her parents. Her father was wrapped up in his land, and her mother loved garish colors, but they were both wise, kindhearted people who loved their children. It was unfortunate that their one blind spot seemed to be her happiness.

Everdon, she noted, seemed to fit in at Missinger. In this relaxed gathering of people who were comfortable with their situation and one another, he was unobtrusive. She would have thought he would find it boring. Deirdre wondered what his own home was like. Apart from his mother, she did not think he had close family. Then she remembered he'd had a brother, who had died in Spain. At Vittoria, she thought.

For these, and a host of other reasons, she found herself mellowing a little toward Don Juan. He spoke like a sensible man and behaved courteously to all. He had a pleasantly easy manner with her brothers, despite their occasional silliness, and certainly did not encourage them in impropriety. If his words had any effect at all, it would be to steer them into a good way of life.

Nor was there that manner of shocking for effect that she had sometimes observed in men and women with an unsavory reputation, as if they were anxious to prove just how bold they were.

Everdon, she thought, did not appear to be anxious about anything.

Conversation over the meal generally flowed easily, but she noted that if it faltered, Everdon could take any conversational ball and keep it rolling, could find a new one if need be. And this was not, she thought, so much expertise as a desire to make things easy for others. A natural courtesy.

She concentrated on her strawberry flan, wondering why she harbored these strange thoughts. If she didn't take care, she'd find herself liking the wretch.

Perhaps that was his aim, but if he employed such a method of seduction, it was exceedingly subtle and would be difficult to fight.

Seduction?

Her spoon froze in the act of cutting into crisp pastry. No, even Everdon would not go so far as that in his mischief.

After dinner Deirdre played the piano while her mother and the dowager chatted, both over needlework, though of a very different nature. The dowager was now engaged in a design of birds on fine lawn; Lady Harby was working a geometrical design in tapestry-stitch for a new kneeler for the church.

Despite this difference, they appeared to be rubbing along very well. Deirdre couldn't help thinking how well these two families would blend.

She let her fingers wander over familiar melodies and turned her mind firmly to her future with Howard. She knew little of his family other than that they lived in Leicester, where his father was a solicitor. She rather thought he had mentioned a sister. Doubtless after the wedding, the Dunstables would be invited to Missinger and rub along well, too.

As her husband, Howard would certainly be often at the house. He had not been to Missinger yet, for her mother refused to invite him, but once they were wed, it would be inevitable. She was sure he would fit in.

He wasn't a yokel, after all. Certainly he had little in common with her father or brothers, but they would find something to talk about.

They would have to. They couldn't just sit in silence.

Howard, however, would not linger over his port for hours talking crops and sports, but would come to take tea with the ladies. Perhaps he would sit and watch as she played, or sewed.

She realized she had never played for Howard. He had no instrument at his cottage, and anyway, she visited there rarely, feeling it was not quite proper. Most of their time together was spent outdoors, or at other houses in the neighborhood.

Few of the local gentry invited Howard, however, for he was an unrewarding guest, generally being lost in his numbers. A poet could perhaps be brought to recite his work, but no one wanted to listen to Howard explaining equations . . .

Something alerted her. She looked up from the keys and her fingers fumbled into a discord. Lord Everdon was seated on a bench at the end of the piano, gazing at her. She glanced around. None of the other men were here.

He was looking at her in that most disturbing manner.

As if he were enjoying doing it.

She removed her unmanageable fingers from the keys. "Did you want something, my lord?"

He placed his hands—those beautiful hands—on the piano case, and rested his chin on them. "I want many things," he said in a deep, disturbing voice.

Meaningless words to cause her heart to leap into her throat. "I mean, anything I can get for you."

He thought about it. "No. I don't think you can *get* for me anything that I want."

"Some tea," she said brightly, leaping to her feet and heading for the tray. Anything to escape.

He caught her hand as she passed and neatly tipped her off balance down onto the bench beside him. She squeaked, but the other ladies at the far side of the room didn't appear to notice. "What are you doing?" she whispered, jerking her hand free. It tingled, as if she'd just taken part in an electrical demonstration.

"Stopping you from running away. Why are you so afraid of me?"

She folded her hands in her lap and made herself meet his eyes. "I am not afraid of you."

"Then stay and talk to me."

Deirdre couldn't think of a suitable response.

He took her hand again. "I'm hardly likely to kiss you here. What else have you to fear?"

She snatched the hand back. "You are capable of anything, my lord," she said tartly. "You have just manhandled me in public."

"Is that what you call manhandling? It is clear a man has never handled you at all well."

Deirdre raised her chin. "Lord Everdon, you will not speak to me in such a way. It is not decent, and I will not tolerate it."

He smiled. "Bravo! It is pleasing to challenge a spirit such as yours. Pray tell me, Deirdre, how did you endure all those tedious social affairs? I'm surprised you didn't cut your throat—or someone else's."

She was disarmed by his approval, though aware she was likely being foolish. "I plotted designs in my head," she admitted, "though sometimes I amused myself forming couples into unlikely pairs. Little fat Mr. Peebles with gangly Miss Vere. Chatty Lady Hetty with the equally garrulous Lord Tring. Do you think they would kill each other for the chance to speak?"

"More likely they'd both chatter without paying any attention to the other. That's the dreadful thing about the over-talkative. They never listen." He studied her. "And all this was worthwhile as the price of gaining your Howard?"

She felt her face heat and looked away. "Yes."

"Is he worthy of you?"

"Of course he is." She was on edge again, sensing that he had moved to the attack.

"What first appealed to you about him?"

She fixed him with a look. "I have no intention of discussing Howard with you."

"Have you not? But I have this terrible problem, Deirdre my dear. I take women seriously. I take their welfare seriously. I cannot possibly free you to go to your Howard without being sure he is worthy."

She moved back slightly. "It is nothing to do with you!"

"On the contrary."

"Are you saying you won't arrange the end to our engagement unless it suits you? That is to go back on your word, Lord Everdon."

"I never gave my word."

Deirdre called his bluff. "I don't suppose it matters what

you intend," she said lightly. "You are hardly likely to follow a life of purity, are you? I will merely have to wait until you revert to normal, and catch you at it."

He feigned horror, though his eyes laughed at her. "Lady Deirdre, think what you might see!"

"I will *set* someone to catch you," she corrected tightly, knowing the red flags were flying in her cheeks again. "After all, *I* am going to be avoiding you."

"You'll find that remarkably hard to do. Don't forget our betrothal, and your ever-watchful mama."

Deirdre glanced over and saw that even as she conversed with the dowager, and set her neat stitches, her mother had the situation under her eye. Well, Lady Harby knew Deirdre was being forced into this.

Deirdre rose to her feet and simply walked away from her spurious husband-to-be, and this time he let her go.

Shortly afterward, the rest of the men appeared, and Everdon went off to play billiards with her brothers. Deirdre was very partial to the game and would have gone, too, but she knew she'd be wiser to avoid him.

She took up her needlework—a conventional banding for a baby's gown, for she rarely worked on her more adventurous pieces in public—and joined the older ladies.

The simple stitches required little attention, and her mind was free to wander troubling paths. She foresaw difficult days ahead. There clearly was nothing beyond the boldness of Don Juan.

4

THE NEXT MORNING Deirdre awoke to a visit from her mother. Lady Harby was a somewhat painful first sight of the day, as she had combined an unexceptionable blue-striped cambric with a yellow and brown shawl and a green-trimmed cap.

Deirdre winced.

"It is all arranged," said Lady Harby, as if the bearer of glad tidings. "You are to take Everdon on a riding tour of the estate. Today."

Deirdre sank farther beneath her covers. "Father would do it better."

"Don't be foolish. The man wants to be with *you*, Deirdre. And you are hardly being fair."

"Fair?" asked Deirdre innocently.

Lady Harby gave her a no-nonsense look. "I know you still feel he is forced upon you, but you could hardly do better in the whole of England. He is a charming man. If you would but give him a chance, I am sure he could make you happy with the match."

"He's a rake," said Deirdre mutinously.

"No, he ain't. I told you, dear, and we've checked most carefully. He don't gamble or drink to excess, and that's what makes a true rake."

"The whole world knows one thing he does to excess."

Lady Harby looked a little pink at that but said, "You have to give him a chance, Deirdre. It's only fair. He's doubtless ready to settle down."

Deirdre sat up in her bed. "He *kissed* me, Mama."

"Very proper at a betrothal."

"I mean when he took me driving. And it *wasn't* proper."

Instead of showing shock, Lady Harby's eyes brightened. "You can't expect him to be bashful, dear, a man like that. And a few kisses could well show you which way to go." She twitched up her shawl. "Just remember what I've always said—don't let him inside your clothing."

With that, she bustled off to attend to other duties.

Though that phrase had been Lady Harby's oft-repeated advice to her daughters, it flustered Deirdre now. She could all too easily imagine Lord Everdon's long, deft fingers insinuating themselves beneath her most secure clothing. It was just the sort of thing a womanizer would be skilled at.

She had never even considered such a thing of Howard.

Nor, when she came to think of it, had her mother ever felt pressed to repeat that advice to her in respect to Howard.

That surely meant Lady Harby recognized Howard to be an honorable man.

Didn't it?

Deirdre muttered about her ridiculous situation, and rang for Agatha to ready her for the ride. She chose her old dark gray habit, which her mother hated, but which she knew suited her much better than the dragoon-trimmed red ordered in Town.

She did wear the high-crowned shako, however, for it gave her a little height, and she would need all the help she could find to deal with Don Juan. Deirdre pulled on her gray leather boots with pleasure. She liked the feeling of walking in boots, for compared to slippers, they made an impression on the world.

On her way downstairs Deirdre made an impulsive detour to visit the dowager. She hadn't yet told Lady Everdon that the betrothal was false, half hoping that if she ignored it, it would disappear. Lucetta must have guessed that it wasn't a love match, though. Now, faced with the potent reality of Don Juan in her life, it was time to seek Lucetta's aid.

The dowager was still in her bed, addressing a breakfast of rolls and coffee. She accepted a kiss on the cheek and smiled. "That habit suits you, Deirdre. The severe line brings out your strength."

"Strength?" queried Deirdre, perching on the edge of the bed. "I'm not strong."

"Oh, but you are. Not a blustering strong, but strong inside. That's why I think you will suit Marco very well. He needs a real woman to keep him in line. Like my mother with my father."

"Did she have a whip?" asked Deirdre ironically.

Lucetta chuckled. "Not that I know of, but she had a cutting tongue. More than that, she just had strength. He knew she wouldn't tolerate misbehavior, and it held him in check, for he loved her."

Deirdre looked straight at Lucetta. "I don't love Everdon."

The dowager sipped her coffee. "How could you? You hardly know him."

"And he doesn't love me."

"Of course not. Not yet."

"He never will. Not least because this engagement is a sham." Deirdre then explained the whole sorry tale.

Lucetta put down her cup. "Oh, my dear, I am sorry. Why did you not tell me all this? Then I would never have suggested you to Marco as a bride."

"Suggested?" asked Deirdre in surprise.

Lucetta explained her part in it, leaving nothing out.

Deirdre leapt off the bed to pace the room. "So I am a lottery ticket, am I? The wretch! He set out to marry me when he would scarcely have recognized me if we'd met in the street."

Lucetta's lips twitched. "I doubt not that he'd recognize you now, my dear. Why the heat? According to you, it will soon be over. All the same . . ."

Deirdre swung around to face her. "All the same, what?"

"Nothing," said Lucetta mildly. "But if you and Marco are in agreement that you will soon end this betrothal, why are you in such a pelter?"

Deirdre looked away. "Because he's alleviating his boredom by teasing me to death."

"What is he doing?"

Deirdre drew her crop restlessly through her hands. "He . . . he kissed me . . . and he threatened to do it again, even when I told him I'd hit him if he did . . . And he *looks* at me!"

"Looks at you?" The dowager's tone was innocent, but Deirdre turned back and saw the twitch of her lips.

"It's not funny, Lucetta. Last night he was looking at me in such a way . . ." She shivered. "I can't describe it, but it made me most uneasy."

"It certainly can be unnerving to be stared at. I am surprised Marco would be so discourteous."

"It wasn't exactly a stare," said Deirdre quietly. "It was intent. As if I were important . . . as if he *liked* looking at me."

"Perhaps he did. Despite what you think of yourself, you are not hard on the eyes, my dear, especially when you are out of your somewhat strange London outfits." Lucetta sighed. "You must not blame Marco too much for flirting with you, Deirdre. He has inherited the tendency just as he inherited his brown eyes."

Deirdre faced the dowager. "He makes me most uneasy, Lucetta, and it is merely a game to him. Surely he will desist if you ask him to."

Lucetta studied her. "Are you sure that is what you want, Deirdre? It is, after all, just a game, and one he is very good at. I'll stand guarantee that he would never take it too far. Once you are married to your Howard, the time for such games will be over."

Deirdre bit her lip. It was a silly fear, but she worried that in some way this would all prevent her marriage to Howard. "Yes, I want him to stop."

"Then I will do what I can."

When Deirdre left, however, the dowager looked very thoughtful indeed.

Deirdre discovered that Lord Everdon was awaiting her in the stables, and so she went directly there. She came upon him making the acquaintance of Henry's fine gray gelding, and took the opportunity to study the enemy.

He'd been startlingly handsome in evening clothes and in day wear, but he suited riding clothes, too. The brown jacket and buckskin breeches toned with his skin and hair. They robbed him of some of his fanciful elegance, but replaced it with practical strength.

As if feeling her eyes on him, he turned and smiled a

welcome. "Your brother has offered me this fine fellow, Deirdre. I hope your mount will be able to keep up with him."

"Oh, I think so," she said dryly as the groom led out her own gelding, Charlemagne, a black every bit as big and strong as his mount.

She saw the flicker of surprise on Everdon's face, but he came over and tossed her into the saddle without comment. She appreciated the fact that he didn't make any conventionally stupid remarks about Charlemagne not being a lady's mount, or protest that she would not have the strength to control him.

She led the way out of the stables and down a lane to open ground. "We'll warm them up as we go down to the river, my lord, then have a gallop over to the eastern boundary. I'm afraid we have no romantic features here, though. No monasteries, magic streams, or caves."

Everdon looked around. "Just hundreds of acres of well-tended land. Better than romance any day. I note you do not have much of a park here."

"Mother wanted it, but Father put his foot down. Wouldn't have acres of good land given over to ornamental deer, and artificial lakes and gardens."

"Very wise."

Deirdre glanced at him, aware again that his smooth social manners were disarming her. It was hard to stay wary with someone so courteous. "What is your estate like, my lord?"

He raised a brow. "I have been calling you Deirdre with great boldness. Do you not think you could call me by my given name? We are, after all, conspirators."

She flashed him a look. "Very well. What is your estate like, Don Juan?"

Humor flickered in his eyes. "Don will do. It's what most people call me. Everdon Park, I'm afraid, was extensively improved by my father, but I hesitate to put the ornamental gardens and obligatory deer park to the plow. It's a pleasant place, in fact, but the house is a trifle small. I'm thinking of building an extra wing when I marry."

The word "marry" caused a little frisson in Deirdre, but she reminded herself sternly that she wasn't the bride-to-be. "You should wait and seek your bride's advice on the matter."

"That is my intent."

They progressed along a narrow lane between hedges, heading down toward the river. The sun brightened the scene obligingly, but was not particularly hot. It was a good day for riding. An unwary rabbit hopped into the lane, froze, then darted off. Charlemagne pretended to take offense and sidled. Deirdre saw Everdon come alert, ready to assist her, but he held back, and she controlled the horse without difficulty.

She had to like the fact that he showed some trust in her abilities.

They speeded a little until they came close to the water, silvery-smooth and overhung by trees.

"Your brothers promise me fine fishing," he said.

"They seem to do well enough here."

"You don't care for the sport?"

Deirdre smiled apologetically. "I don't like killing things. I know it's foolish when I'm perfectly happy to eat the trout, or even the roast lamb, but . . ."

"It's a foolishness many share. I can't say killing animals is a favorite pastime of mine, though I have no trouble with fish. Or wasps, for example."

"I can't even face the wasps," she confessed. "I trap them and let them free outside. Everyone thinks me very foolish."

"And so you are, but it's a charming foolishness all the same."

Something changed between them. Deirdre couldn't say what it was, but she felt as if a connection had been made. She knew she would never forget him. When he strolled out of her life, there would be a space—a small space, but one that would never adequately be filled by another.

It was most alarming.

He made no other personal comment, however, but looked around. He gestured to a grassy hill a field away. "What is that mound over there?"

Deirdre grasped the subject with relief. "It's said to be a barrow, an ancient burial site. There may be bones inside, or even pots and such. No one has dug to find out."

"And you said you had no romantic features," he protested. "Can we ride over there? I'd like to investigate."

She obligingly turned and they cantered to the mound, some forty feet long and twenty feet high. The dun-colored cows in the field ambled resentfully away from the invaders.

"I'm going to climb it," he said. "Are you coming?"

"No, I'll wait here." Despite her firm tone, Deirdre couldn't help but remember how much she had loved to be on top of the little hill in her youth. It was hardly an activity for a mature person, however.

He dismounted and tossed her his reins, then went to investigate. Soon he had scrambled up the slope. "It's certainly a man-made shape," he called from the flat top. "If this were my land, I'd get someone in to excavate."

Deirdre suddenly wanted to be up there with him.

Impulsively she slid off Charlemagne, led the horses to the gate, and tethered them there. Then she picked up her skirts and ran over to climb up after him. Halfway up, she discovered that it wasn't as easy as she remembered. Last time she'd done this, her skirts had been shorter, and she'd felt no self-consciousness about revealing her legs. Now her trailing habit tangled her feet, but she couldn't gather it up without being indecorous. She found she was embarrassingly stuck betwixt and between.

He knelt and stretched out a helping hand. After a momentary hesitation, Deirdre took it. His grip was firm, and he pulled her up the last few feet without difficulty, steadied her, then let her go.

Deirdre caught her breath. "Oh, I haven't been up here for years! I used to love to come here as a girl. I felt on top of the world."

"It is not so very high. Perhaps I should take you to the Lakes."

Deirdre hardly paid attention. She stretched her arms out and slowly turned. "I always felt special here. Tall, strong, powerful. Queen of the world . . ."

She kept turning, faster and faster, allowing the world to spin around her and carry her off to dreams . . .

He caught her hands and jerked her to a stop. She fell dizzily into his arms.

"Oh, don't!" she cried.

"You were going to spin off."

The world was still turning around her, but Deirdre said, "Let me go!"

"Wait a moment."

"Let me go!" she cried, panicked by his arms, and the look in his eyes.

He did so cautiously, warning, "If you try to walk, you'll fall over, and end up back in my arms. I'd really have to kiss you then, you know."

She stood there, begging the world to stay still. When she was younger and had done this, she'd collapsed onto the ground afterward and let the sky turn and turn above her. Nothing would induce her to collapse at the feet of Don Juan. "I do wish you'd stop this," she fretted. "You don't really want to kiss me."

"How can you know what I want?"

The world began to settle, and she met his amused eyes. "I'm not the sort of woman you like to kiss."

"Aren't you? In fact, I like to kiss most women."

"That's ridiculous. Do you want to kiss my mother, for example?"

He grinned. "I didn't say I wanted to kiss *all* women. Those that want to be kissed, I want to kiss."

"But I don't want to be kissed. At least, not by you." She ignored his arrogantly skeptical look and added, "Besides, that policy sounds highly dangerous, my lord."

"True, but it wasn't when I was married."

Deirdre nodded. "Ah, I see. And now you are in peril, but like an opium eater, you find you cannot break the habit."

"Precisely. I thought you would be kind enough to let me blunt my appetite by occasionally kissing you, since we are agreed we wouldn't suit."

Perhaps she was still dizzy after all. Deirdre felt most peculiar. Her senses were being deliberately tangled in knots, up here where reality seemed so far away. "But I don't want to be kissed by you," she repeated firmly.

Or at least, she intended it to be firm, but it didn't come out that way.

"Why not?"

"Why on earth should I?"

"It would be fun."

Deirdre took refuge in primness. "Kissing should never be fun."

He laughed. "Now, *that's* ridiculous." He stood, hands

on hips, beaver at a jaunty angle, making the world spin again.

"It is not ridiculous," she defended desperately. "Kissing is for holy purposes. For marriage and procreation . . ." She bit off what she had been about to say, realizing where her unwary tongue was leading her. She knew her face was red and wanted to wipe the amusement off his all-too-handsome face. She could see he was trying not to laugh, but his lips were twitching anyway.

"I hadn't actually intended to go so far so fast . . ." he murmured, and walked toward her.

Deirdre pushed him off the mound.

With a cry, he tumbled over and over down the steep slope and lay still.

With a gasp of horror, Deirdre slid and scrambled her way down to his side, not caring if her habit was soiled or her legs were showing. Her heart thudded madly and chills shook her. What would become of her if she'd *killed* him?

She landed by his still body. He didn't look dead but his olive skin made it hard to tell. Hesitantly she reached to touch his cheek. At the last moment she saw the flicker of his eyelids as he peeped at her.

She leapt to her feet and backed away, her anger returning in full force. "Get up, you wretch. I know you're shamming it!"

With a laugh, he rose and brushed himself off. Then, without warning, he grabbed her, imprisoned her competently in his arms, and kissed her. She tried to kick and twisted her head, but he held her still and laid his lips against hers.

That's all it amounted to, and yet their subtle movements sent a weakness through her. Her limbs lost their strength, her eyes drifted shut, and the world started spinning again . . .

His lips released hers. "Now," he said softly, "I wish to

point out that you hit me first. I was merely claiming that for which I'd paid."

Her eyes flew open. "That isn't fair!"

"Is it not? I would have thought I could claim a great deal more for a life-threatening attack like that."

Deirdre decided it would be much wiser to accept his terms. "Yes, damn you, it is fair. Now, let me go."

"Such language," he teased as he released her.

He started to brush off her habit. She pushed him away.

"And that wasn't a hit," she warned him quickly, "so don't pretend otherwise. When I do hit you, Don Juan, you'll know it. I'm going to knock your block off. I've been practicing."

Devil lights appeared in his eyes. "Then I must certainly make sure the kiss is worth the price."

Deirdre wished she'd learn to keep her mouth shut.

She also wished there were a way of getting back on Charlemagne without him touching her, but she had to allow him to toss her into the saddle.

He took no advantage.

What she disliked most about Don Juan, thought Deirdre, was that he was so devilishly unpredictable. What would he do, or not do, next?

As they resumed their ride, Deirdre knew she had just escalated their teasing contest. The terrible thing was that she was beginning to enjoy the game.

When she remembered that she'd asked Lucetta to call him off, she actually felt a tickle of disappointment.

Lucetta requested that her son visit her in her room before dinner that evening. He arrived looking carelessly, perfectly elegant and kissed her cheek. "Let me hazard a guess. Deirdre has asked you to tame the savage beast."

She shook her head fondly. "Something like that. Marco,

what are you about? She has told me that your engagement is a sham. I confess I am disappointed, but if she has another love, I can accept it. Why cannot you?"

"Do you conceive of me fighting for her heart? Hardly."

She watched him carefully. "Then what are you doing?"

"Amusing myself," he said flippantly, but then sobered. "No, that is not quite honest. It is true that I find it compulsively amusing to challenge Lady Deirdre's spirit. Do you know she is something of a spitfire? I suspect you do. But she is a banked fire. I am just stirring her up, summoning some flames. I won't hurt her."

Lucetta frowned. "Can you be sure of that, Marco? I suspect she is somewhat vulnerable. She does not think too highly of herself as a woman. Lady Harby is in many ways an admirable lady, but her fearsome efforts to turn Deirdre into a beauty have served instead to convince her that she is a hopeless case."

"Then she needs to be shown otherwise. Physical beauty is not particularly important in a woman."

"Strange," mused the dowager. "I have not heard your name linked to any except beauties."

"But what of my more discreet adventures . . . ?" His smile was secretive and, she thought, the kind that would ignite the iciest female heart. It made her want to slap him.

"Don't play your games with me," she said briskly. "I will not tell you to leave Deirdre alone, but I do tell you to watch what you are about with her."

"I don't hurt women, *Madrecita*. Except Genie, of course." Before Lucetta could comment on that, he asked, "Do you know why Deirdre wants to marry this Howard Dunstable?"

"She has hardly spoken of him. Before your betrothal, she never mentioned him or I would hardly have put forward her name. I suppose she must be in love."

He picked up a black silk rose from her dressing table and contemplated it. "Do you really think so? She does not appear to me to be a woman in love. My instincts tell me that he hasn't warmed her soul." He studied his mother, then fixed the rose in the black ribbons of her cap and frowned slightly. "I wish you would wear colors. I remember how beautiful you looked with a red rose in your hair."

"I was more than ten years younger then, dearest. Besides, I will mourn your father all my days, and why would I want to look beautiful except for him?"

He leaned down and hugged her. "So be it. Perhaps I just don't understand the true dimensions of love. As for Deirdre's mathematician, I reserve judgment until I meet him, but I suspect her marriage to him would be an error."

Lucetta shook her head. "How can you make such a judgment, Marco?"

"How can I not? Does she appear to you like a woman afire with love?"

The dowager had to admit that Deirdre didn't. "But, dearest, you must realize some women simply do not have those fires within them."

"Nonsense," he said crisply. "And if there are such women, Deirdre Stowe is not one of them. I am already toasting my toes." At the look in his mother's eyes, he shrugged. "I simply intend to open her eyes to life, so she will look at Dunstable and make a clear-sighted decision. She is far too fine to be wasted on a selfish nod-cock."

"He's supposed to be a brilliant mathematician," she pointed out.

"Perhaps he is, but in all other ways I am sure he is a nodcock."

Lucetta turned away to hide her amusement, and some burgeoning hopes. "But think, dear. If you should manage to shake Deirdre free of her attachment to this man, what can you do but marry her yourself?"

"I wouldn't mind," he remarked carelessly. "She still seems as good a choice of bride as I am likely to find."

"Quiet, plain?" Lucetta queried. "An adequate lottery ticket?"

He grinned. "Well, plain at least. And highly likely to win me at least a minor prize in the lottery of life."

As he escorted her down to dinner, Lucetta enjoyed the realization that her handsome son was experiencing the first twitches of jealousy. It was so strange an emotion to him that he hadn't even recognized it as yet.

❧ 5 ❧

THE NEXT DAY Deirdre took swift action to ensure she couldn't be dragooned into another outing with Everdon. She rose early and announced she was visiting Anna. The truth was, she intended to visit Howard "on the way." She needed a practical antidote to Latin charms, and the three-mile walk to the village of Missinger St. Mary would not come amiss either.

Her mother had never made objection to her visiting Howard as long as his housekeeper was present, and Deirdre chose to assume that the rules had not changed. She knew that the latest housekeeper, Mrs. Leadbetter, was likely to be there. The taciturn woman never left the house except on market day.

It was this matter of housekeepers that had first brought Deirdre and Howard Dunstable together.

They had met at a musical evening at the Durhams', where she had seen him sitting alone. Deirdre was not in the habit of approaching handsome young male strangers, but she felt sorry for his isolation and so sat beside him and engaged him in talk. She discovered he had just moved to Missinger St. Mary, where he had inherited a cottage from an uncle. The uncle had also left Howard sufficient income to pursue some mathematical inquiries close to his heart.

That evening he had even attempted to explain his work, but she hadn't understood much of it. It had been a relief when he'd turned to more everyday matters and told her of his difficulty in finding a good woman to cook and clean for him.

His uncle's housekeeper, Mrs. Islip, was apparently most unsatisfactory. Deirdre had eagerly offered to help. There had been no thought of romance in her head, just kindness and the reward of being useful to such a gifted man.

Her first step had been to try to work out the problems between Pammie Islip and Howard, for Pammie was known to be a good worker. Deirdre persuaded them both to stick with the situation for a while, and encouraged Pammie not to sing or chatter when Howard was working. She began to make frequent visits to the cottage to see how matters were progressing and to give Pammie a chance to gossip.

She came to value her visits to Foote's Cottage very much indeed.

Sometimes Howard was deep in his work, and so she did not disturb him. Sometimes however, if he was pondering matters in his head, he could be persuaded to take some exercise, thus allowing Pammie to sing as she scrubbed. Usually on these occasions Howard would talk to Deirdre of his work—not conversing, but thinking aloud. Deirdre did not mind. By listening to his musings, she began to understand a little more about his studies; enough to convince her that she was in the company of a genius. It made her feel so useful and important to take everyday cares from his shoulders, and then, of course, he asked her to marry him.

The subject had arisen on one of the occasions when she'd persuaded him out for a walk. They had been walking through a field of playful lambs on a perfect spring day, walking in silence, for Howard had been lost in the numbers in his head.

But then, perhaps he had not been working through equations, for he had suddenly said, "Do you know, I think we should marry."

Deirdre had been startled but thrilled. She had said something silly, like, "Oh, Howard!"

"Good. You're a very useful person to have around." Then, disconcertingly, he returned to his calculations and did not mention the matter again.

A few days later Deirdre reminded him of his words, but tentatively, thinking they might have been a fevered dream.

"Yes, of course," he said. "What's the matter? Have you changed your mind?"

"No. But, Howard . . . if we are to marry, you must speak to my father."

He appeared more concerned with the search for a particular piece of paper than with her words. "Surely you can do that, Deirdre."

"Tell my father we want to marry?" she said blankly.

"Yes. Why not?"

"But he'll want to speak to you about it."

"Why? You can tell him all the details. My income is just over a hundred pounds per annum and I own this cottage. I assume you have a portion, but if you want it tied up for your use and for any children, I don't mind."

Deirdre was thrilled at this evidence that he wasn't marrying her for her money, but protested again. "It's not how these things are done, dearest . . ."

"Forget it, then," he said testily. "Where is Babbage's

letter? Has that damned woman been meddling in here again?"

Deirdre was taken aback, but was definitely not about to forget it. She had finally found her destiny and life's work; she was to be helpmeet to a modern Newton.

That night she awkwardly informed her parents of the matter only to see the notion firmly squashed. Her father, she rather thought, would have gone along if Howard had come up to Missinger and stated his case. Her mother, however, was dead set against it.

"I know you've been hovering about him, and I haven't interfered, Deirdre. I judge you to have the sense not to go wrong. Marry him, though? He's a lawyer's son with a hundred a year."

"I love him, Mama."

"Nonsense. He's just the first man to pay you any interest. Creeping around as you do in white and gray, no one even sees you. We're off to London in a few weeks. With some nice bright clothes, and a bit of a push, we can do better than Mr. Dunstable."

Begging had not moved Lady Harby one inch, but so confident had she been of Deirdre's coming success that Deirdre had been able to strike the fateful bargain—that if she returned from London unengaged, she could marry Howard.

Even Howard had admitted it to be a clever plan, and everything had been in hand until Pammie Islip's patience wore thin. Another opportunity presented, and so she gave her notice the very week before Deirdre was to leave for London.

With so little time to find a replacement, and Lady Harby demanding Deirdre's attention for other matters, Deirdre was forced to settle for Nan Copps, though she feared the woman would not do. Everyone knew Nan was a slovenly worker. As feared, Deirdre had returned from London to find Mrs. Copps had moved on to other pastures, muttering about unreasonable buggers.

Howard had been scathing about the woman's inadequacies and quite helpless to cope on his own. It was doubtless this domestic crisis that had muted his reaction to Deirdre's mock betrothal; he was much more concerned about edible food and clean floors.

It had been a blessing from heaven that Mrs. Leadbetter had been looking for a place, old Colonel Grieve having finally died. Mrs. Leadbetter had an excellent reputation for hard work, won prizes for her cooking, and was known far and wide for her taciturnity.

Deirdre felt that at last she had accomplished her task. When she thought that in weeks she would be free of Don Juan and have won her mother's consent to her marriage to Howard, she could not imagine how life could be sweeter. She sang as she walked down the village street, and waved cheerily at the blacksmith, who was taking a moment away from the heat of his forge. He grinned and touched his forelock.

Foote's Cottage was a square stone building fronting onto the main street of Missinger St. Mary, with a long garden in the back running down to the river. Bert Rawston took care of the garden, and it showed a riot of flowers, herbs, and productive vegetables. Deirdre was quite proud of talking Bert into doing the extra work, for he had a number of gardens in his care. Howard, she feared, scarcely noticed how lovely his garden was, for he was not an outdoors person. Perhaps she should point out to him that all the delicious fresh vegetables served up by Mrs. Leadbetter were the results of Bert's skill.

With Bert and Mrs. Leadbetter, and Jessie Cooper doing

the laundry, Deirdre knew she had made Foote's Cottage a perfect home. She looked forward to living there one day soon.

There was a handsome green front door with a porch over it, but Deirdre went down the side path to slip in the back door. She snipped a spray of mint from the plant by the door, and bruised it between her fingers for the aroma.

Sinewy Mrs. Leadbetter was in the kitchen, scrubbing a pot.

"Good morning, Mrs. Leadbetter. Isn't it a beautiful day?"

"Aye, it is, milady," said the woman sourly. "You'd think some folk would go out and enjoy it."

Oh dear. Deirdre took another fortifying sniff of the mint. "Mr. Dunstable does become caught up in his work, I'm afraid. Perhaps I can tempt him out for a walk."

"See if you can, if you please, milady. I've not been able to dust that room for three days."

Oh, poor Howard, thought Deirdre. He really must take better care of himself.

She tiptoed through to the front parlor, which was now called his study, and found her beloved hunched over his desk. He was a tall man, but she feared his study posture would soon rob him of some of his height. He pushed his hand into his honey brown hair to hold it away from his eyes. His hair really did need to be cut, but it wasn't a matter Deirdre could arrange for him. Not, at least, until they were married.

In fact, she rather liked his hair long. It seemed dashing and piratical. She often thought of running her hands through it, and once or twice she had found the nerve to touch it.

The hands holding his hair back and wielding a stubby pencil were broad, with spatulate fingers. They had always impressed her as strong and practical, but now, disconcertingly, a vision of long brown fingers intruded; strong hands pulling her up to the top of the barrow . . .

She coughed.

Howard looked up with an angry scowl on his square-jawed face, but then it lightened. "Oh, hello, Deirdre. I thought you were that woman. I'm glad you're here. I can't seem to make her understand how I like my eggs."

She smiled and walked over to him. "Poor lamb. I'll speak to her."

"I don't think she'll suit, you know. She doesn't seem to pay attention to my wishes at all. Perhaps you should find someone else."

Deirdre kept her smile with an effort. "I'm not sure there is anyone you'd like better, love. Just be patient. Once I've disposed of Don Juan, we can be married and I'll manage your life to perfection."

He rewarded her with a smile, one that crinkled the corners of his blue eyes in a very appealing way. "I know you will. Has he turned up yet?"

"Yes, two days ago."

"How long do you think it will be before you can break the engagement?"

"I don't know. Unfortunately, it's up to him to do something embarrassing."

"You could always go off somewhere with him and then cry rape."

Deirdre stared at him. "Howard, I could never do such a thing!"

"Don't see why not. Everyone would blame him, and you wouldn't have to bother about your reputation because we'd get married. If I didn't hold it against you, no one else would. I really can't stand Mrs. Leadbetter much longer."

Deirdre was appalled by his plan, though touched by how much the poor lamb needed her. That was it, of course. This must all be so hard for him. And he frequently didn't really think of the implications of his words unless they were to do with mathematics.

"We'll have to keep her on, even when we're married, Howard," she said. "But I'll be here to manage her for you."

"I suppose that will have to do."

Deirdre sighed. It was terribly stuffy in the room, for he would not have the windows opened because of the noise from the street. No wonder he was out of sorts. There was also a film of dust on the woodwork that must offend Mrs. Leadbetter deeply.

"It's a lovely day, Howard," she said brightly. "Wouldn't you like to go for a walk?"

He glanced out of the window, appearing surprised to see the sun. "Yes, I suppose. Let me just finish this . . ." He turned back to his papers.

Deirdre sat quietly to wait, taking her needlework from her reticule. The baby's gown again, one intended for her sister Susan's next child. As she worked, she drank in the peaceful intimacy and imagined that she and Howard were already married, and that this work was intended for her own child. How lovely this would be.

Or at least, it would be lovely on a cold winter's evening, with a big fire roaring in the grate. Today really was too fine a day to waste indoors. Poor lamb. He worked too hard.

Howard did look wonderful poring over his papers, though, a sunbeam touching his hair to gold. Deirdre wished she had a talent for portraiture. He was in shirtsleeves, as he usually was to work in warm weather, and wore no cravat. His hair was tousled and curled against his collar.

Definitely piratical.

She noted with concern that he was growing a little pudgy and round-shouldered from so much book-work. She must tempt him to more exercise. If only he would ride, but he had no taste for it. He didn't shoot, or fish. Not that angling gave much exercise, but it would get him out in the fresh air. Cricket? No, she could not imagine it.

He showed no sign of breaking from his work soon, and she wondered whether she dared remind him she was here.

He was scribbling notes, and checking them against other sheets. She knew if she looked, they would be covered by incomprehensible squiggles. She had asked him once to explain them, but he had assured her it was impossible that she understand.

She had always thought herself good at numbers until she'd met Howard. Numbers in Howard's world were something far removed from anything she had learned in the schoolroom.

He was constantly engaged in communication with three other mathematicians, in a kind of friendly rivalry, and he had presented his work to learned gatherings and written about it for publication. Most people in the area did not realize the caliber of person they had in their midst.

Deirdre had certainly never dreamed of marriage with such a man.

The ticking clock told her she had been sitting here for nearly an hour, with Howard showing no sign of leaving his work. Food might do the trick. She tiptoed out and helped Mrs. Leadbetter to make up a tea tray. As she did so, she tried to mediate on the eggs.

"It's more than a body can manage, milady," the woman stated. "They must be boiled. Not a scrap of the white must be runny, and not a scrap of the yolk must be 'ard. How's a body to tell? And besides, anyone who knows anything worth knowing knows that new eggs cook different from old. How's a body to tell?"

"Perhaps he would take them poached, Mrs. Leadbetter."

"Not 'im," said the woman, with a marked lack of respect. " 'As to be boiled. And toast with no scrap of black on it. How am I, all alone, to watch the eggs and 'old the toast, and never get a touch of black? Do you know, he won't eat bread? He reckons the toasting makes it easier on the stomach. I don't know where he gets all these notions."

Deirdre sighed as she picked up the tray. "Please do your best, Mrs. Leadbetter. Perhaps we can hire a girl to help you here."

As she made her way back to the study, Deirdre wondered whether it was true that toast was more digestible than bread. She was sure if Howard said so, it must be. How strange.

She put the tray down on a table near his desk, braced for irritation. But when he looked up, he smiled. "Do I smell fresh scones? Lovely lady."

Deirdre wasn't sure if he meant Mrs. Leadbetter or herself, and chose not to ask. She poured the tea as he liked it, with very little milk, and basked in his approval. "Please try to be more flexible about the eggs, Howard. Think of Mrs. Leadbetter's baking. She wins awards every year for her pies."

He rubbed his nose and gave a disarming grin. "They are very good. I'll try not to be a bear. It's just that a satisfactory breakfast sets a man up for the day."

Deirdre smiled back, feeling mistily that everything was perfect after all. "When we're married," she promised, "I'll cook your eggs myself." She didn't let the fact that she'd never boiled an egg in her life weigh with her at all.

She received another approving smile and became happily lost in visions of serving him perfect eggs, and baking perfect cakes, and receiving perfect smiles . . .

When Howard finished his tea, however, she found she still could not persuade him to a walk, and had to take her leave. Very daring, as she passed his seat, she leaned down and dropped a kiss on his cheek.

He caught her hand. "You into this kissing business?"

Deirdre went red. "Well, as we are engaged . . ."

"I suppose." He cupped the back of her head with his strong hand and pulled her down. His lips were hot and wetly parted, and the pressure on her neck hurt.

He let her go, and grinned. "There. I don't want you thinking I'm a cold fish, not with a Don Juan creeping around and pestering you. Off you go."

Deirdre left the cottage in a daze.

He was jealous. That was wonderful.

She hadn't liked that kiss.

That wasn't wonderful.

It had just been the position, she told herself. He hadn't realized how awkwardly he had pulled her head down to his. Next time, hopefully, they would be in a better position. Standing, sitting, lying . . .

Her mind strayed to the marriage bed and she felt distinctly uneasy. That, she told herself, was normal for an innocent young maiden. It was quite possible Howard was an innocent, too, which would account for his clumsiness. They would learn about it all together.

With that settled to her satisfaction, Deirdre went off to visit Anna, so that her excuse for absence would not be entirely spurious. She found that Anna had driven into Glastonbury with her mother, however, and so turned her steps home.

What a shame she hadn't been able to drag Howard away from his books and papers. It was a lovely day for a walk. The sky was clear, but a breeze cooled the air. Summer was at its best and flowers rioted everywhere, filling the air with perfume. Even the tang of the dung spread in a nearby field was a good country smell. Insects hummed about their business, and birds sang all around. Every one of God's creations, including Deirdre, was happy to be alive.

She strode over the fields toward the house, singing along with the birds, planning her happy future.

Then she heard hoofbeats.

She knew who it would be without looking, and turned with a shiver of unease.

He was cantering toward her on the gray, a welcoming smile on his face. But then he kicked the horse to speed.

In seconds, he was charging at her like a cavalry officer!

With a gasp, Deirdre backed up a few steps, but she was in an open field. It would be ridiculous to run. He surely wouldn't ride her down . . .

Deirdre held her place, her heart in her mouth. He held the horse straight at her.

At the last minute, he let go of his reins, swayed sideways, and scooped her up.

She screamed as everything whirled around her, then she found herself perched in front of a laughing Don Juan as his horse cantered onward.

She hit out at him. "You crazy fool! Who the devil do you think you are? The hero of a Minerva novel?"

His teeth were wonderfully even and white as he laughed out loud, "I'm Don Juan! I've always wanted to do that. Of course, it would be even better if there'd been a dragon poised to devour you."

Deirdre growled as she struggled to arrange her skirts with decency. They were all over the place, showing her shift, her stockings, and even a glimpse of a garter. "If there was a dragon, I'd feed you to it," she snapped. "Put me down, you idiot."

He made no move to obey, but he slowed the horse. "I think dragons are only interested in virgins."

Deirdre glared at him. "Put me *down!*"

"No. I'm taking you home."

"I have legs, Lord Everdon."

He looked down and grinned. "So I see."

Deirdre gritted her teeth and wriggled harder until her skirts were decent. "A *gentleman,* my lord, would not have remarked on that fact."

"True, but he still would have enjoyed the view."

"In fact, a *gentleman,*" continued Deirdre, "would never have thrown me over his saddle bow in the first place."

"No? It seems to happen a lot in books. But if you were truthful," he pointed out, "you'd acknowledge that I didn't. Didn't you appreciate the skill in the way I landed you right side up?"

"No." Deirdre looked away and tried to pretend this ridiculous performance wasn't happening, that he wasn't even there. The attempt was futile when she was sitting on his hard thighs and his arm was strong about her.

He spoke softly into her ear. "Perhaps we should do it again, so you can admire my technique."

"Once you put me down, my lord, you'll not have the chance to capture me again."

He laughed. "I'm almost tempted to see what means you would use to avoid it. But discretion prevails. I have no doubt you'd succeed. I think you would succeed at anything you set your formidable mind to."

This casual praise so overwhelmed Deirdre that she relaxed against his chest. "Good, for I have set my mind to marrying Howard."

They were approaching the stable lane. "Were you off visiting him then?"

"Yes."

"And singing on the way home. He must have made you happy."

"He always makes me happy."

"Lucky man," he said softly, almost wistfully, his breath brushing warm over her cheek. She could not deny that it sent a shiver down her spine. She told herself that to be in the same situation with Howard would give her even greater pleasure.

They were just short of the stable yard gate when he halted the horse. Before she could act to evade it, he captured her chin, and a light kiss tickled her lips. "You did hit me," he said.

"Under great provocation."

But Deirdre wasn't angry. She thought perhaps Everdon was coming to understand just how she felt about Howard. When he really understood, she knew he would cease his teasing and leave her alone.

That afternoon Lord Everdon sought a word with Deirdre's mother. He was coming to understand Lady Harby and admire her shrewd common sense, but he still winced at first sight of her boudoir. It had been assembled impeccably in green and cream—doubtless by one of her daughters—but subsequently "improved" with cushions, cloths, and ornaments in a rainbow of brash shades.

It was overwhelming, but it was so unabashedly in keeping with the lady's wishes that he was inclined to be charmed.

He came straight to the point. "I think it would be wise to invite Mr. Dunstable here for dinner, Lady Harby."

"Invite him here, Everdon? Why, pray? I have no time for the man."

"From what I hear, he is a rival for Lady Deirdre's hand."

She looked a little uneasy. "I don't deny, my lord, that Deirdre has an interest in that direction, and him in her. It will not be allowed to come to anything."

Everdon wondered what course Lady Harby had planned to prevent the marriage if the worse came to the worst. He had no doubt she had something in mind. She and Deirdre had much in common. "If that is the case," he said, "nothing is served by keeping them apart, and I would like to meet the man."

"Ah," she said, nodding. "Know your enemy, eh?"

"Not at all," he replied innocently. "It is just that I have an interest in mathematics."

Lady Harby snorted. "Have it as you wish, my lord. But I won't single out Mr. Dunstable. We'll have a small party in your honor—just dinner and an informal hop." She smiled. "I gather Dunstable don't dance, and has no conversation intelligible to lesser mortals."

Everdon returned her smile. "I see we understand each other perfectly."

Lady Harby fixed him with a look. "Do you intend to have her, then?"

Everdon took a pinch of snuff. "I consider us engaged to marry, Lady Harby."

"That's not what I asked. I reckon she's told you of that foolish agreement I made with her. If you cut loose, she'll end up with Dunstable."

"Lady Harby, I cannot possibly cut loose and still be considered a gentleman."

Lady Harby did not look particularly reassured.

She announced the plan for the evening entertainment at dinner, casually adding that Mr. Dunstable may as well receive an invitation.

Deirdre was startled, and immediately suspicious. After the meal when, as usual, Everdon joined the ladies ahead of the Stowe men, she asked, "Do I have you to thank for Howard's invitation, my lord?"

Deirdre had been sitting on a window seat near an open window that looked out onto a small courtyard full of roses, and he had joined her there. The wall beneath the window was covered by climbing roses, and the perfume filled the air.

"Now, why would you think I am to blame?" he asked.

"Blame?" Deirdre echoed warily. "Why blame?"

"An unfortunate choice of words. I confess, I expressed an interest in meeting the man, that is all."

"Why?"

"Why not? I have an interest in mathematics."

"I find that hard to believe, my lord."

He met her severe look with a pained one. "What will I have to do to bring you to use my name, *querida*? Any of my names."

Why did a foreign language have such an effect on a lady's heart? Deirdre looked away and said, "Is that an endearment? Please don't. And as for your names, I cannot feel comfortable with that level of intimacy."

"Perhaps if I were to kiss you more often . . ."

She turned back sharply, then laughed. "I am beginning to get your measure, my lord. You delight in teasing. I will not dance to your tune anymore."

He said nothing, but leaned out of the window and plucked a spray of rambling roses—soft cream, blushed with pink. He carefully broke off the thorns, then said, "Stay still."

Somewhat to her surprise, Deirdre did as she was told, and stayed still as he tucked the roses into the fillet that held her hair on the top of her head. The feel of his fingers against her scalp was perhaps the most intimate sensation she had ever experienced, more so even than his kisses.

She looked up at his intent face. "I'm sure that looks very silly."

His eyes met hers, and only inches away. "Allow me to know about these things. It looks very well indeed." His hands were still raised, and she felt his fingers travel through her hair. "It is as delicate as silk."

"That's one way of describing it," she dismissed, seeking a brisk tone. "It's far too fine. It's impossible to do anything with it without hours of curling, and heavy applications of oil."

He caught a tendril and curled it around his finger. "I can think of any number of things to do with it, where such ministrations would be decidedly out of place."

Deirdre stared at him, dry-mouthed. "My lord . . ."

"Don."

"Don . . . please don't . . ."

"Don't what?"

Deirdre sidled away, so he had to release her hair. "You know perfectly well what. It is outrageous for you to be saying such things to a woman who is betrothed to another."

"But at the moment, you are betrothed to me."

"A mere fiction. It is unconscionable of you to trade on it."

"But I'm not," he said simply. "I've flirted like this with many women, none of them a future wife. If we really were betrothed, we would have progressed rather further, I think."

She looked at him in shock. "*What*? But you surely wouldn't . . . I certainly wouldn't . . ." She caught herself up.

"Oh, you outrageous man! How do you make me speak of such things?"

His eyes laughed at her. "Do I make you? Then let me take you further." He captured her hand and kissed it, and would not let her flee. "My dear innocent, there is a world of sensuality between that kiss on the hand and the marriage bed, and the betrothal period is the ideal time to explore it. Otherwise, the marriage bed is likely to be somewhat of a shock. You should be traveling these paths with your mathematician."

He turned her hand and pressed a warm kiss into her sensitive palm.

Deirdre snatched her hand free, heart racing. "And probably would be," she said tartly, "if it were not for you."

But in the months since that unorthodox proposal, Howard had made no move to develop intimacy between them until today's clumsy kiss. They clearly did need practice.

The other men were coming into the room. "No," said Everdon softly. "If you had come back from London free to marry Howard, you would not be exploring gently. You would have rushed into it. I don't recommend it."

Deirdre rose, glad of an excuse to interrupt this discussion. "I hardly think your recommendations on marriage are of great value, my lord."

It was only when she was a few steps away that she realized he might take that as a comment on his failed marriage rather than his rakish life. She turned back, an apology on her lips.

His smile was wry. "There you may have a point, *mia*." He carried on, "The advice is sound all the same. Don't we learn best from our mistakes?"

Deirdre was achingly aware that she had hurt him. Before

she could make amends, however, her brothers hailed Everdon to go off to play billiards, and she was glad when he agreed.

Then Henry said, "Why don't you come, Dee? I'd bet you could give even Everdon a match." He turned to the earl. "She's demmed good."

Everdon looked at her. "Are you, indeed? More surprises. Care to accept a challenge?"

Deirdre had been avoiding the billiards sessions, but she didn't see why Don Juan's presence should deny her all pleasures. "Very well, my lord."

As they walked into the hall, which housed the billiard table, he said, "What prize to the winner?"

Deirdre chose her favorite cue and blocked his next move. "I'm not playing for kisses," she said firmly.

"Very well. How about honesty?"

She turned. "What?"

He appeared suspiciously innocent. "The winner is allowed to ask one question and receive a completely honest answer."

On the surface it seemed innocuous—Deirdre did not think she had any dreadful secrets—but she distrusted the look in his eyes.

"Very well," she said. "But only as long as the question is not of an indelicate nature."

"So be it." His quick acceptance revived all her suspicions. What question did he have in mind?

He shrugged out of his tight-fitting jacket and set up the balls. Deirdre found his shirt-sleeved state, even though he retained both waistcoat and cravat, almost as stirring as she found Howard in that condition. Really, the fact that a lady only ever saw a gentleman completely and formally dressed had alarming consequences.

They tossed and he won the right to start. She soon saw he was very good. His action was smooth, he knew just where the balls should contact for greatest effect, and he was pretty good at planning ahead for future shots.

Not as good as she was, though. As soon as she had a turn, she quickly overtook his score. The turn changed a few more times, but she always pulled ahead. This wasn't surprising, for she was concentrating mightily. Deirdre had become quite certain that she did not want to have to answer Lord Everdon's question, whatever that proved to be.

When she executed her winning shot, however, he showed no particular chagrin. In fact, he applauded. "Bravo! Where did you learn to play so well?"

She knew she was flushed with victory. And relief. "I just practice a great deal. I find it a soothing discipline. I never went away to school—none of us girls did—so I've had plenty of opportunity to practice. My father and Rip taught me a little, but mostly I've taught myself."

"It's clearly a natural talent. Very well, ask your question."

Deirdre was taken aback. In her determination not to have to answer his question, she had given no thought as to what she would ask him. To her dismay, the only questions that came straight to mind were decidedly indelicate.

How many women had he made love to?

How old had he been when he first . . . ?

"I need time to consider," she said quickly. "Is it allowed that I claim my prize later?"

"Very well." His lips twitched. "*I* don't mind indelicate questions, you know . . ."

Deirdre quickly called upon her brothers to make up teams—she with Henry, Everdon with Rip. It proved to be an even balance, and the contest went on until the clock struck eleven and Lady Harby shooed them all off to bed.

Deirdre lay sleepless for many hours that night, wondering just what question to ask Lord Everdon.

And what question he had wanted to ask of her.

6

THE NEXT MORNING Deirdre took her mother's list and wrote out the invitations to the party. Then she hurried off to Foote's Cottage to deliver Howard's herself. She was fortunate, and caught him at a moment when he had attention to spare.

"At Missinger?" he said, reading the note. "But I thought your parents wouldn't let me cross the threshold."

"You know Mother doesn't approve of our plans, Howard. But I'm sure this is an acknowledgment that she will soon have to give in." Deirdre thought it best to leave Lord Everdon's machinations out of it.

Howard tapped the letter thoughtfully against his fingers. "Or that she believes she's won." He suddenly smiled at Deirdre in a way that reminded her surprisingly of Lord Everdon. "We'll have to make sure she realizes her mistake, won't we? You *are* very important to me, Deirdre."

He opened his arms, and Deirdre went into them, bursting with happiness. "Oh, Howard. I do love you."

"That's good," he said, and kissed her again.

This was much more like the time Everdon had kissed her by the barrow. There were strong arms around her, but this time she wasn't struggling. His mouth was more forceful.

More . . . sloppy . . .

Deirdre had to repress an urge to struggle. Where was the magic of love? Nothing weakened her limbs, or made her want to surrender to more.

When he'd finished, she felt only a surge of relief.

Despite her efforts, he recognized her discomfort, but it did not upset him. He grinned. "What's the matter, little innocent? Am I too bold for you? You were the one wanting kisses."

"Yes, of course," she said, dragging up a bright smile. "Of course I want to be kissed by you, I mean. See how flustered you make me? It's just I am unused to such things."

"So I should hope." He turned her and sent her on her way with a playful but stinging slap on the behind. "Off you go. I have work to do."

Deirdre found herself out in the street in a daze, resisting the urge to rub her bottom. What on earth had come over Howard?

She headed back to Missinger, thinking that her world became stranger and stranger every day. Lord Everdon made her feel unlike herself, and now Howard, the fixed point of her life, was changing.

In their extraordinary conversation yesterday, Everdon had said she and Howard should be exploring sensuality in preparation for their marriage. Presumably this was what he meant: that it would take time to grow accustomed to each other, to come to enjoy kisses and . . . and other things.

He had clearly been wise when he'd spoken against a hasty marriage. It was certain that she could not look forward to the marriage bed when she hadn't yet learned to enjoy Howard's kisses.

On the other hand, honesty compelled her to admit that she had quite liked Everdon's kisses from the first. What did that imply?

She tussled with this conundrum for quite some time, walking briskly along the path back toward Missinger.

It was, she decided at last, a simple matter of practice. Lord Everdon's skill came from misbegotten expertise, and therefore was nothing to be proud of. Howard's roughness doubtless came of inexperience, and was therefore proof of virtue. Both she and he would improve their skill in time.

She nodded as she walked. That explained it perfectly.

Perhaps she could make an aphorism of it, and distribute it to all young ladies.

Beware the man who kisses well.

She could embroider it on a banner to be hung at Almack's. She chuckled at the notion as she crossed the narrow bridge spanning the stream that divided the fields from the park.

"Happy again? Oh, lucky Howard."

Deirdre started. She looked down and saw Lord Everdon sitting by the stream below the bridge. Today the noontime heat had brought him to dispense with not just his jacket, but with waistcoat and cravat as well. Like Howard, he was in his shirt and breeches, and looked positively dangerous. He had even loosened his cuffs and rolled them up his muscular forearms.

"I am on my way back to the house," she said quickly.

He captured her eyes. "Come and keep me company." When she hesitated, he added, "Please, Deirdre."

Deirdre found herself walking down the gentle slope to sit by his side. At least she had the sense to leave three clear feet of grass between them.

"Now," he said, "tell me what makes you so happy today."

Deirdre knew it would be fatal to her composure to look at him. She concentrated on tossing daisies into the fast-flowing stream. "Just a general satisfaction with life."

"That must be very pleasant."

He sounded almost bitter. Deirdre sacrificed more daisies. "Are you not satisfied with life, my lord?"

"Not particularly. I want a bride, and it appears I do not have one."

She couldn't really believe he was hurt to lose her, and yet his words touched her heart. "I'm sorry. But the resolution is up to you, my lord. You have merely to disgrace yourself."

There was a movement. She glanced quickly sideways, but he had merely lain back, hands under head, to study the infinite blue of the sky. "I must confess, I am shirking my duty, Deirdre. I find myself liking your parents. I don't want to embarrass them by making them throw out a guest."

Once having looked, Deirdre found herself trapped. She hardly listened to his words for studying his body.

It looked even more impressive in the horizontal than in the vertical, and the tanned column of his throat, the vee of exposed muscular chest, were having a quite extraordinary effect on her nerves.

Then she absorbed what he had said and gathered her wits. "Are you going back on your word?" she demanded.

He glanced sideways, and even his dark eyes and lush lashes took on a new power at this angle. "No, *querida*. But I thought it might go easier if we all transferred to Everdon. Well, perhaps not your father—I know how it is with him. But your mother would accompany you, I'm sure."

She distrusted this move. She distrusted all of this, even as she felt him entangling her, just as a spider entangles a juicy fly. She inched a little farther away. "Why should we move? Are you trying to get me away from Howard?"

"Why should I do that?" he asked with apparent honesty. "He can come, too, if he wants."

"Howard? Come to your home?"

He rolled on his side, head supported on hand. "Why not? I have no objection to your courtship. The main advantage of moving this farce to Everdon Hall, Deirdre, is that I know all the available females there. I will be able to stage a spectacle to suit our requirements with no danger of hurting anyone, or creating more of a stir than we would wish. It will also mean that when you sever our connection in outrage, you will merely have to order your coach and depart while I stand gloomily by the door bewailing what I have lost. We need never meet again."

That caused a strange pang. "You are forgetting your mother," she pointed out.

It seemed he genuinely had. "I will try not to come between you. I'm sure you can find ways to meet without encountering me. But then, perhaps not. You will be married, won't you, and doubtless will not visit London again. I would have no objection to your visiting Everdon when I am absent if your Howard will permit it . . . But then there will soon be children . . . Marriage does tend to change things."

Deirdre was taken aback by this vision, even though it in no way departed from her expectations of her marriage. "Yes, of course marriage will change things," she said firmly. "It is not even clear where we will live. We will be at the cottage for a while, but Howard is talking of taking up the offer of a place at Cambridge. He does not want to teach, however."

Everdon appeared genuinely interested in her plans. "What he needs, surely, is a quiet place in which to think. The cottage seems ideal."

"It is, except that it is on the street, so he has to keep the windows shut. That is unhealthy. And it will be small when . . . if . . ." She broke off in confusion.

"When you have children," he supplied easily. "You will be able to buy something larger with your funds."

Her reaction was sharply defensive. "Howard is not marrying me for my money."

"I didn't say he was, Deirdre. But it will be pointless to stay in a cottage when you have half a dozen children."

Half a dozen children? Deirdre had thought in terms of one sweet, smiling cherub of a baby. Now she was prey to a vision of trying to keep the peace at Foote's Cottage with a horde of little ones underfoot. She'd seen enough crowded cottages to worry her.

"Lie back," he said softly.

"*What?*" Deirdre was jerked out of her concerns.

"I'm not suggesting anything dangerous. Don't you ever lie back and look at the sky?"

Deirdre did, when alone. Was he seriously suggesting that she lie down on the grass with him?

"Lie back and study the arch of heaven with me, Deirdre . . ."

He was.

Deirdre thought, however, that this was not an attempt at seduction, but simply what he proposed—a study of the sky.

Somewhat hesitantly she eased back onto the grassy slope, keeping the space between them. A quick sideways glance assured her that he wasn't planning an attack, but had rolled onto his back and was looking up at the sky. He'd put his hands to cushion his head, which made his shirt gape further open . . .

Deirdre hastily turned her own eyes upward.

The sun, fortunately, was behind them a little, and so

there was little glare. There were no clouds today, and no trees just here, and so all she had to look at was infinite blue.

He quoted, "'I have learned to look on nature, not as in the hour of thoughtless youth; but hearing oftentimes the still, sad music of humanity.'"

"Wordsworth," she identified with pleasure, and made her own offering from the same poem, one composed on viewing the remains of Tintern Abbey. "'And I have felt a presence that disturbs me with the joy of elevated thoughts . . .' I'm afraid we have no such noble ruins here."

"There is Glastonbury not so far away."

"True. Do you know they say the young Jesus visited Glastonbury with Joseph of Arimathea? Some even say that the Holy Grail is to be found there."

"Is this the land of Arthur, then?"

"And of Guinevere."

"Who married a worthy man," he said softly, "but was carried off to destruction by the fevered power of romantic love . . ." After a moment, he carried on. "The stars are still up there, you know. They never go away, but we are blinded to them by the gaudy brilliance of the sun."

"But the moon sometimes prevails. Sometimes it can be seen in the daytime."

They lay there looking up at the sky and talking of wonders and little things. For a while they were free of social conventions and polite inhibitions. Then Deirdre looked sideways and found he was no longer looking upward. He was looking at her.

Her heart fluttered madly at the experience of being eye to eye with a man in the horizontal.

"Don't," she whispered.

"Don't what?"

"Look at me like that."

"Like what?"

"As if I were beautiful."

"You are."

"Don't mock me!" She would have scrambled up, but he rolled, and a strong arm and leg trapped her there. Caught in that heated prison, she stared at him, fearful yet excited.

"I do not mock," he said, his rich dark eyes flashing with anger. "Beauty is more than the shape of a jaw, the curve of a cheek. But if you want beauty," he said, and touched her cheek with heated softness, "your skin is beautiful. It has the luminous pallor of a pearl." A finger traced down her forehead, nose, and chin. "And your profile is delightful. I don't suppose you study your profile much. And your voice charms me. It sparkles with your spirit." That wandering finger traced her lips. "And your smile, *mi corazón*, your smile touches my soul."

His face was inches from hers, and his limbs pressed her down. This was more intimacy than Deirdre had expected in a lifetime.

She reached for a defense, any defense. "You can't pretend I blush prettily."

"No," he agreed with a smile, "but it still delights me to make you blush. As you are blushing now."

Her heart was doing a mad dance in her chest, and she felt hot from head to toe. "Oh dear," she said. "You're flirting with me, aren't you?"

His smile turned brilliant. "My dear Deirdre, don't you know?"

"No."

"Ignorance can be dangerous. Perhaps I should instruct you. This, little one, is rather more than flirtation. We are being very wicked."

At that, she made a tentative move to push him off, but her arms seemed to have become as weak as water. "Why are you being wicked with me? You don't really want to seduce me, I know you don't."

He eased his weight over her an alarming fraction further. "Don't I?"

"No," she said, but instead of a firm declaration, it came out as a squeak. "If you did, we'd have to marry."

His knuckles traced the secret underside of her jaw, and that brief touch sent excitement throughout her body. "I wouldn't mind marrying you, Deirdre Stowe."

"Oh dear."

"So if you decide that you and Howard would not suit, you mustn't hesitate to take me up on my offer."

That brought her back to reality. It reminded her that this was just a clever game he played, mostly fueled by boredom. She'd had a lifetime to learn she was not attractive to men, and to this man she was just a lottery ticket, no better, no worse, than any other.

Her strength came back and she pushed more effectively, though she failed to move him. "Get off me! I'm sure you'd like to save yourself the trouble of finding another ticket in the lottery of life, my lord, but I can't oblige."

He laughed, but she saw with amazement that she had made him blush. "My damn mother." Then he sobered and looked deep into her eyes. "No, Deirdre, you are by now far more than a lottery ticket to me."

Under that gaze, Deirdre weakened again. "I am going to marry Howard," she said firmly. "Let me up, please."

This time he obeyed and rose smoothly to his feet. He held out a hand to help her up, but she rose unaided. The farther she stayed away from Don Juan, the better.

He picked up his jacket and waistcoat but did not put

them on. He climbed the bank beside her with them slung over his shoulder. "You will, of course, do just as you wish," he said calmly, as if those heated moments had never occurred. "I am looking forward to meeting Mr. Dunstable."

Deirdre looked back once at the slope, where flattened grass showed where they had lain. The grass would soon spring back and the evidence would be gone, but an impression of this interlude would linger in her heart.

She glanced uneasily at Don Juan. "You are not to be cruel to Howard."

"I am never cruel," he said, and they strolled back toward the house as if they were a conventional lady and gentleman, who would never dream of behaving in any way even remotely improper.

Thoroughly alarmed by the event, Deirdre disappeared in the afternoon to visit Anna. Though Anna had not had the opportunity of going to London, she was much more worldly-wise than Deirdre, and much more practiced in the art of flirtation. Perhaps she would be able to make sense of what was happening. The visit to Starling Hall would also serve the excellent purpose of removing Deirdre from any occasion of further wickedness.

"I don't know how I came to permit it!" she declared to her friend, after having confessed all.

"Well, it wasn't so very terrible," said Anna, who was bright-eyed at the story. She giggled. "It wasn't even as if you broke your mother's law, and let him get his hands inside your clothing."

Deirdre stared into space. "But it felt as if I did," she whispered.

Anna shivered in delight. "I can't wait to meet him. If you truly don't want him, can I have him?"

This drew a laugh from Deirdre. "What a wonderful solution to everyone's problems! But I'm afraid nothing can come of it, Anna. Once he disgraces himself to set me free, your parents will not look kindly upon his suit."

Anna's bright blue eyes twinkled. "Unless he disgraced himself with me."

"Anna!"

Anna was rather pink, but she carried on. "It wouldn't have to be anything too outrageous. If you were to find us in a heated embrace, you'd be within your rights to return his ring, and he'd be obliged to marry me."

Deirdre didn't know why she felt such violent aversion to the plan, but she did. "I couldn't let you make such a sacrifice. And what about Arthur?"

She expected Anna to laugh at that, but her friend sobered. "There is that." She fiddled with her blue satin sash in untypical bashfulness. "There's no comparison in wealth or rank," she said, "but I rather think that in time, I may want to marry Arthur. It would be a pity to be already married to someone else."

"It certainly would," said Deirdre. "And hardly fair to Everdon. He's had one wife run off with another. He deserves to do better this time."

"Yes," said Anna thoughtfully.

"Anna, why are you looking at me like that?"

"Looking at you?" asked Anna innocently.

"*Looking* at me. I know that look. You're planning something. Oh, Anna! Have you thought of someone here with whom Everdon can disgrace himself? I really would prefer not to have to go to his home."

But Anna shook her head. "No, I haven't thought of anyone. Now, tell me who will be at the party . . ." And no amount of urging could bring Anna to confess to plans, or secret thoughts.

Deirdre left Starling Hall an hour later, little wiser as to the ways of rakish men, and with no preventative techniques in her armory. She also now had to wonder what Anna might be up to. Hadn't it been Anna who had locked Deirdre in the buttery with John Ransom, because she thought it would promote a romance?

When Deirdre arrived home she disappeared into the safety of her boudoir, which was more precisely her sewing room. She needed the discipline of her art and the security of privacy.

She took out the watercolor sketches of her wildflowers, and considered how best to portray them in silks. She knew the effect she wanted; that of wildflowers scattered on a dark green velvet cloth. She wanted them to look real, almost as if they could be picked. She began to set stitches in a scrap of fabric, trying out different approaches and different threads . . .

A knock on the door made her glance at the clock. She had been here for two hours. Her mother must have sent up some tea. She called permission to enter and returned to her work.

It was the heaviness of the step that alerted her. She looked up sharply as Everdon put the tray down on a table.

"What are you doing?" she asked, alarmed.

He grinned. "Bringing your tea, milady. And mine. I encountered a maid sent on the mission, commandeered the tray, requested an extra cup, and here I am." He lifted the china pot, just like a worthy matron. "How do you take it?"

"A little milk only, thank you," said Deirdre weakly. Then she added, "Is this how you do it?"

"Do what?"

"Tangle women in knots. By always doing the unexpected?"

He considered it. "I don't think I've ever planned to tangle anyone in knots. Doing the unexpected makes sure people won't grow bored, but I do what I do because I want to." He brought over her tea, and a plate of cakes. "I invaded your sanctum for two reasons, Deirdre. One, because you are hiding from me here. Two, because I want to see your work." He placed her tea and cake on the small table by her elbow, but then stayed to study her embroidery.

Deirdre wanted to shield it, unused to this attention, and sure he would scoff. She had progressed to embroidering over little silk pads, to raise the petals and give them contours.

Everdon looked thoughtfully from the sketch to the velvet. "How real that looks. You have the colors exactly, and even the shape. I feel as if I should be able to pluck the bloom, able to smell the perfume of it. I beg you, don't make it into a cushion. No one will ever dare to lean their head on it."

He moved away to sit and drink his tea.

Deirdre glowed under his praise. Part of her was saying that he only flattered to manipulate her, but she had confidence in her work, and she knew this was good. She took a piece of seedy-cake and nibbled on it.

"Thank you," she said. "As to its use, I don't know what I shall do with it."

"Then give it to me as cloth, and I will decide."

When she looked at him in puzzlement, he said, "It was agreed, was it not, that this was to be my price for setting you free?"

Deirdre took a fortifying draft of tea. "Only if you behaved well in the meantime, my lord."

"And I haven't? In what way have I misbehaved?"

But Deirdre knew that talking about these things was extremely dangerous. She changed the subject. "Have you spoken to my parents about a visit to Everdon Park, my lord?"

"Yes, and your mother is completely agreeable." His lips twitched mischievously. "I confess, I neglected to tell her that I would be inviting Dunstable."

Deirdre almost choked on a mouthful of cake. "You can't do that!"

"It's amazing what one can do if one is shameless enough. Are you all right? Should I slap you on the back?"

Deirdre regained her breath and waved him away. "But she'll be most put out!"

"Put out enough to forbid you to marry me?" he asked hopefully.

Deirdre sobered at that. "I have come to realize that breaking this engagement is going to be unpleasant for you, Everdon. I'm very sorry. If I *could* act in your place, believe me, I would."

He considered her thoughtfully. "As to that, Deirdre, if you were to be found in Dunstable's bed, you would doubtless end up at the altar with him within the week."

Deirdre's mouth went dry and she wondered how she could have made such a foolish offer. He was correct, though. It was the obvious solution. How on earth was she going to bring herself to do such a thing? What would Howard have to say about it . . . ?

Everdon laughed. "I'm teasing, little one. I wouldn't expect you to act in such a way. For a hardened *roué* such as I, it is a mere nothing."

Deirdre's heart calmed, and she felt more kindly toward him than ever before, for she knew that despite his words, it would not be easy for him. Though his reputation was well known, she gathered that his affairs had always been conducted with discretion. She tried to imagine what anyone would feel—*roué* or not—at being caught in intimate disarray . . .

"By the way," he said, "if you don't object, your brothers are going to come along, too. There is a prizefight scheduled between the famous Molineux and a man named Carter. Everdon Park has the blessed fortune to be within a three-hour drive of Twistleton Gap, and so has become a Promised Land."

"No, of course I don't mind," said Deirdre, though she felt rather dazed. "Have you persuaded Father to come, too?"

"No. Do you want me to?"

She raised her brows. "I'm tempted to set you the task, merely to see you go down to defeat, my lord. Only the sacred duty to marry off his daughters ever drags him away from his land."

He smiled and drained his cup. "But I would merely have to ask his advice on the management of my estates . . ."

And Deirdre had to accept that would do the trick.

He gathered up the plates and cups, and assembled them neatly on the tray. Deirdre was astonished that he was so willing and able to play the maid, and that he was willing to go with so little teasing accomplished. "Are you leaving, Everdon?"

"It was my intent. Do you not wish me to?" He invested the question with layers of sultry meaning.

"Yes, of course I do. I want to return to my work."

"I could read to you as you sew. Byron? Mrs. Edgeworth? Wordsworth?"

She could not deny that the notion held some appeal. He had a lovely mellow voice, and the only thing she did not like about her work was the isolation. That was why she had loved her time with Lucetta, for they had been able to work and chat without interruption. Here at Missinger, however, Lady Harby took it for granted that Lady Everdon wanted to spend time with her, and Lucetta was too polite to disabuse her of the belief.

To encourage Everdon, however, would be perilous. "No, thank you, my lord. I just need peace and quiet to work."

He picked up the tray. "I will arrange a suitable room for you at Everdon Park, then. Until later, my dear."

He was gone. That had, all in all, been an unexceptionable visit. Why, then, did Deirdre feel as if it had pushed her world even more out of tilt?

The next day, as Deirdre dressed for the party, she reminded herself that she had always enjoyed these informal local affairs. They were quite different from the horrible London balls and soirées, for here she knew everyone, and most of her neighbors were delightful people. Even the few who were unpleasant, one had learned to put up with.

On this occasion, however, Deirdre found herself approaching it with anxiety.

Having been brought to the point, Lady Harby had gone all the way and invited Howard to dine. He would at last have the opportunity to win over her family, and if he could do that, Everdon would not have to put himself in an embarrassing situation.

In view of the importance of the event, Deirdre's nerves were in a terrible state. It *had* to go perfectly.

Lady Harby had insisted that Deirdre wear one of her new gowns, and so Deirdre and Agatha had spent the best part of the day stripping a pink and purple dress down to simplicity. To her surprise, the gown looked very well when all the trimming was removed, for the cut and material were excellent. Deirdre had embroidered some flowers on the bodice to cover marks left by the trimming, and Agatha had fashioned a sash of an ivory shawl.

The effect was as attractive as possible.

Deirdre hoped Howard would be as presentable.

As Agatha dressed her hair and worked up a few curls with the iron, Deirdre was tempted to rush down to Foote's Cottage to check that Howard was dressing appropriately, and that he had not forgotten the occasion entirely.

Everdon was also keyed up for the evening. Tonight he would meet his enemy. He chose a particularly fine embroidered waistcoat and a fawn cravat, wondering just what approach would be most effective.

"And how are you liking Missinger, Joseph?" he asked his valet.

"A very pleasant, well-run establishment, milord."

"I would imagine the staff think highly of Lady Harby."

"Indeed, though she does have her funny ways."

"And what of Lady Deirdre? Is she well liked?" He had said nothing specifically to his valet about his marriage plans, but it didn't take genius to work out why they were making this visit.

"Very well liked, milord." The valet cleared his throat. "I gather the older girls were inclined to be a bit sharpish with the staff, and the young men are a little wild, but no one has any word to say against Lady Deirdre. Always most considerate of the staff, she is."

"As I would expect." Everdon put the last touches to the arrangement of his neckcloth. "I gather Lady Deirdre has shown a certain interest in a young man. A Mr. Dunstable." He stood so Joseph could ease on his perfectly fitting jacket and caught an uneasy expression on the valet's face.

"I'm sure there's nothing to it, milord."

"But what is known of this man?"

Joseph smoothed the jacket, and brushed away a minute speck of fluff. "As to that, milord, he's considered to be an odd fish. He's a stranger, of course, and you know country people, but I gather he's had trouble finding a housekeeper on account of his finicky ways."

"Finicky?"

"I don't know any particulars, milord."

"Any other views? Any gossip?" Everdon kept the valet under surveillance in the mirror and saw the way his lips tightened.

"I don't hold with thirdhand tales, milord, but as you have an interest, so to speak . . . it's said he visits a lady called Tess Biggelow. A widow."

Everdon turned. "And would this Tess perhaps be the local convenient?"

Joseph colored. "Yes, milord."

Everdon shrugged. "It would be absurd of me to be holding my nose at that, wouldn't it? You have the right of it, though. I have a particular interest in Lady Deirdre, so if you hear anything else that could have a bearing on the matter, I would appreciate your passing it on."

He turned and surveyed himself, considering the suitability of the pearl pin in his neckcloth. "Perhaps the diamond, Joseph. The large one."

Joseph brought the glittering pin, and Everdon fixed it carefully. A trifle gaudy for country wear, but . . .

No, it would not do. He changed it for the pearl.

At the door, he turned. "By the way, Joseph, Mr. Dunstable will be here tonight."

Joseph stared at the door after his master had left, considering that news. Very strange. He'd learned that Lady Deirdre's attachment to Mr. Dunstable was not approved by the family and that the young man was not received.

It was certainly true that the local people did not think much of him, but it was also true that village folk took time to warm to foreigners. He could be a worthy gentleman.

After all, though nothing was said directly in front of Joseph, it was clear the staff at Missinger had their doubts about the Earl of Everdon, too. They knew his reputation and couldn't believe he meant to deal honestly with Lady Deirdre, whom even the fondest of them admitted to be fusby-faced.

Joseph, however, had listened to people who had known Lady Deirdre from the cradle, and decided she was just what the earl needed. He was also watching his master's behavior, and was very hopeful, very hopeful indeed.

Tonight was the first time in years the earl had dithered about his appearance.

❧ 7 ❧

Deirdre was already in the drawing room with her family when Everdon entered. She was forcibly struck by how handsome he looked. She immediately prayed that Howard had taken some care over his dress so that he not be entirely outshone.

When Howard arrived—just after Sir Crosby and Lady Durham and their offspring, and just before the Misses Norbrooke—she breathed a sigh of relief. None of his clothes had come from a London tailor, but his dark pantaloons and jacket were unexceptionable; his hair had been trimmed, and brushed into a fashionable style; and his bow to her mother was perfect.

Deirdre saw her mother react to all this quite favorably. Lady Harby always had a soft spot for a handsome man. Just possibly, tonight would solve all their problems.

Howard looked rather lost, though, poor lamb. Deirdre went to greet him and drew him over to talk to her father.

"Mathematician, eh," said Lord Harby, who wasn't in the

best of moods. He never was when forced into purely social occasions and deprived of his agricultural reading. "What use is it, eh?"

Howard wasn't thrown. "A clearer understanding of mathematical principles has proved useful in the past, my lord, and will in the future. Without geometry and trigonometry, most of our buildings would be impossible, and road building would still be a primitive art. The financial management of the nation demands a sophisticated knowledge of calculation, as does navigation and trade. Warfare would be hindered without the application of mathematics to artillery work."

Lord Harby perked up. "D'you say so? What good is it in agriculture, eh?"

"I am unfamiliar with the subject, my lord, but I am sure any number of calculations are necessary to plan crops and feeding patterns for cattle. It is quite possible that mathematical principles would enable better prediction of future production . . ."

Deirdre slipped away to help welcome more guests, ashamed of the fact that she was surprised that Howard could defend his discipline so well. He would have her father on his side in no time. Lord Harby always appreciated a man who knew his stuff, and one who could apply his science to agriculture was a sure winner. After all, her father had no particular attachment to Everdon. She hadn't seen them cozied up discussing silage and drainage.

Instead, Everdon, she noted, was showing his true colors as a social butterfly, and was surrounded by a crowd of guests. As the stranger in their midst, he was naturally of prime interest, and most knew of his reputation. The young women were visibly fascinated. If they were looking for the wicked Don Juan of Spanish literature, however, they would be disappointed. Everdon was behaving impeccably.

Deirdre well knew that if in the future any of these wor-
thies should meet someone who made a disparaging remark
about Don Juan, they would retort, "All a load of nonsense.
Met the fellow at Missinger and found him a very tolerable
sort. Thinks just as he ought on all subjects."

How confusing he could be.

Deirdre's sister, Eunice, Lady Ostry, had come to the event
with her husband. She, of course, was a typical Stowe—tall,
handsome, and with lush blond hair. She, too, clearly admired Everdon. Deirdre saw them flirting, but it must have
been in an unexceptionable manner, for her husband was
standing by and didn't seem to mind.

On the other hand, Deirdre had always thought Lord Ostry a rather dim-witted man for all that he was a handsome
six foot with a commanding air. One of the first things to appeal to Deirdre about Howard had been the power of his
intellect.

Seeing Everdon raise Eunice's hand for a significant kiss,
and her sister preen and blush, Deirdre had the alarming
thought that the earl might choose *Eunice* with whom to create a scandal. That certainly would throw the fat in the fire.
Didn't he realize Ostry was just the sort of blockhead who'd
call him out?

She took three steps in their direction, intent on preventing disaster. Then she remembered that Everdon was going
to stage the affair at his own home, and that he would be far
too wise in these matters to risk disaster. She diverted her
steps toward the Misses Norbrooke, two delightful old ladies.

She didn't know why she had developed this tendency to
protect Don Juan; a more fruitless occupation was hard to
imagine.

She was to go in to dinner on Everdon's arm—her mother

insisted on it—and so he came to her as the meal was announced.

"Your swain has your father entranced," he remarked. "Is it possible that I will not have to exert myself?"

"I was wondering the same thing. But there is still Mother to consider. Father will rule her if he feels strongly enough, but he has to feel *very* strongly for it to be worth his while."

"I rather thought she mellowed a little toward Dunstable, so the cause may not be entirely lost. He's remarkably good-looking, by the way. I thought he'd be hunched and bespectacled."

Deirdre warmed to him. "He is, isn't he? Not that I let such things count with me . . ."

"Clearly. I'm even better-looking."

Deirdre looked up, prepared to argue, but decided it would be both foolish and ill founded. Simply on the basis of looks, Everdon could beat Howard all hollow.

As Everdon seated her, she said, "Howard will not take sufficient exercise or fresh air. I do try to encourage him."

Everdon took the seat beside her. "My dear Deirdre, don't carry his entire life on your shoulders. His course is his own, and the consequences also."

"But surely we should care for those we love. Am I to watch him harm himself and do nothing?"

A strange shadow passed over Everdon's face. "Perhaps not. But there is a limit to what we can do."

Then the green soup was being served and they could address their food.

The meal progressed smoothly, though Deirdre noted that Howard was improperly silent. He had been seated between the two Misses Norbrooke, which was doubtless a deliberate maneuver of her mother's, as he could have little in common with them. Even so, he should be exerting himself.

Everdon was managing to converse with Lady Durham, a rather silly and mean-spirited lady who could find something to carp at in everything.

Deirdre sighed. Howard was doubtless lost in calculations, poor lamb. If she were closer, she'd try to kick his shins.

Then she saw Miss Georgianna Norbrooke turn and start a purposeful conversation with Howard, and was grateful to the old lady. Even if Howard contributed little, it made him less conspicuous.

From her left, Everdon said, "I am sure he can manage a simple dinner without your focused gaze, Lady Deirdre." It had the edge of a rebuke, and Deirdre colored, aware that her behavior was almost as gauche as Howard's.

"He gets lost in his thoughts, that's all." She faced Everdon and summoned her social skills. "Did you have a good day's angling, my lord?"

"It was too hot for much, but it's always pleasant to pass time near the water."

She glanced at him, and his eyes trapped hers in an awareness of that magical interlude by the stream. Then, in a disastrous lull in the conversation, she heard Howard say, "Will you please stop chattering at me?"

She looked over to see Miss Georgianna turn away, red from the neck up. After a horrified hush, everyone plunged into talk to cover the moment, but Howard was left completely in peace.

Deirdre knew her face was as red as poor Miss Georgianna's. She wanted to hide under the table. A hand firmly covered hers. "You are not responsible for what he does," said Everdon.

"But . . ." Then she collected herself. "But I encouraged him to come tonight when I know he doesn't like chatter, and much prefers to be alone with his thoughts."

She risked another look at Howard. He seemed oblivious of any problem.

"Forgive me for mentioning it," said Everdon, "but doesn't his love of isolation make him a poor candidate for marriage?"

"For some, perhaps. I, however, am very quiet also, and generally much prefer to be left alone with my needlework." Deirdre addressed herself resolutely to her pork, praying that she wouldn't cry, and wishing this whole horrible evening were over.

As the time approached for the ladies to leave the table, Deirdre began to worry about what would happen to Howard. She was unsure what gentlemen did when left alone, other than drink more wine and take snuff.

Everyone was most fond of the Misses Norbrooke.

Could it possibly come to a duel?

She leaned sideways toward Everdon and whispered, "Look after him, please."

His brows rose. "Wouldn't you rather I killed a dragon or two, my fair maiden?"

She just looked an appeal at him, and he shrugged. "I don't know if anyone will say anything, but I suspect he's pretty impervious to words. I'll make sure no one draws his cork." He took her hand under the cover of the table, and his thumb stroked her sensitive skin. Sensitive skin? She'd never thought of her small, capable hands as sensitive.

She looked at him warily, wondering what price he was going to exact for his assistance.

"Don't worry," he said. "I'll take care of everything."

In some way it seemed to encompass more than the matter of Howard's rudeness.

Then her mother rose, and Deirdre had to abandon Howard to his fate.

In the drawing room over tea, everyone fussed over Miss Georgianna, but the cause of the problem was not mentioned, or the reason for Howard being there. Deirdre, however, felt as if she wore a sign around her neck declaring her to be an accomplice to the crime.

Like Saint Peter, she would probably have denied any connection if challenged.

She went to sit safely by Lucetta, but the dowager's attention was soon claimed by another guest. Then forthright Mrs. Treese, Anna's mother, took the seat on the other side of Deirdre.

"That Everdon seems a fine man," she said. "Can depend on a man like that to do the right thing."

"Do you think so?" said Deirdre, longing to raise his reputation as Don Juan. She could not do it, however, when sitting beside his mother.

In any case, she had to accept that Mrs. Treese was right. One could depend on Lord Everdon.

"Any gel would be lucky to get a man like that," said Mrs. Treese. Having made her point, she went on to discuss her younger son's military career now Napoleon was safely on Elba.

When Mrs. Treese left her side, Deirdre's sister took her place. "What a fool you are, Dee," Eunice said frankly. "I hear you're shilly-shallying over snapping up Everdon. I wish I'd had the chance."

"I'm not shilly-shallying at all," said Deirdre. "I'm definitely not going to marry him."

Eunice raised her finely curved brows. "Are you that much of an idiot? You'd give up the Earl of Everdon for that horrible scholar?"

Deirdre reddened. "He is not horrible. He just doesn't like these events."

"Then he shouldn't have come."

"I talked him into it." But Deirdre remembered that he hadn't been reluctant at all.

"Unwise to talk men into anything," said Eunice. "A word from me, Deirdre, don't think you can change a man. You have to take them as they are, and if you want Dunstable as he is, your wits have gone begging." She rose and drifted onward, an image of matronly wisdom, though she was only twenty-one.

Deirdre told herself that anyone would be cynical after two years of marriage to Lord Ostry, though in fact Eunice appeared to be happy with her choice.

Of course Deirdre wanted Howard just as he was. She didn't want to change him in any significant way. She'd just encourage him to do a little more exercise, to go out and about a little more. She'd ensure he visited the barber regularly, and that his coats came from a better tailor. Once they were married, there'd be time for him to explain his work, then when she understood it, she might be able to help with all that tedious figuring. Then there would be more time for other things . . .

Deirdre hastily escaped her thoughts by joining Anna and the other young people. It was not really an escape. The talk was all of Everdon.

". . . so handsome," sighed Jenny Durham. "I could have swooned when he smiled at me."

"He touched my hand," said Anna, adding dramatically, "I felt it all the way to my heart!"

Deirdre rolled her eyes at her friend, knowing Anna was exaggerating in fun. She tried not to acknowledge that she had felt that way in very truth.

Jenny eyed Deirdre jealously. "Rumor says he's courting you, Deirdre."

"You know rumor," Deirdre responded. "Would you like more tea, Jenny?"

"I think he is," the girl persisted. Blond and pretty, she was used to being the local belle. She considered the homage of the eligible men hers by right. "I saw the way he was looking at you. Amazing really when . . ." Then she recalled her manners and did not say what she was thinking. "And I thought you were going to have to settle for that Dunstable man. Oh," she said with embarrassment, for she was not actually a cruel girl. "Yes, please, I would like more tea."

Deirdre summoned a maid to bring it.

Anna said, "It must be exciting to have such a man under your roof, Deirdre. He has such soulful eyes."

"Soulful," scoffed Arthur Kealey. "Makes him sound like a dashed spaniel. I don't know why you girls will go on so."

"I doubt he has a soul at all," said Deirdre. "Be warned, Anna. It is his habit to flirt with any female who crosses his path. So guard yourself."

"If he pesters you, Anna," said Arthur stoutly, "you can depend on me to take care of it."

Deirdre and Anna shared a look at this absurdity, but Deirdre could see Anna was rather touched. Such devotion made her a little sad, though she couldn't think why.

Mary Kingsley giggled. "I don't mind if Everdon flirts with me."

"Mary," said Deirdre. "I thought you were pledged to Captain Hawksworth." How could she get them off this subject?

"So I am," said Mary unrepentantly, "but that doesn't bar a little harmless flirtation."

"I doubt Lord Everdon is harmless," said Deirdre darkly.

Her three female companions leaned forward. "Do tell."

Deirdre had never been so glad of anything in her life as the sudden entrance of the other gentlemen. This appearance was rather speedy, and she suspected she had Everdon to thank. He gave her a knowing look and the trace of a wink. She noted that there seemed to be an invisible circle around Howard.

For a moment Deirdre was reluctant to go over to Howard, to associate with him before the company. She conquered the cowardice and crossed the room to where he stood. He smiled slightly, but seemed abstracted.

She couldn't just stand there like a sentry, and so she began to talk cheerfully of a sequence of light topics. He made no response. Did he even hear her? She stopped abruptly, afraid he would make matters worse by telling *her* to stop chattering, too.

He had done so before, she remembered. She had been making small talk as she'd been trained—for a silence is a terrible thing—and he'd said something like, "Do stop chattering so. I'm thinking."

She hadn't taken offense, for it seemed a reasonable request. She had found it something of a relief to be with someone without the need to talk, and she'd learned how to judge whether he was receptive to conversation or not.

But this was a different kind of occasion. Even her father acknowledged that one could not retreat into a private world when in company. Oh dear, what was she to do? She glanced over at Lord Everdon, but he was engaged in lively conversation.

Her silence finally seemed to penetrate Howard's thoughts. "What's the matter, Deirdre? Are you giving me funny looks, too? I suppose it's because of that old biddy. But really, she was going on and on about her cats. I have no interest in cats. I was devising what could be a most interesting development on Müller's mechanism. You see, if one were to consider . . . But you wouldn't understand."

No, Deirdre didn't understand, and about far more than

geometry. "Howard," she said firmly, "Miss Norbrooke would consider it rude to leave you alone. It is polite at a dinner to talk to the people on both sides."

"I know that," he said brusquely. "But I can't be expected to abandon a significant insight for a discussion on fleas." Then Howard smiled, that quirky, boyish smile that tugged at her heart. "Was I very rude? Should I go and apologize? I could claim to have a toothache."

"Oh yes," Deirdre said in relief. "I'm sure that would be appreciated."

She watched surreptitiously as he went over and bowed to the frosty Misses Norbrooke. In moments the generous ladies were fluttering about him, doubtless offering their patent remedies. Word spread, and Lord Harby gruffly ordered a glass of brandy and ordered Howard to swill it around his mouth well before swallowing. Having followed orders, Howard announced that he was now free of pain, and thanked everyone for their kindness.

The company was now restored to happiness.

Except Deirdre. She thought it all terribly underhand.

Everdon appeared at her side. "A piece of advice," he murmured, his eyes dancing with amusement. "Always check their teeth before you buy."

"There's nothing wrong with his teeth," she snapped, before catching herself. "Oh, go away. This is all your fault."

"Now, how do you work that out, light of my life?"

Deirdre glowered at him.

He shook his head. "Next part of the course—accepting compliments. Anyone would think you'd never received any before."

"I haven't. Except about my embroidery, of course. Though few people really appreciate . . . And my horsemanship . . . I . . . don't deserve—" She bit off that statement.

"At least you realize how absurd that is. You truly are the light of my life—for the moment, at least. I rise each day with enthusiasm, wondering what new wonders it will bring, and they all stem from you."

Deirdre grasped one phrase. "For the moment?"

"But of course. This can only be a fleeting paradise, alas. You are going to marry the man with the bad teeth. Mine are excellent." He stretched his lips in an exaggerated grin.

Deirdre cast a harried look around. "Do stop it!"

"Ah, I hear new arrivals. We will shortly progress to the dancing. I claim the first set."

Deirdre had little choice but to accept.

The dancing did not start for some time, for the new guests had to be welcomed and greeted by all, and gossip had to be exchanged. Within the hour, however, the music began and two sets were formed.

Deirdre was surprised to see Howard partnering Anna. Doubtless Lady Harby had dragooned him into it, for they were a little short of men, but she was surprised he had allowed himself to be dragooned.

He must be on his best behavior for her sake. That warmed her heart.

He was in the other set, so she could not watch him closely, but he appeared to dance quite well.

Everdon, as she knew, danced superbly, and she found the same magic occurring as had happened at the Ashby soirée— she danced well, too. She knew she was capable of it, but generally in public she felt so awkward that she became stiff and clumsy. She knew it was because deep inside she felt so plain as to be almost a figure of fun. Look how surprised Jenny Durham was that a man like Everdon would even consider her as a bride.

With surprise, Deirdre realized that the burden of being

plain had been absent for days. This evening as she dressed, she had not once looked at herself in the mirror and wished her nose were more delicate, or her lips better defined. True, she had been fretting about Howard, but there was more to it than that.

As she joined arms with Everdon and spun around, her eyes met his, and he smiled as if he knew. "'But oh, she dances such a way/No sun upon an Easter day/Is half so fine a sight.'"

Then she was off dizzily into the arms of Sir Crosby.

As soon as the dance was over, Howard was at her side. "If I must dance, it will be with you, Deirdre. You dance surprisingly well."

She was thrilled that he'd noticed, but said, "Only one dance, though. Then you must partner the other ladies and make a good showing. I think you made a favorable impression on Father."

"He shows some sense for a farmer."

"A *farmer?*" she echoed.

"That appears to be his only occupation, so he is a farmer. He did show an interest in my work, but I could wish people appreciated knowledge in other than practical terms. If there were any justice, rich men would sponsor mathematics and science rather than useless painting and sculpture."

"Are not a great many people investing in the sciences and engineering?"

"In the hope of profit," he sneered. "They never get their noses out of the trough."

This was too much. He was as bitter as Lady Durham. "Really, Howard!" Deirdre exclaimed.

He started. She realized she simply did not speak to him that way. For a moment he looked angry, but then his boyish smile appeared. "Are you going to be cross with me, too?" he asked plaintively. "I thought you were different. I thought I could speak the truth with you, and not have to play silly games . . ."

The music started again, and Deirdre was saved from the need to reply, but not from the need to think. Was it her duty to listen to everything without debate, or was he being unreasonable? Of course he wasn't. She wouldn't want him to pretend with her.

As they took their places in the set, she smiled lovingly at him.

He smiled back and said, "It's a pity you aren't taller, for we don't suit very well as partners. I don't suppose you will grow now, though."

For some reason, Deirdre couldn't capture the lightness and ease she had found with Everdon, though he was almost as tall as Howard. Somehow her arm always seemed to be stretched, or their steps did not quite match. And yet Howard wasn't a bad dancer.

"You need more practice," he said at one point, and she had to agree.

When the dance was over, she slipped away, making an excuse of having broken a slipper ribbon, but in fact prey to a great weight of misery. She couldn't understand how everything was going so wrong.

In her room she wiped away some tears and bathed her eyes with cool water. All she needed was red, puffy eyes to add to her catalog of poor features.

She looked at herself in the long mirror and saw the creature she had known all her life—thin, flat-chested, with a long face, too large a nose, formless lips, and dull hair. Her elegant pink gown did not make matters worse, but no gown could make matters better.

Sometimes with Everdon she felt different—not beautiful,

but attractive, charming, clever. It was just a foolish game he played, and she the fool to be taken in by it.

She turned away from the depressing vision.

As to her misery, it was her foolishness to have encouraged Howard to come to such an event. He might have made no protest, but she knew he had only come to please her. She had to accept that he would never move with ease through social waters, but such occasions would play little part in their married life. Their evenings would be spent at home, she working on new styles of embroidery, he working on his whatever-it-was geometry . . .

Deirdre had a sudden disturbing thought.

She had always considered Howard's intense application to his work as being part of this stage of his life, while he was working on whatever it was that would make him famous. But Eunice had a way of being right about things, and she must have more knowledge of men than Deirdre. What if Howard actually *liked* his present way of life—imperfect eggs excepted—and wanted it to continue forever?

For fifty years or so . . .

Deirdre hastily changed her slippers and returned to the party, where music and chatter would block out her thoughts. As soon as she walked through the door of the impromptu ballroom, her hands were seized by Everdon. "There you are. We are to give a demonstration of the waltz."

"What? But I've never danced it in public."

"Never?" he said. "Oh, poor Cinderella. But surely you know the steps."

He was pulling her farther into the room. She resisted. "Yes, Mama made me learn . . . but I only ever danced with Monsieur Decateur."

"Good enough. Ready?"

She was in his arms. The music started before she had a

chance to think, never mind make a serious objection. She fell into a panic with no idea what to do.

"Step back," he said, and smiled at her with a carefree confidence in himself and her that would have made flying possible.

She stepped back and began to recall the moves, aided by his firm direction. They spun and swayed, alone together among others. She gazed into his eyes because then she could forget everything else—what she was doing, what people were thinking . . .

His eyes shone with approval. "I knew it. You waltz like a flower in the breeze."

She tried to remember her insight in her bedroom—that she was plain and awkward, and always would be. "That's because I'm so thin," she said.

"No, it's because you are lit from within. Smile for me, light of my life."

Deirdre smiled.

It was at that moment that Mark Juan Carlos Renfrew, Earl of Everdon, commonly known as Don Juan, decided he had to marry Deirdre Stowe. He'd felt the notion hovering for days, but had hoped it would fade, for he foresaw that it would bring him great trouble.

Now, however, the joy in her face would allow no escape. He knew, without doubt, that no other man would make her glow, especially not Howard Dunstable.

She would be quietly miserable with her mathematician, even if she never realized it. If she didn't marry Dunstable, she would almost certainly live her life as a quietly miserable spinster. Without someone to encourage her, she would cease twirling on the top of hills, or lying to look at invisible stars, or dancing the waltz like an apple blossom in the breeze.

Yes, he would have to marry her. The question was, how to bring her to agree.

Everdon knew it would be fatal to press her at this point. He didn't doubt that if he employed the full range of his arts, he could befuddle her, or even seduce her, but it would not solve his problem. If he inveigled her into bed, he could carry her to the altar on a wave of guilt, but he didn't care to contemplate the married life that would follow. Deirdre would not soon forgive that kind of scheming.

No, in the end she would have to see Dunstable for what he was, which would be easier to bring about at Everdon Park.

Their waltz ended to enthusiastic applause. Everdon focused one of his most powerful smiles on Deirdre and kissed both her hands with all the artistry at his command. He registered her flustered blush with satisfaction, then handed her without de-mur to young Kealey, who was most anxious to try the dance.

After a quick assessment, he bowed before Anna Treese, whom he judged to be the sort of girl who acted like a gig-gling ninny but who in fact had a very sensible head on her shoulders. Besides, he'd seen the looks she flashed at Arthur Kealey. Though the young man might not realize it, his fate was sealed.

She was not naturally a good dancer, but by the time the music stopped, she was beginning to get the idea.

"Goodness, Lord Everdon," said Anna, fanning herself. "That is not nearly as easy as you and Deirdre made it ap-pear. I am not sure I care for it, either. It seems quite strange to have a man holding one so."

"I think in time ladies will become accustomed, Miss Treese. It is also the case that your feelings may change with your partner."

She endorsed his earlier assessment by flashing him a very shrewd look. "I suppose that could be true."

He gently took her fan and plied it for her. "The waltz offers delightful opportunities for flirtation."

"Really?" she said, with a teasing look. "But you hardly spoke to Deirdre, my lord."

"But then, I am hardly at the flirtation stage with Lady Deirdre, am I?"

"Perhaps you should be."

He raised a brow. "You mistake me, Miss Treese. Deirdre and I are beyond that."

She was not put out, but smiled. "Good."

Arthur Kealey appeared jealously at their side, and Everdon put the fan into his hands. The young man looked at it blankly. Anna bit her lip on a smile, and chose to look demure. Everdon left them to sort it out for themselves and went off to ask Mary Kingsley for a dance.

When it was over, Anna came over to him. "Deirdre's not here," she said.

He looked around and realized she was right.

"And nor is Dunstable," she added.

"Any idea where they might be?"

"No, but I did mention to him how strange it was that Deirdre dances beautifully with you, and badly with him. And how she smiles at you in a way quite differently to the way she smiles at him . . ."

"Miss Treese, what are you up to?"

She unfurled her fan and plied it gently. "Just repaying you, my lord, for teaching Arthur a thing or two."

He shook his head. "I could pity Arthur."

She was taken aback. "Really?"

He smiled. "No. He's a very lucky young man."

He set off in search of Deirdre and Dunstable, wondering just what Anna's meddling had achieved.

• • •

He went into the hall and considered matters. He didn't think Deirdre and Dunstable were likely to be carried away by passion. If she was amenable to being seduced into marriage, however, it wouldn't do to let Dunstable get the jump on him.

The only innocent place for them to be was in the hall, and they were not there. A maid passed through with more lemonade for the dancers, but he did not inquire of her. Instead, he wandered, ears peeled.

He detected them at last in the morning room, with the door half-shut. Or half-open, thought Everdon, wondering if he should be optimistic or pessimistic. At the sound of his name, he did not hesitate to listen to their conversation.

"You can't be jealous of Everdon," Deirdre was saying. She sounded distressed.

"It seems to me to be entirely reasonable." Dunstable's voice was coldly accusatory. "He's an earl, and wealthy, thus more of your station in life. And after the way you danced with him, I cannot think you indifferent."

"It's just that he dances so well."

"Are you saying I do not? If our dance was less successful, it was because you had all the grace of a bag of sticks."

Everdon's hand fisted, but he controlled the urge to go in and knock the oaf out. That would not help Deirdre.

"I know that, Howard," she said quietly. "But I care nothing for Everdon. I will not dance with him again."

"Very well," said Dunstable. Then his tone softened. "I am only thinking of you, Deirdre. If he's pretending to care for you, it can only be for your dowry. A man like that wouldn't really be interested in a dab like you, and he'd never stay faithful. Don't forget he's called Don Juan."

"I don't forget that, Howard." Deirdre's voice was scarcely more than a whisper.

Everdon wanted to horsewhip the insensitive cad, but he also wanted to throttle Deirdre for putting up with such treatment. She was spirited enough with him. What hold did Dunstable have over her? Love? He couldn't believe love led to this kind of . . . slavery.

"There, there." Everdon guessed that Dunstable had taken Deirdre in his arms, and he was even more tempted to interrupt, but he needed to understand what was going on here if he was to rescue her. "I'm sorry for upsetting you, but you know how important you are to me, Deirdre. I don't know how I'd get by without you."

She chuckled. "Nor do I, love. You'd be skin and bone in weeks."

"Have you looked for a new housekeeper?"

"Oh, I'm sorry. I've been so busy . . ."

"Running around with Everdon."

"I am supposed to be engaged to marry him, Howard," Deirdre said apologetically. "But I am sorry. I'll look into it tomorrow . . ."

Everdon gritted his teeth. Where was her backbone? Where was the woman who'd threatened to knock his block off?

"The sooner your engagement is over, the better. When will he arrange it?"

"He wants us all to visit Everdon Park. He says it will be easier to arrange there."

"What? He's trying to separate us."

"Why would he do that, Howard? As you say, he has no real interest in me. Besides, he says he will invite you, too."

There was a silence. "How strange."

At the note in his rival's voice, Everdon reminded himself that the man was no fool. He might well be lacking in social graces, and even in kindness, but when it came to putting two and two together, a mathematician would surely be able to make four.

Deirdre spoke softly, pleadingly. "He knows you are important to my happiness, darling, and he is a kind man in his own way. You will come, won't you? I couldn't bear to be weeks without you again."

"I don't see why it should take weeks," Dunstable said peevishly. "All he has to do is to be found in a woman's bed. He could drag one of those giggling chits out of the ballroom and get it done."

"Howard! He'd never seduce an innocent. And besides, then he'd have to marry her, which would be no part of his plans."

"Serve him right," said Dunstable. "Oh, very well. But I *will* come, and I'll keep an eye on him and you. You women are too foolish where such a man's involved. I wouldn't be surprised to find he's decided to taste you before he lets you go, and you'd be fool enough to let him."

"Howard!"

Everdon waited for the sound of a block being knocked off. When it didn't come, he sighed and pushed open the door.

He coughed.

Dunstable and Deirdre sprang apart. Deirdre looked rather relieved, which didn't surprise Everdon. He had not thought that kiss a masterly example of tenderness. Aggressive possession, more like.

"What the devil do you want?" asked Dunstable.

Everdon toyed with the notion of letting Dunstable pick a fight—he'd enjoy drawing his cork—but discarded it. Deirdre would see her hero as the victim. "People are wondering where Lady Deirdre is," he said smoothly. "We don't want to cause talk."

Dunstable looked as if he would argue, but Deirdre laid a pleading hand on his arm. "Please, Howard."

Everdon said, "Why don't you go back, Dunstable? We'll be along in a moment. If we all return together, it will look as if I'm shepherding back the erring sheep."

Dunstable flashed him a cold look. "Don't think you can play your games with Deirdre, my lord. I've warned her about you."

"I'm sure Lady Deirdre is far too honest and intelligent to fall prey to such as I, Mr. Dunstable."

"Intelligent? Good Lord, she's a practical little thing, but she don't even know algebra."

Everdon almost began to feel sorry for the fool. "I don't suppose you know bullion work from couching, Mr. Dunstable, or how to get rust stains out of linen."

Dunstable stared at him blankly. "What the devil has that to do with anything? It's my opinion you're more than half-mad." He flashed a look at Deirdre. "I'll leave this room, but if I'm to be denied the only pleasure of the evening, I'm for home. I could not bear more of that inane company, and I want to get my thoughts down before they're lost in a welter of feline fleas. Make sure you don't stay here long with him."

With this terse command, he stalked out of the room.

When they were alone, Deirdre made no move to obey Howard and rush back to the dancing. She looked away toward the empty fireplace, and Everdon suspected she was fighting tears. She was certainly distressed, and well aware that her beloved had not shown well. He wondered what made a woman endure a man like that for a moment, never mind a lifetime.

He took a thoughtful pinch of snuff, and asked, "Would you like some?"

She turned to face him. "What?" Her eyes were a little damp.

"Snuff," he said, extending his mother-of-pearl box.

A bemused smile flickered on her face. "Ladies don't take snuff these days."

"Very wise. It's a vile habit, and becomes compulsive in times of stress." But he still extended the box to her.

She looked at the powder. "What do I do?"

"Take a little pinch, hold it in your nostril, and sniff."

With an uncertain glance at him, she followed his instructions. She sniffed, then sneezed, then said, "Good heavens! Oh, my eyes are watering . . ." After a moment, she added, "I feel as if my head is expanding."

He smiled and put the box away. "More space for rational thought, perhaps. We should go back in case your devoted admirer is hovering. I don't want to duel him. It would probably be logarithmic tables at twenty paces and he'd beat me hollow."

She chuckled and blew her nose, then grimaced at the brown stain on the handkerchief. "I don't think I shall take to snuff, my lord."

"Can I not lead you into even a minor vice?" he asked, and gained an honest laugh.

"I fear not. I am destined for a life of sober industry."

"Caring for Howard Dunstable." He kept his tone very neutral.

"Yes," she said, equally blandly. She came over to his side and looked up pleadingly. "He is brilliant. Now you've met him, you do see, don't you?"

He placed her hand on his arm, and they turned to leave the room. "Oh yes, Deirdre. Now I've met him, I do indeed see."

Everdon was summoned to his mother's room before retiring. She was already in bed and he perched next to her.

"You cannot allow Deirdre to marry that man, Marco," she said forthrightly.

"Is not that what I said when we discussed this last?"

"I had not met him then."

"But, *Madrecita,* can you blame the man for not being interested in fleas?"

"What?"

He described what had occurred in the morning room. "Now, you tell me, what makes Deirdre put up with the man?"

Lucetta sighed. "Oh dear. It is hard to explain, but it happens. I think it is perhaps that once a woman commits herself, it is hard for her to abandon someone."

"Not in my experience," he said bleakly.

She covered his hand. "Genie was an unusual woman, dear. Deirdre is nothing like her."

"I know that. So how do I make her prove unfaithful to the man she has pledged to love forever?"

Lucetta frowned over it. "I am not sure. The best course, if it is possible, might be to make him reject her."

Everdon shook his head. "That would hurt her terribly. I want her to knock his block off."

"What?"

"Never mind. There must be some other way."

"Then try to find it. But if she believes he loves and needs her, she will stay with him despite his petty cruelties."

"It makes no sense."

Lucetta smiled sadly. "It does, in a way, to a woman. And think of it another way, Marco. Would you forgive her for a cruelty? And would you expect her to forgive you? Where should it stop?"

Everdon wandered off to his own room, thoughtfully contemplating the fact that some of the qualities he most admired about Deirdre Stowe—her fidelity and determination—were what bound her to a man who did not appreciate her at all. If the only way to free her was to destroy those qualities, could he do it?

Should he do it?

He supposed he could in some way let her know that her Howard used a whore, but if that ruled out marriage, he was a dead duck.

He poured and drained a large glass of brandy, plagued by the fact that for the first time in his adult life, he was at a loss as to how to handle a woman. Even if he made Deirdre fall passionately in love with him, there was no guarantee that she'd abandon Howard; nor, as his mother pointed out, would he want it any other way.

He valued fidelity above all things.

❧ 8 ❧

THEY TRAVELED to Everdon Park in two coaches and two curricles. Henry, Rip, Everdon, and Howard shared the curricles, though Howard did not drive. Lady Harby, the dowager, and Deirdre traveled in one chariot; the personal servants traveled in and on the other. A number of Everdon's servants attended on horseback to smooth their way.

The journey took two days, but under Everdon's organization, it was without incident. The best horses were always brought out at a stage—previously selected by his men. Their stopping places were always prepared for them; and the Bear in Reading, where they spent the night, was virtually overhauled for their comfort. Feather pillows and Persian rugs had been sent from Everdon Park, along with a special firm mattress for the dowager, for she found a soft one bothered her hip.

The meal was superb, though whether that was extraordinary or not, Deirdre had no way of knowing.

After the meal Lady Harby and the dowager took seats in

the garden to chat in the evening sun, while Henry and Rip sauntered off to explore the delights of the town.

Deirdre was inclined to join the older ladies, but she was not at all sure she should leave Howard alone with Everdon.

Howard had as usual been abstracted throughout the meal. Now he suddenly addressed a maid who was clearing the last of the meal. "Is Sonning Eye near here, girl?"

"Aye, sir. It's but a mile north."

Howard turned to Deirdre and Everdon. "Quentin Briarly lives there. I'd very much like to meet him. He wrote an interesting paper on the Leibniz-Newton controversy. I think I'll walk out there."

"Excellent idea," said Everdon genially. "And these long nights, you won't have to hurry back."

"True."

To Deirdre's astonishment, Howard set off without apparent concern that he was leaving his future wife to the tender mercies of a rake—a rake of whom he had been jealous quite recently.

Deirdre definitely decided she wanted to join the older ladies, and rose to do so. Everdon caught her hand, staying her. "Do you really want to sit again, after sitting all day? Why not come for a walk with me."

Deirdre hesitated. She was strongly tempted, but by the chance to stretch her legs, not the company.

Everdon met her eyes. "I give you my word, Deirdre. No kisses, no flirtation, nothing to disturb you at all."

"Are you capable of it, my lord?" she asked with an edge, for even then his thumb was making tiny circles on the back of her hand. She allowed herself to be persuaded, however, and they set out to stroll about the town.

It was not a particularly remarkable town, and being on

the Bath road, the High Street was very busy. They soon turned away from the thoroughfare to take a path that ran beside the River Kennet.

There it was more peaceful, more suitable for a summer evening stroll. Ducks paddled and bobbed in the river, and feeding fish made little circles in the glassy smoothness. Insects buzzed among wildflowers, and birds chirped and sang in the heavy trees.

They walked in companionable silence for a while, then Everdon said, "You need insects."

"I beg your pardon?"

He gestured to drift of wild phlox, busily worked by bees. "Your wildflowers need insects on them."

She focused and saw that he was correct. Whoever saw wildflowers without insects about somewhere? She cast him a teasing look. "Greenfly, perhaps?"

He didn't rise to the bait. "If it pleases the artist in you."

"It's your cloth."

"I'll hold you to that."

Deirdre looked back, studying the scene. She soon saw that in addition to the fat bees with the full yellow leg-sacks, there were smaller ones—or perhaps they were wasps. There were also ladybirds, and some little flies with bronze iridescent wings.

"Now, how would I get that effect?" she wondered, and crouched down to study them closer. She disturbed a grasshopper, and it leapt, bright green, out of her way.

"Poke your nose any closer," said Everdon in amusement, "and one of those bees will think you're a blossom and mine you for nectar."

She laughed, and let him help her to her feet. "Not very likely."

He steadied her with hands on her shoulders. "Very likely

indeed. I'd like to mine you for nectar. May I break my word?"

The look in his eyes made Deirdre want to say yes, but she shook her head.

"Shame." He sighed and let her go. "I must beware in future of foolish promises." He tucked her hand back in his arm, and they strolled on.

To cover the moment, Deirdre said, "You're right about the insects. I must look for a book on them, for I cannot collect them."

"Yes, you can. One nets them, then pins them into a box to be studied at leisure."

She shuddered. "I couldn't do that."

"Consider that a blood sport, do you?"

She met his eyes. "Tease as you will, Lord Everdon, but if I can't swat wasps, I certainly couldn't stick a pin through a ladybird."

"I suppose not. I believe we have a collection of insects at home. Work of an uncle of mine. You could have that, if your stomach is up to it."

Her smile was rueful. "Is it very foolish? I confess I wouldn't mind if the pinning is long since done."

"I enjoy pork, but I leave the slaughtering to others."

They turned to retrace their steps, but halted to watch a kingfisher dive in a flash of blue, then emerge triumphant with a fish flapping desperately in its beak.

"It's a cruel world, isn't it?" said Deirdre.

"So there's no reason to look for extra trouble."

Deirdre took a deep breath and faced him. "Does that refer to Howard?"

Everdon was very serious. "Yes. He won't make you happy, Deirdre."

"You must allow me to be the judge of that."

"I cannot do anything else, but I'm laying my cards on the table. I don't think he's the right man for you, and I hope you will come to see it. Then you will marry me."

Deirdre wished he weren't doing this. This stroll had been a halcyon time, but now he was scarring it. "If I came to see it as you wish, I still would have other options than marriage to you."

"Am I so objectionable?" She could swear she saw hurt in his face. Don Juan, hurt by her? Surely not. All the same, she felt compelled to kindly honesty.

She looked away and softly said, "No, you are not objectionable, Everdon."

"So if you decided not to marry Dunstable, you would marry me?"

It was an honest question and deserved an honest answer. Deirdre stood in thoughtful silence, looking over the river to the meadow beyond, trying to imagine marriage to this man.

"I might," she admitted. Then she turned and added more firmly, "But don't think you can play tricks on me. I intend to marry Howard, so the question will not arise. You may as well set about choosing another bride immediately. After all, it can make little difference to you."

"Can it not? But I do want to marry you, Deirdre."

"Not to the exclusion of all others."

He considered it carefully. "I suppose not, but that's because I haven't met all others. Of the women I have met, I think you would suit me best."

Breathing was becoming more and more difficult. "Why?"

"Begging for compliments?"

She refused to smile. "You know me better than that, Everdon. I am begging for reasons."

She expected a quick and facile response, but he pondered it, frowning slightly.

"I enjoy being with you, Deirdre," he said at last. "In silence and in speech, apart or in one another's arms. Can you think of a better reason for marriage? Looks will change with time, passion cannot last a lifetime, but I believe I will always enjoy your company and your discourse."

Deirdre stared at him. "Goodness."

"I don't know why it should surprise you. Many people like you. I like you. I don't think Howard Dunstable does."

Deirdre was thumped back into harsh reality. "That's a terrible thing to say!"

"It's the truth. I'd tell you to ask him, but he'd be bound to assure you that he does like you—not from dishonesty, but because anyone would. But look to his actions. He doesn't behave as if he likes you at all."

Deirdre turned and started briskly back to the inn. "You don't know anything about the way he behaves. Just because he's not always trying to kiss me . . ."

He kept pace with her, damn him. "That has nothing to do with it. I'm not talking about lust, Deirdre, but liking. When has he ever sought to spend time with you?"

Never! echoed in Deirdre's head like a tolling bell. She clapped her hands over her ears. "Stop it! Stop it! Stop it!"

Everdon grabbed her and pulled her against his chest. She struggled feebly, both against his hold and against tears. "Oh, Deirdre, I'm sorry. Don't cry. I won't say any more."

Deirdre gritted her teeth to conquer the tears, but nothing could conquer the words he had planted in her head. She pushed, and he let her go. She turned away, rubbing at her eyes. "You're horribly cruel."

"I don't want to see you unhappy."

"Howard won't make me unhappy." It was like a litany, a mindless declaration of faith.

The silence stretched so that it rasped at her nerves. What

was he doing? How did he look? She turned. He was very sober and concerned.

He sighed, took her hand, and kissed it. "Just be sure of your happiness, Deirdre, for my sake."

Then he placed her hand on his arm and they continued their walk, but did not speak again all the way to the inn.

Deirdre desperately wanted to talk to Howard, to investigate all these doubts, and to erase them, but he was still out. Rip and Henry were playing piquet, and she didn't want their jovial company anyway. Both her mother and Lucetta had retired. She certainly didn't want to speak to her mother about this, and she suspected Lucetta wanted her to marry Everdon.

She retreated to her own room and prepared for bed, then she dismissed Agatha and sat by an open window to face her problems.

Why on earth was Everdon attacking her like this? In another man, she could suspect the sort of mischief-making that comes of boredom, but she knew Everdon wasn't that sort of man. She had to suppose that it was simple misunderstanding. He clearly didn't like Howard, and could not imagine how anyone else could. He truly believed that Howard would make her unhappy, and being of a kindly disposition, he wanted to help. It was ridiculous, but that must be it.

She suspected, however, that Everdon would drag his heels about setting her free until he changed his mind. She would just have to work at convincing him that she and Howard were ideally suited. At Everdon Park, where they would all be living in the same house, that should be possible.

After all, Everdon was basing his doubts on that one disastrous evening at Missinger. That wasn't the real Howard, as he would see.

However, as Deirdre settled into bed, the traitorous

thought crept into her mind that it *would* be very pleasant if Howard just once waylaid her as Everdon did, seemingly just for the pleasure of her company. Then she fought it away, furious with the earl for planting these corroding notions in her head.

Everdon watched Dierdre flee and wondered whether his actions were fair, or even effective. He'd never been involved in such a case before, and had no notion of how to go on. To him, Deirdre appeared to be intelligent, spirited, and generally wise. Why could she not apply those qualities to her own situation?

Dunstable had been Everdon's traveling companion for part of the day, and he had come to know him a little. The younger man had been an unexceptionable companion—if one did not care for conversation. Everdon had been determined to draw him out, however.

He had known that a question about mathematics would elicit some response, but he had no particular desire for a lecture, and so he raised the subject of Cambridge.

"You were there, too, my lord?" Dunstable asked.

"Yes. Pembroke."

"King's," said Dunstable, giving the name of his college. "I don't suppose our times overlapped."

"No, I left in 1805."

"Then we didn't miss by a great deal. I went up in 1807."

Everdon flicked him a glance. "Are you older than you look?"

"I don't think so. I went up when I was fifteen."

Everdon concentrated on steering the curricle at speed around a tricky corner. He wished Dunstable would prove to be a posturing nonentity, but he suspected nothing could be further from the truth. The man was almost certainly brilliant, but he still was no husband for Deirdre, perhaps for any woman.

"And when did you take your degree?"

"I took my first degree in 1811. I could have been speedier, but there were many intriguing sideways. I was not sure at that time what direction would suit me best."

"But you have now decided on pure mathematics. Is that the correct phrase?"

"It's as good as anything. I pursue knowledge for its own sake. I am wondering, my lord, if you have thought of being a patron of the sciences."

Everdon almost laughed. No wonder Dunstable had deigned to converse. Was he incredibly brash? No, just oblivious to any subtle nuance outside of his own narrow vision.

"A patron of the sciences?" Everdon mused. "Of you, sir? But was it not then a little unwise to take me to task over Lady Deirdre?"

Dunstable looked at him blankly. "What has one thing to do with the other?"

"If you have annoyed me," said Everdon plainly, "then I am unlikely to provide you with financial support."

"Well," said Dunstable severely, "if you wish to reduce matters to that petty level, there is no more to be said. I will not grovel."

"I don't think I asked for that. And what of Deirdre in all this?"

It seemed as if Dunstable would not reply, but then he said, "It is Deirdre I am thinking of. I am well aware of the difference in our rank and fortune. I would prefer to be able to keep her in a comfortable manner."

Despite the words, Everdon received the distinct impression that Deirdre had not been in the man's mind at all until Everdon had raised the subject. Dunstable wanted extra income so as to be able to pursue his work without distraction. Deirdre was more likely a means to comfort, not someone to be made comfortable.

However, Everdon suspected that trying to persuade Dunstable of the selfishness of his actions would be like trying to persuade a fox that it shouldn't eat chickens.

Everdon then asked some mathematical questions—in his role as potential patron—and eventually decided he was correct in all respects. Dunstable was quite incapable of considering anyone else's wishes or feelings. He was also brilliant, and very likely to take humanity forward in knowledge.

In fact, thought Everdon that night as he went to bed, he would probably be doing humanity a service by preventing Dunstable from cluttering up his life with a wife and children.

Deirdre faced the next day with trepidation, but that turned out to be needless. Everdon staged no more assaults, and Howard had so enjoyed his scholarly visit that he was almost jovial. The weather held fine, and they made good speed toward Everdon's Northamptonshire home.

At the last stage, where they stopped for light refreshments, Rip challenged Everdon to a race.

Everdon raised his brows. "You young creatures. After a day on the road, you're up for this?"

"Pooh. What's a few hours' driving? You're a notable whip—I know that, Everdon—but I reckon I can beat you."

Everdon gave a lazy smile. "Indeed? How can I resist? So be it."

But Howard said, "I have no intention of risking death. I will ride in the coach."

"You can't," protested Rip. "Henry would have to join you to make the weight even, and there's not enough room."

"And I'm dashed well *not* sitting out," said Henry. "In fact, I want to take a turn with the ribbons."

"Stubble it, whelp," said his brother. "Not in a race. Dunstable, you'll have to come."

"I'd rather walk," said Howard simply and irrevocably.

It appeared to be an impasse, and Rip and Henry glowered at Howard in a way that would have shriveled a lesser man.

Everdon looked at Deirdre. "What about you? Are you willing to risk death?"

"Travel in your curricle?" she asked, wide-eyed. Her glance flickered between her mother and Howard, gauging their reaction. Lady Harby frowned slightly, but seemed unwilling to object to anything that threw Everdon and her daughter together. The matter seemed to be passing over Howard's head entirely.

Deirdre didn't know what to do. Common sense told her that she should avoid Everdon, and that curricle racing was dangerous. Her soul wanted to do it for the sheer excitement. At least one fear was clearly foolish; Everdon would have no time for flirtation or even innuendo while driving to an inch.

Her instinct told her he would keep her safe.

"Very well," she said.

There was a bit of further debate about weight differences, but Everdon solved this by having a few bags moved to the boot of his curricle. All was set.

As everyone went out to the vehicles, Howard seemed to finally realize what was toward. He frowned slightly, but all he said was, "You are being remarkably foolish, Deirdre."

Deirdre waited for more, but he just walked away to take her seat in the carriage. If only he had taken her in his arms and said, "You will do such a foolish thing over my dead body!"

She sighed and took her seat in Everdon's curricle, prepared to hang on for dear life.

"Don't worry," said Everdon, "I'll let your brother beat us hollow before I endanger you. One learns at some point what is important in life and what is not."

"And winning isn't important, my lord? Shame on you. *I* want us to win."

His eyes sparkled. "Then we will. But with some precautions." He called over to Rip, and it was soon arranged that Rip and Henry would leave ten minutes ahead of Everdon. The victory would be based on time.

"This way," said Everdon, as the brothers disappeared in a swirl of dust, "we at least are not jockeying for position on the road."

"But how will we know if we're gaining or not?" Deirdre was almost bouncing with the desire to be off in pursuit.

He had his watch out, and was keeping track of the time. "We won't. I'll just drive my damnedest. Calm down, *mi corazón,* or I'll think I should harness *you* up. Do you drive?"

"Yes. Mostly the gig, though I have driven a curricle."

He passed her the reins. "Walk them, then, while we wait for the time to be up."

Somewhat nervously, Deirdre guided the horses down the road, then turned them back. It was silly to be nervous of such a routine matter, so she flicked them up to a trot. They were Everdon's own horses, sent here to await him, as were the pair Rip had. They were fine cattle, and she relished the feeling of power at the end of the reins.

Everdon clicked his watch shut. "Right. Off you go."

"*What?*"

"Go." He took the whip and urged the horses up to moderate speed. Deirdre concentrated on managing them, though in fact, the road presented little challenge just here, being smooth and straight.

"You're mad!" she cried, but grinning all the same. "We'll never win with me driving."

"Yes, we will." He set the whip back in her hand. "I'll take over in a while—your arms won't take this for eight miles—but you're doing marvelously. Just watch out ahead. There's a hidden dip."

Deirdre steadied the team and felt her stomach lurch as they went down, then up. "Criminy! I'll go odds Rip and Henry almost tipped out there." She urged the team to speed again.

She spared a glance at her companion, and saw him lounging back in a way that spoke eloquently of confidence in her. She couldn't imagine who else in the world would trust her with this team, though in fact, years of managing Charlemagne meant she was not nearly as fragile as she appeared.

The wind of their speed was dragging at her bonnet, and the dry road was blossoming dust, but Deirdre didn't have a care in the world. She let the horses have their heads, and took a gentle corner like a bird in flight.

She let out a whoop of pure delight, then had trouble as the horses tried to flee this howling monster behind them. She regained control, but wasn't regretful when Everdon said, "Better let me have them now." She steadied them down to a slow pace, and passed the reins and whip over.

He brought them up to speed again and set to catching the challengers.

He was a marvelous driver. The horses seemed to be an extension of him, and his eye for the road was impeccable. Of course, he must know this road well, but that wouldn't help him anticipate the branch that had fallen on one side, or the sudden appearance of a trio of runaway piglets.

Deirdre relaxed to enjoying the thrilling speed, straining her eyes ahead for any sign of Rip. "I can't see them. They're still ahead!"

"Of course they are. I don't hope to catch them before the park gates. The driveway is a mile, and very open. I hope we'll overtake them there. If not, I promise we'll wipe out most of their lead."

He was almost exactly correct. In fact, they came up with Rip and Henry just before the gates to Everdon Park, but on that narrow road there was no question of passing. Once through the gate, however, the wide, smooth, gently curving avenue made it a pure test of speed.

Rip, it was clear, had pressed his team too hard. When he asked more of them, it was not there. Everdon, on the other hand, had merely to urge his team on to sweep by and up to the doors of his home.

Deirdre let out another whoop, and this time the team were too tired to object.

Grooms ran forward, and Everdon leapt down. He turned to assist Deirdre. He put his hands at her waist and swung her a full turn before setting her, breathless, on her feet.

As the grooms led both teams off to cool down, Rip and Henry came over, shaking their heads, but grinning. "It was a fine race," said Rip.

"Indeed. And most enjoyable," said Everdon.

"And damned fine driving," said Henry. "You made up the whole ten minutes, Everdon, and with a female squealing alongside."

"I most certainly did not squeal," Deirdre protested.

"Yes, you did," said Everdon. "Once just now when we won, and once when you brought the team up to speed."

Rip and Henry both gaped.

Henry said, "You let *Deirdre* drive? In a *race*?"

"She drives very well."

Both young men stared at their sister as if she'd grown pink horns.

Rip cleared his throat. "Er, sure you're right, Everdon. Nothing against Deirdre and all that, but I'd rather this didn't get out, don't you know. Beaten by you is one thing. Beaten by a chit of a girl . . ."

Deirdre's heart was touched by his anguish. She put her hand on his arm. "I only drove for a little way, to warm up the horses, Rip. It was Everdon's fine handling that did the job."

Rip laughed in relief. "Bound to be. Know what? You're a good little thing, Dee. Take my advice. Marry this one."

Deirdre couldn't even take offense to that. Rip would urge her to marry any man who could acquit himself well in sporting activities, regardless of any other qualities.

The coach would be some time behind them, and so they all made their way into the house.

Everdon Park House was, as Everdon had once said, quite small. It was a plain three-story cube without wings. As a consequence it had solidity, and Deirdre rather liked that. Moreover, the architect had been skilled, and the lines of the building were very elegant. Without facade or addition, they were unspoiled.

As they mounted the five steps to the front door, she turned to Everdon. "I like your house."

"Thank you. I'm quite fond of it myself, though it will have to be enlarged. Even a moderate house party such as I have assembled now stretches its capabilities. I hope to do it without destroying its purity."

They entered a pleasant square hall with tiled floor and paneled walls. In a somewhat strange voice, Everdon said, "I fear its capacity is going to be stretched a little further."

Deirdre looked around to see a young gentleman emerge

from a room. He was tall, thin, and dressed amazingly in yellow. Dull yellow jacket, bright yellow pantaloons, yellow and bronze cravat . . . As his hair was chick yellow curls, the impression was a little overwhelming.

"Deirdre," said Everdon, "may I introduce my cousin, Kevin Renfrew, also known as the Daffodil Dandy. Kevin, this is Lady Deirdre Stowe, and her brothers, Lord Ripon and Mr. Henry Stowe."

The young men all greeted one another with familiarity, so Deirdre had to assume this apparition led a moderately normal social life.

He bowed to her. "Lady Deirdre. Charmed. Came to lend a hand." His face was too long and thin to be good-looking, but there was an amiable charm in his expression. Deirdre suspected he might be simple.

They shook hands. Servants came forward to take away outer garments.

Everdon said to his cousin, "Lend a hand? With what, pray?" But he didn't sound annoyed, merely resigned.

"Oh, anything," said Renfrew vaguely. "Did you know you have mayapples growing in the sunken garden?"

Everdon steered them all into a room, which turned out to be a wainscoted saloon hung with family portraits and furnished in a motley manner. The contents seemed to be the casual accumulation of generations, and as such, it held an air of being well used and comfortable, rather than a room reserved for guests. Deirdre rather liked it.

"No," Everdon said to Renfrew. "I did not know about mayapples, but then I don't know the half of what I have in the garden."

"Quite rare, mayapple is. Your gardener was going to pull them up."

"I assume he's changed his mind."

"Oh yes. Very reasonable sort of fellow."

"I've always found him rather jealous of his territory."

Deirdre had been admiring a stunning portrait of the dowager as a young bride with wicked, flashing eyes. Now she turned, fascinated by the strange conversation.

"And how's Ian?" Everdon was asking. "The last I heard, he'd rallied a little."

"Yes. Stopped by there the other day, but didn't stay. Fusses him to know I'm next in line."

This was said without resentment, but Deirdre could sympathize with Sir Ian Renfrew, the Daffodil Dandy's older brother. She'd heard talk of the sad case; Sir Ian was stricken by a wasting disease from which he would not, it seemed, recover. Not yet thirty, he would leave a widow and three young girls. No wonder the thought of the Daffodil Dandy inheriting his property and the responsibility for his family was bad for his health.

"Stopped by?" asked Everdon. "Have you not been there these last months?"

"No. Like I say, it does him more harm than good." Renfrew's lips quirked in a sad little smile. "Though I did wonder whether my hanging around might perk him up, give him even more need to get well. There's nothing in it, though. He's done for, Don. Don't seem any point in fussing him. I've been in the Shires most of the year, doing over a place Verderan inherited there."

"Piers Verderan? The Dark Angel? You've been decorating a house for him?" Even Everdon was beginning to sound bemused.

"Yes." Kevin Renfrew drifted over to a pier table and absently rearranged the three figurines that stood on it. "Rather interesting actually," he said. "The foundation in the northwest corner is crumbling."

"Then if you were doing the house over, you should have looked to it."

"Not there. Here," said Renfrew. "I'm reading about gilding." With that he wandered off.

Deirdre shared a hilarious look with her brothers. Everdon, however, rang the bell.

When his butler appeared, he gave orders for refreshments, but then said, "Has the foundation been checked?"

"I did take the liberty of making that arrangement, milord. It appears work is necessary."

"Put it in hand, then." Everdon turned to Deirdre. "I think you would like to remove the dust before tea. I'll have a maid take you to your room."

Deirdre had been staring at the three figurines that Kevin Renfrew had rearranged, realizing with astonishment that their new placement was subtly, but clearly, more pleasing than the old. Now she started, and glanced in the mirror above the pier table. She gasped at the sight she presented. She was turned almost dun brown with dust, and her hair was escaping its pins and the bonnet in all directions. "Heavens! I look a perfect sight!"

Everdon's eyes met hers in the mirror. "Yes, you do." His smile, however, gave the words quite a different meaning, and their gaze held for a breathless moment.

Deirdre fled the room in a flustered state, flustered by more than casual flattery. The assaults on her stability seemed never-ending. She'd end up as daft as that Daffodil Dandy.

What was she to make of Kevin Renfrew? He appeared to be lacking a large portion of his wits, and yet Everdon had taken his words about the foundation perfectly seriously. And with reason.

She wondered if there *were* mayapples in the sunken garden.

As she took off her bonnet and cloak in her small but pleasant room, she felt a new range of insecurities.

She hadn't anticipated the effect of being in Everdon's home. It drew her to him in a disturbing way. She certainly hadn't anticipated the introduction of a fey daffodil. There was something in the air in this house.

It felt like a place where things could change.

❦ 9 ❦

B Y THE NEXT DAY, however, Deirdre had decided that her
anxieties had been the result of weariness, or too much
sun. Everdon's home was surprisingly simple and old-
fashioned, but it was comfortable and well run. There were
no strange undertones at all.

Everdon had a number of matters awaiting his attention,
as he had not spent more than a night here for some months,
and so he arranged for his guests' comfort, then disappeared.
Deirdre had expected an attempt to keep her away from
Howard, and was perplexed that this was not so.

Howard, too, perplexed her. Perhaps it was that he was
away from his cottage, but he was not himself; for one thing,
he did not appear to be working at all. He was completely
available for walks in the grounds, games of cards, and even
angling. Deirdre knew she should have been delighted by
this evidence that he could enjoy such normal pursuits, but
it just made her feel even more uneasy.

Perhaps that was because she had the impression that

Howard was not really enjoying himself, but joining in these activities for a purpose.

He even agreed to join Rip and Henry in cricket practice.

As she stood in the shade by the lawn, watching Howard face a cricket ball tossed by Rip, the Daffodil Dandy appeared at her side. "Clever chap, that."

"Yes. Brilliant." Her heart did not, however, swell with pride. Anyone coherent would appear brilliant to Kevin Renfrew.

"Cares a lot about you."

"Do you think so?" she said, heart swelling despite her earlier thoughts.

"Oh yes. Wouldn't be out here knocking a ball about if he didn't. Very purposeful man." He wandered off to stand by Henry, though whether he was fielding or not was unclear.

Deirdre looked at Howard and realized that, of course, he had no interest in knocking balls about. And his purpose was plain—he was trying to please her, poor lamb.

When the game was over, she linked arms with him as they wandered over to the table where a footman was serving ale and lemonade. "I'm sure you must be longing to return to your studies, Howard."

"True, but I don't mind taking a few days off. I have things to think about."

"If that's what you want, of course. But I just wanted you to know that I don't expect you to dance attendance on me. I know how important your work is."

He smiled warmly and patted her hand. "I know you do. That's one reason I know we'll suit. I probably will spend some time in my room this afternoon making some notes. That Renfrew chap said some interesting things this morning about negative numbers."

"Kevin Renfrew?" Deirdre asked blankly.

"Yes. Strange fellow. Didn't know what he was saying, of course, but triggered an idea or two."

So, after luncheon, Deirdre was deserted. She took the opportunity to visit Lucetta. Here, even more than in Missinger, it was Lucetta's duty to be with Lady Harby, but on this occasion Deirdre's mother had developed a headache and was lying down in her room.

Deirdre went into the dowager's suite and looked around with pleasure. "Oh, how lovely!"

Lucetta smiled. "I think so. My husband had it decorated this way for me, to remind me of home."

The boudoir was painted white, and the floor was tiled in a mosaic of reds and golds. Gilt-framed pictures of Spanish scenes decorated the walls, and ornate grilles covered the two long windows, softening and diffusing the bright sun.

"In Cordoba, where I grew up, there is a lot of Moorish influence," said Lucetta. "There is also a lot of sun, so we hide from it. In the English winter those screens come down so I can appreciate what sunlight the good Lord sends this northern land."

Deirdre looked at a bas-relief of the Madonna and child. "Was it hard to leave your land, your family?"

"It was not easy," admitted Lucetta, "and my English was not good then. When I had Marco, I spoke to him almost entirely in Spanish, which is how he came to know the language so well. By the time Richard was born, it was less the case. And then he was the one to go to Spain . . ."

Lucetta's eyes turned to a small portrait on the wall, and Deirdre looked, too. It showed a smiling man in regimentals, clearly Everdon's brother, who had died at Vittoria. He and Everdon must have been very different, for Richard Renfrew looked more like Kevin—a longer face and paler coloring.

"I'm glad the war is over," said Deirdre, feeling it was an inadequate expression of sympathy, but not knowing what else to say.

"As are we all. My poor Spain . . . But," Lucetta said more briskly, "it was doubtless a blessing that I came north with Marco's father and escaped the horrors."

Deirdre wandered the room thoughtfully. "I'm not sure if I could leave England to live in a foreign land."

"Not even with Howard?"

Deirdre paused and frowned. "But why would he want to leave?"

"Who can say? There are famous universities in Germany, for example. He might wish to study there."

Deirdre felt a creeping unease. "Then I suppose I would go."

"Of course you would. Marriage is always a cause of change, and a change of country could be part of it. I found it hard to come to England, but I would have found it harder to have separated from John."

She indicated another, larger portrait, and Deirdre went over to look at Everdon's father.

"He was so special to me," Lucetta said softly. "Only a poet could have expressed it. You can see that he was not terribly handsome, nor did he have a golden tongue. He had honest eyes, though, and what they said to me was very precious."

Deirdre felt tears in her eyes as she looked at the portrait. John Renfrew, Earl of Everdon, had been a young man when this was done, but his wigless state showed a hairline that already receded. His face was long, rather like his second son's and Kevin Renfrew's, and his mouth was wide and humorous. His blue eyes were doubtless honest, but they were saying little of importance to the portrait painter. But he had been deeply loved, and Deirdre did not doubt he had loved deeply in return. Lucetta would have left her home for nothing less.

"Everdon doesn't look like him," she said.

"No, but there is a great deal of John in Marco. Marco looks just like my family, but he has the English restraint. It can be dangerous. He holds things in, covers them up, so that even those who love him do not see what is inside. My family," she added dryly, "concealed nothing, held back nothing."

Deirdre moved on to a portrait of a young Don Juan, done perhaps when he was twenty or so. He was standing by a tree in country clothes, riding crop in hand. His hair was rather long and curling, and his dark eyes bright with laughter. His stance was both relaxed and supremely confident. He was handsome now, but something had disappeared that had been caught in this picture. A sense of invulnerability, perhaps.

"That was done in 1804, when he was little older than you, Deirdre. Just before his father died."

Was that what had tarnished some of the gold? Grief and responsibility?

Lucetta spoke again, deliberately. "And before his marriage, of course."

Deirdre looked around. "Is there a portrait of his first wife here?" Then she could have bitten her tongue for such a tactless, stupid question.

"I would hardly keep one," said Lucetta dryly. "There was a miniature. I do not know where it went. Perhaps it was returned to her family with the rest of her possessions."

Deirdre knew this subject was best left alone, but she felt a pressing need to know more. Lucetta, she was sure, had raised the subject with some purpose. She faced the dowager. "He must have been very young when they married."

Lucetta looked down at the embroidery in her hands. "He was twenty. She was seventeen."

"So young?" Deirdre said in surprise. "Why . . . ?" She swallowed what she had been about to say.

"Why did I permit it?" Lucetta queried wryly. "You are contemplating marriage at eighteen, Deirdre." She sighed. "But you are right, it was not wise. But they were very much in love."

Deirdre felt a stab of pain at that. "I understand she was very beautiful."

"Very."

Deirdre hesitated to ask, but she had to know. "What happened?"

Lucetta laid down her work and looked up. "You will have to ask Marco. I do not know the whole, and it is not my story to tell. But Iphegenia Brandon was a wild flame destined to burn bright and fast. I should have realized that. Soon after the marriage, she made it clear that she found Marco lacking in some essential way."

"I find that hard to believe." The words escaped Deirdre before discretion could stop them. She colored and turned away from Lucetta's perceptive eyes. "He's handsome and charming," she added quickly. "What else did she want?"

"What else do you want?"

The words were a challenge.

Deirdre sucked in a deep breath, but something in the moment demanded honesty. "I want to be crucial to someone's life," she said quietly.

"Ah."

Lucetta said nothing more, and so Deirdre turned. Her friend was now sewing calmly. "Ah? Is that all you're going to say?"

Lucetta glanced up. "What else is there to say? I do not

know if you are crucial to the life of Marco or Howard Dunstable."

"Everdon would scarcely notice if I were to disappear," Deirdre said firmly. "Howard certainly would. Then he'd never get his eggs cooked correctly." She bit her lip. More words she wished unsaid. "I mean, that's not important. It's just that he needs me in so many little ways. He'd be miserable without me, and then he'd never get his work done, and I'm sure it's dreadfully important . . ."

"I'm sure it is, too," said Lucetta calmly. "You didn't bring any needlework with you? If you wish to sew here with me, you will always be welcome."

"Thank you," said Deirdre, feeling that she had yet again failed to convey the reality of her relationship with Howard. Why was it always so difficult? "I think I need a walk just now, though."

"Very well." As Deirdre turned to go, Lucetta picked up a piece of paper. "This account needs to go to Marco. Do you think you could put it in his study?"

Deirdre took it. "Yes, of course." She was no fool. She knew Lucetta was hoping Everdon would be there, and was throwing them together. But Deirdre did not intend to avoid him. To avoid him would be to admit that being with him could endanger her feelings for Howard. That was simply not true.

All the same, when she knocked on his study door and his voice said, "Enter," she felt a frisson of doubt.

He was sitting behind a desk thick with ledgers and papers. He was not alone. A plump young man rose, blushing, from behind another desk.

Everdon rose, too, a smile lighting his face. "Deirdre. What a delightful excuse to rest from my labors. Morrow, why don't you walk down to the agent's cottage and see if he has those missing records? The fresh air will do you good."

The young man's eyes flickered between them, and he made himself scarce. He carefully left the door wide open.

"A young gentleman of unimpeachable rectitude," remarked Everdon with a smile. "I don't know how he bears with me."

Deirdre held out the paper. "Your mother asked me to give you this."

He took it and raised a brow. "She clearly thinks I've been neglecting you."

"Not at all . . ."

"Don't you think so?"

"No."

He tapped the paper thoughtfully. "Where's Dunstable?"

"Working. He had an insight."

"Excellent."

Deirdre considered the earl suspiciously. She didn't forget the way he'd encouraged Howard on his little jaunt out of Reading.

He smiled blandly. "I want all my guests to be happy here. Do you have everything you need?"

"Yes, thank you."

He tossed down the account unread. "Have you had the grand tour of the house? No? Come on."

Deirdre found herself swept along, but wasn't reluctant. She was feeling edgy and unable to settle. A tour of the house seemed just the ticket, and in such a small and crowded building, there could be no real danger.

She had, of course, seen the drawing room, the dining room, and the breakfast room, but he took her through them again, pointing out items of interest. For the first time she realized how unplanned the rooms were, how old most of the decor and furnishings.

"No one in your family seems to have been inclined to modernization," she remarked.

"No. The last major work done inside the house was my mother's rooms. Would you want to change everything?"

The question seemed to have singular importance, but Deirdre responded lightly. "No. I think it charming."

"That's as well. It would cost the earth."

She gave him an uneasy look, but he said nothing more.

They looked in the library, which was only moderately stocked, and gave nodding recognition to a small, bleak reception room that was surely only used for unwanted visitors.

Then they went to the back of the house to a small garden room. This had glass doors that opened onto a tiled patio edged on two sides by rose trellises. Beyond was the west lawn.

"This is lovely," Deirdre said, and leaned over to smell a red rose. It was strongly perfumed, almost too strongly.

He plucked a pink one and gave it to her. "Red roses are for my mother. This will suit you better."

She held it close to her nose and found the perfume was indeed more subtle and to her taste. She glanced at him over the petals. "You think you know me very well, don't you?"

He shook his head. "No, Deirdre. I don't know you at all. Otherwise I would be able to make you do just as I wish."

She shivered. "I'd hate that."

He smiled. "I don't think I'd care for it much either. Keep your secrets, *querida*. It doesn't take magical powers to see that red is not your color."

He led the way back into the darker coolness of the house. As Deirdre passed a chaise in the garden room, she noticed that it was quite badly frayed along one edge so that the stuffing would soon start to escape. Distracted by that, she almost tripped when the toe of her slipper snagged a hole in the carpet.

Everdon did not see her stumble, but Deirdre was made strongly aware that his house was, in fact, quite shabby. After a hesitation, she asked, "Why did you mention cost before? You are surely rich enough to refurbish your house if you should wish."

They had moved into the hall and begun to mount the stairs. "If I wished, of course. But it is a matter of priorities. Foundations and land drainage come first. That ugly picture, by the way, is a portrait of me as a baby by Aunt Jane."

Though she had not received a satisfactory answer, Deirdre politely paused to study the strange little oil. "How fortunate that your eyes eventually settled in their correct positions."

"Yes, wasn't it? And that slightly better painting is her depiction of the park before my father landscaped it."

In this picture, Everdon Park House stood square in the middle of a small formal garden and flat meadows, peopled by rather unlikely cows. It looked stark.

"I think the changes were an improvement," she said.

"It's hard to tell. Don't forget, Aunt Jane painted that picture, too. The better artwork is along here."

A corridor with windows along one side formed a small gallery. Deirdre inspected the obligatory ancestors, noting the general trend toward the long, thin Renfrew face. Then she came across a family portrait surely executed not long before Everdon's father's death.

The former earl stood proudly behind the chair in which Lucetta sat, a Lucetta unfamiliar to Deirdre. She was some ten years younger, of course, but she fairly sizzled with life. Her gown was white muslin, but she wore a vivid red and black shawl as a sash, and a red rose in her black hair. Her husband had his hand on her shoulder, and her hand covered his.

She was looking up at her sons, who stood close together, smiling at their parents. It was a startlingly cohesive group, and it brought tears to Deirdre's eyes to think it had been torn apart.

As if he knew, Everdon said, "Within the year he was dead."

"How?" she whispered.

"Typhus, probably caught from a prisoner when he was serving as magistrate. He cared too much. Sometimes, if he wasn't satisfied with what happened in court, he would go to the jail to question a felon further. He died in three days."

Impulsively Deirdre turned and took his hand. He returned her grip, and they stood there, looking at each other.

He drew her along the corridor, swung open a door, and then released her hand. He stood back to let her precede him.

Deirdre walked through, then halted.

"My bedroom," he said, confirming her fears. He leaned, arms crossed, in the open doorway, not blocking her escape.

Daring her.

That powerful moment of shared grief had left Deirdre shaken and adrift. She walked a few paces farther into the lion's den but promised herself that if he closed the door, she'd scream.

"A pleasing chamber," she said, tolerably calmly, "but yet again in the old style."

"As you say," he replied, in a tone that did not sound particularly natural. "Lucetta's suite is, of course, next door. My first wife and I felt no need of separate rooms, but perhaps that is not wise. This time we will knock through a door on the other side. There would be no question, of course, of Lucetta moving out of those rooms, or leaving the house."

"No, of course not," said Deirdre. Then she looked at him sharply. " 'We'?" Her heart was running at an alarming rate, which was doubtless why she felt rather light-headed.

"There will presumably be a 'we' when the matter arises. Do you want to see the kitchens or the attics? Otherwise, I'm afraid the tour is over."

Silence fell except for the birdsong floating in through the open window.

Deirdre broke the moment by turning away to look down the wide drive along which they'd raced just a few days before. She was finding it remarkably difficult to think clearly, and yet knew she must. She turned and saw a small book-shelf by his bed. Chaucer, something Spanish, Locke and Southey's *Life of Nelson*. She noted that his bed hangings were threadbare in places.

She faced him. "I've decided what question I want an honest answer to."

For once, she noted with satisfaction, she'd thrown him off balance. "Question?" he queried in wary perplexity.

"The billiard game," she reminded him. "You owe me an answer."

"Ah, yes." He moved away from the doorway, and came to stand a few feet away. "And your question, *mia?*"

Deirdre summoned her courage, for the question was undoubtedly impertinent. "Why is money a matter of concern to you? Are you not as rich as it would seem?"

"That's two questions," he pointed out, but then shrugged. "I am, in a sense, not as rich as it would seem. Land is wealth, and I still have plenty of land, but much of the income has to go back into it. But that doesn't answer your question, does it? You asked why. The answer is, quite simply, the park."

He gestured toward the view of the beautiful park. "When my father took it into his head to re-create this corner of Northamptonshire, he spared no expense. It became a madness with him. It is very beautiful, but it almost ruined us all. When he died I found immense debts and mortgages. We have reclaimed everything, but there is still not an abundance of ready money. New furnishings have not been particularly high on my list of priorities."

"I'm not surprised. It must have been hard to cope with all that when you were so young."

"Yes, but it was losing my father that was harder."

She felt the strongest urge to go to him and hold him, as if that would comfort him. It was silly, for he was a grown man, and Don Juan, but if it hadn't been for Howard, she might well have done it.

Instead she moved toward the door. "I must go, my lord. Thank you for the tour."

"Thank you for your company, Deirdre."

Deirdre found herself inexplicably frozen, facing him across the faded carpet. "I'm sorry for asking such a question."

"Don't be. I give you carte blanche. You may ask me anything."

"Do you not have anything of which you are ashamed?" she asked in a spurt of irritation.

"Yes."

"What?"

He laughed. "A low blow, indeed. Your carte blanche has just been rescinded. You can't go on fishing expeditions. Do you have a precise question?"

Deirdre didn't, unless it was to ask why she was still in this dangerous room, alone with him.

After a moment, he came carefully toward her. "If you were to hit me, *cara*," he said softly, "I'd be obliged to kiss you."

Oh, so that was why. Deirdre took a deep breath, made a fist, and thumped him in the chest.

His hands settled on her shoulders, gently sensitive to her skin and nerves. "You are a very violent young woman." He laid his lips softly over hers.

Deirdre stood there, heart racing, wondering what on earth she was doing. This was wrong. This wasn't what she wanted. Not really. Her lips moved against his.

His hands slid up her neck and cradled the back of her head, turning it slightly to make a more interesting angle, to deepen the intimacy.

Her hands were held defensively against his chest poised virtuously to push him away. They lacked all power. Then strength returned, but only to slide up to his shoulders, and from there to the soft edges of his hair and the skin of his neck beneath . . .

He opened his lips. Instinctively she did the same, as if speaking against him softly of secrets. Their breath mingled, moist and warm, an intimate taste she had never experienced before. Openmouthed, he just brushed his lips against hers, sharing, somehow, more than breath.

She sobbed softly somewhere in the back of her throat.

He drew back, heavy-lidded, and trailed a thumb along her jaw. "You taste of eternity, Deirdre Stowe."

Deirdre swallowed, trembling. "It's just expertise. Yours, I mean, not mine."

"No."

He made no move, but Deirdre knew that in time he would kiss her again, more deeply, more shatteringly, and she wanted it.

At last she found the strength to push him away. "I must go."

He did not resist. "You should," he agreed.

It was like moving against a storm, but Deirdre turned and walked away.

She walked steadily out of the room and down the corridor past the paintings. She steadily made it to the safety of her own bedchamber. Once there, she collapsed, shattered, on her bed.

There was no room in her heart anymore for deception.

Howard would never kiss her like that; she would never experience with him what she had experienced with Everdon. But she was pledged to Howard, he needed her, and this hunger within her was just base lust.

She wept.

When the tears were over, she paced her room, wishing she could leave Everdon Park today. She struggled for ways to force Everdon to end their engagement quickly, but it would have to be achieved without her having to speak to him alone. She was determined never to be alone with him again. She could not think of any way to speed matters, though, except to do as he had once suggested and compromise herself with Howard. The notion was now even more repugnant.

She simply had to trust Everdon to honor their agreement and release her.

Alarmed by the danger, however, Deirdre discarded all notion of encouraging Howard to work, and demanded his almost constant presence. She tried in every way she could to convey to the world—and in particular to Don Juan—that she and Howard were destined for perfect happiness.

"Really, Deirdre," said Howard three days later, "I don't know what's come over you. You're always hovering over me. It's almost as if you don't trust me out of your sight."

"Of course I do," Deirdre said with honesty. She never doubted Howard. She took his hand. "It's just that I like being with you." Greatly daring, she added, "Don't you like being with me?"

As Everdon had predicted, he said quickly, "Of course I do." But he pulled his hand free. "I don't think we need live in one another's pockets, though, Deirdre. You distract me."

They were in the garden, in the shade of a chestnut tree. Howard had some papers, and Deirdre had her needlework.

"I'm just sitting here, Howard. I'm not doing anything to distract you."

"You distract me just by being there." Deirdre found this rather touching until he added, "I always feel you want me to talk or something." He turned back to the papers.

Deirdre rose from the wicker chair. "Very well. I will leave you in peace."

Instead of arguing, he said, "That's a good girl."

Deirdre marched miserably toward the house. As she drew closer, however, she thought she saw someone in the window of Everdon's study. Was he watching for her, lying in wait? She hurriedly turned and walked off down the drive, tussling with her problems.

Was she wrong to want Howard to lie in wait, to seek her out? He had, after all, given her the most powerful sign of devotion by asking her to marry him.

But then, so had Everdon.

Was she wrong to be hurt that Howard wanted to concentrate on his work while Everdon seemed willing to put his responsibilities aside at any moment? She should value Howard's dedication, and despise Everdon's distractibility.

At the gatehouse, Deirdre waved to the gatekeeper, and

walked out onto the narrow lane. It felt strangely liberating to leave Everdon Park, and so she strolled along the lane. There was little view here, for the hedges grew high on either side, but it was peaceful. She let her mind go blank.

Soon she came to a place where three lanes intersected, and a neat white signpost directed people to Kettering, Cranston, and Everdon Park. There seemed something strangely symbolic about this parting of the ways, so she stood beneath the post, considering her future.

She had three choices: She could marry Howard, she could marry Everdon, or she could remain a spinster. Not long ago, the prospect of being a spinster all her life would not have bothered her. She certainly did not believe that there was a special place in hell reserved for such women, where they would lead apes forevermore.

Now, however, something had been woken in her that spinsterhood would leave unsatisfied. Was it the companionship of a man, the sharing of work, the caring for his needs? Or was it the touch of a man, the moist heat of his lips, the magic he could work on her senses?

The shiver that passed through her suggested the answer.

Was this wickedness or a natural part of life?

Would Howard ever be able to satisfy that part of her that Everdon had brought to life? Surely, in time . . .

She was jerked out of her tangled thoughts by the sound of wheels. For a moment she could not decide from which direction they approached, and so she hesitated. Then a gig appeared on the Cranston Road, driven by an elderly, harsh-faced woman with a groom beside her.

The gig halted. "Are you all right, young lady?" the woman asked.

Deirdre blushed, well aware how peculiar she must look wandering about without her bonnet. "Yes, thank you, ma'am. I am a guest at Everdon Park, and I strolled down here."

The woman's face pinched. "You're the next victim, are you?" she sneered. "A fine substitute for Genie, you will be."

Deirdre just stared, and the groom sat there, arms folded, like a statue.

The woman suddenly thrust the reins into the man's hands and climbed down. She was thin, haggard, but with very good bones. "You're only a child," she said to Deirdre. "What on earth are your parents thinking of?"

"I beg your pardon?"

The woman clucked. "I am Elizabeth Brandon, my dear. Mother of Lord Everdon's betrayed first wife. I refuse to acknowledge any closer relationship than that."

Deirdre knew then that she had fallen into a dreadfully embarrassing situation. "I'm very sorry about your loss," she said faintly.

"Loss? We lost our treasure over ten years ago when that profligate enticed her from her home!"

"But he was only twenty," Deirdre protested. "And they married."

"Only twenty? But foreign," she spat. "We all know how they are abroad. Look at what happened to Genie."

Deirdre cast another desperate look at the groom, but he was doing an admirable representation of a painted dummy. Did Lady Brandon behave this way frequently? "Lady Brandon," she said gently. "I know you must be deeply distressed about your daughter, but I am sure it is unfair to place the entire blame on Lord Everdon. Your daughter did leave him of her own free will."

"What would you know of it, miss? Genie was driven away by his cruelty! He was mad for her, but once he had her, he cared nothing for her feelings, nothing at all. And she . . ."

The woman's voice broke. "She . . . she loved him so. It was her love that drove her away! And what did he do or say to stop her, to get her back? Nothing. *Nothing!*"

Deirdre wanted to ask what he could have been expected to do, but knew it was wiser to keep silence. Her face must have revealed something, however, for the woman carried on. "I see he has cozened you with his fair appearance. But if he was innocent, why did he never seek a divorce?" She stabbed the air with a sharp gloved finger. "Because she would have returned to defend herself, that is why. All would have been revealed!"

Deirdre stood there, appalled, staring at that finger.

"He sent all her possessions back to us," snarled Lady Brandon. "Just swept her out of his life."

What was he supposed to do? Deirdre wondered, trying to imagine Everdon at twenty, facing that situation.

The woman suddenly sagged from anger to grief. "Then, just weeks ago, he rode up cool as you please to show us that . . . that *horrible* letter . . ."

Again, Deirdre wondered, what was he supposed to do? She also had some glimmering of how hard it must have been for Everdon to go to his wife's parents to break the news. She had seen no sign of his distress. As Lucetta said, he was too good at concealing things.

"Dead," the woman moaned, putting a hand to her head. "Dead so young, alone in a foreign land. And now he is finally free to destroy another young innocent."

Deirdre could see only one way to escape this horrid confrontation. "I'm afraid you have made an error, Lady Brandon. I am not to marry Everdon. I am promised to another young gentleman at Everdon Park, Howard Dunstable."

Lady Brandon frowned at her. "But I had heard . . ."

"False rumors."

Lady Brandon looked her over. "More than likely. You haven't the looks for Don Juan. Genie was the most beautiful girl in England. He will marry again, though. He needs to now his family is failing all around him. Serves him right," she added viciously. "It's a judgment of God. His brother. Now his cousin. May all the Renfrews rot, every last one . . ."

Deirdre backed away. "I must bid you good day—"

"You watch out for him," the woman shrieked after her. "They don't call him Don Juan without reason. He destroys women for his pleasure!"

Deirdre turned and fled back toward Everdon Park.

Once out of sight of the crossroads, she slowed to catch her breath and steady her nerves. She knew she should have sympathy for a mother's grief, but she could only think how horrible it must be for Everdon to have that kind of hate living close by all these years, how horrible it must have been to have to face them.

What on earth had happened between him and his wife all those years ago? One thing she knew, though, he did not destroy women for his pleasure.

Deirdre hurried back inside the park, hoping she was hiding her distress from the gatekeeper. Howard was still under the tree, lost in numbers. She passed him by gingerly, not wanting to speak to him just now. She smiled grimly at the very idea that he might demand her presence.

There was no watcher to be seen at the study window, and so she slipped into the house and went up to her room.

She washed her face and composed herself, looking around and wishing the walls could speak.

Why had Genie fled?

Why had Everdon never sought a divorce?

Did it, in fact, argue a guilty conscience?

❧ 10 ❧

Deirdre escaped her thoughts by seeking out her mother. Lady Harby was wise, and might be able to throw light on the situation. Lady Harby, however, was deep in the novel *Marmion,* and clearly not in the mood for company.

"Why don't you go and find Everdon, Deirdre? You've hardly spent a moment with him for days. I thought you were coming to your senses."

Deirdre scurried off to Lucetta's rooms. She, at least, was available, but Kevin Renfrew was there.

"I'm sorry," Deirdre said, prepared to retreat.

"Don't go, dear," said Lucetta. "I've seen so little of you these last days. Where's Howard?"

Deirdre took a seat cautiously. There was a strange atmosphere in the room, and the Daffodil Dandy was drooping a little. She had the uncomfortable feeling that she was intruding.

"Howard's in the garden. He's working on something,

and he says I distract him just by being there." She tried to make her distractive force sound positive.

Renfrew straightened and gave her one of his vague looks. "Mathematics do tend to take over a man's head," he said. "Newton was a strange fellow. Not easy to rub along with at all."

Deirdre was beginning to realize that Kevin Renfrew's oblique comments generally carried a point, and thought she saw the direction of this one. "He *was* married, though," she said.

Renfrew nodded. "Noble woman."

Deirdre couldn't think how to respond.

Lucetta intervened. "I'm sure Howard feels guilty for neglecting you, my dear, but it is to my benefit, for now I have the pleasure of your company. I have been feeling that both Marco and I are neglecting our guests. I don't know what Marco can be thinking of."

"We're all perfectly happy," Deirdre assured her. "Rip and Henry have been enjoying cricket or the river, and today they're off to that prizefight. They will doubtless return in transports of delight, loaded with gruesome accounts of the event. Mother is plundering the novels in your library, and Howard and I have time to be together. It is all quite wonderful." Even as she said it, Deirdre could hear the strident overemphasis in her voice.

Lucetta smiled approvingly, but the smile did not quite reach her worried eyes.

Renfrew rose abruptly. "I must take my leave."

Lucetta turned to him. "God go with you, Kevin." She opened her arms, and to Deirdre's surprise, the young man accepted a hug. She knew then that his brother must be near his end. She tried to imagine what it would feel like to lose one of her sisters or brothers, especially when the death would bring so many changes and responsibilities.

Renfrew headed for the door, but stopped and faced Deirdre. There was nothing vague in his manner at all when he said, "Marry Everdon." With that he was gone.

Deirdre pulled her gaze from the closed door and looked at Lucetta. "His brother?"

Lucetta sighed. "Yes. Poor Ian. I never expected there to be so many untimely deaths in my life. Kevin has the right, of it, though. You should marry Marco."

Deirdre felt bludgeoned. "I am pledged to Howard."

Lucetta threw up her hands. "My dear, what can I say? Self-sacrifice is so hard to do well."

Deirdre erupted to her feet. "I'm *not* sacrificing myself! I *love* Howard." But now the words almost choked her, and she knew they were not true.

Lucetta knew it, too; it was clear in her frowning gaze.

Deirdre said, "I met Lady Brandon a little while ago."

"Here?" Lucetta asked in surprise and dismay.

"No. Out in the road. I was walking."

"Ah. Poor woman."

"She is very bitter. Does she have reason to be?"

Lucetta sighed. "I do not think so. But if, in that bad time, Marco had shot himself, I, too, would have been bitter. It is the nature of mothers to adhere to their children's cause."

Deirdre didn't want to ask, but needed to know. "Why did he never seek a divorce?"

"As long as Richard and Ian stood in line, he had no great need to marry again, and I know he did not relish a public airing of the matter. Beyond that, I do not know. As I have said, he keeps a great deal to himself."

Deirdre wanted to ask if Everdon had done anything to drive his wife away, but she could not ask that of Lucetta.

Lucetta broke the moment by posing a question about silks for her work. Deirdre was pleased enough to leave unpleasant subjects alone. There was too much dark intensity hovering in the house today, and too many unpleasant thoughts lurking in her head . . .

A knock on the door interrupted them. A maid presented Deirdre with a note.

She opened it, puzzled. It said simply, *You are needed in the study.* She frowned over it. It was unsigned, and she did not recognize the handwriting, but then there were few hands in this house she would recognize. She supposed it could be from the secretary—Morrow. But why would she be needed?

Lucetta was looking at her with a question in her eyes. Deirdre stood. "My mother wishes to see me," she said, knowing it made little sense.

Once in the corridor, she stood in thought, unsure what to do. Would Everdon send such a note to trap her? It simply wasn't in his style. Perhaps there was some business matter that needed her attention . . .

Then she had a startling thought. Perhaps this was Everdon's play at last. Perhaps she was to find him in a compromising situation. With whom? she wondered faintly. A maid?

Now the moment was come, she did not want to go through with it. It was going to be horribly embarrassing, but there was more to her reluctance than that.

She was going to marry Howard—she accepted that—but as long as this mock betrothal existed, Everdon was part of her life. Once she interrupted his immorality and threw an outraged fit, it would all end. Not just the engagement, but all contact between them for all eternity.

She remembered him saying, *You taste of eternity* . . .

But this was their agreement, and it would free him as much as it would free her; free him to seek a true bride. Deirdre wiped her damp hands on her skirt and marched off to the study.

She paused and listened. It was as if the room were empty. Could wickedness be so silent? She raised her hand to knock, but then realized that would not do at all.

She turned the knob and marched in.

Everdon looked up sharply.

He was alone.

He was seated behind his gleaming desk, cradling something in his hands. A bedraggled letter lay open before him.

The object in his hands was a miniature portrait, perhaps four inches across. He hastily put it down and rose, but he put it down faceup, and Deirdre saw that it was of a startlingly beautiful girl.

It was surely Genie, his first wife. Alerted by her expression, he flipped the picture over.

Dieirdre's chest and throat began to ache in a way that could only be eased by tears, tears she was determined not to shed.

Dear Lord, but he looked grief-stricken.

He still loved Iphegenia Brandon, the most beautiful girl in England. Even a glimpse had told Deirdre that Lady Brandon had not lied about that.

"Did you want something?" he asked in a strangely wooden voice.

Deirdre knew she should go, she should leave him to grieve in peace, but instead she closed the door gently and walked toward the desk, seeking words that would comfort him.

He held her eyes for a moment, and she could see the effort it took, then he buried his face in his hands and wept.

Deirdre froze, appalled. More than anything in her life, she wanted to enclose him in her arms as she would a hurt child. All her civilized instincts, however, told her she must ignore something of which he would surely be ashamed.

She began to edge back toward the door.

He looked up, grimaced, and wiped his face with his handkerchief. "My apologies. My damned Spanish half escapes every now and then." He rose sharply to his feet and went to a table to pour himself a glass of brandy. He knocked it back and poured another.

He looked at her. "Want some?"

She shook her head.

"Steadies the nerves." His voice was still rough with emotion.

There was a silver snuffbox on his desk. Deirdre picked it up, and with unsteady hands, presented it to him. He took it, placed it by the brandy decanter, and opened it.

"Your wrist, if you please," he said, still in a voice unlike his usual mellow tones.

Deirdre looked, puzzled, at her wrists, then extended her right hand. He captured it, turned it, and placed some snuff on the pale, veined underside. His hand warm beneath hers, he raised her wrist to inhale first in one nostril, then the other. His eyes closed as he savored the effect. Deirdre stared at him, wondering how her wrist could be so intimately connected to her heart.

Eyes still closed, he said, "If you don't intend to marry me, Deirdre, you should not have come here today."

Deirdre glanced anxiously at the closed door. "It won't matter."

His eyes opened. "That's not what I mean."

He pulled her into his arms and kissed her.

It was nothing like any kiss Deirdre had experienced before. It was an elemental force that offered no escape.

He trapped and molded her to him in a shockingly intimate way. His hungry lips demanded union, a union her body craved. She was a willing puppet in the arms of a master of sensuality.

She pressed closer and opened her lips; he deepened his burning possession. She ceased to be a separate person and became part of him, and he part of her. She had a shattering insight of how it would feel to be skin to skin and more.

And wanted it.

Alarmed at last, she pushed away.

He resisted.

She struggled in his arms.

Abruptly he let her go.

Deirdre staggered back. She collided with a chair and collapsed into it, staring at her wild-eyed lover.

Passion. She had never known such passion existed.

He drew on control like a dark cloak. "Should I apologize?"

She hugged herself and shook her head. Apologies certainly didn't seem appropriate.

"Have I disgusted you?"

She shook her head again. Words just didn't seem possible.

"Frightened you?"

Another shake of the head. Yes, she was frightened, but not of him.

He moved swiftly to kneel in front of her and captured her hands. "Speak to me, *cara*. You're frightening *me*."

Words were still impossible, but she squeezed gently on his hands. He loosed her fingers and placed a kiss first on one palm, then the other. "I can't let you marry Dunstable."

That broke the dam. "You can't stop me." But when she tugged her hands free of his, it was with reluctance.

"I could seduce you. Here. Now."

Deirdre looked into his dark, passionate eyes and knew it was the truth. "You won't."

"No," he said softly. "I won't." He recaptured her hands,

and it was as if he tried to seize her soul. "Why in God's name are you so bent on marrying him?"

"Because he *needs* me."

"I need you, too."

"Not as he does, and I have given my word. Would *you* break your word? What good are you to me, to any woman, if you would pledge your word and then break it?"

He shook his head. "It's not that kind of situation, *mia*."

"Is it not? You have powers to attract, Don Juan, and I am attracted. I confess it. But am I to turn away from Howard to chase the first more attractive man who crosses my path? Is that honor? That, surely, is what your wife did." She used it as a weapon and saw it strike home.

"You could be right," he said steadily. "But I gave Genie cause to leave me, as Dunstable is giving you cause to leave him. I do not blame her."

"What cause?" she asked.

He shook his head. "It's ancient history. But in my way I loved Genie, Deirdre, and Howard does not love you."

"Yes, he *does*." Deirdre was no longer quite sure of this, but what else could she say? In honor she was bound to Howard.

"No, he doesn't love you," said Everdon firmly. "If I prove it to you, will you marry me?"

How could she believe that a man like Everdon really wanted to marry her? As Lady Brandon had said, his taste ran to beauty. But clearly in his belief that she should not marry Howard, he would do anything, even to pretending to love her.

Deirdre had this horrifying image of them all going in circles saying conventional, meaningless things, spiraling down into disaster. She rose to face him. "You won't be able to prove that Howard doesn't love me, because it isn't true."

"But if I do?"

"I still won't promise to marry you. Our betrothal is a sham. We always intended to end it."

He took a deep breath and ran his hands through his hair. "If I prove to you that Dunstable doesn't love you, will you at least promise not to marry him? Please, Deirdre."

She looked down at her hands. "He asked me to marry him. Why would he do that if he doesn't love me?"

"You find him housekeepers."

It was like a sword to the heart. She looked up at him, knowing the pain of it would be on her face.

He met her eyes. "Go on, hit me. I'm owed one for that kiss."

She swallowed tears. "No, I gave you that kiss. But can't you see, Don? You're trying to make me like Genie. The man she ran away with—I don't know who he was—he probably said to her the things you say to me, and played on her desires and disappointments as you play on mine. But I will *not* be like Genie. There has to be honor above desire. I have given my word to Howard, and I will keep it."

She turned and fled the room. She raced to her bedroom to collapse on the bed there, and weep with a depth and agony she had never believed possible.

The pain she felt must surely be the pain of a broken heart.

Back in his study, Everdon sank into his chair and buried his face in his hands. He was determined not to weep again. No wonder Deirdre wanted nothing to do with him after such an un-British display of emotion.

But that wasn't what had driven her away.

You're trying to make me like Genie.

Was that what he was trying to do? Genie had said she loved him, had agreed to marry him, had tangled with him in bed in some of the most frighteningly intense passion he had ever known. Then she had met someone who pleased her better and left, leaving only a note saying she was bored, and unhappy, and couldn't be expected to stay.

Was he asking Deirdre to do the same thing?

There has to be honor above desire.

But he had loved Genie almost beyond reason. He had honestly tried to cherish her. Dunstable did not love and cherish Deirdre.

He moved his hands and flipped the miniature. Genie looked up at him with that heavy-lidded, secretive gaze that had driven him mad with desire. Her soft, perfect lips were parted slightly as if ready for a kiss. And she'd been a virgin when this had been done.

Abruptly he swept the miniature away to shatter against the far wall.

But then he regained his English sangfroid, and carefully picked up the pieces and placed them in a drawer.

As he did so, he saw a piece of paper on the floor and realized Deirdre must have dropped it. He picked it up and found the note. He recognized the writing.

Kevin. What the devil had this been about?

He'd shown Kevin the letter he'd just received. What a hellish postbag today's had turned out to be—a letter about Ian's failing, and Genie's last words.

He had not received the consolation he had expected. Kevin had his mind on his own problems, true, but it wasn't that. . . .

He picked up the letter—another stained and weary missive from Greece, delayed even more than the news of Genie's

death, for this had been written shortly before. It shocked him
how weak and wandering her writing was, but the words
shocked him more.

> *. . . How could you have cast me off, Don? It was always*
> *you. I didn't really want to leave, but you worked so hard, it*
> *was no fun. You should have come for me, and beat me if I*
> *strayed. Di Pozzinari whipped me if I looked at another man,*
> *and I stayed with him. Next to you, I loved him best. He died.*
> *Why did he die?*
>
> *Why wouldn't you change for me? We were so happy until*
> *you became so dull. Mortgages. Debts. Crops. Rents. I hate*
> *them all. I only wanted to enjoy life . . .*
>
> *Why didn't you love me? You couldn't expect me to stay*
> *when you were unkind. You were supposed to come after*
> *me . . .*

It wandered on in this vein over the whole sheet, crossed,
and the message kept repeating. *You were supposed to come af-*
ter me.

In his pain and tortured pride, it had never occurred to
him to chase after his faithless wife. It had certainly never
occurred to him to drag her home and whip her into sub-
mission. He had thought she wanted to be free.

Kevin had only said, "Poor Genie. She loved the wrong
man." What the devil had that meant?

Everdon took the letter up to his mother.

Lucetta read it soberly. "She was doubtless out of her mind.
The pox does that."

"But there's truth there. Why did it never occur to me to
drag her back?"

"Marco, you were twenty years old. She rejected you, hurt

you, made a cuckold of you. If you had made any move to rush off to the Continent after her, I would have had you forcibly restrained."

That summoned a bitter laugh. "But don't you see . . . ?" He went over to the window and stared out. She thought he would say nothing more, and looked with bitter dislike at the straggly writing on the page.

"I didn't want her back." It was said so softly that she almost missed it. His voice was clearer when he said, "My pride was hurt, and I missed the passion, but I'd tired of her tantrums. I abandoned her just as much as she abandoned me. And it killed her."

"Ten years later."

"She never would have died as she did if I'd kept her safe."

"With a whip?" Lucetta asked caustically.

He turned and leaned against the wall, but his face was shielded. "Perhaps that's what she liked. Wasn't it my duty as her husband to give her what she liked?"

"No." He frightened her in this mood. Her husband had sometimes, rarely, retreated into this kind of shell, but Lucetta had known ways of breaking through her husband's icy shield that she could not use with her son.

"I was her husband," he said quietly, "and I should have tried harder to be what she needed. That, surely, is part of the marriage bond. I knew she wanted gaiety and excitement, but I trapped her here in this decrepit house."

"You had no choice. If you'd lived as she wanted, we'd all be in the workhouse."

"So," he continued as if she hadn't spoken, "she realized she didn't like me anymore, and left, and I hated her for it. But I already knew I didn't like her anymore, and I'd abandoned her in spirit, if not in fact. As Deirdre said, doesn't

honor require that we not take the easy way out once we have
given our word?"

"What has Deirdre to do with this?"

"She has accused me, convincingly, of trying to do to her
what di Pozzinari did to Genie in seducing her away from me."

Lucetta tossed down the letter. "Deirdre and Dunstable
are not yet married."

"And does that make it right?"

"Yes."

He rubbed a hand over his haggard face. "I don't know
what's right and wrong anymore."

"*Santísima!*" Lucetta spat, and for her it was swearing. It
brought his head up, surprised. "Can you break their engagement?" she demanded.

"Yes."

"Then do it. If you can do it, there were deep flaws there
anyway. As there were in your marriage. But don't force her
into marrying you."

"It will hurt her."

"Think of it as the surgeon's knife."

"Lord, but I have no taste for it."

"Think of it as reparation then. You did not rescue Genie,
but you can rescue Deirdre."

"With a whip?" he said with distaste.

"At the very least, with a scalpel."

Everdon returned to his study and spent some time in
thought. Then, with a sigh, he sent a footman with a message
for Howard Dunstable. He paced the room in restless indeci-
sion as he waited for the man to come.

Then Dunstable entered. "Yes, my lord?"

The man's bland unawareness of any undertones decided
Everdon on his course.

"Have a seat, Dunstable. Brandy? Wine?" The amenities over, Everdon looked at the man, trying to dislike him and failing. He didn't like him, but Dunstable was merely charting his own course.

"I have been thinking on your comments about patronage of the sciences," Everdon said at last. "I would like to do what I can to facilitate your work."

Dunstable straightened. "I confess, I am surprised."

"Are you? Why?"

"I didn't think you liked me."

"Liking has little to do with it. You don't like me, but you are willing to take my money. From speaking with you, and from inquiries I've made, I'm convinced you have a remarkable ability. It deserves to progress unhindered. I am willing to cover generous living costs that should ensure your comfort—and therefore a lack of distractions. I will also allow for traveling expenses. I understand there are interesting centers of mathematics on the Continent."

Dunstable blinked. "That is remarkably generous. Where am I to live? Here?"

"No," Everdon said firmly. "Where would you like to live?"

Dunstable considered. "Cambridge, if I don't have to teach."

"Very well."

Dunstable crossed his legs and eyed Everdon. "This will make Deirdre's life more comfortable as well."

Everdon refused to be goaded. "I suppose it may. However, I must make it clear that I will provide enough funds for a single man to live well. There will be no extra allowance for wife and children. How you stretch the money is up to you."

They studied each other calculatingly. Everdon remembered: logarithmic tables at twenty paces.

Then Dunstable said, "Children. I hadn't thought of children."

"Tends to be the natural result of marriage, and I gather you are not of a naturally celibate disposition . . ."

Dunstable's eyes narrowed. "Been spying on me?"

"Just servants' gossip, Mr. Dunstable."

"Children," mused Dunstable again.

"Noisy little creatures. Then there are doctors' bills, and schooling. Of course, I'm sure you could teach them at home . . ."

Dunstable blanched. "I don't have a gift for teaching." He showed his brilliance, it only took him a moment or two to weigh it all up. "I don't suppose Deirdre would much care for travel, actually, and some prolonged visits to the Continent would help my work."

"Certainly travel with children in tow would present problems. I have drawn up some figures and signed the agreement." Everdon pushed the paper across the desk.

Dunstable read it and nodded. "Do you want me to sign anything?"

"There is no need. You can spend the money on opium for all I care. I judge, however, that mathematics is every bit as much of an addiction as any drug."

"You could be right." Dunstable stood. "I will achieve something remarkable, my lord."

Everdon nodded. "I believe it, and you'll do better without a family."

"You're undoubtedly correct. Will you marry Deirdre, then? Is that what this is all about?"

"If she'll have me."

"Course she will. Be a fool not to. I don't see why you'd want her, though."

Everdon raised his brows. "For the same reasons as you, perhaps?"

"I hardly think you need a good housekeeper."

Everdon closed his eyes briefly. "Mr. Dunstable, the sooner we close this discussion, the better for all concerned. Please inform Deirdre of your change in plans."

"Oh, you can do that."

"No, I cannot," said Everdon with icy precision. "Let me make it clear. Our arrangement will start when you have informed Lady Deirdre of your intentions, whatever they may be, and left this house. If you intend to marry her, and she is still willing, take her with you. A coach will be at your disposal whenever you command it."

Dunstable eyed him. "I'm very tempted to call your bluff, you know."

Everdon met his gaze. "By all means."

Dunstable shrugged and left the room.

Everdon sat for a moment, fists tight on the top of his desk. Then he leapt to his feet and swept two vases, a candlestick, and an ormolu clock off the mantelpiece.

The shattering crash was remarkably satisfying.

Deirdre heard the distant crash, even in her room, and ventured out into the corridor. Her mother popped out of her room, cap askew. "What was that?"

"I don't know. A disaster in the kitchens, perhaps."

"I haven't heard kitchen noise before. Go and check, dear." Then Lady Harby focused on her daughter. "You look a bit peaked, Deirdre. Are you catching a cold?"

"Perhaps. I do feel a bit sniffly." Then to avoid her mother's shrewd eyes, Deirdre hurried down the stairs.

She met Howard coming up.

"I heard a crash," she said. "Do you know what it was?"

"No." He sounded hurried. "I want to talk to you, Deirdre. Come out into the garden."

Deirdre followed him, thinking that this was the first time she could remember Howard seeking her company. Perhaps things were finally looking up.

They went through the garden room to the rose-walled patio. Her heart began to beat faster. He'd even chosen a romantic spot. Deirdre wondered if Howard would pluck her a rose, and whether it would be pink or red.

He paced, hands behind back. "The fact is, Deirdre," he said, "I've decided it wouldn't be fair to you if we were to marry."

Deirdre stared at him. "What did you say?"

"You heard me. You're not going to be silly and accuse me of jilting you, are you?"

She sought control of her wits. "No, of course not . . . But why on earth would it not be fair to me? Am I not the best judge of that?"

"Evidently not. Your parents have seen the truth all along. I can't offer you much of a life, Deirdre. There'll never be money for elegancies."

"Howard, I don't care for such things. Has Everdon been at you?"

"No," he said sharply. "You're being rather stupid about this, Deirdre. I simply don't want to marry you." Perhaps her pain showed, for he quickly added, "It's not you particularly. I don't want to marry anyone. I certainly don't want children."

Deirdre felt light-headed, but was bitterly aware that this was the most direct and meaningful conversation she and Howard had ever had. "Why did you ask me to marry you, then?"

"Are we going to hold a postmortem? Dissect the putrid corpse? Very well, if that is what you want. You are quite a tolerable woman, not much given to chatter, anxious to please, and truly grateful for even small attentions. Your family connections are excellent. I thought marriage to you would be an improvement in my circumstances. I was uncomfortable, and you seemed to add to my comfort. Now that Everdon is to be my patron, I can buy all the comfort I need."

"Everdon?" she echoed faintly.

"Yes. And if you detect ulterior motives, you are quite possibly correct. He, too, wants to marry you, doubtless for very similar reasons. He doesn't need a housekeeper, but he does need an heir. After his disastrous first marriage to a beauty, doubtless someone quiet and plain seems safer. Now, can we decently inter the corpse and get on with our lives?"

Deirdre stiffened her spine and summoned her pride. "Yes, of course." She willed her lips not to quiver and held out her hand. "I wish you all success, Howard."

He looked mildly exasperated, but he briefly shook her hand. "I'll be leaving within the hour, Deirdre. If you want my advice, take Everdon. He's a good catch for you and he won't expect too much."

Deirdre watched Howard Dunstable walk out of her life, then thumped down onto a bench, surrounded by the musky perfume of roses.

Everdon had been right, damn him. Howard had never even liked her, certainly never loved her. *Truly grateful for even small attentions.* The shame of it was brutal. She buried her burning face in her hands. She supposed that was how Everdon saw her, too.

After his disastrous first marriage to a beauty, doubtless someone quiet and plain seems safer.

That was doubtless true, and would explain the purposeful way he had pursued her. She was grateful, and safe—not the sort to run off with a foreign seducer, because no one would ever want to seduce her. Deirdre wished she, like Howard, could leave within the hour.

She rose to her feet, intending to hurry to her mother. They must return home, at the latest tomorrow. She must be allowed to end this impossible engagement.

Then she saw a figure in the garden room, and froze. She couldn't face Everdon just now. She *couldn't*. She whisked out of sight behind the trellis and ran.

She ran off into the park. Away. Away from the house. Away from Everdon, who doubtless thought he had won.

Damn him. Damn him. Damn him.

The butler closed the French doors, which someone had carelessly left open, and continued the work of seeing a guest comfortably on his way.

❧ 11 ❧

EVERDON SAW DUNSTABLE off the premises. The man said he had made a clean break with Deirdre, so Everdon retreated to his study and waited anxiously for the repercussions. He wasn't sure what form they would take.

She would probably burst in on him like a termagant, blaming him for Dunstable's defection.

There was a faint hope that she would appear sweetly ready for love.

It only slowly dawned on him that she wasn't coming at all.

He made inquiries and discovered that over an hour ago, even before Dunstable had driven away, Deirdre had been seen running across the park toward the wilderness. She had appeared upset, but the undergardener who had encountered her had not thought it his place to report such a matter.

Everdon cursed and set off in pursuit. He'd known she would be a bit upset, but not deeply. Had her feelings for Dunstable run deeper than he'd thought?

He had this frightening image of her running out of the park, away down the road, out of his life. Another woman fleeing him . . . This time he would follow and bring his beloved back.

He entered the wilderness calling her name. The carefully designed area of winding paths, streams, and little craggy hills seemed populated only by birds and insects. If Deirdre was hiding here, it would be next to impossible to find her.

What if she wasn't?

He looked with concern at the small pond, which was easily deep enough for someone to drown herself in if she were determined on it, but then dismissed the notion. His Deirdre had too much courage and honor to take her life over such a matter.

But she could thoughtlessly put herself in danger.

After a last fruitless bellow of her name, Everdon hurried back to the house. He told his garden staff to keep an eye out for Lady Deirdre, particularly around the wilderness, and then had his best horse saddled. He spent the next hours riding the boundary of his estate, questioning people.

No one had seen Lady Deirdre Stowe.

He returned to the house to hear that Lady Deirdre had come in from her walk and was in her room.

Everdon almost collapsed with relief. Now the only trial was to see how she would treat him when they met.

Deirdre had huddled among some bushes when Everdon appeared, calling for her. She couldn't face him. She wished she need never face anyone again.

Both her mother and Everdon had been proved right. Howard didn't care a fig for her. What a fool she had been.

No man was ever going to fall in love with ugly Deirdre Stowe. The best she could ever be was convenient.

And of course, she had made matters worse by running away; she had shown what a blow it was. If she had thought, she would have pretended she didn't care. Too late for that now.

But for Everdon to find her hiding behind a rhododendron bush with mud on her skirts and tears on her face would be the absolute bloody limit.

When he'd gone, she crept out and made her cautious way back to the house. When she passed one of the gardeners she tried to look as if she were just enjoying the sun.

Back in her room, however, she let the mask fall. She had never been so miserable in her life. It wasn't Howard's defection that was torturing her—Deirdre was aware that she was almost relieved to have that commitment ended. It was that he had ripped away the pretty illusion she had constructed about Everdon.

She tried to recall those heated moments in Everdon's study, to believe again that he had desired her, but now she could only see another clever man determined to get what he wanted. Well, she wouldn't be used anymore.

She just wanted to leave Everdon Park and put the whole sorry business behind her. She blew her nose. She would remain happily single and dedicate her life to her embroidery.

That brought a thought. What about her promise to her mother? She leapt to her feet. Her mother surely would not hold her to it now.

Would she?

Deirdre hastily washed her face and changed her gown. When she studied her reflection, her eyes were puffy, and her nose was red. She looked a fright, but then, that was nothing out of the ordinary. She *was* a fright, and always would be. She dusted a little powder on her nose to try to disguise her misery, then headed for her mother's room.

"Deirdre."

Deirdre froze as she passed the head of the stairs. She looked down to where Everdon stood, one foot raised onto the lowest step. He began to climb the stairs. She turned and ran to her mother's room, slamming the door behind her as if fiends pursued.

Lady Harby took one look, and sat her down. "What's happened, dearest?" She opened her arms.

Deirdre fell into them gratefully and burst into tears again on her mother's ample chest. Lady Harby rocked and soothed her until the tears were over. "Now, love, tell me what's amiss. It can't be worthy of all this."

Deirdre blew her nose, but she was already feeling a little better. Her mother's presence had a way of doing that. "Howard doesn't want to marry me anymore."

"Well, you can't expect me to shed tears about that, dear."

Deirdre twisted the handkerchief. "He never really wanted to. I was just . . . convenient."

"Ah. Well, I never did think him a downy one. Not, at least, as far as people go. What changed his mind?"

"Don Juan," Deirdre spat. "Everdon's going to be his patron. Look after everything for him. I suppose he'll even find someone who can cook his . . . his damn *eggs* right!" She started crying again, but conquered it and blew her nose fiercely. "I will *not* become a watering pot."

"Very good. Don't see what you have to cry over anyway. Now the coast's clear for you to marry Everdon."

Deirdre looked up sharply. "I will *never* marry Lord Everdon."

"Why on earth not?"

Deirdre found it hard to say. "He doesn't care for me, Mama."

"It looks to me as if he's gone to some lengths to win you."

"Convenience again. I'm just a suitable . . . a suitable broodmare."

"Deirdre!" But Deirdre could see her mother was rather amused. Lady Harby considered her. "We had an agreement, Deirdre."

Deirdre flushed. "But that was different."

"What was different was that you thought you held all the cards. You had Howard in your pocket, you didn't think you could attract a suitable man, and you thought Everdon would behave badly enough to shock me. Now you find you've lost an ace. That doesn't mean you can welch on the bet."

Deirdre gasped. "Mother, this is my life. You *can't* make me marry a man I don't . . ."

"Don't like?"

Deirdre met her mother's shrewd eyes. "A man I don't want to marry."

Lady Harby nodded. "Probably not. But I'm not going to let you jilt him either. Not yet at least. Fair's fair. At last the man has a chance."

"*Chance!*" Deirdre wanted to indulge in a fit of the vapors. She remembered Eunice, when thwarted of something, lying on her back and drumming her heels on the floor. She finally saw the appeal. "He's still mourning his first wife, Mama! I came upon him grieving over her picture. And according to her mother, he drove her away with his cruelty. *And* he as good as admitted it! I want to leave here tomorrow, and never see Lord Everdon again."

"No," Lady Harby said flatly, and would not be moved.

Deirdre thought again of a tantrum, but remembered that when Eunice had behaved in that way, Lady Harby had thrown a jug of cold water over her. She retreated back to her room to seek some other way of sorting out her life.

Everdon stood in the middle of the wide staircase, stunned by the blank misery on Deirdre's face, by the cold way she had looked through him. God, how had his simple plan come to this moment? How had he hurt her so?

He went toward his bedroom with a good mind to get thoroughly drunk, but instead he went to report to Lucetta.

"Your instructions have been followed, Dunstable has bowed out, and Deirdre's heart is broken. What now?"

Lucetta eyed him. "It is not entirely my fault, Marco, so I hope some of that snarling is for yourself. And for Dunstable, if it comes to that." He made a sharp movement, and she added, "If you start smashing my valuables, too, I will be very annoyed."

He beat a fist against a white wall. "I feel extremely destructive."

"It's your Spanish side, dearest. My mother kept a lot of cheap earthenware for just such occasions."

"I have never been of a violent temperament. I didn't smash anything when Genie left."

"By then, you didn't love Genie."

He turned sharply. "Are you saying I love Deirdre?"

Lucetta put down her needlework. "Mother of God, Marco. Surely you realize that!"

He collapsed into a chair. "No . . . no, I don't think . . . How can I love her? She hates me."

"I doubt that, dearest. And the two points have nothing to do with each other."

He slid back with a sigh. "Very well. You're the one with all the answers. What do I do now?"

"What did you do about Dunstable?"

"Bought him off." He explained what had happened.

Lucetta nodded. "Well done. It still would have been possible for him to have married Deirdre and lived tolerably if he'd wished to. A strange young man, and dedicated to his muse. It would never have done."

"Tell Deirdre that. She looked at me as if her heart was broken, and I was responsible. What do I do now?"

Lucetta considered him. "I don't know, but I want a promise from you, Marco."

He straightened. "That I'll make her happy? I'll do my best, though my record in that regard is not promising. Perhaps I can only cope with women on a flimsy basis."

"Don't grow maudlin on me. I want your promise that you'll tell her, and convince her, that you love her before you marry her."

He stared at her. "Why?"

"I am not a believer in the magic of words, but in this case, I think that is essential. Your word?"

He steepled his hands and rested his brow on them. "What on earth *is* love?"

"Ah, Marco, what is the sky? Love is when another person is essential. If you could wave Deirdre good-bye, even with regret, and in a few months choose another and be content, then you do not love her, and should let her go."

He looked up. "If I let her go, she'll probably never marry."

"*Dios!* You are certainly *not* to marry her out of pity. No wonder she wants nothing to do with you!"

He erupted to his feet. "I don't know what I feel, damn it!"

"Then go and find out," she snapped back. "And find something to smash at the same time!"

He stormed out and slammed the door. Huddled in her room, Deirdre heard the raised voice and the slam, and wished desperately that she were safe at home.

Everdon prowled his home restlessly, wondering what to do, what he wanted. It dawned on him that the place was unnaturally quiet, and when he saw a maid glimpse him and whip out of sight, he knew the servants, at least, were avoiding him.

He stopped and laughed bitterly. He was the kindest and most indulgent of employers. Were they now frightened of him?

He stalked to his room and rang fiercely for Joseph.

In a few minutes the man came in. "Yes, milord?"

"What the devil's the matter with everyone?"

"The matter, milord?"

"The house is like a tomb."

"The young gentlemen, I understand, are at their pugilistic match. And Mr. Dunstable has left."

"What of the servants?"

Joseph looked at him with quiet confusion. "What of them, milord?"

"They are not there, damn it! I just saw one hide from me."

"They generally do, milord. It is considered proper behavior."

Everdon realized that Joseph was correct. Except when engaged in a specific duty, the servants did keep out of the way of the family and guests. He was going mad.

He ran his hands through his hair. "I suppose that is true." He glanced in a mirror and saw that he looked a state. His clothes were rumpled and his hair was standing on end. Perhaps Deirdre's painful look had not been heartbreak and reproach but mere shock at his appearance.

He stripped off his coat. He was not a man to shirk necessary steps; he had to talk to Deirdre. "Fix me up, Joseph. I need to go a-wooing."

"Yes, milord," said Joseph fervently. "It will be a pleasure.

Once more a picture of sartorial elegance, and resisting a disturbing tendency to wreck it all by running his hands through his hair again, Everdon went first to Lady Harby's room.

He found her indulging in Walter Scott and bonbons.

Her look, however, was direct and disapproving. "Ah, Everdon. Glad you came to see me. You have upset my daughter."

Everdon knew he was flushing like a boy. "How have I done that, pray?"

"Don't play me for a fool, my lord. I'll say no more, but I have a question."

"Yes?"

"Are you still mourning your first wife?"

"No." He looked keenly at her. "Does Deirdre think I am?"

"How should I know what Deirdre thinks?"

Everdon found he was pacing the room. "Lady Harby, I wish with all my heart to win Lady Deirdre's affections. I believe I can make her happy."

"I believe it, too, Everdon, but I tell you honestly, if you can't convince her, then the match will be off. I'll not force the girl to the altar. Nor can we stay here many days if you can't bring her around."

Beyond that, however, she would not be drawn on the matter. Everdon left with the small assurance that Lady Harby would not drag Deirdre away the next day, but all too aware that his time was finite. Once Deirdre left Everdon Park, his chances of winning her would be slim.

He stood in the hall, finger tapping against the glossy oak banister, considering his predicament. Was his motive pity?

There was an element of compassion in his feelings. If Deirdre did not marry him, she might never marry at all. That would be a shame, but not a tragedy. She was a woman capable of living a full life without a husband. He knew, however, that she had qualities that would die if not tended, and that he was one of the few to see and cherish them. It did seem a pity that she go through life thinking herself unappealing to men.

He knew, too, that he was partly driven by convenience. He had little taste for starting a new search for a wife.

He imagined the scenario his mother had placed before him. How would he feel if he had to wave farewell to Deirdre, and woo elsewhere?

His hand tightened on the banister, driven by a surge of primitive possessiveness. Never. Bring another woman to be mistress here? See Deirdre, perhaps, wed to another man?

Never.

He loved Deirdre Stowe!

He took a moment to relish the full recognition, as he would relish the first taste of a magnificent Tokay wine, knowing that there was a pipe of it in his cellars.

Then he raced up the stairs two at a time and dashed to her door. He pulled himself to a halt, heart pounding, hands rather unsteady. This would not do. He was Don Juan. He could please any woman. Pray God, he could please the one who mattered.

He knocked. When there was no answer, he walked in.

Deirdre had been sitting miserably by the empty hearth. She turned, shocked that someone would invade her privacy. At the sight of Everdon, she felt the blood drain from her head.

"For God's sake, don't faint on me."

His harsh voice snapped back her wits a little. "Please go away, my lord. There is nothing to be said."

"Is there not, indeed? Why all this coldness? Of what am I accused? Do I not deserve to hear the charges?"

Deirdre rose to her feet, almost afraid of him in this mood. "I have no charges, my lord. It is just that everything is over."

"On the contrary. We are engaged to be married."

"A mere stratagem . . ."

"Nonsense. I told you earlier, Deirdre. I want to marry you."

"No!" She found she had retreated behind her chair as if she expected him to attack her.

"Why the devil not?"

"Stop *shouting* at me!"

They stood facing each other, breathing heavily with their anger.

She saw him take a deep breath. "I love you, Deirdre."

"Oh, very pretty, my lord. Am I to be twisted around your fingers by three easy words?"

"Easy! Damn it, Deirdre—"

"And stop swearing at me."

"Why the devil should I? You're enough to drive a man to drink. I love you. I love you. You are essential to my happiness. What else do you want to hear?"

"Good-bye?" Deirdre heard the cruel word escape her lips, and winced. But, oh, she wanted him to be gone. Surely without him in front of her, this pain would lessen: the pain of cutting free of a man she loved, but who did not love her.

"Why?" he asked quietly, all anger leashed.

His gentleness weakened her. Deirdre turned away. "I can't marry you, my lord, not least because you don't really want to marry me. You don't love me, though you are courteous enough to pretend. It's just that I'm quiet and won't be any trouble. And I'm here, which is easier than finding someone else . . ."

"Deirdre, for heaven's sake—"

"And I suppose that you were right. You proved that Howard didn't really love me, and so now you feel an obligation . . ." She made herself turn back. "I am grateful, truly I am. You saved me from a disaster, and now you're trying to mend my hurts. It is not necessary, though. I will mend well enough on my own."

"Will I?"

Deirdre shook her head. "Please stop trying to be noble, my lord. I know what I am, and I am not the sort of woman that men suffer for."

"You are a complete fool."

Deirdre flinched under his sharp tone, but she would not fall to brangling again. She went to her jewelry box and took out the diamond ring—the ring that she had only worn for a few brief hours. She held it out to him. "Please take this, my lord. I find we would not suit."

He took it thoughtfully. "It surely isn't so easy. What of your mother?"

"She will understand . . ." But Deirdre could not make it convincing. She wasn't sure what her mother would do.

"Will she? The suitor she does not favor has left. But the suitor she does favor is still committed."

"Oh, but surely . . ."

"But surely," he said. "If you truly wish to be free of this engagement, Lady Deirdre, I think we will have to go through with our original plan."

"You will arrange to be found with a woman?"

The thought of catching Everdon entangled with another

woman, even a maid, made Deirdre almost sick with misery. But it would serve to free him of his obligation, as well as to allow her to go home. She nodded bravely. "Very well. What must I do?"

"I will put it all in hand. Just come where and when I summon you. Promise? I don't want to go through this for nothing." There was even some humor in his tone.

"I promise."

"Just remember, Deirdre. I am doing this for you."

She felt like Joan of Arc on the pyre. "I will not blame you in my heart, my lord."

"I'll hold you to that."

With that he left, and she could be miserable in peace. How right she had been. Just a little token protest and he had agreed to set her free. Don Juan clearly felt nothing particular for her, and soon would be delightfully happy with a pretty bride.

" 'If it were done when 'tis done, then 'twere well it were done quickly.' " Everdon found himself muttering the line from *Macbeth* and really began to fear for his sanity. What was he supposed to do with a little fool who wouldn't believe she was loved? Couldn't believe she was desired.

Within a few hours her brothers would be home. He felt no surety that she wouldn't persuade her mother to leave on the morrow. Once out of sight, she could be snapped up by some other man.

Had she forgotten that kiss they had shared? How could she discount that passion?

Clearly she could, so he must try some other measures. Risky ones.

Everdon gave some careful instructions to his staff: when they should keep out of sight, and when a couple of them should appear. Then he wrote three notes to be sent to the three ladies of the house.

That done, he went to the garden room. To set the scene, he stripped off his jacket, waistcoat, and cravat. On such a hot summer's day, it was a dashed good idea anyway.

He did not feel comfortable, though. He felt like a green lad engaged in his first assignation. What if she did not react as he expected? What if he had misjudged her feelings? Well, at least he would find out before they were committed beyond redemption.

When he sat on the sofa his restless fingers found a thread-bare spot where the stuffing would soon work through. He looked around with new eyes. He hadn't realized quite how shabby some parts of his house had become. There was a damp stain above the glass doors and a hazardous hole in the faded carpet. His affairs had been in order for some years and it was clearly time he paid attention to his home. One of his wife's first duties, he decided, would be to help him refurbish his home.

One of Deirdre's first duties . . .

Deirdre crept tentatively in. Seeing him alone, she stopped, reddening with embarrassment. "Oh, I'm sorry . . . I must be too early . . ."

He stood, praying for all his skill. "No. I want to talk to you first."

"What about?"

He held out a hand and was much heartened when she trustingly placed hers in it. He thought perhaps it was going to be all right.

He drew her just a little closer. "When you are free, Deirdre, I am hoping you will look for a husband more to your taste. I think you will be better able to choose a husband if you know more about kissing. Now, while we are still betrothed, it wouldn't be entirely improper for me to show you."

"But we did . . ." She was deliciously pink and flustered, and he could feel the strain of keeping the situation light.

"Alas. I was upset. It was hardly my most skillful effort. Let me show you properly."

"Oh, I don't know . . ." But she did not retreat, and the longing in her eyes betrayed her.

He drew her into his arms, gently, slowly, giving her every chance to escape. "Please, *mi corazón.*"

With a visible sigh of surrender, she nodded. "Very well, then."

He took a deep breath of relief and backed to the sofa to collapse there, with her in his lap.

She balked a little at that. "My lord! Don! What of your . . . ? What if she . . . ?"

"She won't." He raised her small hands between them and kissed them with reverent care, concentrating on their pleasuring.

It was the kind of thing a woman liked, the kind of thing he'd done a hundred, a thousand times before, but now it was so hard. He did not want to use his skilled seducer's steps. He wanted to embrace her with all the passion of this morning, to kiss her, to lose himself in her forever . . .

Deirdre looked down at his glossy hair, felt his lips tease her palms, and knew she was a fool. What pain she was creating here. The memories of this moment would be thorns in her heart forever, but she wanted them all the same.

How could kisses on the hand be so wonderful? Now his tongue was on her fingertips . . .

"Oh my . . ." She had whispered it aloud.

He looked up, and his dark eyes seemed darker and

frighteningly intense. His arms encompassed her, and his lips wandered over her face—her cheeks, her chin, her temples, her eyelids—so that she felt she was drowning in kisses.

"Don . . ." It was intended as a protest, but Deirdre could hear the longing in it.

Now his hand was wandering over her body. It was not bold enough to summon a protest, except that she thought perhaps she should protest. Except that she did not want to. At least he wasn't inside her clothing . . .

"I thought you were to teach *me* to kiss," she managed to say.

"So I am, Deirdre. I have been demonstrating. Now, you kiss me."

She stared at him for a moment, then began to kiss his face as he had kissed hers. Oh, how she had wanted to do this; to pay homage to his lean cheeks, his perfect nose, his beautiful eyes . . .

He slid back so she was on top of him. His shirt stood open at the neck, so she kissed his warm skin there. She was aware of his hands traveling over her back. Through her fine muslin it almost felt as if they touched her skin.

"Bite me," he said softly.

She looked up. "What?"

"Just little nips. It's another form of kissing. Like this." He captured her hand and took the fleshy part of her thumb in the gentle pressure of his teeth.

Deirdre sucked in a sharp breath. Then she surveyed him. "I feel like a diner choosing the most succulent piece of meat." Deirdre realized she was smiling at him. How could she be smiling at a time like this?

He grinned back. "I wait to be eaten."

She sank her teeth into his neck, but didn't think she hurt

him. She relished the taste of his flesh, but when she released him she saw that she had made a dark mark there.

"Oh dear . . ."

"Marked me, have you? Fair's fair. You must let me mark you."

Deirdre swallowed, but nodded. A dim, distant part of her mind reminded her that she had come here for some other purpose, but nothing short of Armageddon could stop her from enjoying every last moment of this tryst.

He pushed her away slightly, surveying her as greedily as she had surveyed him. The very path of his eyes made her tremble.

He put out a hand and traced the low bodice of her dress, easing it down to uncover the upper swell of her breast. She captured his hand.

His eyes dared her. "Fair's fair, and you wouldn't want the mark where it could be seen, would you?"

With a mental apology to her mother, Deirdre released him, and his mouth wandered across her chest to settle on the spot he had marked, just an inch or two inside her neckline. She swayed back against his arm, and her own hands came to hold his head to her. He nuzzled lower and lower. His fingers brushed her thigh, and it felt as if he really was touching her bare skin . . .

"Good God!"

Her mother's voice shocked Deirdre back into her senses. She twisted her head to see her mother standing in the doorway, staring at her. Lucetta stood behind, looking amused. The butler and Joseph peered in from a distance.

Deirdre squeaked, and grabbed Everdon's head to pull him off her.

He was deliciously flushed and disordered, and for a moment she lost awareness that they had been caught.

"Lord Everdon," said Lady Harby awfully. "Remove your hand from my daughter!"

Deirdre looked down and found that his hand covered her right breast, but it was the only thing that did. She hastily tugged up her gown, and he eased his hand away as it became unnecessary.

"Oh, criminy . . ." Deirdre muttered. She would have leapt to her feet, but he was still all over her. She whispered frantically, "Get up, my lord!"

"Calm, light of my life. There is an art to this."

Deirdre realized that more than her bodice was disarranged. Most of her skirt was, too. His hand really *had* been on the naked skin of her thigh. Somehow—years of practice?—he pulled her to her feet and rearranged her clothing in one smooth movement, and turned them to face their accusers, keeping her safe in his arms.

"Well," said Lady Harby severely. "I've told you, Deirdre, let them inside your clothing and it's the altar for you. And we'd best not wait until September by the looks of it."

"We will certainly wait until September if Deirdre wishes to," said Everdon firmly. "There is no reason for haste."

"We'll at least have the betrothal in the papers immediately," countered her mother.

"Of course."

Deirdre looked between them and collected her wits. "Stop! I am not marrying Lord Everdon."

"You most certainly are, miss, after a scene like that. Look at the pair of you!"

"He tricked me!"

"Tricked you? How, pray?"

Deirdre turned to Everdon for support, then the truth dawned. Rage bloomed, and she swung back and clouted him with all the strength in her arm. She cried out at the pain in her hand, but she had the satisfaction of seeing him knocked backward. Of course, he would not have fallen if his heel had not caught in a hole in the threadbare carpet, but there was great satisfaction in seeing him tumble to the floor.

She stood over him, arms akimbo. "I told you I'd hit you."

He lay there laughing. "I knew you were a woman of your word. Marry me, Deirdre. Please?"

"Why?" It was almost a wail.

"I haven't finished the kissing lessons."

She hurled a musty cushion at him. She looked for further ammunition and threw his jacket over his face.

He pushed out from under it. "Is that a hint that you want me to dress, dear heart?"

"That's a hint that I want you to stop making fun of me!"

He leapt lightly to his feet, but there was nothing light about his expression. "I truly want you to marry me, Deirdre. You have every quality that I wish for in a wife, but in addition, I adore you. Think back over the last fifteen minutes or so. That was not a mild, convenient passion, Deirdre. That was deep desire. I desire you, body and soul."

Deirdre looked anxiously at the watchers, for though Everdon seemed unaware of them, she was. She saw that the servants, at least, had gone. "Why on earth did you stage this farce?"

"To show you what we have here. You could have stopped me at any time, but you wanted that as much as I. But also to compromise you. This time, one way or another, I will keep you with me."

"You are trying to trap me!"

"Yes. But what am I to do? I can make you happy, *cara* . . ." Then he spread his hands and sighed. "I fool myself. I cannot hold you like this. Even in your own interests I cannot use the

whip. No one here will speak of what they have seen, Deirdre—
I promise you that. You are free. If your heart is free."

Deirdre sucked in a breath. This final gesture, the act of
setting her free, was the one that broke the chains. "You
truly do love me," she whispered in wonder.

"To distraction. As I have never loved before."

"But why? I am not pretty."

"If I were to be scarred tomorrow, would you cease to
love me?"

"No, but—" She glared at him. "I have not said I love you,
sir."

"Do you not? If you don't, I will find a way to make you
love me as I love you."

Deirdre was overwhelmed that he would say these things
before others. "I don't know . . . *Why* do you love me?"

He reached out and touched her cheek. "Why do you love
me? I love you for your courage, and your honor. For the way
you dance, and the way you smile. I love the child that is still
in you, and the woman you are beginning to be. I love you as
you are. What more can I say?"

There was almost a plea in that, and Deirdre answered it
by going into his arms. "This frightens me a little."

He held her close. "It terrifies me," he admitted with a
laugh. "But to be without you would terrify me more."

Deirdre had to ask. "And your first wife? Is she still in
your heart?"

"Oh, love, my heart and she parted long ago. I wept for
the person she might have been, in another time and another place, and for the misery of her passing. There is no
one but you."

Deirdre had no choice but to believe. He produced the diamond ring with a question in his eyes. Blushing, she extended
her hand and let him slip it once more onto her finger.

At that moment Rip and Henry burst in. "Where is every-body?" Harry demanded. "What a day. What a fight!"

"Yes, wasn't it?" murmured Everdon.

"Thought it'd go on forever!" declared Rip. "Wasn't sure of the outcome at all."

"Neither was I," mouthed Everdon, and Deirdre bit her lip against a grin.

"Until the victor landed that blow," said Henry. "What a right!"

"Sent him crashing to the floor!" said Rip. "Wouldn't have missed it for the world."

Everdon turned Deirdre in his arms, and stood with his chin resting on her head. "My sentiments entirely, Lord Ripon."

"What?" said Rip. "You weren't there, were you, Everdon? Corking contest, wasn't it? Touch and go. Some clever maneuvering, but plenty of close work. They really went at it toward the end."

Deirdre could feel Don Juan shaking with the laughter she was fighting down. She elbowed him, and he kissed her cheek.

Rip looked around. "Why's everyone in here, anyway? Not to be discourteous or anything, Everdon, but this room ain't your best spot. Could do with a bit of refurbishing. There's a hole in the carpet there that could cause an accident."

"How true. Deirdre will doubtless see to it."

"Not at all," said Deirdre sweetly. "I shall preserve it as a valued memento."

Rip stared at them in bemusement, then his gaze became fixed on Everdon's neck. "I say . . ."

Lady Harby interrupted. "It lacks but fifteen minutes to dinnertime, Ripon, and you are in all your dirt. Get along with you. And you, too, Henry." She turned to leave with

Lucetta, but turned back. "And you, too, Everdon. And I'll thank you to behave yourself until September!"

They were alone again. Everdon turned Deirdre gently in his arms and they collapsed together in helpless laughter.

When she recovered Deirdre gasped, "I don't feel at all like myself."

He hugged her. "I don't feel like Don Juan, either. Will you mind being boringly domestic, and attending to my rather tattered home?"

She smiled up at him. "I can think of nothing I'd like more, Don. Except, perhaps," she added with a sliding look, "another kissing lesson?"

His eyes darkened, but he pushed her away. "Oh no, sweet temptress. That will have to wait until September."